Now the Darkness Gathers

Shaun Lewis

First published in 2019 by Endeavour Media Ltd.

In memory of Dr John Archer, who died in February 2018. An eminent historian.

Table of Contents

Now the day is over,
Night is drawing nigh;
Shadows of the evening
Steal across the sky

Now the darkness gathers,
Stars begin to peep,
Birds and beasts and flowers
Soon will be asleep.

From a hymn by Sabine Baring-Gould, 1867

PROLOGUE

September 1898

Sir Herbert Kitchener, Sirdar of the Egyptian Army, seemed pleased to receive the two scruffy Dervishes and had even offered them hospitality. This struck his aide-de-camp as odd. Both visitors were dressed in the manner of the followers of the Mahdi, that is barefoot and semi-naked apart from the curious headgear, and yet they had claimed to be British officers. The ADC found this hard to credit, given the disgustingly black colour of their skin, and yet they both spoke faultless English with no accent. There was, also, something disconcerting about the taller of the two. He was probably three or four inches taller even than his own height of six feet, but it was not his tallness that commanded obedience. It was the eyes. They were deep-set and dark, like two railway tunnels. Meeting the stare, the ADC had felt he had been looking into the stygian darkness of Hades itself. Somehow he had felt compelled to announce the visitors to his general, despite his disquiet. Now the Sirdar had asked to be left alone with his guests and the chief of intelligence, Colonel Wingate. Something was up.

****

'How certain are you of this information?' Kitchener asked of the tall naval commander seated before him in the disguise of a Mahdi warrior.

'We cannot guarantee any of it,' William Miller replied. 'But Lieutenant Kensett and I are very confident that the attack tomorrow will be a feint. Al-Taashi's real intention is to lure your army into the Surgham Hills where his main army will await you. He has 17,000 men there and another 20,000 of his followers further to the north-west … about here, behind the Kerreri Hills.' Miller stabbed a finger on the map spread out between him and the general.'

'But you have your doubts, Miller?' Kitchener had dozens of agents in Omdurman and Khartoum, but these two officers from the Royal Naval Brigade were his best. Miller had his own network of spies that had penetrated the inner circle of the Khalifa, Abdullah al-Taashi, and the

9

intelligence provided so far had been vital as the Egyptian Army had made its slow, but steady, progress down the Nile.

'No, sir. Not on that score. We just haven't been able to penetrate the army of Muhammed Sherif, the commander of the Army of the Red Flag. He's the one protecting al-Taashi's right flank between the Surgham Hills and the Nile. We've discovered very little about the strength or disposition of his forces.'

Kitchener slowly stroked his moustache and studied the map for the hundredth time. His army of about 25,000 troops was centred on the village of El Egeiga with its back to the Nile and the precious navy gunboats and transports that made up his fleet train. He knew he was outnumbered by the Mahdi troops, but he had more modern weaponry, including field artillery and Maxim guns. His troops would also be trying out for the first time in battle the new hollow-point bullets made in the arsenal at Dum Dum. He was confident of victory in daylight, but he worried about a surprise attack by night. He would not then be able to maximise his technological advantage.

Whilst Kitchener deliberated, Wingate offered the two naval officers a cup of thick coffee. Miller tasted it and immediately winced.

'Is the coffee not to your liking, old boy?' Wingate asked suspiciously.

'I'm sorry. I find it too sweet, that's all. I suppose over the last couple of months I've become more used to the Sudanese style.'

'It's fine by me, sir,' Kensett cut in. 'I find the sweetness quite refreshing in this heat.'

Kitchener interrupted the social pleasantries. 'Wingate, what have you to say about this information?'

Wingate paused before replying. 'It seems fairly consistent with what I've heard from other sources, sir, in terms of the numbers. My understanding is that the Khalifa has split his forces into five forces and I suppose Azrak's attack might be a feint.'

'But why not make a surprise attack tonight? If al-Taashi waits until dawn, we'll murder his Ansar.'

'I honestly don't know, sir. I think you have to trust to the information from Commander Miller, sir.'

'Sir,' Miller interceded. 'Whilst our information suggests the attack will be at dawn, I see your difficulty and have a suggestion to make. Why not bring up the gunboats closer and use their searchlights to sweep the line of your overnight defences? You could land a few lights in key positions, too.

If al-Taashi's men do have any thoughts of a night attack, it will make them think twice about presenting an easy target for your pickets.'

Kitchener looked across to Wingate questioningly. Wingate just shrugged in reply and pursed his lips non-committally. Kitchener made his decision. 'Very well, gentlemen. I will discuss it with Commander Keppel.'

****

Lieutenant Winston Churchill felt the thrill of battle course through his veins. Up to now the infantry and artillery had had the best of the battle. At dawn, the Dervishes had swept down the hills and past the front of the Anglo-Egyptian army position. Then they had turned and launched a full-frontal assault on the defending army. It had been carnage. The superior firepower of the British had mown down the Mahdists in their thousands. The attack was shattered and the savages were withdrawing from the battlefield. After four hours of watching the infantry and gunners gain all the glory, Lieutenant Colonel Martin, the Commanding Officer of the 21st Lancers, had just received orders to cut off the enemy's retreat across the plain to Omdurman.

As his squadron commander followed the colonel's lead in increasing the pace of the pursuit, from a walk to the trot, Churchill found the noise amusing. Kitted out for all eventualities in the desert, the troopers' pots and pans clanked in a cacophony of noise. It was a bizarre sight and odd musical accompaniment to war, he thought. Some of the wags in his troop had described it as 'Christmas Tree Order'. It didn't matter. After decades of inaction in India, the 21st Lancers were going into a fight. No longer would the rest of the army mock them that their regimental motto should be: '*Thou shall not kill*'.

He reined back his Syrian mare. She, too, was being caught up with the infectious excitement of going into battle and had trotted too close to the squadron commander ahead. Like Churchill, beads of sweat ran down her head, attracting the flies. Ahead, he saw the enemy for the first time. A few hundred Mahdists were in full flight, but others were being made to halt and turn to face the oncoming cavalry. The colonel and squadron commanders had seen them, too, and without orders the regiment increased its pace to a canter. The horsemen began to spread out and Churchill's squadron was to the left of the others, only a few hundred yards from the bank of the Nile.

The horses' hooves kicked up whirls of dust and Churchill had to turn his head to one side to spit out the sand that was clogging his throat. Or was this the dryness of fear? He had heard fellow officers of his earlier regiment, the 4th Hussars, talk of parched throats on entering battle. He saw a red flag fluttering on the crest of a ridge before him and a file of Dervishes armed with rifles, swords and spears in a ragged line abreast it. He was close enough to make out the square, black patches sewn on the front of their white tunics. He glanced across his right shoulder and saw the sunshine reflecting off a forest of lances and drawn sabres. It was a magnificent sight. This was the way to fight a battle. Not for the 21st Lancers the impersonal firing of lead and shrapnel from a range of several hundred yards. This would be point against flesh, although he had opted for a Mauser pistol in preference to the sabre. The pounding of the hooves of hundreds of horses at the canter seemed to reverberate in unison. He suddenly found the smell of horse, sweat and leather intoxicating. This was the thrill he had always craved since his childhood.

Some of the Mahdists opened fire on the approaching cavalry and he could make out the bearded faces of his enemy about 200 years ahead, just as he heard the trumpet major sound the three 'Gs' from his bugle, the signal for the regiment to charge. There was no time to feel fear. The adrenalin took over and, as one, the regiment began the gallop.

Within seconds, the 350 lancers swept through the line of Dervishes, overwhelming them as waves pour over the beach. Then Churchill discovered their horrible mistake.

The ridge was in fact the bank of a khor, a dry watercourse four to six feet deep and in which were carefully hidden thousands of angry Dervishes. The 21st had been drawn into an ambush. With only a slight stumble, his mount found her footing, but was hemmed in by the seething mass of Dervishes feverishly stabbing at the lancers and horses with their spears and short swords. All around him he could see green or white banners covered in the strange script of the Orient and, at the far end of the water course, more Mahdist troops joining the battle. Several lancers had been unhorsed by the fall into the khor and were being hacked to death without mercy. Those that had retained their mounts were desperately trying to fight through to the other bank.

He spurred his horse forwards and fired his pistol point-blank into the faces of those who tried to impede his progress. Suddenly, and for the first time in his memory, he felt afraid.

He spotted his troop corporal 100 yards away, being brought to a standstill by a horde of the enemy and in imminent need of help. Like a mounted policeman in a riot, he and his horse waded through the frenzied mob and he fired the remainder of his ten rounds at his corporal's attackers. Hurriedly, he loaded a fresh clip into the pistol, but the enemy recognised his temporary helplessness and lunged towards him and his horse. He just had enough time to realise the loneliness of his position when he heard, rising above the inhuman howls of the Dervishes, the sound of a bugle and, as he looked up, he knew he would always be grateful for the sight: a dismounted troop of another squadron had rallied to the aid of his own.

The lancers began to pour fire from their carbines into the mob below and from a range at which they could not miss. The Dervishes were shocked and momentarily stunned into inaction. It had had the opposite effect on a section of the troop to Churchill's left. Under the quick-thinking command of their sergeant, several lancers who had made it to the opposite bank, also formed up to open fire on the ambushers. In the narrow confines of the gulley the effect was devastating and too much for the Mahdist army. They quickly turned and ran.

Churchill's emotions instantly changed from astonishment to gratitude that his life had been spared. He knew the battle was now won and suddenly he felt tired and emotionally spent. The charge must have lasted only two minutes, but those minutes had been the most exciting of his life. Brushing down his uniform, he realised that he was filthy from the dust of battle and incredibly thirsty. Leaving his fellow lancers to mop up the remaining Dervishes, he led his mare and ascended the river bank in search of water.

To his shock, a few hundred yards away he saw a gunboat, from the stern of which proudly, but lazily, flapped the ensign of the Royal Navy. With a start, he spotted only yards from him, two men standing in Dervish costume. In a panic, he reached quickly for his Mauser once again, but was stunned to be addressed in English by the taller Dervisher.

'There's no need for that.' The taller man bowed slightly to him and again addressed him. 'Commander William Miller of the Royal Naval Brigade and temporarily appointed to Her Majesty's River Boat *Melik*. At your service, sir. Allow me to introduce you to my second-in-command, Lieutenant Philip Kensett, also of the Royal Naval Brigade.'

For a few seconds Churchill was too surprised to speak. He quickly recovered and replied, 'Lieutenant Winston Churchill, attached to the 21st Lancers. But, sir, what are you doing here?'

'It's too long a story to relate right now. But judging from my recent observations, I suspect you are sorely in need of a little light refreshment to wash away the remnants of battle. If you will wait but a moment, I have some champagne chilling in the river.'

CHAPTER 1

August 1909

The long-suffering wife of Superintendent Stanley Clarke, of the Home Section of the newly formed Secret Service Bureau, or SSB, had planned that the Clarke family would spend this beautifully sunny August day by the sea at Bognor Regis. It had, accordingly, been difficult to avoid an argument when, earlier in the day, he had announced that he been called to a crime scene at a flat near Soho. Despite the transfer to his new department, Clarke had been careful to keep in touch with his former colleagues at the Yard. On arrival, together with one of his men, Detective Jackson, he addressed the back of a short, bowler-hatted man talking with a group of uniformed police officers.

'Good morning, Hitchins. What's the situation then?'

Detective Inspector Hitchins of Scotland Yard immediately detached himself from the other officers and shook the hand of Clarke vigorously. 'Morning, sir. I'm sorry to call you so early in the day, though it seems straight forward enough. One of the neighbours reported a gunshot coming from this flat in the early hours of the morning. A couple of lads from the local station come round and forced an entry. They found the corpse of the occupant, a rent-boy well known to us, lying in the corner of his bedroom. He'd been beaten to death.'

Clarke raised an eyebrow. 'So where does the gunshot figure in this, Hitchins?'

'I was just coming to that, sir. The lads also found an unconscious man suffering a bullet wound to the head. I reckon the wounded man 'ad beaten the rent-boy to death and then shot himself. Maybe it was in remorse, or more likely to avoid the scandal of a public trial for the murder.'

'And have both men been removed?'

'They 'ave, sir. They're in the Charing Cross. If the gunshot victim lives, we'll question 'im and in all probability charge him with the murder. The thing is, sir, from 'is effects we've identified him as a German national, one Friedrich von Trotha. That's why I called you.'

'I see. Perfectly reasonable … and I thank you for it, Hitchins. What else can you tell me of the suspect?'

'Judging by 'is effects, sir, he's living in some apartments in South Kensington. Seems a well-heeled sort of bloke, if you ask me. Here's 'is wallet, some letters we found on him with his address … and his keys. Do you plan on checking out 'is address, sir?'

'I think I will. Do you need a hand here?'

'We'll be fine, thank you, sir. As I said, it seems pretty routine and we're just about done here now, anyway. How's your new department, by the way?'

'Less exciting than life at the Yard, I can assure you. I spend most of my time on wild goose chases, but one has to be seen to be taking all these spy scare-stories seriously. I owe you one, thanks.'

****

It was still only late morning and neither Jackson nor Clarke had turned up anything interesting, that was, anything out of the ordinary, in their search of the apartments of the suspected murderer. Clarke began to wonder if it had been worth incurring the wrath of Mrs C. However, duty called and he prided himself on being a thorough and conscientious detective. His attention to detail and doggedness were two of the reasons he had been transferred from Scotland Yard to the SSB. Perhaps, if they concluded their search now, he could make amends and take the kids to the zoo for the afternoon. It seemed a pity to waste Mrs C's picnic.

''Scuse me, sir, but what exactly we lookin' for and why're we 'ere any'ow?' Jackson asked.

'Use your loaf, Jackson. Documents, photographs, anything that might suggest that Herr Frederick von Trotha is no ordinary German citizen.'

'Yeh, but, sir. Just 'cos 'e's furrin don't mean anythin'.'

Clarke winced inwardly, as he always did at Jackson's murder of the English tongue. But the man was a little ferret in a search, so he bore it stoically.

'Quite right, Jackson, but all these penny novels on German invasion plans are frightening the great British public. Believe the newspapers and every German waiter and seaman is a spy. If Captain Kell judges it worth a cursory investigation, then who are we to argue? After all, we've hardly much else pressing.'

'Fair enough then, sir, but there ain't much of in'erest 'ere, I reckons. Looks like 'e wuz heducated in this country, though. See the photographs 'ere.'

Clarke saw what Jackson meant. Both on the desk and on the walls of the library were several photographs and mementos of what looked to be von Trotha's life at a British public school. Clarke wasn't that surprised. Several of the German aristocratic families favoured the English education system. He cast his eyes over the family photographs and one in particular drew his especial attention. This might be significant and justify this search, he thought. Von Trotha clearly had a connection with the German military. A family group included an older man in the uniform of the German Army, probably von Trotha's father.

He searched the desk for any documents or other photographs that might offer the slightest hint of espionage. Suddenly, he was brought up short. Maybe this wasn't a wild goose chase, after all. One of the photographs in the desk was of a large yachting party and, if he was not mistaken, one of the group was a Royal Navy officer. And it wasn't just any naval officer either. He recognised the man as being one of the founders of the SSB, Captain Miller from the Admiralty's intelligence department. What was his connection with the German military? He slipped the photograph into a large envelope and continued his search.

Detective Jackson was checking out the bookshelves and Clarke moved over to help him. Judging by the library, he decided that von Trotha was well-read and cultured. The bookcases included several works of great English literature, including the novels of Joseph Conrad. Perhaps it was Jackson's wry humour over his present employment, or perhaps, through a sixth sense, but seemingly absent-mindedly, he picked out Conrad's latest book, *The Secret Agent*. As he started to leaf through the book out of idle curiosity, he suddenly called out.

'Hey, Mr Clarke. Come and have a butcher's at this. I think I've found something.'

Clarke examined the book and discovered what had attracted Jackson's attention. The book was a box in disguise. He put on a pair of gloves and tried to open the lid, but nothing happened. He examined the three gold-edged sides that should have been paper, but there was no sign of a catch. The edges were smooth and he slid his fingers along them.

'Eureka!' he called out.

To his astonishment, the lid of the box had sprung open to reveal a secret compartment hiding various letters.

'Well done, Jacko. This is interesting. Put your gloves on. I don't want your smudges over any of these letters, right?'

He and Jackson carefully examined and read the letters.

'How's your German, Jacko?'

'Ain't got none, sir.'

'Nor I, but some of these are in German. I'll take a quick look and pass them to 'K' for translation and further examination. Here. Take these. They're in English.'

Both detectives examined the documents and letters before them for several minutes.

'Fuck me, sir. Fritz is a fuckin' ponce! These letters is disgustin'. I 'ate ponces.'

'Just keep reading, Jackson, and mind your language. I need to concentrate.'

Clarke focused on the other letters, written in German. He hadn't expected to derive much from them, but the signature of the sender of two of them caught his eye. 'Brose, Karl Brose,' he muttered to himself. 'Where have I heard that name before?'

He searched his elephant-like memory for the name and it finally came to him.

'Right, Jacko. That's enough. Leave everything as it is. As soon as I've reported to Captain Kell, I'm going to have a specialist team take this flat apart.'

'But why, sir? What yer found?'

'Only that our Herr von Trotha has been corresponding with Karl Brose, the Oberstleutnant heading Abteilung IIIb, the military intelligence service of the Imperial German Army. Well done, Jacko. You've hit the bloody jackpot! Now stay here until I return and nobody enters the flat, right?'

As Clarke left the flat to head for the offices of the SSB, he was troubled by the photograph in his pocket. What was the connection between Captain William Miller VC of the Naval Intelligence Department and a German spy? He shuddered at the possibilities.

CHAPTER 2

Since his return from Berlin the year before, as the Naval Attaché to the Courts of Berlin, Copenhagen and The Hague, Captain William Miller had tried to make it a rule to take the whole of the month of August as summer leave at his country estate in Lancashire. The Royal Navy continued its commitments worldwide throughout the year, of course, but in a time of peace, the affairs of the Naval Intelligence Department could generally be left in the more than capable hands of a commander. Whilst the NID now ran four agents in Germany, for whom Miller was personally responsible, they were run jointly with the War Office and their reports were unlikely to require his urgent attention. Miller was, consequently, surprised to have his leave interrupted by Kell's urgent summons by telephone to return to London.

Miller placed the secret document back on his unusually tidy desk at the Admiralty for a moment. Normally, the desk would have been covered in charts, drawings and files, but for the duration of his leave, everything was locked in the large, green safe in the corner of his office. As he happened to be in the office, one of the clerks had passed him the file containing Agent TR6's latest report from Germany. It contained disturbing news, but Miller paused its perusal to reflect on his meeting with Kell that morning. He shifted his chair back from his desk a little and picked up one of the few other objects on his desk, a photographic portrait of his two eldest sons. It had been taken when Richard and Peter had been, respectively, just eight and four years old. Both boys had been page boys at a family wedding, dressed proudly in the uniforms of naval cadets. It pained Miller and, he knew, the boy himself that Peter had been rejected on account of a problem with his middle ear from following his elder brother to Dartmouth. Vertigo was a great disadvantage to those required to climb masts and rigging, and no doubt Peter would have suffered chronic sea sickness. Miller replaced the silver-edged frame on his desk with an audible sigh of regret and picked up his cup of tea instead. One sip was enough. Having sat on his desk for fifteen minutes it was cold – and he hated cold tea.

He had been piqued to be recalled from his leave, but Kell had been correct to call him over this von Trotha business. Counter-espionage was not his affair. It was a concern of the Home Office, but Kell had been right to enquire of his connection with the dead man. It saddened him that the son of his old friend had met his end this way. He and Oberstleutnant von Trotha had campaigned together against the Boxers in China. Since then the Millers had enjoyed the hospitality of the von Trotha family many times in Germany. Von Trotha came from a wealthy Bavarian family of landowners and, such was the friendship, von Trotha had even sent his only son Friedrich to join Peter at Charterhouse. Miller had naturally asked Peter to look out for Friedrich and help him settle into the alien culture.

He found it hard to believe what Kell had said about the lad's attempts to turn against the country that had given him his education and he was puzzled as to how this could have come about. Kell and his team had had the same thought, but in the week that it had taken young Friedrich to die, they had not been able to turn up much concrete information, despite working day and night to build up a picture of von Trotha's recent activities. All 'K' had established from Brose's letters was that von Trotha felt some bitterness towards the British establishment and this had led him to offer his services to the German Embassy as a spy. The German military attaché had put him in touch with Brose and, after some cursory confirmation of von Trotha's identity and background, Abteilung IIIb had accepted his offer to work for them. Kell's SSB men at von Trotha's bedside had desperately wished for him to regain consciousness, so that they could question him on the depth of his involvement with the German intelligence service, but, disappointingly, he took the information to the grave, leaving Kell and his staff in a quandary.

Miller's musing was interrupted by a gentle knock on the jamb of his office door. The door was open, an old custom from his seagoing days. At sea, officers tended to leave the doors of their cabins open, with a curtain pulled across, when available to their colleagues or men. A closed door signalled the incumbent was in his bunk or otherwise indisposed.

It was the one of the NID staff officers, Captain Temple of the Royal Marines Artillery. 'Come in, Temple.'

'I'm sorry to disturb you, sir, but I heard you were back from leave. I wondered if you had had time to digest the latest report from TR6.'

'I've just been reading it. You're an artillery expert. What do you make of it?'

'TR6 seems to have a real scoop with these results of the German Navy's latest gunnery trials. Judging from his previous reports, I don't think we can doubt the veracity of his information, sir.'

'I agree, but I doubt our ordnance experts will. We now seem to have conclusive proof of the high rate of fire of the German guns. A discharge of three rounds a minute from their 11-inch guns is astonishing enough, but four rounds a minute from their 9.4-inch guns is incredible. According to his report, the Germans are also conducting trials of a "Richtungsweiser", or direction pointer, as a method of fire control, to improve the accuracy of their gunnery... But you knew that, of course, Temple? You've read the report?'

Temple nodded.

'Quite right, Temple. It's always been best to leave senior officers under the impression that they alone are the founts of all wisdom. I'm sorry.'

'No problem, sir. Have you read the bit yet about how much the Germans are investing in gunnery research, sir?'

'I have. Ten times what we are, but he admits it's so far unsubstantiated. I also noted that the practice ammunition allowance was eighty percent higher than that of RN ships.'

'If I recall correctly, sir, did we not receive a report from another agent, that the German Navy is also experimenting with gunnery practice at ranges of up to 24,000 yards? As we're still working on ranges of 10,000 yards, we might be hopelessly outgunned in any future conflict. Is there any way our agents can find out, sir?'

'I'll look into it, but even if they confirm the information, I have my doubts it will be acted on. We've become far too damned complacent about our mastery of the oceans these days. The obsolescence of all other battleships by the Dreadnoughts has enabled Germany to start building a new navy on level terms with Britain.'

Miller signed the docket before handing it to Temple.

'Here. Take the report. Remove the references to the source of the information and send a copy to the Ordnance Department under cover of a note to the effect: *"We have received compelling evidence from reliable sources that ..."* et cetera, et cetera. You know the drill.'

'Aye aye, sir. I'll see to it. Just one thing, though. I hope you don't mind me asking, but why do you call this agent, TR6?'

'Ah. It's only my occasional attempt at humour, Temple. We use "Tiaria" as the fictional enemy in our exercises at sea, so all our agents in

Germany have the prefix, TR. I picked the number at random. We wouldn't want the Germans to pick up on the codenames and deduce the numbers of our agents from the information, would we?'

'Thank you, sir. I feel stupid for asking. Now the Germans are imposing strict censorship of printed material on any naval matter, even what were previously open sources, we could do with a few more agents of TR6's calibre in Germany.'

'Yes … and yet our Fourth Estate now positively revels in its freedom to print whatever it likes about our own naval developments. It's bloody hopeless, but you've heard me say this before.' Miller stood up so suddenly that he startled Temple.

Temple changed the subject. 'Are you returning on leave this afternoon, sir?'

Miller opened the solid-gold case of his hunter watch, a present from his late father, and calculated he had plenty of time to catch a train back to Lancaster, but it would have to be the sleeper to Scotland.

'No, I think I'll go up in the morning. Anxious as I am to renew my leave, I hate the sleeper. With the constant noise and all that jolting, I hardly get a wink of sleep on the train. Besides, it wouldn't be fair to turn out my coxswain in the middle of the night, to meet me with the automobile at Lancaster Station. I'll take dinner at my club and spend the night at my town house, should you need me. I presume the Admiral has already gone on leave?'

'Yes, sir. He's down in Devon collecting specimens for his garden.'

'He should meet my mother. She loves her garden, too. Never mind. I'll be on my way in a few minutes. Carry on.'

Miller thought it a pity that the Director of Naval Intelligence, Rear Admiral Bethell, was not in. Like many of his naval colleagues, Miller had spent time in Germany, both on leave and on duty, visiting shipyards, dockyards and factories to keep pace with her naval developments, but such visits were now banned. The NID needed a network of suitable secret agents in place with legitimate cause to travel about Germany. He had wanted to ask Bethell if there was any news yet of the appointment of Kell's opposite number in the SSB. Before going on leave, Bethell had agreed to interview a retired boom defence officer, living on the Hamble, who Miller had suggested for the post. However, another vague thought occurred to him instead. He reached for the telephone and gave the operator a number to call.

'Kell, Miller here. I'm glad I caught you. Do you have any photographs of von Trotha before his death? ... You do? Good. I'll be right over. I'd like to look over them. ... No, it's nothing important. A strange notion has crossed my mind and I'd like to have time to explore it fully before I explain it. I'll be at your office within half an hour.'

He looked out of the window overlooking St James' Park. It was still a fine day so he thought he would walk to Victoria. The fresh air would help him think and the news of Friedrich's death disturbed him. However, if his germ of an idea worked, the Germans might not have lost a potentially valuable intelligence asset in Britain after all.

CHAPTER 3

September 1909

The Parisian prostitute was surprised by the appearance of the lonely diner seated above, at the only table on the gallery, overlooking the bar and main dining area of the bistro. Situated in a side street off the Champs Élysées, it was not a regular spot for the 'quality'. The gentleman was anxious and clearly waiting for someone who was either late for the assignation or no longer coming. One of the tricks of her trade was eying up potential clients and Annette, although only nineteen years of age, already had six years of experience in identifying likely prospects. The man was handsome, with dark hair and dark skin to match. He's probably from Spain or Italy, she thought. His suit was well cut, in the style of the English, so she concluded he might well be Italian. In any case, he looked wealthy and in need of company. After a cursory look at her reflection in the mirror of her compact, she mounted the rickety stairs to the gallery.

****

Peter Miller was suffering from post-holiday blues. He had enjoyed a wonderful summer holiday at home in England and, at a dance in Lancaster, had even met an attractive young lady of whom he hoped he might see more. Alas, that had all ended a month ago and he was back into the routine of work. He loved Paris, but not the life of a Third Secretary in His Britannic Majesty's embassy. His main function seemed to be to read numerous papers produced by the French Ministry of Agriculture, summarise any points he thought HMG's Board of Trade might find salient, and present his summary in the form of a weekly report to the Head of Chancery, Mr Raymond Stokes.

The previous week, he had sought to enliven his otherwise tedious report by including some commentary he had gleaned from various French newspapers. Unfortunately, that had resulted in a humiliating interview with Stokes this morning, at which he had been told to resubmit his report without the offending commentary. In Stokes's words: '*Stick to the facts, old boy. There's no place for conjecture.*'

Accordingly, it had come as a welcome surprise to receive the news that his father was staying at the new and luxurious Hôtel de Crillon, on the Place de la Concorde, and wanted to meet. Surely Papa was meant to be on leave at Marton Hall, but he was grateful for the interruption to his routine. His father's choice of venue was another surprise. It was very nondescript and, as such, he had never previously frequented it. Papa was not known for his epicurean tastes, but even so, he might have chosen any one of several other more fashionable establishments between here and the hotel. Although prepared to eat anything on the plate before him, Papa did have exquisite taste in wine and enjoyed imparting his knowledge to Peter and his elder brother, Richard. Perhaps this little bistro kept a decent cellar.

After announcing his name to the proprietor behind the bar, he was immediately ushered up a short flight of stairs to a small mezzanine floor overlooking the main body of the bistro. Disappointingly, there was no sign of Papa. He sipped the glass of white port he had ordered and surveyed the bistro. There was only one table at this level, so he presumed it a good place to transact private business. The table was well apart from the hearing of other customers, but that was not his concern this evening. Although only set with two places, it was large enough for a party of six. The bistro was quite dark, despite the glow of the gaslight outside coming through the large window overlooking the narrow street. To the right of the stairs below, a number of customers were seated at the brass-edged bar. Behind them were about ten or twelve tables clad with white cloths, only half of which were occupied. He wondered why the restaurant seemed so dark, as it was brightly lit by a large lamp hanging overhead. Perhaps it was the effect of the dark-coloured furniture, or maybe it was the fug of cigarette smoke rising from the bar and dining tables. The smell assaulted his nostrils. As a rule, he did not mind the smell of tobacco smoke. In fact, ever since compiling a report on the French tobacco industry, he had become interested in the product. His economic research had revealed that the following year, France would have two of its own cigarette brands, Gauloises and Gitanes, but for now, he was experimenting with a pipe. It seemed to have a certain cachet amongst the younger elements of the embassy. Even so, he found the smoke in the bistro quite acrid and was glad that Papa had reserved this table on the mezzanine. Again he consulted his watch and observed that Papa was now twenty minutes late for their appointment. Normally, Papa was such a stickler for punctuality.

Could Papa have suffered an accident? He wondered how long he ought to remain. He decided to give it another twenty minutes.

His situation offered a good vantage point to observe the comings and goings of the fellow diners. He glanced down to the bar and noticed an unaccompanied, very pretty girl drinking a glass of wine. From the relative height of the gallery he had a good view of the cleavage between her small, but plump, pale breasts, barely contained within the low neckline of her dress. The girl looked up and seemed to view him quizzically. She smiled and he automatically smiled back. The girl checked her make-up in a mirror and, to his surprise, stood and ascended the stairs towards him.

On climbing the stairs to reach the gallery, the girl approached him and, after wishing him a good evening, asked if she might join him. Taken aback by her forwardness, he agreed politely. After exchanging a few brief pleasantries, during which she introduced herself and he was able to correct Annette's misconception that he was Italian, Peter once more cast his eyes in vain over the dining area for signs of his father's arrival. Papa was now twenty-five minutes late and he was embarrassed by the presence of this girl, Annette. It dawned on him that she might well be a 'lady of the night'.

'Are you waiting for a young mademoiselle to join you, sir? Or, perhaps, your wife?'

'Oh, no!' he spluttered. 'I'm not married. I'm just expecting my father,' he answered quickly and added, 'He should have been here half an hour ago.'

To his horror, Annette confirmed his suspicion about her virtue by exchanging her place for that alongside him, on the banquette on which he was sitting.

'Perhaps I could keep you in company instead, sir? May I compliment you on your French. I would never have guessed you were a foreigner.'

As she spoke, Annette started to stroke his inner thigh. He froze. Nobody had ever done this before to him. Very quickly, Annette's nimble and practised fingers rose to his groin and found the rising swelling. Expertly, she started making circular strokes of the sensitive spot.

'There's a room through the back if you would like to come with me, sir.'

Increasingly aroused, Peter knew this had to stop. Although the sensation was pleasant, his Roman Catholic upbringing told him this was a sin. Sex was only for the purpose of procreation, and in any case, Papa might yet arrive. Summoning his resolve, he firmly grasped Annette's slender wrist and forcefully removed it from his thigh.

'No, mademoiselle. I have an engagement to fulfil. Good evening.'

Annette stood up. 'You English talk too much. No wonder you are such poor lovers.' She picked up her glass and flounced back down the stairs to the bar, passing Captain Miller at the foot of the staircase. He bowed before her, in the exaggerated fashion of a Tudor courtier, and spoke quietly to her. She laughed, stroked him on the shoulder affectionately and returned to the bar.

'Hello, Peter, old son. Sorry I'm late. Or was I just in time?' Miller cocked his head in the direction of the bar.

Peter had initially been both relieved by his father's arrival and embarrassed that he might have witnessed the connection. Now he was intrigued.

'Hello, Papa. Forgive me for asking, but do you know that lady.'

'Annette? Why, of course. Many's the time she has rendered me some little service. It's one of the reasons I come here.'

Peter was shocked by what the answer implied. Although it was his Swiss mother, Mutti, who was the strict Catholic, nonetheless he had always thought of Papa as a very honourable and upright man. Moreover, his parents had always seemed to have such a strong marriage. He was disturbed to see his respectable father in this new light. However, he cautiously decided that, for now, he would not question the nature of Annette's services. It could be another of Papa's teases.

'Have you ordered, or did you wait for me?'

'Er, no, Papa. I barely had time to look at the menu whilst I waited.'

'Fine. To be honest, Peter, I'm a little pressed for time. I have to meet someone later. Would you mind if I ordered for you? This isn't the best place to eat in town, but Madame la propriétaire has her strengths.'

'Papa, I'm in your hands. I'm just pleased to be in your company.' He wondered if he had just seen Papa set up this pressing engagement.

As he had suspected, the food was not terribly good, but it was passable. It was served by the patron, whose wife had prepared the dishes. Papa had chosen two very fine wines to accompany the first two courses and the evening passed convivially as he was transported back to England by the latest news of his family. His father also questioned him closely on his life in Paris and work at the embassy. Peter felt comfortable enough to confide his growing disillusion with the Diplomatic Service and his father took the news calmly.

'Look, old chap. I know you had your heart on the navy, but you must have had good reasons for choosing the Diplomatic. Do those reasons not still hold good?'

'I'm not sure they do, Papa. I joined primarily because I was interested in foreign languages and relished the opportunity to visit far-off places. I also had a notion that my role would be part of a wider plan to develop mutual understanding of other nations' cultures. I'm starting to feel I was naïve. It all seems so stuffy … and independent thought is very much frowned upon. I'm not sure I see myself in thirty years' time as a mandarin with a God-given right to rule other people.'

'Have another glass of the Château d'Yquem. I have an idea that might interest you. If I could arrange it, would you be interested in a move to the navy?'

'Of course, Papa. It would be my dearest wish, but I could never be passed for sea-going duties.'

'Well, that wouldn't matter for what I have in mind. I'm thinking more of a commission in the Voluntary Reserve, for special duties.'

'If you are thinking of me joining as a Paymaster, Papa, forget it. I've had enough of being in an office already.'

'No, I was thinking of something very special and a damned sight more interesting. Tell me, do you still keep up with Brassey's, *Naval Annual*?'

'Every now and then, but since you introduced me to Mister Jane, I've tended to be more interested in his books, *All the World's Fighting Ships*. Why do you ask, Papa?'

'I may come to it in due course. Tell me how you would distinguish the Nassau and Helgoland classes of German Dreadnoughts.'

'You mean quite apart from the fact that the later ships have three funnels, rather than two? Come on, Papa. That's too easy.'

'How else would you tell the difference, Peter?'

'All right, Papa. The Helgoland has a main armament of 30.5 cm guns to replace the earlier 28 cm guns. She has an improved triple-expansion propulsion system capable of producing an extra 6000 horsepower, increasing her maximum speed from 22 to 23.6 knots. Do I get a coconut, Papa?'

'Don't be smart. You've made your point. What do you remember of your old school chum, Friedrich von Trotha?'

Peter was surprised by the question and the change of subject. On reflecting on his relationship with Friedrich, he realised that he had not seen or heard from him for just over three years, since they had both left Charterhouse.

In respect for his father's wishes concerning the son of his late friend, Peter had done his best to help the son to fit in as best as he could. However, von Trotha had not been popular with the other members of the school. His Bavarian arrogance had seemed extreme, even by the standards of the progeny of the British nobility in the school at the time. This had served to set him apart from his fellows, but Peter had persevered in trying to build a friendship with the young Bavarian. Both boys were very alike in looks and many people, including the masters, often confused the two. On several occasions, it was only when one of them spoke, to betray their native accent, that they could be differentiated with any certainty. In fact, both had a facility for languages and eventually learned to mimic each other so that even their voices and speech patterns could be made to sound alike.

Peter and his father laughed as he recounted fondly some of the scrapes they had entered into and pranks they played when they swapped identities. Poor Matron and a particular French student master, whose name he could not now recall, had often been the particular butt of their humour. Shockingly, in June 1904, when Oberst von Trotha was serving on the defence staff at the German Embassy in Washington and the boys were in the Cricket Quarter of their final year in the Lower School, news had come through that both von Trotha's parents had been killed tragically in a shipping accident off New York.

Miller continued to question his son on his school days and, perhaps in the hope that it might spoil his father's later engagement, or through the effect of a good dinner and fine wine, Peter was happy to expand.

It had been a surprise to many when von Trotha had returned to school for the Oration Quarter of the new school year after attending the funeral of his parents at the end of the previous term. It had been assumed that he would remain in Germany to continue his education. However, von Trotha had told Peter in confidence that as well as being an only child he had no immediate family and so he could not see any purpose in remaining in Germany. The family's attorney was taking care of his late parents' affairs and arranging for the sale of the farms and estates in Bavaria. Von Trotha had confided that the winding up of his family's affairs would supply more than enough capital and interest to provide him a healthy income for the rest of his life. Von Trotha had, therefore, planned to follow his education at Charterhouse with study for a degree at Cambridge.

It had not been long, though, before many fellow Carthusians had noticed a distinct change in von Trotha's behaviour. It had been almost as if he had considered that, in the absence of both his parents, he was answerable to nobody. Initially, this had manifested itself in an even more arrogant and unapproachable attitude, but this had not been the worst of it. Von Trotha had started to display a marked partiality for some of the younger boys. To some, he had appeared to be unusually kind and, it had been rumoured, unhealthily friendly. Yet to others, or even to his supposed favourites, he had been unusually cruel, even sadistic. The Lower School had never known which way the wind would blow.

Despite the loyalty he had felt towards his father, Peter had found it untenable to continue his friendship. He and von Trotha had started to go their separate ways and this had left von Trotha completely isolated in the Upper School. The fluctuation in behaviour had not gone unnoticed by the masters in the Brooke Hall common room and von Trotha had not been judged worthy of appointment as a monitor for his year. Peter had never known the full story, but there had been rumours that the monitors had thrashed von Trotha in response to some indiscretion with a younger boy that, had it come to the ears of the masters, would have led to von Trotha's permanent expulsion from Charterhouse. Peter had concluded that the rumours had probably been true since, in their final year at Charterhouse, von Trotha had abandoned his intentions of studying at Cambridge and, moreover, become increasingly and vehemently opposed to the school way of life, the British class system and its form of government and colonial service. This latter piece of information seemed of particular interest to Papa.

'Have you heard anything from your old pal Friedrich since leaving Charterhouse?'

'No, nothing. Why do you ask?'

'Because he's dead.' Miller outlined the details of the discovery of von Trotha's corpse, including the information about the letters found hidden in the apartment.

'It's hard to credit. I can't say I'm overly surprised to hear Friedrich was a homosexual. One heard rumours of some indiscretion at school. But to offer himself up as a potential spy. Why would he do that? After all, you and his father were good friends, Papa.'

'We each have our hidden depths, Peter. Perhaps he was motivated by revenge or maybe he was just bored. He may even have thought it a means to become important. I doubt it was inspired by patriotism. Would you consider yourself a patriot, Peter?'

'Why, of course. You surely don't need to ask.'

'I'm afraid I do. Indeed, I need your help. Peter, I'm in the process of setting up a new department. It will work for the Admiralty, but be outside it and independent. You don't seem terribly struck on life in the Diplomatic Service and I wonder whether you might be game for a little adventure. I could arrange you that commission and you would be serving your country in a more direct way than by writing economic digests. What do you think?'

'And what does this department do, Papa?'

'It keeps an eye on German naval developments, only we can't always find the information we need from *Jane's* or *Brassey's*. We need some enterprising young men to keep their ear to the ground, as it were.'

'You mean, become a spy? Is that what you are, Papa?'

'Me? No, I'm just a pen-pusher in the Admiralty and the new department will be run by somebody else.'

'Is it not dangerous? I don't see myself as some kind of hero. What about training? I assume I would have to live in Germany.'

'Peter, you've never lacked courage, but we're not looking for heroes. We need people who appear ordinary, who don't attract attention. Often the job merely involves reading the journals and newspapers, or listening to sailors talking in bars. It would involve visits to yards and factories, or meeting others with legitimate access. I promise you it's far less exciting than Le Queux's novels on the subject. I grant that if you're not careful, you could end up in trouble with the local authorities, but it hasn't happened yet. My people would organise a cover for you being in Germany. As for training, that could be arranged, too. We already have a couple of good men out there, but that information is between you and me. Do you still keep up with your piano practice?'

'I still play most days and I'm giving a solo recital at the embassy next month.'

'Capital. We could arrange for you to become a salesman to one of the German piano manufacturers. Steinway have a factory in Hamburg and it would give you the perfect excuse to travel around Germany without suspicion.'

'But why me, Papa? How do you know I could do whatever is required?'

'Peter, you are my son. Of course I know you well enough to judge you capable of this. You have a grasp of detail, a retentive memory and an abundance of common sense. I am sure you would have the necessary initiative, too. Moreover, and very importantly, you speak German like a native and that will keep you out of trouble. I will not lie to you. You will undoubtedly experience fear and no doubt a large measure of tedium, but think of the opportunities. You would be your own man, acting on your own initiative, with rarely an office in sight.'

Peter felt the hairs rise on the back of his neck. The opportunity did seem intriguing and even alluring. He relished the idea of being independent, but also a part of a potentially exciting new branch of the navy. He sipped his wine carefully and looked down at the other clientele of the bistro. He would miss the life in Paris, but not the fixed routine of desk work at the embassy. Perhaps it was the wine mellowing him, but he was certainly tempted to accept his father's offer.

'All right, Papa. If I accepted this proposition, when would I leave for Germany?'

Papa smiled broadly. 'I cannot honestly say, as it's not within my control. We would like you to start by impersonating Friedrich for a little while, and then take it from there.'

Peter was in the process of draining his glass and nearly choked on the wine. 'What? I couldn't do it.'

'You could do it. You told me yourself how you often used to change places with him at school, a far more intimate environment, and yet you pulled it off. We just want you to make contact with the Germans, play along for a while and see what they're up to. There's nothing dangerous or heroic about it. You'd just be playing a part.'

'But what if I'm then asked to find out things? How would I find the information? I've had no training. Supposing I went to Germany and met somebody who has known Friedrich more recently than I. How would I explain my absence to Mutti?'

'Look, Peter. You'll not be doing this on your own. I told you, the people I know will give you the training and support you need. In any case, Friedrich would have been just as much an amateur. Come on. You're surely not going to be weak and duck a challenge are you? It might only be for a couple of months and it would be an entrée into the Department. I can square it with your mother.'

Peter felt the familiar gaze of his father's eyes into his own. As he looked into those dark eyes, the goose bumps and hairs again rose on his skin and he shivered. The fixed and steady eyes were hypnotic. They seemed to paralyse him, much as the cobra's hood fixes its prey before the snake strikes. All his life he had been awestruck by, if not frightened of his father, and he knew he would again have to submit to his iron will.

He answered more cheerfully and airily than he actually felt. 'Very well, then, Papa. If you can arrange for me to be excused my desk and a commission in the RNVR, I'll give it a go.'

'Stout fellow. Let's have a glass of cognac to celebrate. The patron has a special bottle put aside for me. And one thing more. Your mother is never to know what you're really up to. She would never forgive me.'

As Papa tried to attract the eye of the waitress, his attention was diverted by the entrance of a strange-looking man, wearing a dirty, grey Homburg hat. The man looked around the room, carefully observing each of the diners on the ground floor, before approaching the bar and ordering a small beer. Peter noted that the stranger had an unattractive face, with sallow, rough skin and looked like a Jew. He was intrigued. There was something odd about the chap. Why's the fellow's standing with his back to us, clearly watching the door? 'ay up! That Annette's given Papa a slight nod.

'I'm sorry, Peter, but I have to go to my next engagement. There's no hurry for you to go, though. I'll fix you a cognac and coffee before I go. Leave the bill. I have an account with the patron and he'll sort all that out. I'll be in touch very soon. Good to see you, as always, and thanks for your co-operation.'

Peter shook hands with his father and watched him approach the stranger at the bar, mutter something to him as he passed, and leave the bistro. The Jew finished his beer, left some coins on the counter and, after an interval of two minutes or so, also left the bistro. Peter was intrigued and began to wonder whether Annette's services to her father were innocent after all. Then again, he thought, it depends on your definition of innocence. It had been quite an evening, but it would be best not to discuss it with Mutti.

CHAPTER 4

Captain Miller checked his watch again. He was long past the point of considering this meeting at the SSB's offices as quite tiresome. It had already lasted over an hour and he decided it time a resolution was reached. Kell had thought it a good idea that Peter should impersonate his former school friend, but Commander Mansfield Smith-Cumming, the naval officer designated to be Kell's opposite number in charge of the Foreign Section of the SSB within a few weeks, was proving difficult to persuade. Miller had only involved Cumming out of courtesy, but Cumming was already showing he might be too much his own man.

'Surely, Commander Cumming, you can see the benefits of the plan. If we could keep von Trotha's death a secret, there might yet be further contact from Abteilung IIIb that we could follow up,' Kell stated.

'But I still don't see why have you sought my opinion on this, Kell?' Cumming asked. 'I would have thought this more a contre-espionage operation and outside my bailiwick. If you are so keen on the idea, then you hardly need my support.'

'At first sight, certainly. But look at the potential to gain an insight into the modus operandi of your German opponents … if this was to pay off.'

'Possibly. But I appear to be desperately short of agents at present and will not have the resources of your section. You can at least call on the help of the War Office and local chief constables. I will barely be able to count the number of my agents on one hand. I'm more interested in obtaining intelligence on specific subjects than learning how the Germans operate. What's the Admiralty view on this, Captain Miller, sir?'

Miller stood before answering. He liked to stand whilst thinking. 'At least initially, I agree this is within Kell's purview. But we don't know where this might end.' Miller closed his eyes for nearly a minute whilst he thought over the problem. Neither of his subordinates felt comfortable to break into his thoughts.

'As I see it,' Miller continued, 'it's all down to the Germans' plans for von Trotha. If they have him in mind as a spy in Britain, which would seem an obvious notion, then knowing their plans is very much of interest to you, Kell. On the other hand, supposing they were to think it too obvious, that we might already be on to von Trotha? Then they might choose to deploy him elsewhere. After all, he could pick up valuable—'

'But, sir!' Cumming interrupted. 'You seem to discount the possibility that the Germans are not taken in by your son's subterfuge. They cannot be stupid.'

'But I do discount it, Cumming, and not because I deem the Abteilung to be stupid. 'K', are you confident that there is no possibility that news of von Trotha's suicide may have leaked?'

'Absolutely, sir. Clarke has an excellent relationship with Scotland Yard and has assured me that von Trotha's identity is known only to three of their detectives and he guarantees me they can be trusted to be discreet.'

'There you are then. There is no reason for the Germans to be suspicious and I know my son well enough to know he can pull off the impersonation. He's done it many times before, after all. Satisfied, Cumming?'

'Very well, sir.' Miller could see there was no enthusiasm in Cumming's response, but that would do, he thought.

'Good. Now, as I was saying. Our von Trotha would be well-positioned to pick up intelligence on our navy that would interest the Germans greatly. However, he could do the same on our ships in any foreign port. And let's not be arrogant enough to consider this country the main target of German intelligence-gathering operations. France is a much more likely target and we know von Trotha spoke fluent French as well as English. In such circumstances, Cumming, his tasking would be of equal importance to your department as any information one of your agents recovered on the Germans. Knowing what the Germans want to know would be quite valuable. Do you see my logic?'

'I hadn't thought of it that way, sir,' Cumming replied guardedly.

'Sir, you surely don't imagine running your son as a double agent abroad?' Kell exclaimed. 'I had no idea you had such a thing in mind. If the Germans had a notion to use von Trotha in the manner you suggest, then he would surely have to go to Germany for briefing for a start.'

'Quite possibly.'

'How would young Peter impersonate von Trotha in Germany? Naturally, he's intimate with the life of von Trotha during his school days, but in the absence of any communication since their intertwined lives at Charterhouse, he couldn't possibly know who von Trotha had since met and what had passed between them. Impersonating von Trotha at

Charterhouse was an innocent jape with no great risk. Taking his identity as a German agent would not only be far more difficult, but failure could lead to a firing squad. If Peter were to leave these shores, then he would be beyond our protection.'

'Steady on, 'K'. It might not be as difficult as it looks. The main obstacle has been cleared in that there are no complications concerning family connections. However, let's not rush our fences. We don't yet know the Germans' plans for von Trotha, but the opportunity to penetrate the German intelligence services is surely too good to forego. I propose that, for now anyway, 'K', you run Peter until we see whether he is accepted by the Germans as von Trotha. If that works and he is tasked to stay in England, then it's a straightforward counter-espionage operation. He should help you identify the existing spy network over here at the very least. If the case should develop along a different path, then it would be for Cumming and me to make the call on subsequent steps. Either way, I will, naturally, be keeping a close eye on events.'

Miller fixed each man in turn with his intense stare. 'Are we agreed, gentlemen, that we should let our little *ruse de guerre* run its course?'

Cumming nodded immediately, but Kell clearly had doubts.

'Sir, over the past few weeks I have greatly valued your assistance and direction in setting up this department. I assure you that I hold you in the highest esteem. But for God's sake! I cannot understand how you could be so ruthless as to expose your son to the risk we are contemplating. I urge you to reconsider.'

Miller and Kell stared hard at each other for several seconds before Kell broke off eye contact. Miller settled the issue. 'I'm sorry, Kell. My mind is made up. There's too much at stake.'

CHAPTER 5

October 1910

The proprietor of the Hôtel Jean de Luxembourg, Monsieur Gustave Lecuyer, hung up the room keys of the three Dutchmen and wished them a good day before he returned to the piece in his newspaper on the Tour de France. Lecuyer was not a bicyclist, but had been a fan ever since he had seen the riders pass by that July on the first stage to Roubaix. The Tour had gone on to include a stage through the Pyrenees for the first time. Now, according to the newspaper columnist, the 1911 tour might take in the Alps, too. This seemed odd. Surely the riders would have to get off and walk part of the way. How could it then be called a bicycle race?

Lecuyer folded his paper and mused over his three foreign guests. They struck him as odd too, but then were not all foreigners? He found the two gentlemen quite civil, but he did not care for their valet. Indeed, he was surprised that they continued to employ him, considering how little work he appeared to do. They seemed to have no less need of the hotel staff for their daily needs, despite the presence of a valet. He had heard them excuse his eccentric behaviour by saying that the valet was an excellent cook, but then why stay in a hotel and frequent the dining room or the local restaurant and cafés? However, after more than thirty years in hospitality, he had learned to keep his thoughts to himself and ask few questions. Moreover, he was grateful for the business. So far from the coast, the hotel did not generally have many guests after the summer season and these foreigners had been with him for nearly three months. Better still, they paid their bills regularly.

Lecuyer knew Herr Kleisters better as he spoke excellent French. Like his colleague, Herr Rutte, Kleisters was tall, slim and athletic in build. Kleisters was an architect with a special interest in 16th and 17th century buildings. He had expressed great delight in the work of Vauban's great citadel at nearby Arras and was now making regular visits to the mediaeval town of Montreuil to examine and draw its many fine buildings. His friend Rutte, on the other hand, was blond, moustachioed and a keen artist. Rutte, along with the valet Kuyper, spoke very little French. Lecuyer had learned through Kleisters that Rutte was a devotee of the earlier Hague School of landscape painting. Apparently it was known also as the 'Grey School' for the muted tones of the colours and Rutte had decided that the grey skies of the French Flanders countryside were perfect for this genre of painting. Lecuyer thought this daft as usually the grey skies heralded rain and who could paint in the rain? When he retired, he planned on moving down to the warmer and sunnier climes of the Auvergne or Limousin.

Glancing out of the window to check the weather, he noted with grim satisfaction that the sky was quite leaden and he was certain that rain could not be long off. In doing so, he saw his guests being driven off by Kuyper in the trap they had hired for their daily visits to the local countryside. Kuyper's one merit seemed to be that he was good with horses and an excellent coachman. Although short in height at about one metre seventy-five centimetres, he was powerfully built with a huge barrel chest. His completely bald pate was compensated for by enormous dark whiskers and a huge moustache. Lecuyer didn't favour their chances of getting much painting done today, but there would be plenty to take their interest in Montreuil.

****

The Dutchmen were not too worried by the likely lack of opportunity to paint today. Their main medium for recording the local landscape and architecture was camera film, supplemented by sketches and detailed maps of the area, as well of any military fortifications that could be employed for defence against an invasion from across the Belgian border. For six months, Kleisters and Rutte had successfully used the architect and artist story as a mantle for their activities in surveying large areas of the Flanders, Pas-de-Calais and Picardy regions. For the past three months, they had been accompanied by the only member of the party to speak Dutch, Staff Sergeant, or "Vizefeldwebel", Semper of the 1st Royal Saxon Field Artillery Regiment. Semper was a South African Boer by birth who had fought the British and, after the Boer Wars, had moved to Saxony. He was now driving the trap in his alias as Kuyper. His passengers were also members of the Imperial German Army and all three were currently assigned to the military intelligence division, Geheime Nachrichtendienst des Heeres, or ND. In charge of the party was Hauptman Maximilian von Hoffman of the 13th Royal Bavarian Infantry Regiment, a gifted amateur artist, and, thus, well suited to play the part of the artist Rutte. His companion was known to them as Leutnant Friedrich von Trotha of the 2nd Railway Regiment.

****

That evening the two officers discussed their operation over dinner in low voices to avoid being overheard.

'I have finished decoding the letter I received this afternoon, von Trotha. It seems our masters are pleased with the results of our work so far and have asked me to return to Berlin to brief the General Staff on our findings. The photographs have apparently come out very well, but they now wish to see the full plans, sketches and maps. I am to return the day after tomorrow.'

'It seems rather sudden, sir. What are their plans for Semper and me?'

'You are to remain here for a few days. I'll tell the proprietor that I have to go to Amsterdam to discuss a potential exhibition of my work. You can then say that you have, accordingly, decided to cut short your holiday. Say you are going to have a few days in Amiens before returning home. In reality, you and Semper are to travel to Albert and make a survey of the local area whilst you await either fresh orders or my return. Send me a telegram with your address when you get there.'

Sub Lieutenant Peter Miller RNVR of Britain's new Secret Service, alias Friedrich von Trotha, delayed replying for a moment whilst the waiter cleared the table and then he ordered them both a coffee and a cognac.

'I don't relish being left on my own with Semper.'

'I agree he is a coarse fellow and I don't suppose he's had a bath for a month, but he's an excellent cartographer with a good eye for the topography. Moreover, his artillery experience is invaluable. I'm sure you'll work things out between you.'

'He is most certainly coarse and even brutal. It's not just the smell of sweat that offends my nose, but he only ever seems to eat the local garlic sausage. It's clear he doesn't respect my lack of formal military training and, to be honest, I don't trust him. I'm sure he has been stealing wine from the hotel cellar.'

'Von Trotha, my dear fellow, take a piece of advice from me. It's not necessary to like your men to lead them. Take the time to work out their strengths and weaknesses, and then harness the strengths and show them you respect these qualities. That way you will get the best out of them. Of course, Semper will be wary of you. You've been an army reservist half a year to his twenty and, forgive me for saying so, but you know what Academy officers call reservists?'

'Yes, sir. They call us "civilians with extenuating circumstances".'

'Quite right. You are still new to this line of work, whilst he has been doing it for nearly five years. Show him you are competent and he will learn to respect you. Semper has worked his way up the ranks the hard way. That makes him feel he is entitled to respect from his officers. As for his honesty, you may be right. He's a good locksmith and I suspect he is using these skills not just to the profit of the Fatherland.'

Peter considered his superior's words. He respected and even liked von Hoffman. He was a good officer and a very decent man. Peter felt uncomfortable about deceiving him and it was difficult to regard him as a potential enemy. During his time as the Naval Attaché in Berlin, Papa had built many friendships with German officers and Mutti even had German relatives. To Peter, the Germans were people just like the English. Even the royal families of Britain and Germany were related. It seemed unthinkable that the two countries might one day go to war against each other and yet, he, of all people, knew the hostile intentions Germany had towards Britain's neighbour across the Channel, France. He did not yet see war with Britain as inevitable but, if it did come, he knew he might have to fight and hoped he would not come face to face with honourable men such as the likes of Hoffman. Men like Semper would be a different matter.

****

Peter bade farewell to von Hoffman at the pretty timber-faced railway station in Abbeville, leaving Semper at the hotel to start organising their baggage to go ahead of them to Amiens two days later. Much as he enjoyed travelling in a horse and trap, on a wet day such as today it was a pleasant change to make the return trip in the automobile he and von Hoffman had hired for the occasion. Peter thought it polite to compliment the vehicle.

'Am I right in thinking, sir, that this is from the Renault factory?'

'Absolutely, sir. It is a Type AG ...'

The driver began a lengthy discourse on the merits of the automobile and Peter regretted his feigned enthusiasm. In truth, it was not as impressive as his father's Mercedes. However, he was genuinely pleased with the relative speed and comfort of the vehicle versus the trap. The rubber tyres certainly made the heavily-potholed French roads more tolerable, but as the driver prattled on, his mind began to wander.

His life as a double agent in the guise of Friedrich seemed to have made him more an agent of Germany than Britain. After all, he was spying on France and Belgium and none of the information he had gathered so far seemed of any use to the SSB. Even so, he faithfully recorded his actions and regularly submitted a coded report back to London through an address in Switzerland. This was disguised as an innocent letter to an old school chum from Charterhouse, now living in Geneva. Naturally, although such a person existed, Cumming's men at the SSB had an arrangement to intercept the letters and send them on to London via the diplomatic bag.

'... I grant you, it was a great risk to borrow from my family to raise the sum to purchase this vehicle, but it has been a prudent investment, sir. I have almost repaid the loan. At this rate I will be able to give up my smithy. I have had a few bookings for weddings. That all started when I ...'

Peter continued to utter a few 'umms' and 'ahs' to keep the conversation going as the Picardy countryside rolled by. It struck him as odd that there were so few hedgerows to delineate the fields. It was all so tame and far removed from the perilous life he had previously imagined an agent of the Secret Service would face routinely. If he was honest, he was now enjoying the life. It had taken the German Intelligence Service a full six tedious months to recruit him, during which he had kicked his heels in London and Berlin, living the life of Friedrich. Then he had been disappointed to be sent to Belgium, but the surveys were interesting and he liked working for von Hoffman. But it didn't have any relation to the navy and he wondered if there was any point in him continuing the deception. He resolved to raise his future employment in the remainder of his next report to London.

'We have arrived, sir.' Peter was jolted from his private thoughts by the driver applying the brakes rather sharply outside the hotel.

'I have so enjoyed our conversation, sir. It is so nice to meet a fellow enthusiast. Believe me, invest in the new Renault and you will not regret it.'

Peter checked his pocket watch and observed that it was already late afternoon. He still had time to finish his latest report to London before he would need to shave and change for dinner. Prior to paying the driver for his fare, he went over the arrangements for taking him and Semper to Amiens in two days' time. After entering the hotel, he mounted the stairs quickly and breezed into the living room of his suite. He froze in astonishment.

He had fully expected to see his portmanteau packed neatly and the remainder of his clothes and possessions stored away tidily, much as he had left them. Instead his room had been ransacked and all his belongings were strewn about the place in chaos. No sooner had he taken in the surroundings than he smelt the sour mixture of wine, sweat and garlic sausage that he knew heralded the approach from behind of Semper. He turned to remonstrate with him for the state of his rooms, but before he could do so, was struck on the head by a heavy object and he collapsed onto the floor semi-conscious. Whilst he lay on the floor, a cloth was roughly stuffed into his mouth, his hands were quickly bound behind his knees and his ankles tied together, leaving him in a sort of foetal position on his back. It had all happened very quickly and he was powerless to resist. Slowly his vision returned and the blurred shape of his attacker came into focus to reveal the malicious face of Semper, just before receipt of a violent kick in the ribs. Semper picked him up like a doll and threw him into a corner of the hotel room.

'So who are you really, you treacherous little piece of shit?' Semper snarled.

Peter was shocked by this sudden attack. His brain tried to engage to appreciate what was happening, but for the moment, his thoughts were focused on the throb of his head and he didn't react to Semper's question until Semper half lifted him by his lapels and shook him violently.

'You're a filthy spy. Come on. Who are you working for?'

Peter was completely taken aback. 'I don't know what you are talking about,' he stuttered in reply.

He quickly surveyed the room, looking for an explanation of Semper's extraordinary behaviour. His eyes rested on the dressing table and the blood seemed to drain from his head and chest into his stomach, and yet at the same time his face and temples flushed with a surge of heat. Carefully placed on the dressing table was one of his boots with the heel twisted through ninety degrees, an unfolded piece of paper and a pile of gold coins. The full horror started to dawn on him and Semper spotted the signs.

'Yes, you little fucker. I've found you out and here's the evidence. I've always known there was something not quite right about you, so I checked your baggage and look what I found. A coded letter written in secret ink hidden in the heel of your boot and fifty gold coins stitched into the base of your trunk. So don't deny it, you prick.' Semper finished his sentence with another hard kick, this time to Peter's groin.

Peter nearly gagged as he gasped with the pain and tried to spit out the cloth to allow him to swallow properly. Semper positioned himself to aim a further kick at Peter's groin.

'Make no mistake, I'm going to kill you, but not before you've answered my questions. It's just a matter of how much pain you opt to endure before I put you out of your fucking misery, you traitor.'

Again Semper's boot landed in Peter's groin, despite his attempt to roll out of the way. As he fought the excruciating pain, he also fought the urge to vomit. With the gag in place he would be in danger of choking in his own vomit and he did not think Semper would much care. He knew he had to think and think quickly or else he was going to die, but the pain overcame him and he drifted into unconsciousness.

CHAPTER 6

Peter Miller's consciousness returned when he found himself roughly shaken and slapped across the cheeks. He had no idea how long he had been unconscious, but would have preferred to have remained in that state. The pain in his groin was still sickening.

On opening his eyes in response, he finally grasped the situation. Semper was waving his half-finished coded report in front of him. The report was written in a synthetic ink of British invention, hidden in Peter's shaving stick. The secret message became invisible when dry, but could then be exposed to the recipient by exposure to iodine vapour. Pretending not yet to be fully conscious, he surreptitiously, but carefully, studied the objects on the dressing table and looked at the mess around him. To his intense relief, he noted that whilst his shaving items were scattered over the floor, Semper had not cut up his shaving stick to reveal the ink powder hidden within it. Now opening his eyes fully to look at the paper Semper was holding so gleefully, he was comforted to see that it contained only the black ink characters of the letter to his former school pal and none of the brown writing between the lines that iodine vapour would have revealed. He had been a careless fool to have left the message in the stout boots he had worn the previous day. As the report was not yet finished, he had stupidly hidden it away and forgotten to transfer it to the boots he was wearing today for his trip to Abbeville. He cursed his slackness, but maybe there was a chance of redeeming himself. He motioned with his eyes to Semper to remove the gag to allow him to speak.

'All right, I'll take out the gag for a moment, but one cry out of you and I'll ram it so far down your fucking throat to kill you. Go on. Speak.'

Peter knew that Semper's threat was not empty and he fought himself to remain calm. 'Semper, you're mistaken in your interpretation,' he croaked. 'I'm not using secret ink. If I was, you would have developed a hidden message by now. We both know how to do it.'

He saw in Semper's eyes that he had clearly tried to find such a message and failed. It offered some hope.

'Then why take the trouble of hiding such a letter in a specially made compartment of your boot? And why write the letter in French? Are you working for the Froschfresser?' Semper made to kick him again.

'No, wait!'

Peter's brain had never worked so fast in its life as he desperately sought an explanation other than the truth. He tried to buy time by taking the part of the innocent.

'You had no right to be searching my baggage when you should have been packing it? That letter is private and I merely hid it in my boot to hide it from the chambermaids. You can see it is in French and why not?'

Peter began to gain confidence and with it his indignation increased. 'My friend is Swiss and lives in the French speaking part of Switzerland, so naturally I write to him in French. Once the Hauptman hears of this outrage …'

Semper's abusive reply was accompanied by a vicious stamp on Peter's right kneecap. He nearly passed out with the pain, but Semper shook him back to full consciousness to his intense discomfort.

Semper's head was now so close to Peter's own that he could smell the rancid, garlic-ridden breath. In itself it was almost too much to bear. Semper growled, 'I know you think I'm stupid. I've seen that contemptuous look in your eye often enough. Just because you're an officer. Let me tell you, you high and mighty little fucker, I was killing English swine in Africa when you were still in kindergarten. So how do you explain the Gold Roosters?' He slapped Peter hard across the left cheek.

Peter had not been expecting the blow and had bitten his tongue, but he detected some diminishing of certainty on Semper's face and relaxed a little despite the pain of his tongue and smarting cheek.

'They are mine in case of emergency. Surely you recognise that in our work it is not always easy to draw large sums of cash from a bank in a hurry. When my parents died, they left me well provided for and I choose not to leave all my assets in a bank.'

Peter's tongue began to swell and speech was becoming difficult, but he forced himself to keep talking. He couldn't take much more pain and his mouth was filling with blood.

'As for hiding it, I would have thought the reasons obvious.' He saw the rising uncertainty in Semper and regained his earlier confidence. He spat out a mouthful of blood.

'Now if you are not satisfied with my explanation, I suggest you raise it with the Hauptman on his return. I certainly intend discussing with him your outrageous behaviour. Indeed, you'll be lucky to avoid a court martial. Now untie me and start cleaning up this mess.'

To his intense relief, his explanation and the mention of von Hoffman were sufficiently persuasive for Semper to give way. Peter was sure that Semper was not convinced, but couldn't take the risk that he was telling the truth. Sheepishly, Semper started to untie Peter's bonds.

'I'm sorry Herr Leutnant. I hope you will accept my apology and that I was only doing my duty. I am sure you would agree that one can never be too careful in our business.'

Peter thought he could not have agreed more with the last part of the statement.

****

As Peter lay in his bed that evening, his brain was too active to allow him any semblance of sleep. He knew that Semper was no fool and was only biding his time before the return of von Hoffman to report the incident. Whilst von Hoffman might appear to accept Peter's account of the items found in his luggage by Semper, Peter was sure that he would face more intense scrutiny once back in Germany. Somehow, he had to avoid Semper making his report and that could only mean one thing. It was him or Semper. For hours he turned over the problem in his mind.

He tried to bring on sleep by listening to his heart pumping and monitoring the pattern of his heart beat. He could hear it thumping away in his ears more noisily than normal. For a few seconds it would beat regularly and then the rhythm would suddenly change. The last beat of the sequence seemed to be replaced by a nauseous convulsion in his stomach. There was no chance of falling asleep. Even had his mind not been so active, his ribs, testicles and kneecap were giving too much pain to allow the relief of sleep.

Eventually, the solution was obvious. Semper had to die. The method was the problem. Semper was a huge man and Peter did not see how he could overpower him without a firearm. Even if he used a knife, he would need the element of surprise. Furthermore, where do you stab a man to kill him in one thrust of the knife? Murder hadn't been part of his training, either in England or Germany. Semper was too powerful a man to be given a second chance. Peter had no doubt that even a severely wounded Semper would be capable of killing him with his bare hands. And there was another thing. Even assuming he was successful, it would have to be done in a way that would not draw suspicion on him or their mission. To make matters worse, it had to be done soon, as he had no idea when von Hoffman might return or the orders arrive for their recall to Berlin.

It crossed his mind several times that the task was too great. He was not a trained killer. The largest mammal he had ever killed, without the aid of a rifle or shotgun, was a rabbit. Nonetheless, each time his resolve to kill Semper failed him, a cold sweat overtook his body as he imagined the consequences should his cover be blown. He thought of bolting back to London and abandoning his mission, but then he imagined the interview with Papa as he was forced to admit his failure and cowardice. Outwardly Papa would appear to be understanding, but they would both know the truth. He really had no choice.

Slowly an idea started to form itself as to how he might use Semper's avarice to his own advantage. The light of the new day had already started to filter through the drawn shutters of his room before he fell into a fitful sleep, in which he was alternately tormented by visions of Papa, Semper and his potential fate in Berlin.

CHAPTER 7

For the following few days Semper was much more civil and compliant, but still suspicious and very watchful of Peter. He, for his part, remained badly shaken. It had been a salutatory reminder of the hazards of his trade and he was now much more careful. His kneecap and testicles had swollen to twice their normal size and he was unable to walk even with the assistance of the crutch lent him by the local doctor. He had kept silent on the injury to his groin, but had explained away his other injuries by a tale of how he had drunk far too much and fallen down a flight of stairs during the night. The doctor had seemed satisfied with the explanation and everyone in the hotel had had a laugh at his expense. His injury did at least give him a legitimate excuse, both to delay leaving for Albert, and to avoid Semper's company for a few days, whilst he worked through his assassination plan. It is hard to look a man in the eye when you are planning to kill him.

For the purposes of his plan, it suited him to exaggerate his handicap and he readily submitted to the doctor's instructions to remain in bed to rest his damaged knee. Indeed, the swelling of his testes prevented him from walking anyhow. He wondered if he had suffered permanent damage and might never father children. Semper, in his turn, seemed happy to go out alone to survey and update his maps of the area.

For three days, Peter spent much of his day exercising his knee and hatching his plot to kill Semper. In his report to 'C', he mentioned that his identity was under suspicion and requested he be withdrawn at the earliest appropriate time. He also sent a coded report to von Hoffman in Berlin, explaining that he had fallen and, due to his damaged knee, would be unable to leave the hotel for at least a week. He practised again and again how to remove the tight bandages around his kneecap and to replace them quickly. As soon as was able, he also spent much of his time walking up and down his room until he was able to do it quietly and without the aid of a stick or crutch. In the evenings, after the hotel staff had retired, he rehearsed going down and back up the hotel stairs as silently and quickly as his knee would allow.

On the fourth day, he at last felt ready both physically and mentally. His plan was not fool-proof, but it had the virtue of simplicity and, more importantly, he would not have to face Semper when he made his strike. Soon after Semper had left for the day's survey, he announced to the hotel staff that he intended to attempt a short walk in the vicinity of the hotel with the aid of his crutches. With much fuss and great difficulty, the hotel staff assisted him to descend the main staircase to the garden. Frequently, he had to rest on account of his weakness and obvious pain, and yet he remained steadfast in his objective, drawing many plaudits from both the staff and fellow guests at his apparent courage.

It was not a pleasant day outside. The sky was dark with clouds that threatened rain before long and the south-westerly wind had a cool edge to it. It was of no consequence, for he did not intend to take the air for long, just long enough to demonstrate his invalidity to the hotel staff and to collect his murder weapon.

He walked with exaggerated difficulty on his crutches along the gravelled paths through the hotel garden. At this time of year the gardens were well past their best and looking neglected, but this was of little concern to him. At the far end of the garden a previous generation of gardeners had set up a coastal garden, such as might be seen anywhere along the northern French coastline. The upturned rowing boat had long decayed through the combined attacks of the weather and wood-chewing insects. Around the boat somebody had laid a bed of shingle and pebbles on which lay an adornment of some fishing floats that had suffered a similar fate to the rowing boat. It was whilst gazing on this sad-looking example of the pride of one generation being followed by the apathy of another, that Peter's damaged knee gave way and he first stumbled and then collapsed with a loud cry.

****

The young Dutchman's fall was spotted by two of the hotel staff and a fellow guest. As he lay prostrate on the ground, they rushed to his assistance.

'Sir, are you all right?' they asked in unison.

The casualty gritted his teeth before replying, 'I'll be fine in just a moment. Just give me a minute to rest. I think you will find my pride is more hurt than my knee. I do feel a little foolish.'

'Allow us to help you up.'

With some difficulty, the porter and his colleague were able to lift the young man to a standing position again. He had by now been joined by a little crowd of onlookers, intent on gaining first-hand knowledge of the drama.

'Thank you, gentlemen, for your solicitude. I think I should manage well enough now.'

Herr Kleisters tried to use his crutches to take a step forward, but immediately he tried to place any weight on the damaged knee, he collapsed once more to the crowd's cry of 'Ooh la la.' Despite the young Dutchman's obvious courage, it was clear to the sympathetic audience that no matter how reluctantly, he would have to give in to his injury and suffer the indignity of being carried back to his room on a stretcher. By now the hotel proprietor had arrived on the scene, but he was immediately despatched by the guests' entreaties to call a doctor. The poor Kleisters vainly protested that he did not need the assistance of a doctor.

'My God,' the circle of sympathisers voiced. 'The courage of this young man. He is an example to us all. How can we help?'

****

It was no less than an hour later that Peter was left alone to rest his knee on the bed. No sooner had the party left, than he leapt to his feet and emptied the contents of the inside pocket of his coat. He felt pleased with his surreptitiously gathered haul of large pebbles and hid them in one of the socks contained in a drawer of the clothes chest. Act One was complete. His objectives had been achieved and it was now time for the main act.

CHAPTER 8

As had become his custom for the past few days, Peter took his evening meal in his rooms rather than in the hotel dining room. In a departure from his normal custom, however, he had issued an invitation to Semper to join him after dinner, to discuss his recent activities over a drink.

'I am sorry, Vizefeldwebel, for the enforced delay in leaving this place. I am pleased to see that you have used the time profitably. These maps are very, very good and you did well to gather the information on the French 75 mm field gun.'

'Not your fault, Herr Leutnant. I'm of course to blame. I heard you were out for a walk outside today. I hope you've recovered from our unfortunate disagreement and your knee is not too painful.'

Perhaps it was through guilt or more likely through the effects of a couple of glasses of fine cognac, but Semper seemed to be genuinely concerned about his welfare.

Semper continued, 'I had no idea that the French 75 mm could achieve such a rate of fire. Fifteen rounds a minute is bad enough, but imagine the effect on our infantry of thirty rounds a minute...'

Peter was naturally aware of Semper's zeal for discussing artillery matters and realised too late that he was in for a lecture on the subject, but it suited his purposes to gain Semper's confidence this evening.

'... Of course, I knew there was no need to realign the gun after every shot, but this braking system of the French could give them a devastating advantage in the hands of skilled crews. According to the boastful young pup I spoke to yesterday, a four-gun battery can deliver 17,000 pieces of shrapnel a minute over a piece of ground 400 metres by 100. Thank God I'm no infantry man.'

Although bored by it, Peter was pleased to note that the more Semper talked on the subject, the more cognac he drank. It was a very fine cognac, indeed a Camus La Grande Marque of 1890, and had cost him a fine sum. Normally, he would have resented Semper's treatment of such a fine vintage. Semper was bolting each glass of the precious liquid as he would his beloved schnapps. Still, such coarse treatment of the cognac was having the planned effect and he noted Semper's eyes were starting to glaze and, similarly, he was beginning to struggle with his speech. Semper's enthusiastic explanations of the "abattage" and "fauchage" capabilities of the French artillery pieces versus those of the Germans had become increasingly wearing. It came as a great relief when, inevitably and not long after the clock had chimed one o'clock, Semper drained the decanter dry with obvious disappointment.

'Oh. Sorry that I can't offer you another glash of this del … this delish … this very fine brandy, Herr Leutnant,' Semper slurred.

'It is indeed a pity. I am very much enjoying your discourse on the efficacy of our artillery units. But I have an idea.' Peter searched in his pockets and withdrew a gold 20-franc coin. 'Perhaps you could use this to rouse one of the hotel staff to bring us another bottle from their excellent cellar. Were I not somewhat *hors de combat* at present, I would of course do so myself. Would you mind, my dear fellow?'

Semper eyed the gold coin greedily and Peter observed his brain slowly whirring into action. The greedy gleam in Semper's barely focused eyes clearly indicated a plan being formed in his drink-crazed brain to obtain the coin for himself. Rising unsteadily to his feet, Semper almost fell on his back, but managed to correct his balance in time.

'It would be a pleashure, zir, to rouse one of those lazy frog-eaters from his pit. Just leave it with me, sir. I'll be back before you know it.' Semper tapped the side of his nose conspiratorially and set off with a rolling gait, stopped at the door, turned and saluted Peter.

'Leave it to me, sir,' he repeated and headed down the hotel corridor.

Within seconds of Semper's exit, Peter was on his feet and removing the dressing from his knee. He kicked off his shoes and rummaged in his chest of drawers for the sock containing the pebbles. After picking up one of the walking sticks leaning by the door to the hotel corridor, he listened carefully for sounds of Semper's receding footsteps. Hearing nothing, he gingerly opened the door and peeped down the corridor. There was no sign of Semper or indeed anybody. Quickly, but silently, he advanced down the corridor, past the main staircase and through a side door leading to the staff staircase. To his dismay, it was shrouded in darkness.

He scolded himself for not thinking of this possibility before. His previous practice runs had been conducted earlier in the day and the staircase had been lit on these occasions. Briefly, he thought about returning to his room for a candle, but quickly dismissed the idea. There would not be time. Fortunately, in this short time, his night sight had developed and he noted that a glimmer of light through a window downstairs was giving just enough light to illuminate a path down the steps. As quickly as he dared without risking a fall, he descended and cautiously entered the corridor leading to the hotel kitchen and pantry.

His heart pounded from his exertions and the fear of being detected in his activities. He stood still in the shadows whilst he brought his breathing under control. The corridor was dimly lit by lamplight and, just as he had suspected would be the case, he saw the huge outline of Semper by the wine cellar door. He flattened himself against the wall and barely dared to breathe. Exactly as he had hoped, Semper had decided against disturbing the hotel staff for a bottle of cognac and was picking the lock of the cellar door with the intention of helping himself to the bottle and keeping the twenty francs for himself. Peter could not believe his luck, but the most difficult element of his plan still lay ahead.

With a grunt of satisfaction, Semper opened the door of the cellar and made to descend the cellar steps. Peter immediately rushed towards the open door and nearly had heart failure as Semper suddenly reappeared in the corridor. All Peter could do was freeze. There was no time to withdraw into the shadows or flatten himself against a wall. A feeling of terror paralysed him as he started to fear the consequences of Semper finding him fit and fleet of foot. Now he really was going to die.

He need not have worried. Semper must have had only one thought in his head and he unhooked one of the lanterns on the wall of the corridor, turned round and re-entered the cellar. Any thoughts or reservations Peter may have had about his ability to kill a man in cold blood were long gone by now and he sprinted after the retreating Semper. He caught up with him four steps from the top of the stairs leading down to the cellar and struck Semper a mortal blow on the back of the neck with his home-made cosh of pebbles in a sock. Almost simultaneously, he pushed Semper hard in the back and barely waited to hear Semper's body cartwheel down the steps to the floor of the cellar. The noise was bound to rouse attention and he had to return to his rooms, fast.

He dashed back up the corridor and had only just started to mount the staircase when he heard sounds of activity behind him. Fortunately, the commotion was not audible upstairs and he was relieved to recover the sanctuary of his rooms without discovery. Still he had no time to relax. He emptied the contents of the sock out of a window and threw it and its pair onto the fire. After applying his dressing back on his knee, binding it tightly and replacing his shoes, he sat and waited for news of Semper.

The wait was agonising. Several unwelcome thoughts entered his head. What if Semper was still alive? If so, would Semper have known his assailant? If Semper was dead, would the suspicion for the attack fall on him from other quarters? Had he been seen? Why had nobody reported the accident or murder by now? As the adrenaline was spent, he felt incredibly tired and drifted off to sleep.

Soon after three o'clock, he was gently roused from his slumbers by the hotel proprietor. For a few moments Peter was confused and surprised to see Monsieur Lecuyer in his rooms. It was only when he recognised the form of the doctor that he remembered, with a start, his deeds of just two hours earlier.

'Herr Kleisters, I am sorry to disturb you. There has been a terrible accident.'

Peter's brain grasped the word 'accident' like a sailor reaching for a lifeline. It was now time for Act Three and he was going to have to play the performance of a most consummate actor if he was to save his life.

'I'm sorry,' he replied. 'What accident? Why are you calling me?'

'It's Herr Kuyper, your valet. I very much regret to inform you that he is dead.'

'Dead? How could he be? I was talking to him only a short while ago. What time is it?' Peter glanced across to the clock and started to dare that his evil plan may just have come off. It had helped that he had been genuinely asleep when the two men had called and he was relieved to see no gendarme present.

Both Frenchmen stared at the empty decanter and two glasses on the table before Lecuyer elaborated. 'Herr Kuyper seems to have fallen down the cellar steps and broken his neck. I cannot account for his presence in the cellar or how he opened the door as I locked it myself before retiring for the evening.'

The doctor took up the tale. 'There is no doubt about it. He is quite dead. I came as quickly as I could, but death would have been instantaneous. He had clearly been drinking and lost his footing on the steps. His neck is cleanly broken and he has some grievous injuries to his skull where it struck the stone steps on his way down to the cellar floor. I'm afraid he is not a pretty sight.'

'Have you called the police?' Peter asked.

'Of course,' Lecuyer replied. 'However, Sergeant Foy is not the most active officer and he resented his sleep being disturbed. He saw no reason to investigate what, on the face of it, is a simple accident in the middle of the time God has granted to him for his beauty sleep …'

'You mean he's not coming?' Peter asked, hardly daring it to be true.

'No. He will drop in later in the morning, but is more interested in what Herr Kuyper was doing in the cellar at one in the morning, than the accident. It is indeed a very strange affair.'

Peter mused on this information for a short while before responding.

'I think I can offer an explanation of his presence in the cellar. He and I were having a few drinks together to celebrate some good news I have received, but as you can see from the empty decanter, I ran out of cognac. I'm embarrassed to say that I gave him a 20-franc piece and asked him to find a member of staff willing to supply me a bottle of that rather splendid 1890 vintage you keep. Perhaps he was unwilling to disturb anybody and, therefore, intended to retrieve a bottle himself. He is a very faithful servant.'

'That seems plausible, sir, but he doesn't have a key to the cellar. I keep it on my person. Look.' Lecuyer proffered the key. 'I know I locked the door last night before going to bed. No, sir. That does not explain the facts.'

'I'm sorry to have to raise this, Mister Lecuyer, but I have a suspicion that a locked door would be no barrier to my valet … sorry, late valet. Kuyper often seemed able to afford drink beyond the paltry salary Herr Rutte and I pay him. I fear we have kept our suspicions about the source of his supply a secret to avoid scandal. Perhaps if you were to search Herr Kuyper's room, you might find some evidence that your cellar has been pilfered.'

Lecuyer digested the information for a minute and then replied, 'Thank you, sir. That could make sense. I will pass on the information to Sergeant Foy in the morning. Now I think we should leave you to spend what little remains of the night in sleep. Might Doctor Le Brun and I assist you to your bed?'

Here Le Brun interjected, 'Since I am here, might I first check your knee, Herr Kleisters? You had a bad fall earlier today.'

'Oh, it is fine now, doctor. I just turned a little awkwardly and it gave way, but I sense it is healing well.'

'That is for me to judge, young man. Let me see,' the doctor replied as he started to unbind the dressing. On examining the knee, he noted it was still quite swollen and tender to the touch. In fact Peter was quite pleased that it was so. The exertions of the evening had placed quite a strain on the knee and, whilst he was more mobile than he admitted, his knee was genuinely painful and a horrid mix of black and yellow hues. With his activities of the night apparently successful, he could afford to give his leg some proper rest over the next couple of days.

As the two Frenchmen helped him to bed, Peter had a final thought. 'Gentlemen, I wonder if one of you would be kind enough to inform the local Dutch consul of the unfortunate events of this evening. I am sure there will be an inquest and many arrangements to be made before we can repatriate poor Kuyper's body back to his family in Holland. In my present condition I would welcome some assistance.'

CHAPTER 9
November 1910

Peter left the relative warmth of the U-bahn station building at the Berlin Zoologischer Garten and was immediately chilled by the icy blast of the easterly wind blowing across the Hardenbergplatz and zoological gardens beyond. It was snowing hard and the combination of wind and snowflakes was uncomfortable on the eyes. Pulling up his muffler to protect his exposed face from the wind and adjusting his hat to shield his eyes, he turned right out of the station after only a cursory glance to ensure he was not being followed. He had plenty of time before his meeting, but wished to ensure his rendezvous would not be observed by his colleagues in the German Intelligence Service. One advantage of the foul weather was that there were fewer people on the streets of Berlin and any tail would be more obvious. However, the visibility was also poor, so proving the absence of a follower would also require more attention. As a result, he decided that, despite the cold, he would make a detour and turned into Kantstrasse. Once he had satisfied himself that he was not being followed, it would only be a short walk to the Kurfürstendamm, Berlin's answer to the Champs Élysées. Immediately on turning into Kantstrasse, he was thankful to have the wind to his back. Nonetheless, he could still feel its sharpness cutting through his Austrian Loden overcoat.

Two weeks earlier, he had returned to Berlin from France for debriefing. He had thought it best to report the incident with Semper in case the Boer should have passed a private message of his own back to Berlin, but it seemed that he had kept his suspicions to himself. Peter had chosen to adopt a magnanimous view that whilst Semper had overreached himself, he was a loyal and efficient agent who had acted in what he saw as the best interests of the Fatherland. This attracted him much credit amongst his fellow officers of the military intelligence division. Back in France, a lackadaisical police investigation and inquest into the death of Semper had drawn the conclusion that he had died an accidental death whilst under the influence of a considerable quantity of alcohol. Following the inquest, all assistance had been given to repatriating the corpse. This had not automatically eased Peter's worries. Quite apart from the knowledge that he had had a close call, his conscience was extremely uneasy about his actions to murder a fellow human being in cold blood. It helped that he regarded Semper as a despicable oaf, but nonetheless, his death had arisen merely from his zeal in doing his job to the best of his ability, in the cause of his country. Peter could not damn a man for his patriotism. He worried he could no longer be sure his nerve would hold and he had lost no time in sending an emergency message to his controller to facilitate his withdrawal from Germany and the abandonment of his mission. London had responded by arranging for him to meet with one of the SSB's agents in Germany and he was now on his way to keep the appointment.

He stopped at the Theater des Westens to check he had no shadow and it was a good opportunity to shelter from the weather. After searching for any possible tail, he glanced at the programme of forthcoming performances. Sadly, he had been in France for the visit and performances of Diaghilev's itinerant Russian ballet company. He had heard it had been a resounding success. Happily, he had been in Berlin for the performance of Enrico Carouso five years earlier, when his father had taken a box for the whole family. Captain Miller had then only recently taken up his appointment as the British Naval Attaché in Berlin. Peter remembered how much fun they had had that evening. Mutti and Papa both loved opera and for days afterwards, had been almost childlike in entertaining each other with various arias. Peter had then still been a Specialist at Charterhouse and it had been one of the last care-free holidays he had spent with his family. How his life had changed since then.

He took advantage of the brief respite from the wind his shelter afforded to survey the street and buildings of Charlottenburg. There was no question that Berlin was thriving and Charlottenburg was now not just a very affluent residential area with its newly built broad streets and avenues, but in effect a suburb of the main city of Berlin. A number of industrialists were setting up factories in the north-east of the area, creating jobs and more prosperity. This improving affluence brought with it pressures on housing and Peter had already noted with disappointment the appearance of large housing blocks to meet the demands of the rapidly increasing population. He could not help reflecting ruefully that Germany's rising industrialisation and wealth were being achieved at the expense of that of

Great Britain. Germany as a nation was now developing a great self-confidence and starting to see itself as the new leading nation in Europe.

He of all people now knew only too well that an increasing militarism was also taking root. There was talk that, having already developed the biggest army in Europe, some Germans had started to imagine a day when the Imperial German Navy might even rival that of Britain. It was common knowledge that the Kaiser dreamed of ruling his own empire and, to achieve this, Germany would need a powerful navy of her own.

Now certain that he had not been followed and, after checking his pocket watch, he noted that the hour of his appointment was nigh. Taking care to avoid the busy traffic as he crossed Kantstrasse, he headed south down Fasenenstrasse past the building site of a new Jewish synagogue. He was a little surprised to see a synagogue being built in such a prominent location as in his experience they tended to be hidden away in back streets. Perhaps this was yet another sign of a change in the times and Germany was becoming more favourably disposed to the Jews than Britain.

As he reached the Kurfürstendamm, he turned right again to present his back once more to the easterly wind and head in the opposite direction of the Gedächtniskirche, the church the Kaiser had had built in memory of his father Wilhelm II. He had plenty of time to walk the length of the Ku'damm for his appointment.

Despite the weather, the wide avenue was thronged with busy Berliners darting into the many shops out of the cold, in their search for Christmas presents and luxury items. Whilst the snow was starting to ease, the sky was dark and leaden and the gaslights were starting to glow in the late afternoon gloom. The visual effect was quite unearthly. With the benefit of the wind behind him, Peter was able to lift his head to survey the scene before him in full. The effect of the snow, driven before the wind, was constantly affecting the visibility and caused the bright lights of the gaslights beneath the dark sky to appear as a lane of floating candles bobbing in and out of sight on a rippling river. He saw himself as travelling a never-ending corridor of flickering light towards an unseen destination. That final destination offered him hope – hope of escape from his fears of being unmasked by the German Intelligence Service.

After the long walk, he reached the address he was seeking. It was a private mansion, faced with grey stone and appeared to have been built only recently. He thought it unprepossessing and modern for his taste. After one last surreptitious glance for any suspicious passers-by, he briskly approached the main door and rang the bell. The door was promptly answered by a tall footman bedecked with a magnificent moustache. Peter addressed him in his fluent German.

'Herr von Trotha to see Doktor Schmidt.'

'One moment, sir. You are expected. Please follow me.'

Peter followed the footman into an opulent entrance hall, decorated in the latest art nouveau style. At the centre of the ornate plastered ceiling hung an enormous and grand candelabra with very expensive leaded glasswork. The marble walls, from which hung huge, ornate sconces, were decorated with gilt mouldings. It was clear that no expense had been spared on the interior furnishings and he knew enough about German furniture to recognise that all the pieces in the hall were antique. As he mounted the richly carpeted staircase after the footman to the first floor of the house, he noted a complete absence of wall art. The art seemed to have been confined to the coloured glass decorations in the window that lit the half-landing. He was surprised at the pleasing effect on the eye of this mixture of the modern art nouveau style and the traditional furniture. His surprise then gave way to shock as he was ushered into the drawing room on the first floor. After the footman closed the door behind him on leaving the room, he suddenly noticed the contact from the SSB, standing in the bay window overlooking the street. Almost simultaneously his heart leapt with joy and a medicine ball thudded into his intestines. His contact was none other than Papa.

CHAPTER 10

'Papa, I had no idea I would be meeting you. It is so good to see you again.' Peter rushed up to his father to embrace him warmly.

The two men exchanged pleasantries before seating themselves in the sumptuous armchairs.

'I have taken the liberty of having tea prepared for you, Peter. It's the old Royal Blend from Fortnum and Mason and I doubt you can obtain anything like it in Germany. May I pour for you?'

'It would be most welcome,' Peter replied warmly. 'It's months since I have enjoyed a cup of tea. I still cannot accustom myself to the continental taste for coffee.'

'That's because you've never tasted real coffee, my boy. For that you need to visit East Africa.'

Peter sipped appreciatively the mix of Ceylon and Assam tea, first blended for the late King Edward eight years previously. After so many months of drinking bitter French, Belgian and German coffee, the honey flavours reminded him of a fine white burgundy. It was a typically thoughtful deed of his father. Peter was reflecting on how his father so often seemed to know exactly the right thing to do when he suddenly remembered the purpose of this meeting. With this thought his stomach chilled. He had expected to meet one of 'C''s men. It was going to be so much more difficult to explain his fears to his father.

After some conversation on the health and state of the family, Miller came directly to the point. 'So, Peter. I read your latest message. It seemed so important I decided it best to hear for myself just what has been going on. Tell me your problem.'

For the next hour, interrupted only occasionally by questions merely for the purpose of clarification of facts, Peter related his account of the circumstances leading to the murder of Semper. He was relieved that Papa listened patiently and offered no judgement on his actions. It was the first time he had been able to speak of the recent events and it seemed as if some of his fears were being washed away by the process. Even so, he ended his account with a plea to be released from his mission and to be allowed to start a new career or return to the Diplomatic Service. He knew he was opting out, but this convivial meeting with his father over tea made him feel homesick for his comfortable life in England with his family. Papa seemed to be taking it well, he thought. Only once he had finished did his father speak.

'Do you think this von Hoffman accepted the account of Semper's death?'

'Of course I cannot be sure, but I think so. Von Hoffman is a pretty decent sort of chap and he seemed more cut up that Semper's brutality might have caused me serious injury.'

'So why are you so worried?' Miller responded.

'I'm sorry, Papa, but the whole incident has shaken me. I honestly thought Semper was going to kill me. Just one more stupid slip and I could face a firing squad. Now I'm back in Berlin, the risks increase that I meet an old acquaintance of von Trotha and my cover could be blown. I feel I've done enough.'

'Enough, you say?'

Something in Papa's tone made Peter shiver. He worried that he might have gone too far. Sure enough, Papa visibly bristled with anger, but quickly controlled it and resumed his conciliatory tone once more.

'Peter, I know you are facing risks, but the work you are doing is vital to our country's interests. We both know that Germany is preparing for war with France and the information you are providing could give us the warning we need to counter the offensive when it comes. It might even save thousands of lives.'

'I understand that, Papa, I really do,' Peter replied sorrowfully, although he had never seen his mission in that light. 'But what's it to do with you or I? Surely this is a French or Belgian matter. Why don't we leave them to do this sort of work? It's not as if Germany poses any great threat to Britain is it?'

Again he witnessed his father flush with anger and fight to control his temper. This is what he had dreaded, but he had come so far he had to push on. The dull ache in his testicles reminded him what was at stake.

After pausing to complete his thoughts, Miller asked quietly, 'Do you really think that is true, Peter?'

Deep down Peter did not think this entirely true, but then he knew nothing emphatic to the contrary. Even so, and knowing he was grasping at straws, he continued to play the innocent.

'I have only ever heard the German military speak of Britain with respect and have encountered no serious discussion of war with us. After all, the Kaiser and the Queen are blood relatives. Of course, they despise the French and feel they have an old score to settle. Only a few years ago, Britain was on poor terms with the French, too ... No, Papa, let me finish.'

Peter could not believe his boldness in cutting off Papa's interruption, but his blood was up and he was gaining confidence.

'But there's no doubt that thanks largely to Bismarck, the new Germany is now a powerful nation. The military believe that their young nation is entitled to some respect internationally and merely wishes to be given the freedom to follow in the footsteps of France, Britain and even Belgium and Italy, in building an empire of its own. My sincere belief is that whilst the Germans now see themselves as worthy competitors of Britain economically, they do not see Britain as an enemy.'

'Have you finished now?'

Peter nodded. He had said his piece, but could feel his heart racing and hear his pulse in his head. *Any minute now and I'm for it. Papa's going to blow.*

Miller stood and walked over to the bay window and looked down onto the shoppers scurrying about below on the Ku'damm. It had stopped snowing and was now completely dark. With a sigh, he drew the heavily-brocaded, thick curtains and returned to the armchair.

'Peter, my boy, not only do I know you received an excellent education in European history at Charterhouse, but even the humblest clerk in the Foreign Office has a better appreciation of foreign affairs than that, let alone a former Third Secretary in our Paris embassy and a Secret Service agent. But let me tell you again what it has to do with us.'

Peter was relieved that his father's tone was calm, but it contained an edge. He hardly dared breathed as he listened.

'For the last couple of hundred years, successive governments have been committed to maintaining the most powerful navy on earth to defend both the empire overseas and prevent an aggressor invading our shores. Our armies on the other hand have only been maintained at levels not much more than sufficient to garrison the empire. Instead, it has been our policy to support other European countries to counter any nation likely to become a dominant power on continental Europe. We stood up to Philip II of Spain and sent an army to the continent to prevent the Low Countries and its coast falling to Louis XIV. More recently, we fought Napoleon when he aspired to hegemony in Europe. If we allow Germany to overrun France, it is an absolute inevitability that we will soon be faced with not just a powerful army on the shores of the North Sea and across the English Channel, but a formidable navy capable of contesting our command of the seas, too. We cannot let that happen.' Miller had raised his voice during the last two sentences, but he paused and, with more control, continued more quietly.

'So any conflict with France will involve Britain as well. My experience of the Boer War is that hundreds of thousands of men on both sides would be slaughtered in the barbed wire by today's artillery and machine guns. It would be a long war. You know all this, of course, so what is the point of this dissembling?'

Peter flushed at the question and stood up suddenly. He could tell that Papa was angry, but he was past the point of no return.

'Can you not see, Papa, that I've had enough? When I agreed to play the part of von Trotha, I knew it had its dangers, but it didn't seem that bad. Now I've had a thug half cripple and very nearly kill me. I'm afraid that there *will* be a next time and then the very best outcome will be a firing squad. I resign. I want you to get me out of here. I'm finished with it all. Can you not understand that?'

Peter instantly regretted his outburst. His father stood up again, suddenly, to respond to him. Peter recognised the signs of a volcano about to erupt. He had always feared his father's temper. Miraculously, Papa seemed to be maintaining his anger in check, but Peter could see it welling up inside him as he replied.

'You do not see how vital your work is, do you? Throughout Europe we have agents placed to report on Germany's military and naval armament. They, too, are risking their lives, but none is as well placed as you. The Service needs you to hold your nerve. Pull yourself together.'

Peter started to panic. He felt he was going to burst if he did not get out of that room. He had to do something, anything, to make Papa understand. If Mutti had been there, he would have thrown himself on her lap and cried his eyes out, much as he used to as a small child when he was frightened. Seeing Papa standing there, so tall, strong and impassive, started to terrify him. He realised he was not going to win this argument and it became clear that Papa stood in his way to escape the clutches of the German Intelligence Service. A feeling of hatred rose from his gut to his head. Losing all control he started screaming at his father.

'It's all very well for you to say these things. You can sit in London planning your games to save Europe. You've spent your life being a hero and winning your medals. I'm not built like you. I'm scared. Every day you keep me here, working for the Germans, you increase the risk to my life. You don't care about me. I'm just a tool in your hands. For God's sake let me go.'

His hysteria was suddenly interrupted by a powerful and painful slap across the face from his father.

'How dare you?' Miller snarled angrily. 'I have only ever done my duty to this country and tried to bring you and your brothers to share my values. I cannot believe that a son of mine could be such a coward. I'm ashamed of you.'

Miller strode out of the room, slamming the door behind him. Peter did not notice the pain of his cheek, but collapsed on the rug sobbing uncontrollably and shouting to anybody that would hear, 'I hate him! I hate him!'

Miller did not hear Peter's cries. He stood at the top of the stairs and tried to recover his emotions. He also tried to slow his rate of breathing, finding himself drawing short, sharp breaths, as if he had just run a 100-yard dash. He was angry with himself for striking his son for the first time in at least ten years. He knew he should not have lost his temper, but the sight of his favourite son cringing and wailing like a pathetic child had been too much for him. Where had he gone wrong as a father? He was truly shocked by his son's behaviour. There was no doubt that Peter was starting to crack up. How could he be so weak? Peter of all boys. The one he thought most like him. But if Peter gave way, the whole mission was in danger, something he could not ignore. He would have to deal with it, however distasteful. He returned to the drawing room.

Peter was still lying on the floor, but by now sobbing quietly to himself. He looked so frail and Miller wanted to pick him up, to comfort him much as he used to when Peter was a young boy. However, the emotion was countered by equal feelings of revulsion and embarrassment that the pathetic creature before him had let him down so badly. He had once had one of his officers court martialled for cowardice and could not bear the reality that his son had proved himself a coward, too. The emotions of the loving father gave way to those of the ruthless commander he had so often proved to be in the past.

'Sub-Lieutenant Miller, stand up,' he barked.

The words of command stirred Peter, but he remained on the floor. He stopped sobbing though, and looked up at his father in a dazed and unfocused manner. Miller could see that Peter's brain was not fully engaged and that shock tactics were required.

'Stand to attention when you are ordered by a senior officer.'

Miller gave full force to the order and this time it was effective. Peter leapt to attention like an automaton. Having gained his son's attention, Miller went on to state firmly, 'Sub-Lieutenant Miller, I am your commanding officer. Listen carefully. I have taken note of your plea and will take the necessary action to relieve you of your duties and return to you to London. However, the arrangements will take a little time and you are to continue with your previous orders until then. This is to include reporting any changes to your tasking by the Geheime Nachrichtendienst des Heeres or any change in their attitude towards you. Is that clear?'

'Aye, sir,' Peter replied. It was a conditioned reaction, but that was the best Miller could hope for right now. Peter was clearly still in some form of shock, but Miller knew from experience that discipline would soon take over. He no longer regarded the confused and frightened young man before him as his son, but as an agent whose nerves were shattered and in danger of imperilling the organisation he had so carefully built up. Bewildered by his mixed emotions of anger and shame he quietly withdrew from the drawing room, leaving the man he had once so proudly loved standing alone at attention.

CHAPTER 11

Just three days later, Peter was again standing at attention. This time he was in full uniform alongside von Hoffman in the outer office of one of the five Assistant Chiefs of Staff or Oberquartiermeister of the Imperial German Army. His face was still bruised, swollen and painful from the blow from Papa. He had suffered further indignity from the ribbing of his colleagues in the military intelligence department. Notwithstanding his protestations that he had tripped and fallen, the favoured interpretation was that he had come off worse in an encounter with a young maiden defending her virtue. He occasionally smiled to himself at the irony as he continued to suffer the pain in his groin. He was still not sure he would ever be up to much with the opposite sex. However, conscious of Queen Gertrude's line in Hamlet, *'The lady doth protest too much, methinks,'* he said nothing to quash the ribaldry.

It was a rarity for him to be wearing the German uniform once again and he felt very awkward. Both he and von Hoffman had been surprised to have received the summons to the office of General Kuhn, the Oberquartiermeister responsible for collating all intelligence on fortifications in France and Western Europe. Peter was pleased to note that von Hoffman seemed equally discomforted by the occasion. Fortunately, they did not have to wait long before being shown into the magnificent office of the general. Von Hoffman seemed equally surprised to see amongst the officers present, not just their commanding officer, Oberstleutnant Heye, the head of Abteilung IIIb, the General Staff's department for counter-intelligence, but a naval captain. Colonel Heye darted forward to greet them and present them to the general and captain.

Bewildered by the welcome, both von Hoffman and Peter did what came naturally to any German officer in such circumstances. They snapped to attention with a click of heels in unison and saluted the general smartly. He returned the mark of respect with a beaming smile and addressed them.

'Gentlemen, on behalf of the Fatherland, I congratulate you on your excellent work of this past year. Thanks to the skill and courage of you and other like-minded loyal members of Oberstleutnant Heye's department, we now have a clear picture of the terrain, railways, obstacles and forces that will face us when we implement General von Schlieffen's master plan for the invasion of France. It is my great pleasure to reward you both for this dedication and loyalty. Hauptman von Hoffman you are promoted to Major and I award you the Roter Adlerorden 4th Class with crown.'

With these words his aide-de-camp stepped forward with a tray on which sat two small red leather boxes. Peter noted from a sideways look that von Hoffman seemed equally relieved and surprised by the announcement. Kuhn quickly extracted a military decoration with bright orange stripes on the ribbon from one of the boxes and pinned the badge of the order on the left side of von Hoffman's chest.

Shaking Hoffman's hand warmly, he added, 'Congratulations, Major. I am pleased to inform you that you will be joining my planning staff. Your knowledge and experience will be invaluable.'

It was then Peter's turn to receive his award, also the Order of the Red Eagle 4th Class, but lacking the distinction of the crown. He was too dazed to hear the general's opening words of congratulations, but just caught him say, 'You, too, have been promoted, to Oberleutnant with immediate effect. You are being transferred to 'N' division of the Naval Staff, but such is the secrecy with which this service operates, not even is the Oberquartiermeister permitted to know why it demands the services of one of my officers.'

The general looked across at the naval officer peevishly. Both the newly decorated officers were then swiftly ushered out of the general's office by the ADC and the whole business had been contracted in fewer than three minutes.

Perhaps sensing some surprise in both von Hoffman's and Peter's reactions to the briskness of the proceedings, Heye explained: 'The Oberquartiermeister is naturally a very busy man and I am sorry he was only able to spare you a few minutes. It is an indication of the importance of your work that he insisted on sparing the time, no matter how small, to bestow these decorations on you himself.'

Heye beckoned them to follow him. 'Now, perhaps, if you would like to join me in my office for a glass of schnapps, we can make arrangements for your farewell, von Hoffman. I will be very sorry to lose you. As you heard just now, von Trotha, I am also losing you to the Admiralstab. The naval captain in the Oberquartiermeister's office is Kapitan zur See Tapken, one of the directors of the Naval Intelligence Service. You are to report to him this very afternoon. Now, gentlemen. Let us enjoy this glass of schnapps. Prost.'

****

Peter was genuinely sad to say farewell to von Hoffman. He admired his professionalism and leadership qualities. He suspected that von Hoffman would quickly rise to command his own regiment in time for the conflict that seemed increasingly certain to arise with France. It was unlikely that the two men would cross each other's paths again. After they had bid each other farewell, Peter left the headquarters of the Imperial General Staff and headed for the address he had been given by Heye.

Unlike the headquarters of the General Staff, the Admiralstab was spread out across a number of buildings over central Berlin. The office of the Nachrichten-Abteilung, the Naval Intelligence Department, was co-located with some other departments of the Naval Staff at Koniggratzer Strasse. Reporting to Captain Tapken's office at the appointed time, Peter was unable to hide his surprise that the entire department comprised only four officers, including its head, 'N'. Abteilung IIIb was vast by comparison. Tapken seemed amused by Peter's reaction.

'I can see that you may feel you have stepped down in the world, von Trotha.'

Peter flushed with embarrassment that his thoughts had been detected.

'I am sorry, Herr Kapitan. I was merely surprised that the intelligence department's growth has not matched that of our navy.'

'Ah well, we are the poor relation of the Naval Staff. Indeed, we are fortunate to be here at all. The Naval Office resents our mere existence and our chief, Admiral von Fischel, has had to fight hard to ensure we are located within his staff. However, such affairs of state are beyond our control. I am sure you are keen to know why you are here. Coffee?'

The two men sipped their coffee in silence. Peter felt uncomfortable and completely out of place in his army uniform. Moreover, he was acutely conscious that Tapken was staring at him and obviously judging him from his demeanour. It was not the junior officer's place to open the conversation, though. He instead studied his reflection in the mirror behind Tapken and stole surreptitious glances at Tapken in turn. The man who returned his looks from the mirror was young, tanned and healthy with dark, close-cropped hair in the fashion of the Prussian Army. His eyes were tired and the bruise across his cheek was only now starting to fade.

69

For the past few weeks Peter had felt his left eye twitch continuously, but he was pleased to note that it did not show in the mirror.

Tapken reminded him of his Uncle Franz. He, too, had short, dark hair, combed smooth with Macassar oil and parted to the left. Like Uncle Franz, Tapken sported a Van Dyke-style beard and moustache, but there the similarities ended. Tapken's upturned moustache and beard had already turned grey, in marked contrast to his hair colour, but it was in the eyes where the difference was most striking. Whereas Uncle Franz was always jovial, had twinkling blue eyes and never seemed to have a care in the world, despite any business worries he might have, Tapken's eyes were dull and creased with worry lines. He was obviously a man under pressure.

After draining the contents of his cup, Tapken eventually spoke, and to Peter's surprise in English.

'You have been to an English public school, Charterhouse, I believe. Do you think the English ready to fight a European war?'

Peter thought it best to respond in English too. 'I am not sure, sir. Before the Entente Cordiale of 1904 I would not have been surprised to see Britain go to war again at some point with France. Since then I have formed the impression that Britain just wants to hold the ring as it were, to ensure a stable Europe. It's always possible that the death of King Edward earlier this year could bring about a change in attitude, but I have not been back in Britain in the past year.'

'You may find yourself back there very soon.'

Peter fought hard to hide his emotions at hearing the words in light of the argument with his father just a few days earlier.

Tapken continued, 'It might surprise you to know that my wife is English and I have a great regard and fondness for the nation. My own impression of the English is that they like a comfortable life compared with the standards of the German people. By and large, they do not seem to be willing to exert themselves to any great sustained effort if they can avoid doing so, unless it is likely to impair their way of life or security directly. There are exceptions of course, but this craze to reach the South Pole first seems to demonstrate my point. The English know they have become too comfortable and so feel it necessary to prove to the world that they have not. However, England is still a rich and powerful country and has the industry, resources and wealth of its empire at its disposal. It is, thus, like a sleeping lion that it is best not to disturb.'

Tapken paused to reflect for a few moments. Peter wondered where this conversation was going, but decided not to interrupt.

'The Kaiser has been greatly influenced by a book written by an American naval officer and has decided that if the new Germany is to build a great empire of its own, then we must have a great navy. We are in the course of building such a navy, but at some point we will come into conflict with England and the Royal Navy. The Naval Staff have conducted a series of war games and concluded that our cruisers are still no match for those of the Royal Navy. It is, therefore, vital that we gather information on the Royal Navy's ships, its capabilities, latest tactics, building programme and state of its armaments. That is the prime role of this department. Whilst there is little love lost between the Naval and General Staffs, I have at least learned from Colonel Heye that plans are now well advanced for an inevitable war with France. He has been kind enough, as a personal favour to me, to keep me abreast of your contribution to these plans. May I congratulate you on your promotion and award of the Order of the Eagle? Few officers of your age and rank receive such prestige in peacetime.'

'Thank you, sir. I only did my duty to the Fatherland and was privileged to serve under such an able officer as Hauptman von Hoffman.'

'Your modesty does you credit, von Trotha.' Tapken had reverted to German and Peter was left wondering whether Tapken had just been practising his English or perhaps testing Peter's command of the language.

'It is the earnest hope of both the General and Naval Staffs that when we go to war with France, England will remain neutral. If we have summed up the English character well enough, then provided we can assure the country that she is under no threat from Germany, the English will return to their gardens and take the view that there is no need for them to become involved in somebody else's war, especially one involving *l'ancien ennemi*. Do you follow me, Oberleutnant?'

'Yes, sir.'

'Good. With the benefit of good intelligence we can strengthen our navy to the point that it serves as a powerful threat to the Royal Navy and its ability to defend the empire. In that way, even if there is a national call for intervention on the side of France, then the English Government can be persuaded it would not be in their national interest. The Imperial German Navy does not need to achieve parity with the Royal Navy for this, in the same way that a bishop can pin a king on the chess board. I can tell that you speak English faultlessly. My wife is forever telling me that my accent is too thick, but you could easily pass yourself off as English. Is that not so?'

If you only knew the truth, Peter thought. 'You honour me, Herr Kapitan, with the compliment, but it is only the product of several years of the English schooling system. I am, of course, more comfortable in my native German.'

Peter spoke calmly, but his mind reeled from the interpretation of Tapken's words. From his work over the past year he was already well aware that Germany intended going to war with France and Count von Schlieffen's plan called for access to France via Belgium, with the chance that if Belgium resisted then she, too, would be brought into the war. This was the first he had heard that Germany was contemplating war with Britain, if necessary. Recalling the words of Papa earlier in the week, he realised how foolish as well as cowardly he must have appeared to him. If he understood Tapken correctly, then he was about to be asked to spy on his own country to give advantage to the Imperial Germany Navy in the event of an armed conflict with the Royal Navy. With a shudder he recalled vividly Papa's words: *'I cannot believe that a son of mine could be such a coward. I'm ashamed of you.'* He now felt ashamed of himself, too. He shivered and blushed unconsciously.

Tapken had been observing Peter's reactions closely and followed up by saying, 'If I have interpreted your emotions correctly, von Trotha, you appear excited by the prospect of helping us gain an advantage over the English. This is where you fit in.

'You can see how small is this department. Tirpitz has restricted our budget from the 150,000 marks a year we need, to little more than 10,000. Our resources are consequently targeted almost entirely on England. Whilst we obtain very little cooperation from the Abteilung, whose focus is much more on France and Russia, we do receive help from our friends on Wihelmstrasse to identify potential agents in England. Our negotiations with the directors of the Hamburg-America Line have also proved effective in identifying large numbers of loyal seamen willing to assist us. We want you to go to England to co-ordinate this network of volunteers and identify others who may be in a position to assist us. At this stage we merely require men willing to act as reporters, the "Berichterstatter". You must select your men carefully as the contract cannot be cancelled later. Do I make myself clear?'

'Yes, Herr Kapitan.'

'To maintain secrecy you will be their main correspondent, the Hauptberichterstatter. You in turn will deal only with a colleague, Gustav Steinhauer. He is well regarded both here and in England, having helped save the Kaiser from a Russian assassination plot whilst he attended the funeral of Queen Victoria. Steinhauer will brief you further. I believe he has already recruited an Irish sailor to assist you. How soon can you leave?'

Peter took his time in replying. He was still stunned by what he had just heard and was unsure how to react. It hardly seemed conceivable that the Germans had already started establishing a network of agents to spy on Britain and this was demonstrable proof that Germany regarded Britain as a potential foe. This in itself was vital information for Papa and the SSB. More startling, perhaps, were the opportunities this new assignment afforded the British to uncover the identity of each member of the spy ring.

All of a sudden Peter recognised that Germany now posed a real threat to Britain and the people he loved. She had to be stopped and he could no longer stand by and allow others to take the risks. Again his father's words echoed in his mind and he recognised the truth of them. He felt quite stupid and anxious to make amends, but nervous of the inevitable meeting with Papa again.

'I have little to keep me here and am anxious to serve the Fatherland to the limits of my ability. I need a little time to arrange my affairs, but I expect to be ready to leave for England next week.'

CHAPTER 12

December 1910

Commander Mansfield Smith-Cumming had been born as Smith, but had adopted his new name on his marriage. He had finished his boom defence duties earlier in the year and was now fully committed to the SSB. Cumming felt sure that after a difficult first six months in office, his new department was making its mark. This was reflected in the report he was now presenting to his superior at the Admiralty. He waited patiently whilst Captain Miller left his office for a few minutes to attend to some urgent business. As always, Miller's desk was strewn with heaps of untidy papers, charts and notebooks. Cumming thought it out of character for somebody with such a tidy mind. In contrast to the clutter on the desk, the office was sparse and almost devoid of furniture and home comforts, save for some photographs of Miller's wife and sons.

Whilst he sat alone in Miller's office he reflected how he always felt more comfortable visiting the Admiralty than the War Office. Both were his customers and naturally, as a retired naval officer, he was more familiar with navy blue than khaki, but it was more that the War Office always seemed to keep him at arm's length. He was rarely granted an audience with Lieutenant Colonel MacDonagh, the Director of Military Operations and Intelligence or DMO, to whom he was also partially responsible. Indeed, he had been asked merely to leave a copy of his six-monthly report with one of MacDonagh's staff. The army's only requirement of him was for notice of any intended mobilisation by the German Army. Until now this had been done to their satisfaction through his agent, TR21, but Captain Miller had just advised him of the need to extricate his son from Germany.

MacDonagh had made it clear that, the reports from TR21 apart, any of the War Office's other intelligence requirements could be met by his own staff. He seemed to have a much closer relationship with Kell's section. The General Staff regarded him as one of their own and perhaps thought Kell should be heading up the whole bureau. This troubled Cumming.

After all, Kell was an experienced intelligence officer and a gifted linguist. The grandson of a Polish count, Kell was fluent in German and French, and had also made the effort to learn Russian and Chinese. He, by contrast, could not speak any foreign languages, but had started to teach himself German. Whenever the War Office did take an interest in the Foreign Section, he saw plots to take it over and make it solely accountable to the DMO.

The Admiralty, on the other hand, seemed anxious for any reports his department could deliver. That was not to say that the navy was any better at seconding officers to him to run his office or act as agents. As soon as the navy had a more pressing need for its staff, they were whisked away. Moreover, on more than one occasion his few and, therefore, valuable agents, had taken time, pains and risk to collect certain information that it transpired had been in the hands of the NID for some time already. Worse, the NID was still running its own intelligence operations, not just independent of his own office, but frequently with little or no consultation. A case in point was an NID-sponsored tour of the German North Sea coastal defences that summer by a Royal Marine officer, Captain Trench, and his naval surveying officer colleague, Lieutenant Brandon. He had only learned of the operation when the two officers had been caught. Both were due to be tried in Leipzig shortly. Certain quarters still failed to realise that the type of intelligence now required could no longer be obtained by the amateur efforts of the professional naval officer on a spot of leave. The work required tradecraft, by men who could lie low in Germany for long periods without arousing suspicion. It made it all the more disappointing that TR21's tasking was about to change.

Notwithstanding these frustrations, he considered Admiral Bethell and Captain Miller very supportive. Both had stood their ground and garnered the backing of the Foreign Office to maintain the independence from the War Office of what had become termed the Secret Service. Even so, he didn't feel relaxed in his meetings with Miller. For some reason he always felt as if he was being carefully studied by a large predator with a view to his potential as a meal. Almost immediately the beast returned to his lair.

'I'm sorry about that, Cumming. It was a matter that couldn't wait. Where were we?'

'You had just explained your reasons for wishing to extract TR21 from the ND, sir.'

'Quite.' Miller hesitated. Cumming had already observed that Miller was discomforted by the discussion. He decided he would have to tread carefully if he was to persuade Miller to give up the idea. He knew already that Miller was not a man to be crossed once his mind was made up.

'I wonder if you're not being a bit hard on the lad, sir. Life as a double agent must have imposed immense pressure on his nervous system and he's managed to stick it nearly a year, already. He's not the first, you know.'

'He's not the first what? Do you mean the first to crack under pressure? Or to fly into a blue funk?'

'That's not as I see it, sir? Two similar instances come to mind, sir. One of my best men suffers from neurasthenia. I've offered him leave in England, but he deems excitement to be the best palliative for his condition and, as a consequence, suffers all the more during the frequent periods of tedium his work entails. Another agent, only last month, convinced himself it was all up and he was on the point of arrest. He duly sent the emergency telegram and caught the next train to Holland. It was only once he'd crossed the border that he recognised it as a bad case of neurosis. We then had to set up a plausible reason for his sudden departure. When he returned to Germany, he discovered that everything was normal. I don't think anybody understands the strain under which our agents are working, sir.'

'Absolute rot, Cumming. You forget that I do have experience of working long periods undercover. If I or my men had been caught, it wouldn't have been to face a civilised trial in a court of law like Trench and Brandon. We would have been tortured mercilessly and then chopped to pieces, little by little. The fact of the matter is that he has become a liability and is no longer of any use to us. I leave you to work out the details for getting him out. Is there anything else we need to discuss?'

Cumming considered this harsh indeed and decided it would be prudent not to reveal that TR21 was already on his way back to London, under his own steam, or rather that of the ND. He had received the coded message only that morning and had incorrectly assumed that this was the reason he had been summoned to Miller's office. There seemed little point in continuing the conversation. Miller might be his superior, but only he would run his agents and it would be done his way.

'No, sir. Leave the arrangements to me. I'll let you know when it's done.'

****

A week later, Peter Miller was meeting with 'C' in his rented apartment at 12 Park Place, St James. Cumming had taken a new office, separate from that of 'K' in Victoria Street. His rationale was that he bumped into too many colleagues, outside the Army & Navy stores opposite, to maintain the discretion of his office and position. Instead, he had taken a flat in Ashley Gardens on Vauxhall Bridge Road. Even so, he never met agents there and rented the St James' apartment for this purpose.

Peter had never before met Cumming. He had left for Germany just as Cumming had taken up his position the previous October. He was surprised by what he saw before him. To him, Cumming appeared a kindly, stout, old man and not at all how he had previously imagined the head of the Secret Service. He was grey-haired, clean-shaven and wearing a monocle. His weather-tanned face incorporated keen grey eyes, a long nose and, most strikingly, a broad smile.

'As you requested, Miller, I haven't yet told your father you are back in London, or how your return came about. He told me the reasons for your resignation and it's a damned pity, too. You've been one of my better agents.'

'Thank you, sir. But I've had second thoughts about my resignation. That is, if you really think my service has been valuable.'

'Don't be a fool, man. Of course you've been valuable. Thanks to you, we now have the full Order of Battle and the detailed plans for the German Army's invasion of France through Belgium. Moreover, this latest tasking by the Nachrichten-Abteilung, and the summary of your interview with Tapken, is priceless. It's the first positive news I've had of Germany's intentions towards Britain. Even the War Office will see the value of this information.'

'Thank you, sir, but I don't know how much my father may have told you of our last meeting. The fact is that I'm rather ashamed of my actions. He said something to me that cut deep and I'm keen to redeem myself in his eyes. I now see I've been a little naïve and I regret my hasty resignation. I'm ready to go back to Germany should you require it, sir.'

Cumming rose and paced the width of the room with his hands behind his back in typical naval fashion and deep in thought. It appeared to Peter that something was troubling him. At length he approached Peter and sat on the edge of his desk.

'Miller, let me ease your mind on one matter. Your father only told me the bare facts leading to your decision to resign. I know nothing of what passed between you. I can say that I well understand your reasons. You had a nasty scare and I've had other agents get the wind up for less.'

'That's very good of you, sir—'

'Hear me out, Miller. As for going back to Germany, there is nothing I would like more. I'm desperately short of professional agents, but there is no question of it. It would be too risky, right now. Besides, you still have an important role to play as a double agent here. Your latest tasking is most intriguing. I'll speak to my opposite number, Major Kell, about it. Between us we should be able to cook up a plan. If you could identify the German's spy network in this country, we could turn it to our advantage in selecting what we allow them report back to their masters in Germany. It would be jolly handy to have some idea of what they want your network to find out. You'll have to give us some time to work out the details.'

'I am in your hands, sir. I just need to make amends for some foolish words I exchanged with my father.'

'Then leave it with me, young man. Is there anything else?'

'Actually, there is something else, sir. After my interview with Captain Tapken, I was invited to join some dozen other officers in attending a "Bier-Abend", a dinner, in honour of von Hoffman's decoration and promotion. As usual on these occasions, the beer flowed freely and, once the cigars were lit after the meal, we ended up singing. The talk afterwards started off sentimental, but then turned quite bellicose as the officers berated the late King's policy for the "encirclement of Germany" as they see it, and the Entente Cordiale. Soon, much of the assembled company began to display outright contempt and hatred for the French.'

'I presume there is a point to this tale of a typical officers' mess function, Miller?'

'I beg your indulgence a little longer, sir. Some of the officers then started to talk about the von Schlieffen Plan and how they would smash the French and take Paris within six weeks. You know, to release the troops to meet the Russian mobilisation to the East and all that?'

'I'm listening.'

'Their cheerleader was an infantry major. Somebody then countered by pointing out that the plan would fail if the German Army was delayed by the great Belgian forts at Liège and Namur. This is where the conversation became very interesting. An engineering officer mentioned that he had studied these forts and could not see how the army's 12-inch howitzers would make much progress against the 9-inch armour plating covering the forts' great gun cupolas, or against the 4ft-thick concrete walls of the shelters. The infantry major scoffed him and referred to the existence of some 16.5-inch howitzers at Essen …'

'Did you say 16.5 inches?'

'Yes, sir.'

'Good Lord! This is interesting. I shall make a note. Pray continue.'

'I learned that these massive guns seem to have been designed with the express intention of pulverising the Belgian frontier forts. Before the major could go on further, von Hoffman put a stop to this loose talk and he and the major afterwards had a heated discussion in a corner of the room. I maintained my customary von Trotha aloofness and took no part in the discussion.'

'Bravo, Miller. My, you certainly kept your wits about you. It could all be an exaggeration, but I think I will have somebody do some sniffing around Essen, very soon. For now, though, I'd best be letting you go about your business as a new German spymaster. Where do you plan to start your work?'

'I've been given the name of a German hotelier in Norfolk. I thought I might start there with the apparent intention of finding sympathisers willing to report on naval activity on the east coast. Perhaps you could give me a couple of days to leave London before informing my father of my latest plans.'

'As you wish, old chap. Just keep the reports coming via the usual methods. In the meantime, I'll talk to Kell. Good luck, Miller, and keep up the good work. We'll be in touch, before long, I promise.'

CHAPTER 13

June 1911

'I need to see the Home Secretary.'

The porter looked up from his newspaper at the tall, grey-whiskered man who had addressed him. He noted from the dress, grooming and clothes of the stranger that he was obviously a gentleman. However, the porter was less impressed by the pool of water that was collecting on the tiled floor of the Reform Club's entrance hall. Despite being late June, it had been raining hard all day and the rain was streaming off the stranger's cloak and broad-brimmed hat. The visitor had clearly arrived at the club on foot.

The porter straightened himself to his full diminutive height and replied stiffly, 'I'm sorry, sir, but the Home Secretary is attending a private function and cannot be disturbed.'

'Damn your eyes, sir,' replied the stranger abruptly. 'I'm here to see the Home Secretary on a matter of the utmost importance. Interrupt the party and tell him that Captain Miller is here on urgent business.'

The porter, an ex-army man himself, cast his eye nonchalantly over the full figure of the visitor. He noted his six-feet-four-inch height and, despite the outer clothing, the slim build. He judged the stranger's age to be about fifty and long retired from the army to have progressed no further than the rank of captain. He had no time for pompous officers who held on to their relatively junior rank for the rest of their lives. Whilst he sensed from the force of the captain's personality that he was beaten, he was, nonetheless, unimpressed and felt compelled to make one last effort to protect the privacy of a club member.

'Very good, sir. If you would be kind enough to leave your card, I will inform the minister as soon as he is free that you desire …'

Before he could finish his sentence, he suddenly found himself staring into the twin-barrels of two cold, deep, merciless, dark eyes the colour of anthracite, drilling into his brain less than six inches from his face and with such force that the hapless porter suddenly knew how a rabbit must feel in the carriage lights of one of the new-fangled automobiles.

'No, my little weasel,' the captain growled quietly in a voice that had often carried across the open bridge of a cruiser in a force ten gale. 'I wish to see the Home Secretary now, and I mean now. Either you go and fetch him, or stand aside and I will call him myself. When matters of national security are at stake I am in no mood to tolerate petty obstructions. So it's up to you, little man. How do you wish to play it?'

The porter, conscious of the six-inch height advantage of his interlocutor and his obvious wiry strength, quickly decided that submission was the order of the day.

'Very well, sir. If you would like to take a seat and wait here a few minutes, I will take your card to the minister.'

Mustering his last vestiges of dignity, he then retired, none too swiftly, across the hall. At each step, his boots squeaked, adding to his self-consciousness. At the bottom of the grand staircase he met a liveried footman. Before passing over the captain's engraved card he was surprised to note that the captain was in fact not an army man, but a naval gentleman, and more astonishingly, the post-nominal VC. Curiously there was no address shown, but the words, "Remember Omdurman!" had been written across the face of the card. As the footman placed the card on a salver and mounted the staircase, the porter returned to his desk to find the visitor had removed his hat and cloak and was sitting reading the day's newspaper.

At the top of the staircase, the footman cast his eyes over the guests in the Gallery, from which the dull roar of conversation of some of the most powerful men in the empire greeted him. The party was being given by former Liberal Prime Minister, the Earl of Roseberry, and was attended not just by several of the Liberal Party grandees, but also by many of the opposition Conservative Party. However, the footman, a Scot himself, noted with some bemusement that the great man was not discussing politics, but in animated conversation with John McDowall, the Chief Executive of the Scottish Football Association. It took a couple of minutes before he spotted the Home Secretary, his short height accentuated by the towering figure of the person with whom he was speaking. At five feet eight inches in height, Mr Winston Spencer Churchill, Secretary of State for the Home Department, was dwarfed by the Metropolitan Police Commissioner, Sir Edward Henry.

At a convenient pause in the conversation, the footman deferentially interrupted the two men.

'Excuse me, Mr Churchill, sir, but there is a gentleman downstairs who is very keen to see you and has asked that I stress the urgency of a meeting.'

Churchill was visibly annoyed by the interruption, but took the proffered card nonetheless. He did not instantly remember the name Miller, but was impressed by the VC.

'Well, bless my soul!' The words, "Remember Omdurman" brought him up with a jolt.

Wistfully and for several seconds, he was transported to a battle in the sandy wastelands of the Sudan on 2 September 1898 and the cavalry charge of the 21st Lancers at the Battle of Omdurman.

'Excuse me, sir. Shall I arrange for your visitor to be shown into the card room?' Churchill was instantly brought back to the 20th century and realised that both the footman and the Metropolitan Police Commissioner were watching him curiously.

'Forgive me. Yes, please,' he replied to the footman and then turned to his former conversational partner. 'Sir Edward, I wonder if you would excuse me. I have just had an acute reminder of my past. I am intrigued to meet with this visitor. He and I once shared a very exciting and intimate experience, and I am anxious to renew the acquaintance.'

'Of course,' replied Sir Edward. 'Forgive me, Home Secretary, but I could not help noticing the name on the card. I know something of Captain Miller's activities in the Admiralty. With these activities in mind, I wonder if I might join you. I doubt his purpose here is to reminisce.'

Churchill nodded his assent and both men followed the footman into the card room. A few minutes later, Captain Miller was shown into the room to meet them. As Miller entered the room, he surveyed it rapidly before fixing on Sir Henry. After a mere moment's reflection, he nodded slightly to confirm recognition and then switched his attention to the Home Secretary. It was almost thirteen years since he and Churchill had last met, but Churchill was slightly embarrassed to note that whilst he had put on some weight, he barely noted any change in the physical appearance of the man he had last seen on the River Nile. Despite his naval profession, he was wearing plain clothes and had not yet changed into evening dress. Churchill envied the still-full head of now greying hair and the athleticism of his physique. He advanced across the carpet with his hand outstretched to welcome his former comrade-in-arms.

'My dear Miller. What a pleasant surprise to meet you again after so many years. Do sit down. I hope you don't mind, but I invited Sir Edward Henry, the Metropolitan Police Commissioner to join us. Do you know each other? Can I offer you a drink?'

'Yes, we have indeed met occasionally, one way or another. Good evening, Sir Edward. I was informed that you, too, would be here tonight. Your presence is highly convenient. A malt whisky with a splash of water would be very welcome, sir.'

The three men settled themselves into the leather armchairs by the window of the card room and sat impassively whilst a steward arranged their drinks. Before the steward withdrew, Miller, laying a hand on his arm gently, addressed him. 'My business with these two gentlemen is of a confidential nature. I wonder if I might trouble you to leave the decanter and ensure we are not disturbed?'

The steward glanced questioningly over to Churchill, before replying, 'If that will be all, gentlemen,' and retiring from the room.

As the men sipped their drinks, Churchill opened the conversation. 'Your skin has adopted a lighter hue since our days together in the Sudan. I am pleased to see you fit and well, though. May I offer you my congratulations on your promotion to Captain and on your VC in South Africa. I fancy there was a report of some other exploit before then, too. Perhaps it was China, but I cannot recall. I did try to keep up with your career progress, but the last I heard, you were an attaché in Berlin. What is your present employment?'

'I am flattered that you should take such an interest in me, sir. You are well informed. May I, too, offer my congratulations? I have watched your rise in politics with much interest, although I was disappointed at your defection to the Liberal Party. Until your move to Dundee, we could have been said to be almost neighbours.'

'Defection is, perhaps, putting it a bit strongly, don't you think? I hope I might be considered a man of principle and when those principles became more aligned with the policies of the Liberals, why it was only natural that I would ally myself with the members of that party.'

Churchill thought Miller seemed embarrassed by his possible lack of tact and so quickly added, 'How is it that we were almost neighbours, Captain?'

'My family home lies in Lancashire, none too far from your former seat of Oldham. However, I see that your principles have enabled you to achieve high Cabinet office.'

Churchill suspected a jibe was implied, but was well used to such comments and decided to let it go. 'So how might I help you today? I have no doubt that the purpose of your meeting is not to reminisce over the war in Sudan.'

Miller took a large sip of his malt whisky before speaking. 'Since returning from Berlin, I have been working at the Admiralty, in the Intelligence Department, and latterly with the Foreign Section of the new Secret Service Bureau. It is in this connection that I sought our meeting this evening.'

'So you are involved with the SSB, too. I was aware of Kell's position, of course. He and I were at Sandhurst together, and we have met many times in connection with the new Official Secrets Act. All being well, we should have Royal Assent next month. But Kell has been at great pains to stress the independence of his office from my ministry, so how does it come to be linked with the Admiralty?'

'Kell is quite right about his independence, sir. The SSB is not just responsible for working with the police to monitor foreign espionage activities in this country. Its other customers are the War Office and Admiralty. Colonel MacDonagh in the War Office, and I, on behalf of the Naval Intelligence Department, liaise over the tasking of the Foreign Section. Given the urgent requirement to ascertain information on German shipbuilding and dockyards, the Foreign Section is run by a naval commander and Kell's Home Section focuses on counter-espionage within these shores.'

'Thank you for the elucidation, Captain. Please continue,' Churchill replied.

'Gentlemen, I will not waste your valuable time with social pleasantries, but will instead cut to the quick. I am here to enlist your help to foil a German plot to blow up the naval magazines at Chattenden and Lodge Hill in Kent ...' Both Churchill and Henry spluttered on their drinks in unison. 'I am sure that I do not need to tell you that ...' Miller continued unperturbed by the reaction of his audience, '... were such a plot to succeed, the Royal Navy would lose its entire reserves of cordite!'

Churchill was the first to recover. 'A German plot, you say. But surely that would be an act of war? Our countries may be rivals in the modernisation of our fleets, but surely not even the Kaiser would contemplate such an act of naked aggression? How do you come by this information and why do you bring me the news, and not the First Lord of the Admiralty?'

Miller calmly helped himself to another whisky and water before replying. 'I came by this information directly from the architect of the plan and leader of the gang that is to execute the operation. I can assure you that the German Intelligence Service is behind the plot and war with Germany is only a question of time. The ringleader of the plot is well known to us and he has gathered around him a network of German spies and saboteurs. I have come to you, sir, as the Home Secretary, since my department wishes the capture and subsequent handling of the saboteurs to be conducted in a certain way. You and Sir Edward have a certain influence in these matters that the First Lord does not. Moreover, both Mister McKenna and the First Sea Lord, Sir Arthur Wilson, are in Orkney, visiting the Fleet in Scapa Flow at present and I have insufficient time to obtain their authority for what I have in mind.'

This time it was Sir Edward's turn to question the naval captain. 'Captain Miller, your reputation is well known amongst my officers in Special Branch. I am still in regular contact with former-Superintendent Melville of the SSB, and although he has a closer relationship with Kell, he speaks very highly of you. As a result, I have no reason to doubt the veracity of what you have said so far this evening. However, how certain are you of your information? Who is this ringleader and how do you know of his intentions?'

Miller rose to look out at the wet June sky. It had stopped raining at last and the birds were singing again. He turned to face his two colleagues, both hanging on his answer. 'I will readily stake my life on the credibility of the information as the man who formulated and leads the plot is my son!'

CHAPTER 14

July 1911

'Sir,' the big Irishman muttered quietly. 'Beggin' yer pardon, but we need to move on.' He looked around him and noted that the crowd of onlookers was growing. 'Come on now, sir. There's nothin' ye can be doin' now for the poor wee thing an' we've a timetable to be keepin'.'

Von Trotha ignored him and continued to examine and comfort the mangled mess of hair, blood and bone lying before him. The dog lifted his head and let out a whimper of anguish. O'Malley was no expert in veterinary medicine, but it was obvious to him that the animal could not be saved. It had run across the road and been hit by an automobile. One, if not two, of the vehicle's wheels had run over to crush the dog and the driver looked on hapless and anguished. O'Malley could not understand von Trotha's behaviour. It was out of character. Von Trotha was a cold-hearted bastard and yet he was quite emotional about this unfortunate dog.

He shook von Trotha's shoulder. 'C'mon, sir. We need to be away from here. There's a bobby approaching on his bicycle and we've reason to be somewhere else.'

Von Trotha lifted his head in the direction of the policeman in the distance. O'Malley saw the pain on his face change to an attitude of practicality. 'You're right, of course, O'Malley. Just give me one more minute to release this poor animal from his suffering.'

Von Trotha shifted his attention back to the dog. Taking the piece of sacking he had removed from the dray cart to support the dog's head, he now wrapped it around the animal's snout. Then, to O'Malley's surprise, he took a firm but gentle grip of the sacking and squeezed it tightly. The dog made to struggle, but didn't have the strength. 'Don't fret, old fellow,' von Trotha said soothingly. 'We'll soon have you out of your misery.'

O'Malley could see tears running down his officer's cheeks as von Trotha gently suffocated the poor animal. Very soon the dog gave one last twitch of a rear paw and stopped breathing. Even so, von Trotha maintained the pressure on the sacking until he seemed sure that the dog was indeed lifeless. At last, he was satisfied and stood up. He turned to the driver of the automobile that had struck the dog.

'Can I leave it to you, sir, to ensure the dog is properly buried?'

'Er … Why, of course … Naturally … Anything. The least I can … There was nothing I could do, you know? The dog just jumped out in front of me …'

'I do know. Explain it to the policeman when he arrives. I have to return to my round.'

Von Trotha returned to the dray cart and re-joined his two nervous-looking colleagues, one of whom was holding the reins of the two horses pulling the cart. He blew his nose and wiped his eyes and face before nodding to O'Malley. 'Come on then. We have a job to do.'

O'Malley climbed back into the driver's seat and set the horses in motion again. He glanced surreptitiously to his left and noted that von Trotha's face had resumed its customary expressionless mask. 'So, Herr high and mighty von Trotha,' he thought. 'There is some feelin' in you after all, you bastard.'

****

O'Malley pulled up at the main entrance to the naval magazine at Chattenden. His way was blocked by the closed gates and two police constables on sentry duty. As previously agreed, he let von Trotha do the talking. He had the English accent.

'What's happened to the usual men?' the first policeman asked von Trotha as he examined his papers.

'They're on another round. We're all working crazy shifts at present. It seems the whole nation is stocking up to toast the new king's health. The boss couldn't let you fellahs and the navy run dry, could he? So he sent us along with this delivery.'

'I suppose that makes sense, although I'll be spending the coronation at home with the wife and her good-for-nothing brother.' The policeman checked the papers of the other occupants of the dray cart whilst his colleague mounted a cursory inspection of the cart's contents.

'Righty-oh then, mate. Everything seems in order. You know where you're going?' Von Trotha nodded. 'On your way then.' The two policemen opened the gates and allowed the dray cart to pass through.

****

The doctor turned into a doorway and, making a pretence of retying one of his bootlaces, looked back down King Street to check he was not being

87

followed. Despite the cool weather, there still seemed to be plenty of people abroad in Gravesend. It had not been the finest of weather for the new King George's coronation, but the British had nonetheless turned out in droves to celebrate the occasion. Several Londoners had clearly enjoyed themselves a little too much and Dr Isaac Jacobs watched with disgust as a drunk vomited on the pavement five yards up the street. Another shower started and several of the milling revellers quickened their pace to return home or even to seek the shelter of the nearest public house. Satisfied that he was not being followed, Jacobs continued up the road and, a few minutes later, turned left and arrived at a terraced house in Berkley Road.

Within seconds of knocking on the front door, it was opened by a dark-haired, moustachioed man of medium height. It was difficult for Jacobs to see the man in detail as the hall light was off and the man was half hidden behind the door.

'Can I help you?' he was asked nervously.

Jacobs responded, 'I understand you have some wounded eagles for me to see.'

The man behind the door was clearly relieved, but asked quietly, 'Are you the doctor from the embassy?'

'I am,' replied Jacobs, 'But may I come in? I am worried I may have been followed.'

Without awaiting a further response, he pushed his way through the half-open doorway. The other man shut the door hurriedly, causing the hall to fall into complete darkness.

He called out, 'Es geht. Er kommt.'

In response, a door at the end of the corridor on the right opened and Jacobs was able to see again. Another man carrying a candle entered the hallway from the adjoining room and beckoned Jacobs to follow him upstairs.

Jacobs noted in the dim light that the pictures on the left hand wall of the stairway were hanging crookedly and the wall was streaked with a dark stain above the dado. Knowing something of the situation, he immediately deduced that one of his new patients had needed help in climbing the stairs. As he turned on the half landing, the man with the candle opened the first door on the left of the first floor and the stairs were bathed in gas light emanating from this room. The bedroom was sparsely furnished with a washstand, a chair and an iron bedstead on which lay a man and beside him kneeled another. The latter immediately rose to his feet and turned towards Jacobs. He was wearing a white, blood-stained shirt beneath a workman's overall. The man spoke, in English, and Jacobs recognised the thick Irish accent.

'It's good of you to come, Doctor. I think it's all over with this fellah, but there's two in the front room who'd more than likely merit yer attention.'

Jacobs approached the man on the bed. He was lying on his back, bare-chested with a blood-soaked bandage to his left side and, with his dark eyes wide open, staring at the ceiling unblinkingly. Feeling the carotid artery for a pulse, Jacobs determined that the man was indeed dead and closed his eyes. The body was still warm and the blood had not congealed, suggesting that death was quite recent. He removed the bandage and noted the entry wound of a bullet close to the heart.

'You did well to get him this far. He has lost much blood. And you? Are you wounded, too?'

'No, Doctor. I was lucky and the other two through there aren't hurt badly. Just scratches like.'

'I will examine them now. Are there any more patients for me?'

'I can't rightly say. Von Trotha was definitely hit and I think the murderin' bastards have killed 'im. Two were caught by the bobbies, but I think the other two got away unharmed. I'm hopin' they'll make their way to the rendezvous all right.'

'My concern is only with the wounded,' responded Jacobs. 'I do not want to know any of the details of your activities. Others will take care of that. I am here strictly as a doctor on humanitarian grounds. Let me see the others.'

The Irishman and the man with the candle led Jacobs through to the other bedroom. The doorman returned downstairs. This second bedroom was larger than the first, but still sparsely furnished. Two pairs of thick, green curtains covered the windows overlooking the street. As well as a washstand, the furniture comprised a double wardrobe, an armchair and two single beds. Both occupants of the room immediately stood to attention and clicked the heels of their boots as the doctor entered. Each was dressed in a shabby, woollen suit and both had an arm in a bandage.

The Irishman, noting Jacobs's surprise explained, 'I patched 'em up as best as I could, Doctor. Some good came out of me trainin' in His Bloody Majesty's Navy, anyhow. Fritz here took a bullet through his hand and Hans got caught in the arm by a chip of brickwork from a bullet. I've dressed both wounds and they're clean right enough, but I'd still like you to have a look at 'em.'

'Would you be so kind as to turn up the gas a little so I may make my examinations?' Jacobs asked. The man with the candle had by now extinguished it and he attended to the gaslight. Jacobs suddenly realised that this man had yet to utter a word in his presence. *So what?* he thought. *The less I know about this foolhardy scheme the better*.

In German, he instructed the two men still standing at attention, 'Gentlemen, please sit down so I may attend your wounds.'

As he worked, he glanced over each of his patients surreptitiously. From their bearing and manner it was obvious that they were military men. Both sat very upright and suffered the pain of his probing their wounds in strict silence. Although he did not really want to know, he could not help but wonder who they were. All he knew was that with the full knowledge of the military attachés at his embassy, these men had clearly been involved in some form of clandestine operation that had gone badly wrong. The Irishman had referred to 'bobbies', the local slang for the police, so that suggested the operation had been conducted against the English. Indeed, the Irishman's very presence confirmed this suspicion. But why would his government choose the day of the coronation of the British monarch to mount a subversive operation? Although rivals, industrially and for control of the seas, the two countries were not at war. Indeed, had not the Kaiser visited London only last year for the funeral of his uncle, King Edward the Seventh? As a member of the German Embassy in London he considered himself well informed on political matters, but this was madness. Then again, had not Clausewitz said that "War is the continuation of politics by other means"? The generals had far too much influence on politics these days.

After removing a few strands of cloth buried in Hans's arm and applying a splint to the hand of Fritz, Jacobs was satisfied that both men's wounds would heal. He applied a fresh dressing to each of the wounds and immobilised each man's injured limb in a sling. He turned to the Irishman.

'I do not know who you are or what you have been doing. I have only been instructed to tend to the wounded and pass you one instruction. If you are fit to move, you are to proceed with your escape plan and catch the morning tide. Depending on his nationality, your dead colleague is to be repatriated or disposed of locally where his corpse will not be found easily. Is there any message you would like me to take back to the embassy?'

The Irishman paused for a moment before replying. 'Yes. I'll see these fellahs and their dead comrade to the ship all right. But ask the embassy staff to inform Mrs Reimers that I'll be comin' too. London's a bit hot for me for the time being, and I need to lay low for a while. Tell 'em that they'll need to watch the newspapers for news of the missing eagles. Have ye got that?'

'Yes. To tell Mrs Reimers to expect you and to check the newspapers for news of your missing comrades. I will pass on the message. Now I must go. It is already late and I do not wish to attract suspicion over my movements at this time of night.'

The Irishman opened the door of the bedroom and called downstairs. 'Wilhelm. The doctor will be leaving now. Will ye show 'im downstairs?'

Wilhelm, the doorman of Jacobs's earlier acquaintance, returned upstairs with a candle and Jacobs gathered up his instruments.

'I'll leave Wilhelm to see you out, Doctor. I'm somewhat wary of showing my face at the front door. Thank ye for your help and God be with ye.'

With this the Irishman shook Jacobs's hand warmly and left the doctor to follow Wilhelm downstairs.

After bidding Wilhelm farewell in the dim light of the candle, Jacobs cast a glance down the street in both directions and then looked more intently at the front garden opposite. In the shadows he had spotted a movement and his heart seemed to stop in panic. Had he been followed after all, he wondered? As his eyes adjusted to the dark, he saw that the movement had emanated from a figure lying slumped in the doorway. He heaved a sigh of relief. It appeared as if the man opposite had over-indulged in the coronation celebrations and been locked out to sleep it off. Breathing normally once more, Jacobs turned left down the street to return to Gravesend station.

CHAPTER 15

Major Vernon Kell, formerly of the South Staffordshire Regiment and now known to everyone in the SSB as 'K', looked out across the grimy streets of Westminster from his office at 64 Victoria Street. He was in a good mood. After all the cool, wet and unsettled weather of the last couple of weeks, it was now a beautifully warm and sunny day. The Meteorological Office was suggesting that the summer was now here to stay and even expounding the possibility of an unusually hot July. It boded well for the coming grouse season and he looked forward eagerly to his August holiday in Durham, as the guest of Lord Barnard.

He returned to his desk and re-examined the folder containing the report of Operation Mousetrap. He smiled to himself as he read the title.

'The person who gave the name to this operation obviously had a sense of humour, Clarke. However, it wasn't good for security.'

Superintendent Clarke was seated the other side of Kell's desk. 'Why is that so, Major?' he responded.

'Hmm, what if the enemy were to hear just the name of such an operation? They might glean too much of its nature. I think, perhaps it would be safer to draw up an alphabetical list of random code words and use these sequentially for future operations. It might be dull, but secrecy is paramount in this department's line of business.'

Whilst Kell made a mental note to discuss it with 'C' when they next met, Clarke remained silent. His air suggested he thought Kell was making too much of it.

Kell returned to the report and scanned it for perhaps the eighth time of reading. It conveyed the details of the recent successful operation to foil the sabotage of one of the Royal Navy's magazines near Chatham. Enormous credit was due to his friend Miller in the Naval Intelligence Department. It had been a capital plan and, on the whole, it had been executed well.

'It's a pity that the Irishman, O'Malley, escaped, though. That wasn't agreed beforehand. With his many years' service in the Royal Navy, experience with ordnance and Irish nationality, O'Malley could be a dangerous weapon in the hands of our opponent.' The opponent to whom he referred was Mrs Reimers, alias Gustav Steinhauer of the Nachricten-Abteilung, 'N', the German Admiralty's Intelligence Service.

Kell reviewed the closely typed narrative of the attempt by a gang of nine Germans or German sympathisers to blow up the Chattenden magazine on the day of King George's coronation. Under the guise of delivering beer to the men on duty in the depot, four men, including their leader, Oberleutnant von Trotha, and Petty Officer Seamus O'Malley, had successfully entered the lightly guarded depot in a dray cart. Having overcome and replaced the unarmed police constables on duty at the gate, von Trotha and O'Malley had laid explosive charges in one of the magazine stores under cover of a diversionary attack by five armed agents in a commandeered taxi cab. Unbeknown to the Germans, the Admiralty and the local constabulary had been forewarned of the raid and had deployed armed police in the depot. After some armed resistance, they had spoiled the German plan and, in the course of the operation, the gang's leader had been killed and two of the agents captured.

'And he wasn't alone in evading your clutches either, Clarke?'

'No, Major. In all, six of the gang escaped, four in the commandeered taxi cab and two on foot.'

Clarke replied in an even tone that gave no hint of any vexation he might feel at Kell's questions. Kell knew he was pushing Clarke's patience. There was no doubt that the operation to capture the German agents had been a great success. Clarke's men had been well supported by the police and no doubt he was expecting Kell be pleased. Indeed, Kell was delighted, but that was no reason to let on to Clarke just yet. He allowed Clarke to continue.

'As it states in the report, Major, two have already been arrested by my men and are being detained securely in a secret safe-house for interrogation. They have both been given the choice of trial for treason and hanging after the undoubted guilty verdict, or co-operating with the SSB to become double agents. It didn't taken either agent long to agree to the latter arrangement and both are now singing like canaries. They just couldn't wait to hand over information on their fellow spies, sympathisers and arrangements for communicating with Berlin.'

'That's something, I suppose. And you're quite sure the others have left the country?'

'Absolutely, Major. My men followed the four at-large agents to their safe-house in Gravesend. Three of them had been wounded, one seriously. I set watch on the house and, as we expected, the doctor from the German Embassy called. One of my men, posing as a drunk in the garden opposite, clearly identified him and noted his time of arrival and departure. That provides definitive proof of the German Government's involvement in the plot.'

'So, four German agents are at large to continue their dastardly plots against us. But the proof of government involvement will come in extremely useful. I'm sorry, I interrupted.'

Kell could see that Clarke was clearly becoming more irritated by the questions, but he remained patient in his replies. Kell silently revelled in Clarke's discomfort. He was not in the least dismayed to read of the four fugitives. It would not take Clarke's men long to commence the next phase of Operation Mousetrap, the rounding up of the rest of Germany's intelligence network in Britain. Cumming's department would then start the feeding of false information on the Royal Navy's defences and movements to their handlers in the German Intelligence Service. If Germany wanted war, then it would find the Home Section of the SSB fully prepared.

'The following morning, two of the agents and O'Malley were escorted by two other German nationals to a boat at one of the piers. Both nationals are known to us, but have been allowed to remain at large as part of the next phase of the operation. The two agents have been identified by von Trotha as members of the Königin Augusta Garde-Grenadier-Regiment Nummer Vier or Fourth (Queen Augusta) Grenadier Guards Regiment.'

'Tell me more about these two German nationals.'

For the first time Clarke had to consult his pocket notebook before responding. 'One of them is a barber, Karl Gustav Ernst, currently residing in Caledonian Road, Islington. The other is his assistant Wilhelm Kronauer.

'But your men lost sight of them at the pier?'

'Not at all, Major.' This time Clarke failed to avoid sounding impatient in his reply. 'We had already anticipated that the Germans would intend to flee by steamer and I had, accordingly, placed one of my men, Detective Jackson, with a patrol from the River Police. He confirms seeing O'Malley and the two guardsmen board the SS *Emden*, bound for Hamburg. O'Malley was carrying, with some difficulty, a long and heavy length of tarpaulin up the accommodation ladder. Jackson believes that this may have been the corpse of the third guardsman, but could not be sure. If he's right, then the Irishman has the strength of an ox. However, in accordance with *your* instructions, Major, my men made no attempt to detain O'Malley as it would have interfered with the plan to allow the guardsmen to return to Germany. You were quite emphatic on the last point.'

Kell laughed aloud. He could not tease Clarke any further. 'Stanley, I'm pulling your leg. You and your men have done a brilliant job. Of course, I would have dearly loved to have captured O'Malley and have him stand trial for treason, but it was imperative that the guardsmen returned to Germany. Were the public to become aware that HMG held in custody serving military personnel of a foreign power who had undertaken an act of naked aggression on sovereign territory, it would cause too many complications and there was the risk that the situation would spiral out of control.'

Kell's remarks lifted Clarke's tension. 'You almost had me going there, Major. Anyway my pals at the Yard will ensure the Home Office blames the Fenians for a random attack by O'Malley and fellow sympathisers.'

'Good. That will not, of course, prevent the Foreign Office from taking advantage of the situation and sending the Kaiser a strongly worded and secret diplomatic note of protest. That should put Stenhauer's department on the defensive for a while. Most importantly, the German Intelligence Service now has credible eye witnesses to the death of their operative, von Trotha. Matters have worked out very satisfactorily and the evasion of O'Malley was a small price to pay. Thank you, Stanley, for your excellent work on this and please also pass on my thanks to your men.'

'I will certainly tell the men. However, I do have one question of my own. Why did we have to pretend that the agent von Trotha is dead? Surely he was a most valuable double agent and well placed to penetrate the Germans' intelligence services deeper?'

'That's something puzzling me, too, Stanley. It was Captain Miller's idea and, knowing him as we do, I think he will have had his own good reasons.'

As the two men shook hands, they were interrupted in bidding each other farewell by the entrance of Kell's secretary with the tea trolley. 'Your next visitors are here, Major. Would you like me to tell them to wait?'

Kell glanced up at his clock and observed that it was just after five minutes to eleven o'clock. As always, the Royal Navy had to be five minutes early.

'No, show them in now, Mrs Elland. I would like Mister Clarke to meet them,' he replied affably and crossed the floor to meet his guests.

One of his visitors was Kell's old friend and colleague, Captain Miller. The other was much younger; a serious-looking man, dark-haired, slim and about six foot in height. Kell shook hands with them both very warmly.

'Captain William, may I congratulate you on a brilliant success, none of which could have been achieved without the daring and courage of this young man.'

Turning to the younger man, Kell saluted him and went on to say, 'Oberleutnant Friedrich Wilhelm von Trotha, formerly of the Second Railway Regiment, I am pleased to see you looking so fit and well. As Mark Twain would have said, "Clearly, reports of your death have been greatly exaggerated." Welcome. Do sit down and tell me all, before you go on a well-earned and lengthy spot of leave.'

CHAPTER 16

August 1911

Captain Herbert Heath MVO Royal Navy, was impressed by his friend's motor car. The 60-horsepower engine was making light work of the many hills between Lancaster and Miller's estate at Marton Hall. The last time Heath had seen the Mercedes Simplex Saloon had been in 1908 when he had seen it loaded onto the ship taking it to England. Heath had just relieved Miller as the Naval Attaché in Berlin. Although the two officers had met frequently since then, it had always been in London or Portsmouth and this was Heath's first visit to Marton Hall where the automobile was kept. Prior to his appointment in Berlin, Heath had commanded the Monmouth class armoured cruiser HMS *Lancaster* for two years. He had returned to Britain twelve months earlier to take command of the Dreadnought class battleship HMS *Superb* and was now enjoying a few days' leave in Lancashire, catching up with old friends made during his command of *Lancaster* and spending this evening with Miller.

'So, Herbert, how was your stay with the noble judges of Lancaster? I heard that such is your distinction, Sir George Pilkington, the High Sheriff was your host.'

'There was too much oratory and port for my liking, but it was nonetheless a convivial evening. My ears and head are still singing. I also met a King's Council who claimed to know your brother well and asked to be remembered to him. His name was Marshall Hall. He seemed to think I should have heard of him. From what I remember of the evening, his claim to fame was that he returned the brief to defend Crippen and reckons if the fellow had only followed his advice, he might have saved him from the gallows. Do you know him, William?'

'I cannot say I do, but I have heard my brother Edmond talk of him. He used to be the Unionist MP for Southport and Edmond met him from time to time at various political functions. Edmond spoke highly of him as a barrister. According to Edmond, he spoke very little in the House considering his reputation as a fine orator. I think he might even have taken over the seat from Sir George, but I cannot be sure. I have to say, I don't envy your evening with politicians and lawyers.'

'Ah, but I certainly envy your motor car, William. It has quite a turn of speed. I might have to upgrade my Riley.'

'Thank you, Herbert. I am very pleased with it. It's a fine example of German engineering. More than a few times I've had to thank God for the double-brake system. Perhaps I should take it to London sometime and show our technical people what they will be up against if one day we do have to fight the Imperial German Navy.'

'At least this recent crisis over Agadir seems to have forced the Admiralty to acknowledge that war with Germany is just a matter of time. I spent all my time in Berlin warning of the growing threat, but it fell on deaf ears as far as Lloyd George and Churchill were concerned. At last the noble Sea Lords seem to have woken up over Agadir and I am finally getting my defects repaired and being allowed to increase my ammunition stocks. Perhaps we can get in some real gunnery practice now.'

'Certainly Lloyd George is convinced at last. Thank God for his Mansion House speech. But for that, I'm convinced the Kaiser would not have backed down. I think you'll find Churchill a convert now, too. It's just as well as I've a feeling that Asquith has him in mind for the Admiralty soon.'

'Churchill as First Lord of the Admiralty! You can't be serious. William, even you must be wrong about that. He's an army man, a publicity seeker and a traitor to his class. Why would Asquith move McKenna anyway?'

'Calm down, Herbert. I've made it my business to study Mister Churchill over the past few months and I have found him highly intelligent and extremely energetic. He's good on his feet, in the House or on a public platform, and that makes him a good man to have on one's side. I agree he's ambitious, but that could be no bad thing. He might even be Prime Minister one day. As for his army background, he can be briefed, but more importantly, he has seen action and is not afraid to speak out against old-fashioned doctrine. He's probably just the man to shake up the Admiralty and Whitehall complacency. As far as moving McKenna is concerned, I suggested it some time ago to a few people in the right quarters.'

'You suggested it!" Heath exclaimed. 'Surely that's a bit beyond the remit even of Intelligence. But why suggest it?'

'My dear friend, if, or indeed when, we go to war with Germany, it will be like no other war that has gone before. Like it or not, Germany is now a great industrialised power. Her army is the strongest in Europe and, in my opinion anyway, more than a match for those of France and Russia combined. We in Britain can only muster six divisions as an expeditionary force, so to win this war, you will no doubt agree, we must rely on the strongest possible navy.'

'We can agree on that, William, but what's it to do with replacing McKenna? I would suggest his record is more pro-Admiralty than that of Churchill.'

'Because, dear friend, without Fisher as First Sea Lord, we need a vigorous figure at the helm to ensure we have the right navy for the right war. I fear that some of our admirals are too mindful about keeping their ships pristine than exercising their ships' companies in gunnery and damage control.'

'That's certainly true.'

'I tell you in confidence, Herbert, had we gone to war over Agadir, the Fleet would not have been ready. We're too weak to maintain our commitments to the Empire and at the same time match the German High Seas Fleet. But you're not here to discuss such matters. You're on leave, remember. Let's stop a short while and you can tell me what you think of the view.'

By now they had ascended the steep hills out of the Wyre Valley and were able to enjoy some marvellous views across the Fylde Plain and Irish Sea coast.

'Just where does your estate start, William?' Heath asked as he admired the view out to sea.

'You're on it now, my dear fellow. That cattle grid we've just crossed marks the boundary. I let out this land for grazing.'

'You certainly have a fine setting for your estate. What a superb view of Morecambe Bay and the Irish Sea.'

As the two senior officers of His Majesty's Navy admired the view, they fell silent for a few minutes. Both men were comfortable in their silence in the way that only good friends can be. It eventually fell to Heath to open the resumption of their earlier conversation.

'I've heard His Majesty state that you get some good shooting round here? He tells me he has been one of your guests on more than one occasion.'

'That we do,' Miller replied. 'We have some excellent pheasant and partridge drives. As you'll see shortly, the valley is a good spot from which to catch them in a high shot as they flee the cover of the woods. To be honest, I do it more for my guests' pleasure than mine. I prefer rough shooting to driven shoots. On Boxing Days, my brother Edmond and I like nothing better than to go out on our own with a couple of dogs and bag something for the pot. It seems more honest toil than the wholesale slaughter of a drive. Moreover, of late, my two eldest lads have started to join us, and sometimes Edmond brings his son and daughter, so we can make it a real family outing.'

'Did your brother not inherit the shipyard from your father?'

'He did indeed. I inherited the estate and house in London and he the shipyard. My father was a shrewd man. He could see that my ambitions lay in the Service and I wouldn't have the time to run a shipyard, so I inherited Marton Hall and the house in Cumberland Terrace. It's an arrangement that has worked out very well since Edmond was always more technical than me and in these days of steam and possibly oil, you need to be an engineer to build ships. Edmond's son seems interested in joining the business, too, so everything has worked out fine. If you look yonder, you can just about see Liverpool. And Miller's Shipyard is just across the Mersey, in Birkenhead. It's not too far for me to visit, to keep up to date with the latest developments in shipbuilding.'

After pausing for a moment of private reflection, Miller continued. 'The arrangement meant I also inherited my mother and she is expected for dinner. We'd better push on or not only will Johanna be worrying where we've disappeared, but my dearest mother will be scolding me. She is very particular about punctuality. Come on, it's not far now.'

Heath enjoyed the next stretch of road. As it crossed the high tops of the Lancashire moors, it undulated in a reasonably straight line and Miller was able to show off the speed of his Mercedes. Such was the roar of the wind in the open-topped vehicle that conversation was curtailed until Miller slowed down for the final two miles to the gates of his estate.

'So how is your ship then, Herbert?'

'Superb,' Heath chuckled in reply. 'Sorry it's an obvious pun. Seriously though, she is an excellent ship and more than a match for anything the Kaiser is building.'

'I understand His Majesty was very impressed by what he saw at the Fleet Review for his coronation. So much so, I hear you will be raising your flag on board next month. Congratulations, Rear Admiral.'

'Is there nothing you don't know? No, of course it's a silly question. I remember all too well the machinations of your department. I used to work for you there, after all. I'm glad His Majesty was pleased. It was good to catch up with him again. I enjoyed hosting him on board *Lancaster* for his cruise of the Mediterranean, and it was quite an unnecessary, but great honour to be awarded Membership of the Victorian Order afterwards.'

'Nonsense, Herbert. The King likes you. If not, he would not, also, have recently appointed you as one his ADCs'.

'Be that as it may be, His Majesty was disappointed, if not a little peeved, not to meet you on board, William. He had been looking forward to catching up with you again. Indeed, I, too, was sorry for your absence. I presume something came up?'

'I am sorry about that, Herbert. You are quite right. Duty called and, as you well know, there are some aspects of my work that come before even my Sovereign. I'm pleased to say though, that it all went off satisfactorily and we could reap the benefits for a year or more. I'm afraid I cannot elucidate.'

'I understand and hope the King will have forgotten it, too. Although I doubt it will boost your own chances of flag rank. How do you rate your prospects? I'm very surprised to have pipped my old mentor to the post. You have an extremely distinguished record.'

'You flatter me, sir. I was fortunate in gaining my cruiser command, but I was never a battleship man. I've spent too much of my career independently engaged in the more clandestine aspects of the Service, to knuckle down to the strictures of fleet manoeuvres. No, the future admirals should be men like you and young Beatty. Besides, I enjoy the freedom of my current role and there is still much to do to reorganise our various intelligence departments.'

'And what might that entail? Assuming you are at liberty to tell me.'

'I can tell an old friend. I'm working on an idea that Cumming's Foreign Section should take on some of my responsibilities and become independent of Kell's Home Section. I thought we might rename Kell's department the Security Service and Cumming's as the Secret Intelligence Service. It would need the approval and promise of funding from the War Office and Foreign Office, of course, but I hope the work will see me out to my retirement. Anyway, welcome to Marton Hall.'

Miller turned the motor-car off the road and they entered through the open gates of Miller's inner estate. Heath looked eagerly for his first view of the main house, but all he could see were woods to his left and a steep valley to his right, with farms on the opposite slope in the distance. It was a full mile later that Heath was first able to glimpse a tall, castellated, gothic tower rising from behind yet more trees. As more of the house became visible, Heath perceived that the tower lay at the corner of a large L-shaped stone-built house. As they turned through another pair of gates and into the main courtyard, Heath was surprised to see the date 1868 carved into the stonework.

'Your abode is more modern than I imagined, William.'

'That's true. My father had it built from scratch when he returned from India. He bought the estate rather than inheriting it. Our family is what is called "new money". My father made his pile in the East and set up the shipyard on the Mersey. He also fancied joining the other nabobs in buying a respectable country estate and so bought Marton Hall for his retirement. My mother still lives here, but now in the original farm house just a half-mile up the drive. As I said on the way here, you'll meet her later as she is joining us for dinner. I think you'll find her quite interesting.'

There the conversation was halted as Miller had parked the Mercedes before the front door and chaotic scenes were being enacted. In stark contrast to the dignified stance of the butler, former Petty Officer Durton, and to Durton's clear disapproval, dogs were leaping about in all directions and barking wildly and John Miller came rushing out into the arms of his father.

'Cadet Miller, have you no decorum or even manners? This is no way to conduct yourself before a guest. Has Dartmouth not taught you how to pay your respects to a commanding officer?'

Miller smiled as he administered the admonishment and tousled the fair hair of his youngest son.

'I must apologise for my son's behaviour, Captain Heath. Snotties these days are ill-disciplined young pups. I promise to make him kiss the gunner's daughter before sunset. Perhaps I could introduce you to the remainder of my family.'

By now Johanna and Richard had appeared at the front door. 'Johanna it's lovely to see you again. I thank you for inviting me to stay in your enchanting house.' Heath kissed Johanna three times on the cheeks in the continental manner.

'Herbert, it is always a pleasure to see you. Do come in and meet my sons. How is Elizabeth?'

'She is very well, thank you, and sends her love. She is quite preoccupied these days with the preparations for our eldest daughter Madeline's twenty-first birthday next February.'

Miller interrupted. 'May I present my eldest son, Lieutenant Richard Miller of His Majesty's Submarine *D2*?'

'I'm very pleased to meet you, Miller. I admire the courage of our submarine service. You wouldn't catch me going on board one, but it seems a pity our submarines do not yet merit names of their own.'

'Thank you, sir. For my part I hope you will not think me impertinent if I say I prefer life in submarines to the bull of battleships and cruisers.'

'Touché.' Heath laughed in response. 'I can tell we will enjoy a stimulating conversation over dinner.'

'We'll move on quickly, I think. My second son, Peter cannot be here today. I believe he may be in Germany on some commercial affair, but ... Johanna where's Paul?'

'I don't know, dear. He was here just a few minutes ago. Paul, where are you?' Johanna called and looked back into the hall perplexedly.

'Here I am. De dah!' Suddenly a figure dropped, as if from the heavens, somersaulted in mid-air and landed directly in front of the two senior officers, causing Johanna to clutch her bosom and shriek with surprise.

'Hello, Pops. I think you were about to introduce me to our guest for the evening.' Paul had climbed out of the landing window and hung in the ivy above as the other introductions were being made.

'Paul, you will be the death of me with your pranks.' Johanna chided Paul good-naturedly, as if such behaviour was common place. Miller was less sanguine about the prank.

'Paul, you knave! I've spoken to you before about these schoolboy antics. I can see we need to repeat the conversation. Shall we say ... in ten minutes? In my study?'

'Oh bother. Very well, Pops.' Paul answered resignedly.

'And don't call me "Pops". Papa or father will do nicely. Anyway, Herbert, this is Paul. He has just left Charterhouse and goes up to Cambridge next term. That's if he hasn't run off to join a circus as a clown in the meantime. I apologise for his extraordinarily eccentric behaviour. If he'd gone to Dartmouth, it would have been beaten out of him.'

'Good evening, Paul. I think you might make a fine gymnast or trapeze artist with such acrobatics. That drop must be all of forty feet. I congratulate you on surviving Charterhouse, too. When my parents put me down for the school it drove me into the navy. So you didn't choose to follow your distinguished father in a naval career then?'

'No, sir.' Paul replied. 'I enjoy foreign languages and see the Diplomatic Service as my metier. When I go up to Trinity College I will be studying Oriental Languages.'

'There's a place for a gifted linguist in the Royal Navy, too, these days, you know,' Heath responded. 'I think your father bears this out. Thanks to Admiral Fisher's reforms, study of a language is now compulsory at the naval college. However, I will not debate the point. And Cadet Miller, what language are you studying?'

'Thanks to Mutti, sir, I already speak German, French and Italian fluently, so I opted to study Norwegian.'

'Norwegian? That's an odd choice. Why not Spanish? I found it very useful in my days as a snottie in Peru.'

'It was something my father suggested, sir.'

Heath gave Miller a quizzical glance, but could read no more in Miller's expression.

CHAPTER 17

The dining table had already been cleared before the sun's last rays disappeared beneath the horizon of Morecambe Bay. The dining room faced west and the setting sun bathed the room with its orange glow. As the candles flickered and the last light of the sun shimmered, Heath imagined that the room had been momentarily engulfed in fire. He was seated at a beautifully polished, long Georgian table of Cuban mahogany. The walls of the room were half-panelled in light oak and above the panelling hung several paintings of seascapes and both Near Eastern and oriental landscapes, as well as a selection of nautical charts and old campaign maps. To one side of the broad expanse of floor-to-ceiling windows, stood a large telescope on a tripod. Heath thought the room surprisingly masculine. Indeed, it would not have been out of place in a wardroom or gentleman's club. It was a strange contrast to the décor of the drawing room which clearly reflected his hostess's feminine and Swiss touch.

When at home in Lancashire, Johanna did not usually follow the convention of withdrawing from the dining room whilst the men sipped their port. She saw little enough of her sons these days and enjoyed participating in their conversation. After twenty-five years as a naval wife, she was well aware that naval officers invariably turned the conversation to naval matters or mutual acquaintances, but she was happy to listen and also confident enough to participate in discussions of world affairs. After all, her father was an international industrialist and she had occasionally accompanied him on his many business trips abroad from Switzerland. Indeed, that was how she had met her husband. In later years, during his service in Berlin, she had invariably accompanied him on his travels to Denmark, the Netherlands and through Germany. She had not shied at taking an interest in the diplomatic conversations. However, tonight she rose to retire from the company of her family and guest. Her mother-in-law was not only stricter about etiquette, but had no interest in naval matters. Mrs Arjumand Roxanna Miller originated from Bushehr in Persia, but had spent much of her life in Calcutta where her father had run a successful chandlery business. It was in this connection that her father had become a client of Captain Frederick Miller, a merchant seaman who had built up a prosperous shipping business trading between Britain, Persia, India and China. Despite the obvious differences in race, colour, religion and culture, somehow Roxanna, as she had become known in the West, and Frederick had married and eventually come to live in Lancashire when their sons had started their schooling in England. As a foreigner living apart from her relations herself, Johanna had a deep sympathy and respect for her mother-in-law. Roxanna was sharp, witty and urbane. Notwithstanding her status as a septuagenarian, she was fit, energetic and still retained some of her good looks from her youth. The two exiles enjoyed a close relationship.

'Madaer, it's a lovely evening. Shall we take a turn in the garden before I walk you home and leave the gentlemen to discuss cricket, steam ships or some other arcane subject?'

'Thank you, Johanna my dear. That would be splendid. I have, as always, enjoyed a very fine meal. Please pass on my appreciation to your cook.'

'Madaer, you know very well that in England it is not correct to praise the cook.'

'So you say, but perhaps that is why, with the obvious exception at Marton Hall, the English enjoy such a poor reputation for their food. Thank you, boys and gentlemen, for your company, but I am a little tired. Captain Heath, it was very kind of you to offer me such a detailed account of the Fleet Review and the arrangements for the coronation. It was so much more interesting than the newspaper accounts. I hope you will enjoy what remains of your leave.'

'Ma'am, it was my pleasure. I, too, have enjoyed the company and I was fascinated by your stories of life in Persia and India. Alas, I have not had the honour of visiting your homeland and I fear there may be insufficient time to remedy the situation in my last few months in command of my fine ship. It will be a lifelong regret.'

'Peter and Paul, I will see you both for your language lesson tomorrow at the usual hour. I hope you have both learned those passages of the Qur'an that I gave you last week.'

'*Yea, we will come to thee to accomplish that of which you have doubt,*' Peter replied in almost perfect Farsi and paraphrasing one of the verses of the Qur'an.

'I'm impressed, Peter. Perhaps you would ask Durton to arrange a lantern for me and to telephone my maid to let her know I will be home soon. As for you, John, I think it is time for you to be in bed. You may kiss me goodnight.'

'But, Grandmama, I was hoping to hear more about life in a Dreadnought.'

'John, your grandmother is quite right. Don't take liberties. It's time you turned in,' Miller said sternly. 'You'll see Captain Heath again at breakfast and tomorrow you'll need your sleep to be in top form for cricket. This time I'll be batting and I want to see those off-breaks, you little scamp,' he added more lightly.

John visibly brightened at the prospect and made to leave the table. 'Yes, Papa. I'm sorry, Grandmama.' Bowing to Heath he added, 'Sir, I have very much enjoyed your company and particularly the tales of your experiences in South America. I hope one day I will have the honour of serving under your command.'

'It would be a pleasure to have such a polite young officer in my wardroom and a treat to have such talent in the ship's cricket team,' Heath replied and shook John's hand warmly before John followed the ladies out into the hall.

****

Johanna and Roxanna each took a shawl and a lantern between them and stepped out through the French windows onto the terrace running along the south side of the house. The three-quarter moon was bright in the cloudless sky and the stars shone clearly to the north and east. To the south-west they could just make out the loom of the Preston gas lamps and to the west the lamps of Blackpool flickered like a long band of fireflies. It reminded them that despite the tranquillity and solitude of the Marton Hall estate, urban life lay only twenty miles distant. However, it was a beautiful sight. There was not a breath of wind.

Johanna broke the silence. 'This moonlight is perfect for your Mughal garden. It was such a clever idea to plant it.'

The Mughal emperors of India had responded to the intense heat of the tropical sun that kept them out of their gardens during the day by planting gardens that could be enjoyed in the cool of the evening hours. They had built magnificent moonlight gardens, filled with the sweet scents of evening flowers, the rustle of exotic grasses and the ethereal glow of plants that captured the moonlight on their leaves. When Roxanna had moved to her new home in Lancashire, she had persuaded her husband to indulge her by allowing her to recreate a reminder of their days in India. Roxanna had made the most of the low, evening light levels by choosing plants with silver foliage or white flowers that reflected the light and appeared to glow. The addition of white stone sculptures and marble landscaping also picked up the light and had created an ethereal aspect to the garden. As well as planting to create visual impact, Roxanna had planted several varieties of flowers and exotic foliage that gave off evocative aromas in the evening air and, to stimulate the senses further, taller plants that rustled in any form of breeze. Clever siting of outdoor candles and lanterns to pick out key features of the garden also created dancing shadows to give a calming and even sensual feeling of movement. After nearly forty years, the garden was fully mature and a treat for guests on warm evenings.

'I love looking at the moon, Johanna, dear. I'll share a secret with you. When I look at the moon, I think of my old home in Bushehr and my relatives all over Persia. I imagine them looking up at this moon at the same time and somehow that connects us. Yet, as we look at this moon, the sun is rising above the Bay of Bengal and more of my relatives are stirring from their beds. It is too easy for the Europeans to forget sometimes that there is another world out there that is not building Dreadnoughts, ruled by the factory whistle or fascinated with naval cadets and postal orders.'

'Do you feel homesick then, Madaer, after all this time?' Johanna's husband had always used the Persian form of address for his mother and Johanna had picked up the habit as a mark of respect. 'After all, you were still a child when you moved to India.'

'I suppose it is a sign of my advancing years. One regresses. However, the feeling has become stronger in the last few weeks. It is to do with my lessons to Peter and Paul. It has been wonderful to speak my native tongue again and I cannot help but feel jealous that Peter is preparing for a posting to Tehran and yet I am unlikely ever to set foot in Persia again. I find myself wondering how my brothers' grandchildren compare with my own.'

'I of all people understand, dear Madaer. I often think about Switzerland and my family there and yet I am able to return home every two or three years. How are the boys progressing in their language lessons?'

'Paul is progressing, but I don't think his heart is in it. I think he does it to please me. He has not had the courage to inform me that it is his intention to study Chinese at Cambridge, but I heard it from John. He must think that I would be disappointed. However, Peter is both gifted and committed. Indeed, he seems to wish to immerse himself in the language and culture, including the poetry and teachings of Islam. No detail seems too trivial and he seems very keen to learn more of his distant relatives and every aspect of life in Persia. It seems deeper than mere preparation for a posting to Tehran next year. He seems driven by a motive beyond the normal preparations for a diplomatic posting.'

'I'm glad he is doing well. He has seemed very preoccupied lately, if not worried. Far from being excited about this new assignment, he seems to dread the prospect. I'm sure he's become disenchanted with the Diplomatic Service. You've known Peter all his life. Can you not see how he has changed in the past two years? He has closed in on himself and perpetually wears a hunted look.'

'What does William say?'

'Oh, he just tells me not to worry. That only makes me angry. I am not some hysterical woman with the vapours. I'm sure William knows more than he is saying and yet he doesn't seem to care.'

'Johanna, there I think you are wrong. I know my son and he cares deeply about all your sons. However, he is English and seems unwilling to show his love openly. His father was the same.'

'Of course, you are right, Madaer. I know he loves all our sons and especially young John. It's just that he seems to push Peter especially hard and Peter seems to resent it. Indeed, I know they have had some fearful rows and I sometimes form the impression Peter is avoiding William when he can.'

'In the world of magnetism I read that two similar poles repel each other whilst opposite poles attract each other. People are no different. Of all your sons, Peter is the most like his father. All your sons are good linguists, but Peter is the most gifted. Like his father, he has a passion for learning foreign tongues. William recognises this and I am convinced that if he has a favourite, it is Peter and not John. As a result, perhaps he is trying to mould Peter to live out a life he would have wished for himself. In that respect it is a pity that Peter was not able to follow his father into the navy. It is ironic as William and my late husband had similar issues. They both shared a love of the sea, but William did not share my husband's interest in commerce and went his own way by joining the Royal Navy.'

'You surprise me. William only speaks of his father with admiration and has never hinted at any conflict, but then there are many subjects on which he is a closed book. I love him dearly, but there are so many topics I wish he would discuss with me. I so much want to share his thoughts and not to be protected from his worries. I want him to trust me. After all, I'm not stupid.'

'Johanna, my dear, you are far from stupid. However, in my experience, men are the same all over the World and you will not change their opinions of women. Come, I'm ready to go home.'

CHAPTER 18

November 1911

'Permission to relieve the lookout, sir?'

It was the responsibility of Officer of the Watch on the bridge of HMS *D2*, to prevent congestion by controlling the flow of personnel up and down the narrow conning tower of the latest addition to His Majesty's submarine service.

'Yes, please,' replied Lieutenant Richard Miller, also the boat's First Lieutenant, through the voice pipe down to the control room. Having safely negotiated the harbour of Harwich, the captain, Lieutenant Harold Johnson, had gone below, leaving his second-in-command to take the submarine out into the open waters of the North Sea. Richard shivered. He wasn't sure if it was through the wind or with the excitement of taking the submarine on its first operational patrol. The trials and work-up earlier in the year were behind them. Now he and the crew of *D2* were going to show the Admiralty and the many armchair critics what the submarine service could achieve.

Richard reflected that even ten years after the launch of the *Holland 1* submarine, the officers of the "big-ship" navy still looked down on him and his fellow submariners. He wished that Jacky Fisher was still at the helm of the Admiralty. Fisher had done so much to shake up the complacency of a navy that had not been seriously challenged in battle for two hundred years. Papa was a big-ship officer, too, but had not stood in Richard's way to plough his own furrow. Papa had even hinted that Sir Arthur Wilson, the current First Sea Lord, might not last much longer in his present position.

Currently, Johnson, Richard and their passenger were the only ones on board who knew the nature of this coming patrol. The identity of the passenger had come as a great shock to Richard. Papa had never disclosed the nature of his work at the Admiralty, but somehow Richard had always suspected he was connected with the Intelligence Department. It was now clear to him that Papa must have had a hand in selecting *D2* as the submarine to carry out this operational test.

The new lookout emerged from the conning tower and Richard moved over to the port side of the bridge to give him room, and focused his binoculars on the martello tower to the south of Felixstowe. Despite the cold winter day, some children were, nevertheless, playing on the beach and he returned their cheery waves. He wondered what they thought of the black, sinister-looking objects regularly passing the point. Did they even know what they were?

He sniffed the air with pleasure. To some, the odour might not have seemed so pleasant, containing as it did a whiff of rotting vegetation mixed with the tang of the brine, but Richard loved it. It was a smell he savoured every time the upper hatch was opened on surfacing and the great rush of sea air washed out the rank, fetid air below. Looking out to starboard, he marvelled at the almost unbroken view of the open sea, interrupted only by the birds and a fishing smack. He would never tire of such a view. At sea he felt closer to God and he loved that feeling. The smack reminded him that the disciples of Jesus had once been fishermen and fellow mariners. That was not a trade he had ever wished to follow. Fishing was far too dangerous. His thoughts were interrupted by the new lookout.

'Joe Egg sent this up for you, sir.' Joe Egg was the nickname of the wardroom mess-man and he had kindly sent up a mug of tea with the lookout. Richard did not know how the seaman had acquired this nickname. His name was not Joe and nor was he egg-shaped. Sailors were a funny breed. It was thoughtful of him to send up the tea, anyhow. The seasonally low temperature along with the combined effect of the wind across the sea and the submarine's own speed all froze the tips of his ears. He was grateful for the warmth of his submarine blazer. It wasn't as warm as his old duffel coat, but more practical in the confined spaces of the boat.

'Lookout relieved. Permission to go below, sir?'

'Yes, please,' Richard replied. He checked his watch to see how much longer he would have to wait before it was time to go to Diving Stations for the first dive to check the trim. After checking the lookout had been properly briefed, he called down to the control room to ask when he should alter to the new course for the Heligo Bight.

****

Down below, Peter Miller lay in a hammock in the fore-ends of the submarine, the forward torpedo compartment, contemplating his brother,

Dick's, world. Slinging a hammock had not been such a surprise to him, but he had expected to be accommodated with the other officers in the wardroom and not with the torpedo crew. He had been astonished to have his leave interrupted by 'C''s urgent summons to London. Apparently, the Royal Marines officer who had originally been briefed to undertake this mission had broken his arm in a hunting accident. According to 'C', he had no other German-speaking agents available and, after all the difficulties in persuading the Admiralty to provide a submarine, he could not waste the opportunity. Peter chuckled to himself at the memory of being welcomed over the brow by Dick. He was not sure who had been the most stunned. Peter had just had time to brief Dick that he was to be known as Lieutenant Whittaker of the Royal Marines Light Infantry, the victim of the unfortunate hunting accident, before he was taken to see the submarine's captain. Peter realised that the next time he and Dick met he would have some explaining to do. At least he might avoid Dick's jibes in future about his soft life as a diplomat, but Papa was unlikely to be pleased that Dick was now in on the secret.

Peter had been gratified to discover that Johnson was quite a civilised officer. Other naval officers seemed to look down on submariners and mocked their willingness, literally, to get their hands dirty and involve themselves with the minute technical detail of machinery and engines. He had heard submarine officers likened to unwashed chauffeurs by their contemporaries on the surface.

During his time with the German Army in Flanders and northern France he had become accustomed to discomfort and even dirty conditions. Alas, he had even been steeled for danger. However, this mission was something else and although he had agreed to it, he was, nonetheless, starting to have some regrets. At six feet in height he was finding the conditions extremely cramped. Dick was an inch taller, so how did he cope continually with the low deckheads? Furthermore, the air was already starting to reek with the smell of diesel and bodies. He knew it would get much worse once the submarine dived. There were no washing facilities on board and the air would not be replenished until surfacing. Not only would that offend the olfactory gland, particularly since a typical submariner's diet seemed to produce unsavoury stomach gases, but the longer the submarine was dived, the less oxygen there would be for all, the concentrations of carbon dioxide would rise and, as if that were not bad enough, high-pressure air from leaking systems would raise the pressure in the boat.

The landing ashore posed its own dangers, but first he had to get there. His new messmates had already regaled him with tales of the hazards of submarine life. These included being run down by merchantmen on the surface, running aground when dived, a fire underwater and mechanical failure leading to the submarine plunging to the bottom of the sea or being unable to return to the surface. These were not hazards to which Dick had ever alluded at home. Indeed, he had always taken pains to allay Mutti's fears on the subject. The first trial, it seemed, would soon be taking place.

'Made your will then, sir?' asked his host in the fore-ends, the TI, apparently the senior torpedo specialist and a Glaswegian.

'I'm sure there is no need, PO. You chaps all strike me as quite competent.' Peter swung himself out of his hammock and leaned against the side of a torpedo.

'Aye, well let's hope our papist Second Captain's done his arithmetic properly, then. If not, we might be on the bottom very soon.'

'I'm sorry, PO. I don't quite follow.'

'The trim dive, sir. The first dive after any period in harbour's always a chancy business. And it dinnae help that Old Misery Guts is a single man.'

Peter hid his feeling of affront at the lack of respect being shown his brother.

'I'm sorry, TI, but you'll have to explain this to a simple lobster.'

'Yeah, sorry about that, sir. Ye forget after a wee while that what ye reckons as second nature can be a bit odd to others. It's like this, sir. In harbour we takes on fresh water, stores, fuel and torpedoes, all of which will have changed the weight of the old boat since her last dive. It's the First Lieutenant's job to make a note of all the changes and calculate the new weight of the submarine correctly. He then has to make the appropriate compensations to the amount of water in the trim tanks. If he gets it wrong, then we could be too heavy an' hit the bottom first dive. We in the crew always hope for what we call a married man's trim. One that keeps the submarine light. It dinnae matter if we takes our time in goin' doon slowly.'

Peter wondered what drove Dick and these men to volunteer for such privations and risk. It didn't seem worth the extra few shillings in the pay. Before he could quiz the TI further, his education was interrupted by the call to Diving Stations.

****

Miller approached the residence of the new First Lord of the Admiralty with some curiosity. The invitation to call that evening intrigued him as he had had no further contact with Churchill since the meeting in the Reform Club in June. As the cab drew up outside 32 Eccleston Square, Miller recalled that the Second Sea Lord, Prince Louis of Battenburg, had once lived nearby at number 37. The houses had been designed by the master builder Thomas Cubitt and offered grand porticos and balconies to the front and spacious accommodation inside. Miller chided himself for taking a little secret satisfaction that the First Lord's house was not on a par with his own John Nash-designed, neo-classical property in Cumberland Terrace off Regent's Park. However, it was still a substantial house and no doubt its Pimlico location was convenient for Westminster Palace. He tipped the cab driver and ascended the steps of the front door.

It was a cold winter's evening and, although not yet late, the temperature was falling quickly. Miller was relieved that the door was opened promptly and he was able to exchange the biting cold for the warmth and shelter of the hall. The butler and footman were clearly expecting him and, after relieving him of his cloak, cane and hat, showed him into Churchill's study without delay or even asking his name.

He was surprised to see that Churchill was not alone as he entered the room. Churchill rose from his armchair and came across immediately to greet him.

'My dear fellow. I'm so glad you were able to come. I know how busy you must be. Can I offer you a drink? I believe you already know each other.' Churchill indicated to his other guest.

Miller's fellow guest was a short, stocky man with a round face. His complexion appeared oriental due to a bout of malaria earlier in life. As his gaze fixed on Miller, his expression betrayed a flicker of recognition, but no other obvious emotion before he spoke.

'Miller, it is good to meet with you again. I trust you are keeping well, although I am disappointed, but not surprised, to note you have still to achieve promotion.'

Admiral of the Fleet John Arbuthnot Fisher, First Baron of Kilverstone, had a reputation for directness. Known as Jacky within the Navy, Lord Fisher had been the First Sea Lord until his retirement on his seventieth birthday in January that year.

'Sir, the pleasure of renewing our acquaintance is all mine, I assure you.'

Miller shook hands warmly with his former Head of Service. Turning back to Churchill he said, 'A large malt whisky with a splash of warm water would be most welcome. It's dashed cold out there this evening.'

The footman supplied a third chair for Miller and retired, leaving the three men alone to their drinks and conversation in privacy.

'How is Lady Fisher, sir?' Miller opened the conversation.

'Oh, she's fine.' Fisher replied. 'She just keeps pestering me to use my influence to advance the careers of our three sons-in-law. I keep telling her it will not do. It is ability and professionalism that must count in the navy of today and not patronage. I've just been allaying the First Lord's fears about an imminent war with Germany. That Agadir business has certainly focused the Government's attention, but I doubt war will come before October 1914. That gives us three vital years to prepare.'

'Really, sir? Why so precise a date?' Miller asked, genuinely intrigued.

'Tirpitz will wait until the new Kiel Canal is open by my reckoning. Time to implement our concept of the Fast Division, don't you think?'

Churchill interjected, 'My dear Lord Fisher, you didn't really explain the concept. Would you be so kind as to do so now?'

'I'm sure this young man can do the honours. It might help you reach your decision. I must go. I promised to look in on Lady Fairfax's ball and must change first. I enjoy a good hop at my age. Thank you for the drink, Minister. I hope what I have said will be of use.'

With that the great man was gone. It was like a squall that had subsided as quickly as it arrived. Churchill seemed taken aback by the sudden departure of his guest, but Miller was familiar with the former First Sea Lord's rushes of energy and activity. Miller was also aware of how much Fisher loved to dance.

After a short pause to gather his thoughts, Churchill remarked, 'He really is a most extraordinary fellow. This is only the second time I have met him, but he has quite overwhelmed me with his energy and passion for the navy. In the short while I have been in my new post I have already received reams of correspondence from him.'

'I and several of my colleagues have a very high regard for him, sir. He was never reluctant to commit his views to paper and views he has many. Both as the Second and First Sea Lord his energy and vision have carried through several reforms that have rendered great service to the Royal Navy and will bode well for the future.'

'You admire him then?' Churchill asked.

'Naturally, sir. I accept that he has a style that has regrettably caused some friction within the Service. It is well known that he and Lord Beresford have often differed on several policy matters. However, Lord Fisher was right to carry forward his reforms on both the training of our officers and the shape of the navy. Our next foe will be very different from the one we fought in the Crimea.'

'Indeed. What would you say if I asked him to come back as First Sea Lord?'

Miller was surprised both at the idea and the directness of the question. He responded guardedly. 'Firstly, I would say that you already have an able Sea Lord in Admiral Wilson. I understand he has no plans to retire before next year. I would also remind you that Lord Fisher is already almost seventy-one years old, but to his suitability to return to his old post, it is not for me to venture an opinion. As the noble Lord reminded me a few minutes ago, I have yet to achieve promotion to flag rank and it would be inappropriate for me to comment even privately on any of my senior officers. Having served in uniform yourself, sir, you must recognise the nature of my position.'

Churchill considered the reply and clearly wanted to pursue the subject, but thought better of it. 'I understand and respect your position. I also accept it was an unfair question. Allow me to top up your glass.

'Thank you, sir. It is a very fine malt. Its softness reminds me of the highland distilleries, but I cannot place it.'

'I'm glad you like it. I collected a case from one of the local distilleries on my recent inspection of Scapa Flow.'

An uncomfortable silence then followed. Miller was aware that Churchill had invited him for a purpose and was clearly searching for an angle to broach a subject. He left it to Churchill to start up the conversation again.

'I trust you were satisfied with the arrangements at Chattenden after our last meeting. I understand some of the bandits escaped to Germany.'

'That is so, sir, but it was a necessary part of the plan to give it some credibility. All in all, the Secret Service Bureau is very happy with the outcome. We now know the extent of the German network and how they are reporting back to Berlin. When the time comes, it should be simple enough to round them up. In the meantime, we also have control over a couple of agents and with this, the means to select what information they pass to their spymasters. Thank you for your part in the operation, sir.'

'I was only too pleased to help. Tell me though. Why was it necessary to fake the death of your son? There were enough genuine fatalities for the purposes of authenticity and would it not have been useful to allow him to escape with the others to continue his heroic deeds?'

'That is a fair question, sir. To be honest, it was a course Kell and I considered. However, you must understand the strain my son Peter was under, first living an alias as a serving German officer amongst the army in Germany, and then as their agent in the Low Countries and France before they sent him to Britain. The pressure was beginning to tell and we could not risk allowing him to return to Germany. Nearly two years of such a life was more than enough. Besides, we have another assignment for him next year. He is now resting and preparing for it.'

'I admit to being intrigued, but know better than to press you for details. Please send your son my best wishes and I hope he enjoys every success. He is a very brave young man, not unlike his father has proved to be on several occasions.'

'You are too kind, sir. I will pass on your good wishes and am sure he will feel honoured.'

'Before we go on, perhaps you would explain to me the concept of the Fast Division that Lord Fisher mentioned.'

'Sir, I regret that this is a subject that would have been better addressed by Lord Fisher. I am no battleship flotilla commander, but will do my best to explain nevertheless. You will be aware that, traditionally, formations of opposing ships would engage each other on parallel courses. The effect was that although part of a formation, the battle was effectively a series of single ship engagements with the heavier ships of the line in the van and matched against the enemy's most powerful ships. Nelson defied this convention by crossing the line, both to rake the enemy's vulnerable stern and to split their formation into three groups, two of which could then be engaged on both sides by the whole of his force of ships. Once he had sunk, crippled or taken a proportion of the enemy ships, it released our ships to engage the remaining section of the enemy line with superior numbers. Are you sure you wish me to go on, sir? It is an arcane topic.'

'Absolutely. I am all ears.'

'The advent of steam, armour and the gun turret has rendered these tactics obsolete and so the convention is once more that battle is conducted by formations in line ahead on parallel courses. Then Admiral Togo, in the recent conflict between Russia and Japan, demonstrated that if one formation can outpace the other, it is possible to overtake the enemy, cross ahead of the leading ships and pass down the other side to achieve the same effect as Nelson's crossing the line. We call this tactic "Crossing the T". The challenge is that to achieve this manoeuvre, we need a five-knot speed advantage over the enemy. This is already achievable by our battle cruisers as, being lightly armoured, they are lighter and faster, but it puts their 7-inch armour up against the more heavily armed battleship with 12-inch armour. It is not an even contest.'

'That I can imagine. I have seen for myself the effect of the Maxim gun on infantry.'

'Quite. The solution offered by the Royal Corps of Naval Constructors is to build a new type of faster battleship, powered by liquid fuel rather than coal. These ships would form a Fast Division. Aside from the advantages of liquid fuel's power-to-weight ratio over coal, it offers a longer radius of action, is easier to refuel, needs fewer stokers and can even be refuelled at sea to provide yet greater endurance to the fleet. The First Sea Lord is very keen that all our new ships be adapted to burn oil in place of coal. Does that explain the concept reasonably clearly, sir?'

Churchill was silent for a few minutes of contemplation before replying.

'Yes, but although I can certainly see the advantages of the concept, I think I detect a flaw in the reasoning. Firstly, this country is blessed with bounteous supplies of high-quality coal. As far as I am aware, we have no such supplies of oil in this country. Such a policy would make us dependent on the supplies of foreigners. I do not relish the prospect of losing our independence. Where are we to find a reliable and regular supply of oil? Moreover, how is this oil to be brought to our shores? Does this not create greater vulnerability on the high seas and, thus, a requirement for more escorts? Finally, where are we to store sufficiently large quantities of this precious oil to ensure we have plenty in reserve in both peace and war? Would not these stores of oil themselves be vulnerable to attack or sabotage? We have seen already in Chattenden something of the dastardly low means to which our potential foe is prepared to resort, to deal us a mortal blow. Answer me that, oh noble Captain.'

'Sir, you have hit many nails on several heads and I admire your perspicacity. These are indeed points that need to be addressed and I suggest you take them up with the First Sea Lord. They are not matters within the purview of my own department. However, with respect to a reliable source of oil, I am aware of an opportunity to secure a supply in Persia. I hope I am not speaking out of turn, sir, but you will soon be presented a proposal to persuade His Majesty's Government to form and finance a company to drill for the oil in a manner similar to the financing of the Suez Canal. Others are better placed to brief you on their thoughts, but my department is currently working on plans to ensure that should the negotiations take place to secure a contract favourable to HMG, then there will be no interference from the Germans.'

'By Jove, Miller. You interest me greatly. Indeed, you astound me with your vision and forward thinking. Fisher said I would be. I will lay my cards on the table as to why I invited you here this evening. But first, let me offer you a refill.'

CHAPTER 19

'Bearing that.'

'Red six-zero.'

'Angle on the bow, red one-twenty. Range that,' called the captain.

'2,500 yards,' replied the periscope assistant.

'Down. Small coaster. Starboard ten. Steer one-eight-zero. We'll leave her to open up the distance off track before surfacing.'

Peter was literally in the dark as to what was going on. He did not understand the staccato exchange between the captain and his periscope assistant and, as the control room of the submarine was in complete darkness to preserve the captain's night vision, he couldn't see anything either. Three hours ago, HMS *D2* had dived after the surface crossing of the North Sea and was now approaching the north coast of Heligoland. He was already missing the comparatively fresh air of life on the surface. Used to a more active lifestyle, he also looked forward to stretching his long legs ashore on the island. The captain had been generous enough to give him unrestricted access to the bridge over the past few days, so he had at least breathed fresh air and seen daylight. Even so, the interior length of *D2* was barely the length of two cricket pitches, so his leg muscles longed to be stretched.

'Lieutenant Whittaker, are you ready?' enquired the captain.

'I am, sir.'

'Good. I plan on running in for another thirty minutes before surfacing and landing you. The sea is calm with a slight onshore wind to assist your paddle. There is a half-moon, but it is quite cloudy, so you might encounter the odd shower on the way to meet your contact. The First Lieutenant will go over the arrangements for picking you up again. I'll see you on the bridge before you go, so I suggest you go and get yourself ready. Up. All-round look.'

Peter found himself dismissed and so he fumbled his way back to the fore-ends. The plan was for *D2* to approach the beach as close as possible without running aground, but Peter would have to paddle ashore in one of the latest rubber inflatable coracles. Unfortunately, these rubber boats tended to crack at the seams, so Peter was apprehensive that he might have to swim ashore. Once beached, he would be dressed as a typical Frisian mariner, but he resolved that for the paddle ashore he would dispense with the heavy sea boots and reefer jacket. He carefully removed the silk map from the lining of his jacket and placed it in his trousers' pocket for now.

A short while later he was joined by Dick, who checked nobody was in earshot.

'When this is all over, Peter, you're going to have to tell me what on earth you are doing. I thought you were a pampered diplomat and between postings. Now I find my little brother is a secret agent.'

'Well, it was meant to be a secret, Dick. For God's sake try to keep it that way. Christ knows what Papa will say when he finds out my cover has been blown. There's been a cock-up along the way.'

'Steady on, younger brother. You know I don't like to hear the Lord's name taken in vain. Anyway, I shall have to be patient for now. Are you all set?'

'As ready as I'll ever be, I suppose. Don't take it the wrong way, Dick. You chaps have been awfully hospitable and all that, but I can't wait to get out of your precious boat. I don't know how you all stand being cooped up like this for days on end. At least your pigeons get to fly home.'

He gestured to the cages of homing pigeons the submarine was carrying.

'Tell me, Dick, why you carry them. I understood your boat to be fitted with the latest wireless equipment.'

'Peter, the feeling's mutual, I assure you. I've had enough complaints from the ship's company about you eating too much food and breathing too much of our precious oxygen, you great hulk. This is the first class of boat to have wireless equipment, but the transmission range is usually no better than twenty miles. Moreover, Johnson would rather sacrifice his wisdom teeth than transmit. He's worried that the Germans will have direction-finding gear to fix the origin of our transmissions.'

'There's something in that I suppose. The Germans seem to be investing quite a lot in DF gear.'

'It seems you would know. Now, let's get down to business. We'll meet back here, on the same beach, in seventy-two hours. Are you happy with the signals?'

'I'm fine with it all. If for any reason I or you cannot make the rendezvous, then we will follow the same routine off the east coast twenty-four hours later, but you can only wait for me two nights. In that case, I bury or destroy the package and walk off the island like a tourist. It's all clear.'

'Do your best to stick to the original plan, Peter. This beach is risky enough, but the water off the east coast is too shallow for us to approach at periscope depth. So stick to your brief and no tourism, right? Good luck, old man. Tell you what. Once this is all over, I'll come up to London and stand you lunch in the Savoy Grill. If you promise to tell me how you came to be mixed up in this cagey business, that is.'

He patted his brother on the shoulder and led him up to the fore-ends to gather his gear. The plan was that, once ashore, Peter would meet his contact and survey the island to assess the feasibility of Britain taking it over and fortifying the harbour in the event of war with Germany. Britain had handed over the islands to Germany only twenty-one years earlier, in the Heligoland-Zanzibar Treaty. Situated only forty miles and three hours' sailing time from the base of the German High Seas Fleet, the two islands of Heligoland could be of strategic importance to Britain as a forward operating base for aircraft as well as ships. However, there were reports that the Germans had started investing in a programme of fortifications and it was important to obtain evidence of how far these preparations had advanced.

Within a few minutes of Richard's return to the control room, word was passed for the submarine to go to Diving Stations in preparation for surfacing. On surfacing, the captain took control of the submarine and slowly piloted *D2* towards the shore. Although the half-moon was frequently obscured by cloud, he could clearly see the stack of Lange Anna to starboard and the white horses of the waves breaking on the beach. There were no other vessels in sight. Johnson closed the beach still more before ordering the speed to dead-slow. *D2* would normally run on the surface on her diesel engines, but for this operation Johnson was continuing on the electric motors. He ordered a leadsman to take soundings from the bows of the casing as he intended to get as close inshore as was safe, in order to cut the distance his passenger would have to row to the beach.

Whilst the casing party prepared the inflatable boat for launch under the supervision of Richard, Johnson bade farewell to Peter on the bridge.

'Good luck, Whittaker. I don't envy you the task you have before you. I hope your German is up to scratch and you meet up with your contact without a hitch. Once I've landed you, I'll lay offshore further out for a bit in case you have any problems. There's still two hours of darkness left, so I'm not in a hurry.'

Peter descended to the casing, removed his clumsy sea boots and, after shaking his brother's hand, clambered gingerly into the inflatable coracle bobbing gently just behind the starboard hydroplane. He paddled away from the hull of *D2* a few yards before turning to wave a last farewell to his shipmates of the last few days.

Thanks to the onshore wind and the captain's consideration in risking a grounding to approach the coast as closely as possible, it was an easy paddle to the shore. Mercifully, although the boat had leaked a little, it had retained almost full buoyancy so he avoided a drenching in the cool North Sea. Having landed safely on the beach and removed his boots, jacket and ditty bag from the boat, he carefully stowed the paddle inside and, using his flashlight, signalled back to *D2* to draw in the tether. He noted that the captain had already manoeuvred the submarine further offshore, but even then she seemed highly visible from the shore. As he started his ascent of the beach, he hoped that there was nobody other than his contact patrolling the cliff tops to his right.

***

Churchill poured Miller a generous measure of Highland Park whisky. 'I wish to make you an offer.' He looked at Miller expectantly, but Miller remained silent and impassive so he continued.

'I had heard a hint, of course, about the proposal to purchase shares in a Persian oil field and somebody suggested I approach you about it.'

'Sir, the proposal is not yet fully drafted and I would not presume to pre-empt it.'

'I quite understand. But I was also keen to learn more about you, Miller. Several years ago we campaigned together. There can be no better reason to trust a man. Following the renewal of our acquaintance in the summer, I have made certain enquiries about you. I was surprised to learn that you are well known even to the Prime Minister. The Foreign Secretary has explained that your department has even had some influence over foreign policy and that both he and my predecessor have trusted you with a great deal of freedom and autonomy. Sir Edward Grey speaks highly of your political instincts and strategic thinking. However, I like to make up my own mind on such matters.'

'I am flattered to hear Sir Edward's good opinion, sir, but I have only ever concerned myself with my duty.'

'The affair at Chattenden has convinced me of the inevitability of war with Germany. As you heard Lord Fisher say, he predicts it will come in the autumn of 1914, once the Kiel Canal is complete. This war will present greater challenges than any we have ever known. Like you, I have seen for myself in South Africa the ease with which men can now slaughter each other in large numbers. It will, therefore, be a long and hard struggle to vanquish our opponent, but one that we must win at all costs. It goes without saying that my new office is vital to these islands' future. I believe I am the very man for the task, but it is clear that the Admiralty resent me and will not willingly embrace some of the changes in policy I feel it necessary to implement.'

'Sir, the loyalty of the Service is your due and I find it difficult to credit that your suspicions of inflexibility are correct. However, I am bound to say, in candour, that your policies and actions whilst President of the Board of Trade were none too favourable to the Admiralty. Amongst the senior officers it is well known that you supported Mister Lloyd George in cutting the Naval Estimates. You can, therefore, readily understand why some officials may be anxious about your plans for the future with the prospect of war looming, but I cannot believe that your policies would be blocked. Indeed, I happen to know that many of my colleagues would welcome some shaking of the Admiralty tree.'

'That is precisely why I asked to see you,' replied Churchill. 'You know who is for modernisation and who might resist it. Now hear me out.' Modesty had impelled Miller to protest. 'You play the innocent in claiming to know little about certain affairs and yet it is already clear from our conversation this evening that you are intimately acquainted with the affairs of the innermost recesses of the Admiralty.

'With your help I could navigate the potential obstacles. I accept your point that in the past my actions have not been conducive to gaining the support of the navy. You must understand that military and naval men alike will press continuously for more weapons, men and equipment ...'

Miller felt impelled to make a comment, but there was no stopping the First Lord in full flow.

'... but it is the job of the peacetime Government to balance these pressures against the needs of the country elsewhere and its means to support its programmes. It is now clear that our national interests are threatened by violence. In these circumstances, the first duty of the Government becomes the protection of its people from such calumny. I am utterly determined to build up our navy to meet the coming crisis and will make the case fervently to my colleagues to gain their support. However, I am a new First Lord and it is true that I do not yet know how the navy operates. There will be some who would seek to take advantage of a new minister's ignorance and inexperience. They would delay necessary and urgent reforms through obfuscation and detours.'

Miller wondered how much of what the First Lord was saying had been prepared. He felt as if he was listening to a speech, but out of deference he avoided interrupting the minister in full flow. In any case, it was a very fine malt whisky and he was savouring it.

'Forgive my bluntness, Miller, but as the First Sea Lord remarked, a man of your record should have achieved further promotion by now and time is running out before you are due for retirement. I have it on good authority that some of the noble Sea Lords are passing you over out of jealousy. They resent you already for your freedom and influence and are loath to offer you yet more power. I, however, hate to see such talent wasted and have a proposition for you.'

'Sir, you do me a great honour in taking such an interest in me. Nevertheless, I am not an ambitious man and am fortunate that I do not rely on my naval career for an income. Like any man though, I am always interested in a proposal, but that does not mean I will accept it. How can I help?'

'I believe I am uniquely qualified to take the helm of the mighty Admiralty as it sets out on its course to achieve complete supremacy over the might of the Imperial German Navy.' Churchill slapped the arm of his chair so hard that Miller nearly spilled his drink with surprise. 'But, from my position, I am not able to watch out for rocky shoals ahead in sufficient time to alter course to avoid them. To know when to reduce speed to pass over shallow water and, above all, where there is open, deep water to allow us to proceed at full speed. Miller, my dear friend, could you be my pilot? Will you help me set the correct course and guide me through the dangerous waters safely? Will you join me on a glorious voyage to victory?'

Miller was a little taken aback by the poetic words of the First Lord of the Admiralty and took his time to finish his drink as he contemplated them. 'What is it you envisage I can do for you that I am not already doing? I can assure you that my loyalty to your position means I will give you every support I can. '

'I want you to become my Naval Secretary in the rank of Rear Admiral!'

There was a moment's silence as Churchill reflected favourably on his own words and Miller considered them with some astonishment.

'Thank you for your candour, sir. Nonetheless, I must decline your kind offer of a new appointment.'

'But why?' Churchill asked a little vexedly.

'To be honest, sir, I enjoy my current appointment. As you have just acknowledged, it offers much freedom and independence. More importantly, the Secret Service and the Admiralty is far from ready to supply the intelligence the exigencies of war will demand, and I consider it my duty to complete the work I have started before I retire.' Miller was amused to see his minister looking so crestfallen, like a child deprived of a present. 'Perhaps I could suggest an alternative name?'

'By all means.'

'May I suggest Rear Admiral David Beatty? You may recall meeting him at Omdurman.'

'I most certainly do,' replied Churchill animatedly. 'A most promising officer. His father was in my old regiment, the 4th Hussars. Daring, charming and generous with the champagne, too, if I recall correctly. However, am I not right in thinking that he is our youngest admiral and more deserving of a sea command? He is certainly a fine fellow.'

'Indeed, sir, but he has fallen out of favour with the noble Sea Lords. He has very unwisely declined the appointment as the second-in-command of the First Division of the Home Fleet on the grounds that he deserves a more senior appointment. He is, accordingly, unemployed at present and, were this situation to continue, as I fear is planned, after three years he will be forcibly retired. Should you be minded to employ him as your Naval Secretary, I think I could persuade him to accept the offer. I know him well.'

'That is good of you, Miller, but I am not sure why you think him suited to serve on my staff, other than it will keep him in the Service.'

'Sir, Beatty is a well-rounded and modern-thinking officer. Like me, he has experience of fighting on land with the army and this affords him a degree of objectivity on strategic matters. He also has recent experience of command of a Dreadnought and how to fight with a battle squadron. He is unconventional and adaptable to new ideas. He has already proved that he is not afraid to cock a snook at his seniors. You would not find him afraid to challenge antediluvian policies presented for your approval.'

'I will certainly look into your idea further, but I cannot help feeling that unless you change your mind, admirable as Beatty might prove to be, I may lose a sovereign to find a crown.'

'I am sorry, sir, but my mind is made up.'

'Perhaps, but I would like to continue this discussion some other time. Now I must look in at the House before the current debate winds up, so I will not detain you further. But I would like you to call on me again. Would that be convenient?'

'I am at your service, sir.'

'Good. I shall look forward to our next meeting.'

The two men rose to leave and Churchill escorted Miller to the hall. After wrapping his cloak tightly around him and donning his hat, Miller stepped out into the cold night in search of a hackney cab to take him home. He wondered if he had just made a powerful enemy. Churchill was a cunning fox and he would have to tread carefully.

CHAPTER 20

Peter was feeling increasingly depressed by this short-notice intelligence operation. He felt certain his mission would be considered a disaster. Right from the start, events had gone badly wrong. He had failed to meet his contact on landing from *D2* two nights earlier; indeed he had mistaken his contact for a German soldier out with his girlfriend. Fortunately, they were the more surprised in the encounter and had not made any enquiries of his presence on the shore at the late hour. He had then discovered the absence of his silk map. It must have fallen out of his pocket during his paddle ashore. Without it he only had a vague notion of where his contact lived. However, his luck had then changed when his guides had, by chance, found him walking towards the nearby village.

For the next two days he had pored over their maps of the island and that of its neighbour, Dune. The guides had taken him all around the island, but due to the recent sea state, he had not been able to get across to Dune. From all he had seen, this little island probably offered the best possibilities for an airstrip, but the main island offered a perfect harbour for a wartime navy. The island's geology was perfect for the building of fortifications to protect the harbour and deter an enemy landing on the beaches. It was whilst surveying the harbour earlier in the day that his luck had taken another turn for the worse.

Yet again, he carefully withdrew a portion of one of the curtains covering the window of the parlour of his hosts. He peered into the darkness outside. There was still no sign of the two visitors he was expecting, but the increasing howl of the wind indicated that the sea state would be rising yet further. Would he manage to get off the island the following night, he wondered?

'Here. Take a measure of this to calm your nerves, young man. Gazing out the window won't bring them any earlier.'

Peter let go of the curtain and turned to face his host, an elderly Heligolander who remained loyal to Britain. The man was offering him a glass of whisky.

'You're right, of course, Niels. Thanks.'

Peter took the proffered glass and sat down, stretching his long legs out before the fire. The light of the fire supplemented that from the lantern swinging from the ceiling above the dining table, one of the few objects in the sparsely furnished room. From the kitchen he could hear Mrs Niels washing the pots after their supper. He took a sip of his spirit and cast his mind back to the events of the morning.

****

Peter and one of his guides were standing on the quayside, looking out over the harbour when he had heard two voices speaking loudly and in English. There was nothing uncommon in that, but the content of their conversation attracted his attention.

'Make sure you get a decent shot of those submarine berths, Manners.'

'Of course I will, Martin. It wasn't me that photographed the gun emplacements with the lens cap on was it?'

Looking beneath him, Peter noticed two men standing in the bows of a small, open fishing boat, one of whom was quite overtly taking photographs of the construction works for the new harbour.

'Hurry up with that, Manners. If we're to visit that seaplane base on Dune and be back tonight, we don't have much time to spare. I don't like the look of the coming weather.'

Peter was shocked by their stupidity. 'Who the hell are you?' he called softly.

The shorter of the two men in the boat spun round to see who had addressed him.

'I don't think that any business of yours, old man,' he replied curtly. 'I might ask the same question of you.'

'For Christ's sake. Have you no discretion? It's perfectly obvious what you're up to. Carry on like this and you're likely to end up arrested for espionage. There's a German policeman standing only thirty yards up the quay, you fool.'

'I say. You're not being exactly civil. Who am I addressing?'

'I'm Lieutenant Whittaker of the Royal Marines. Who are you?'

'Not Hubert Whittaker, of the Light Infantry, by any chance?' Martin asked quizzically.

'The very same,' Peter lied.

'Well that's rot. I may be a Lieutenant in the Royal Marines Artillery, but I happen to know Whittaker. Are you some form of German spy?'

Peter recognised his error too late, but now had no choice but to make a clean breast of things. A couple of German soldiers seemed to be taking an interest in him.

'Precisely the opposite. I cannot tell you my name, but I'm here on a survey operation on behalf of the Admiralty.'

'Why, this is a turn up for the books, old man. We're working for the same outfit then. I'm Eustace Martin. Manners, here, and I are on a spot of shooting leave, as it were. We thought we'd organise our own private tour of these islands and report our findings to the Admiralty. It's good sport, what?'

'Keep your bloody voice down then. It would do no good to advertise your intentions to the whole of the island. They still speak some English here, you know.' Peter was perturbed to see a couple of soldiers walking towards them. He thought quickly.

'Where are you staying?'

'In some gasthof on Elbestrasse. I forget the name. I say, perhaps we should work together.'

'Shut up, you fool. I'm thinking.' *Not bloody likely*, he thought. Turning to his guide, he asked in German, 'Do you know this place?' The guide nodded. 'Could you bring these men to meet me at the Niels's home after dark?' Again the guide nodded.

'Right, Martin. This man will meet you outside your gasthof at 20.00 sharp. He'll bring you to see me. For God's sake don't be late or attract further attention to yourselves.'

For the first time, Manners joined the conversation.

'Look, I'm not sure I like your tone. We're here on the King's business. Who the hell are you to be giving orders?'

'Don't be so deuced stupid, you idiot. I'm here for the same purpose, but unlike you, I'm here officially and your presence and activities might well have jeopardised my mission already. We'll talk about it later. For now, get back to your rooms and keep out of the way.'

Peter turned on his heels and walked smartly away before his interlocutors could remonstrate. He could not help but notice that the two soldiers were now in animated conversation with the policeman, and pointing to him and the fishing boat as he passed.

****

Peter almost jumped out of his skin at the sound of the heavy knocking on the back door. He checked his pocket watch and noted it was not far short of quarter to ten. Could this be the police or German Army? Then again, why come to the back? He did not have to wait long before he heard English voices, at the sound of which his heart recommenced its steady beat. Niels showed the Englishmen into the parlour and discreetly withdrew to the kitchen with his wife and the guide.

'Thank heavens you're here, but why so late?' Peter asked.

'Steady on, old man, you might at least wait until we've been fixed with a drink first, before the interrogation,' Martin replied.

Almost immediately, Niels entered the room with a tray on which stood a bottle of schnapps and three glasses. 'I am sorry, gentlemen, but I have very little whisky. I hope this will suffice.'

'Thanks awfully, old man,' Martin replied affably. 'We're developing quite a taste for this local moonshine. It takes one back to one's days in Queenstown.' Martin took on the duties of host and after filling the three tumblers, sat down in front of the fire. Niels repeated his discreet exit.

'What the bloody hell are you two playing at?' Peter demanded angrily.

'Hold hard. You're forgetting your etiquette, old man. Allow me to present my good companion, Lieutenant Algernon Manners Royal Navy. Manners, moreover, is an hydrographer and, unlike me, speaks German. Manners, this is, er ... Lieutenant Whittaker, a fellow Royal Marine, but of the Light Infantry.'

Peter shook Manners's hand and eyed him coldly.

'Fine. The civilities are over. Now tell me what's going on and why you arrived so late?'

'All in good time, old boy. As I told you this morning, we're on a spot of leave and thought we might embark on a ripping adventure by taking a tour of this island and, perhaps, Mellum, Nordern and Borkum, too. I mentioned it to the Marine officer in the NID and he seemed to think it a good idea, provided we didn't claim any expense on the Admiralty. As I don't speak German, I persuaded Manners to accompany me and, bless me, what a stroke of fortune that was. Naturally, Manners here is a great cartographer. We've been here a full week and just about finished a full survey of the islands. When we saw you this morning, we were just off for another jaunt to Dune. As it happens, we are grateful for your incivility, since otherwise we would have faced a very choppy outward journey and might yet be stranded across there. So there you have it. Now you know our story, pray tell us yours whilst I pour us all another glass of the moonshine. Come on, raise your elbow. You haven't touched your glass.'

Reluctantly, Peter briefly explained how he had arrived on the island and his purpose. He omitted details of his rendezvous with *D2* the following night. Both Martin and Manners seemed awestruck by his landing from a submarine.

'Golly, Whittaker. You're a brave one,' Manners uttered. 'You wouldn't catch me in one of those tin cans for all the tea in China. To think we merely caught the ferry.'

'You still haven't explained why you arrived late this evening.'

'Ah yes. Good point. We had a spot of bother after you left. Manners and I were returning to the gasthof as you so peremptorily instructed us, when we noticed we were being followed by a couple of German soldiers. We didn't worry about it, but as we were tucking into the local bratwurst and pickles over luncheon, we were rudely interrupted by a policeman demanding to see our passports and to know the nature of our visit to the island. You can be sure we made our feelings known to him and he withdrew, but we could tell he was suspicious of us. After what you said, we thought it best not to queer your pitch, so we spent the afternoon collating all our information and drawings, before hiding them in the lavatory cistern.'

'Oh my God,' Peter interrupted. 'You haven't left them there, have you?'

'Of course not, old man. What do you take us for? A couple of blithering idiots?'

Peter thought it prudent to make no comment.

'I admit we had planned to leave them behind. After all, who would think of searching the heads? It was just that as we were leaving to meet your man earlier, we noticed a couple of strange fellows opposite taking an interest in us. We beat a hasty retreat to our rooms and regrouped. Manners here then had the splendid notion of leaving the gasthof by the fire escape at the back. He tipped the porter to inform your guide of where we were, the guide met us and, hey presto, here we are.'

'Are you sure you weren't followed?'

'Absolutely, old chap. Your fellow saw to that. In any case it's too bloody dark and windy to see beyond fifty yards or so. It meant that we came the long way round, though, and hence our tardiness.'

'Did you destroy the maps and drawings before leaving?'

'Come on, old chap. What do you think? Credit us with some sense.'

'Thank God for that.' Peter exhaled loudly in relief. 'Then you're free to leave the island and the Germans can't pin anything on you. I just hope they can't find the link between us. I'll have to lie low all tomorrow which means I won't be able to finish my survey, but never mind.'

'Well you don't need to worry about finishing the survey. We've done it for you. Here.' Martin fished a large package from within his coat. 'We couldn't risk the Germans finding this on us, so we brought it here.'

Peter eyed the package as if it was an unexploded bomb in danger of going off at any minute. 'You brought the incriminating evidence here? Are you both mad? What if you had been arrested on your way here? What if the Germans are waiting outside this very minute?'

Peter doused the lantern and rushed to the window. He peeked behind the curtain and scanned the field of view available to him. He could see nothing. It was too dark. His hand trembling, he took a glass of the fiery schnapps and downed it in one. The harshness of the liquid burning his throat calmed him, so he took another tumblerful. He was trapped. There was nothing he could do. If the two bumbling idiots before him had led the Germans to his door, then there was no escape. All he could do was hope.

'Naturally we brought the stuff here. Following the day's events we thought it best to curtail our visit and leave on the morning ferry tomorrow. We don't want to risk being caught with it on us and nor do we want to waste a week's work. There's something you should know.'

Peter sat down. He felt tired, deflated and above all, irritated by Martin's insouciance.

'If the chaps at the Admiralty still have a notion to take these islands, then they'd better think again. The Germans are ahead of them. You explain, Manners. You have the lingo.'

Manners helped himself to another drink and unwrapped the package of drawings and maps. Included within it were some rolls of camera film. Peter's fear and anger started to give way to awe at the quantity of material Manners was carefully laying out on the dining table.

'You will have seen for yourself that the island is crawling with the German Army and the work going on down at the harbour. According to the locals, it's all part of a huge programme of works under way by German Army engineers to build a harbour, dockyard, coaling station and a secret network of tunnels linking fortifications to be built all around the coast. Apparently, work began only last year. The work going on in the harbour is the start of preparations for the construction of two huge moles extending perhaps 1,300 feet or more from the south-eastern shore of the island to form a spacious harbour. I've managed to obtain copies of plans to build twelve large berths for warships and several short piers for submarines and torpedo craft. I also overheard a senior officer boasting that the Kaiser planned to spend thirty million marks to make Heligoland a fortress to rival even that of Gibraltar. He referred to plans to evacuate the small island population in exchange for a garrison of troops. Naturally, that does not dispose them too well to the locals, especially those who were once British subjects.'

Peter marvelled at the detail that lay before him. The information was a veritable treasure trove and far more than he would otherwise have been capable of obtaining in just three days. Martin was right in saying that Manners was an expert cartographer. What Martin had not said was how skilled an artillery man he himself was. The drawings of the fortifications under construction and their potential arcs of fire were masterpieces. He took his hat off to these two idiots after all.

'Very well, Martin, Manners. I'll take the package and try to get it off the island. Stick to your plan to leave tomorrow, but forget visiting the Frisian Islands. It's too dangerous. Instead nip smartly back to London and report your discovery to the Admiralty, just in case I don't make it off the island or have to destroy the package.'

'What? There's no need for melodrama, old boy. Of course you'll get off the island, all right,' Martin exclaimed. 'You cloak-and-dagger boys do love to exaggerate the dangers you face.'

CHAPTER 21

The following night, Peter scanned the horizon to the north of Heligoland with eager anticipation. Given that there were so many members of Germany's army and navy on the island, he was grateful to the British sympathisers for sheltering him. With such a small population, the people of Heligoland formed a tight-knit community and strangers were obvious. It would not have taken much for his presence to have been reported to the German officials. The decision to land and recover him from the north-west corner of the island had proved a divinely directed choice. Anywhere else and *D2*'s operations would have been widely reported. He wondered how Martin and Manners were faring. On his advice, they were abandoning their little adventure and returning directly to London to pass on as much of the information they had gleaned as could be retained in their memories. He shuddered at their naïvety. To them this had just been an exciting game.

However, he had still to get off the island. He patted the priceless oilskin-wrapped package strapped to his chest. There was no way it would be lost the way of his silk map. Once more he anxiously scanned the horizon for signs of *D2*, but the visibility was poor on account of the light rain that had started to fall. He felt lonely and vulnerable. Long ago his guides had left him hidden in a shallow cave formed in the sandstone of the cliff. It afforded little shelter from the developing rain and rising wind, but at least it did not betray his presence to anybody walking the cliff top.

As he waited anxiously the signal announcing *D2*'s arrival, he reflected on the strategic importance of these islands to Britain and Germany. He was not well informed on the provisions of the Heligoland-Zanzibar Treaty so was not sure what Britain had gained from it. He vaguely remembered something about recognising British interests in East Africa. In 1890, of course, there had not been much prospect of Britain and Germany going to war. Now it was obvious that Heligoland was a keystone in the defences of the German bases of Wilhelmshaven and the rest of the Bight. Were the Germans to place batteries of 12-inch guns on both the island and the mainland, their long range would leave only a narrow corridor navigable for the Home Fleet, and such a corridor could be mined and covered by torpedo boats and submarines. Under such conditions it would be impossible to bottle up the German High Seas Fleet in the newly enlarged Kiel Canal, let alone mount a seaborne invasion of the German coast.

Peter checked his watch for the hundredth time. Where was Richard's submarine? She should have been here four hours ago.

****

Johnson was worried. He was late for his rendezvous to pick up Whittaker and the weather was worsening. Moreover, the reason for his tardiness had led to one of the electric motors burning out. Earlier in the evening, on passage from their patrol area in the German Bight to return to Heligoland, they had dived to avoid detection by several steamers plying their trade along the coast between the Frisian Islands and that of Denmark. Suddenly, the submarine had stopped and it had become clear that she was entangled in some form of underwater obstruction. Richard, who had the watch in the control room, had immediately stopped both motors. He had checked the chart for any marked hazard, but the chart had showed over 300 feet of water beneath them. Meanwhile, the boat had started pitching up and down and the scraping noise along the hull had confirmed Richard's suspicions. *D2* had become entangled in a fishing trawl. By this time, Johnson had entered the control room and ordered full astern. This had had some effect, but it had been obvious that the boat was still held fast. Whilst still going astern, Johnson had alternately ordered the after-tanks flooded and pumped in the hope that the changes in the angle of the boat might have some effect. When this had failed, he had ordered full ahead in an attempt to break through the net. After an hour of such manoeuvring, all that had been achieved was a waste of battery power and a burnt-out motor. There had been no alternative but to surface.

Richard had detailed two men to stand by at the forward hatch with axes and prepared to go to the bridge on surfacing. Johnson had ordered the tanks to be blown and the submarine had bobbed to the surface. Sure enough there had been a trawler about 1,000 yards astern. Richard had seen from its deck lights that the crew were already well advanced in cutting the trawl themselves. It must have been no less worrying for the trawler men to have a trapped sea monster thrashing away in their towed net. Indeed, Richard had realised that the crew must have feared being dragged under. Losing a trawl net was an expensive business, too. No doubt there would be some fierce complaints to the German authorities.

Whilst the men of *D2* had set about cutting the wires of the trawl, Johnson had relieved Richard on the bridge. Before he had climbed down onto the casing from the bridge, Richard had seen that the trawler had at last extricated itself from its net. However, that had still left *D2* a prisoner of the trawl and he had been disappointed to see that it had also fouled the starboard hydroplane. Fortunately, although the wind was increasing in force, the sea state had not yet been too high and, now that the net was free of the trawler, the tension on the hawser had relaxed and it had become a reasonably straight forward job to clear the trawl.

The men on the casing had worked quickly and Johnson had been extremely relieved to dive before the trawler had had the opportunity to approach them to remonstrate over the loss of their valuable net or to establish their identity. Johnson suspected that the poor trawler may have fouled its propeller in a part of the trawl after releasing it. No doubt the local German Naval Command would soon be on the receiving end of an undeserved complaint, but he had other worries. He was already late for his rendezvous and the absence of a motor was going to delay him further.

****

Peter was now very concerned. He was also very wet and cold, but that was not what worried him. It would start getting light soon and too late for *D2* to take him off the island. Although Johnson had promised to return the following night, that would mean spending another day on the island with the attendant risk of being arrested as a spy. It was too dangerous to stay on the beach during the day, but nor could he return to his guides. It would be simple enough to bury the oilskin package to avoid being caught with it, but it was vital to get it to London somehow.

'C' was going to be very annoyed when he heard of the antics of Martin and Manners. It was not unusual for Royal Marines officers to volunteer for this sort of work because it released them from the normal routine of regimental duty or appointments on board the navy's capital ships. In the absence of any significant conflict in which to draw favourable attention to themselves, it also offered a prospect to earn early promotion. 'C' had shared a different opinion with Peter, though. 'C' reasoned that in this modern era, for spying – for that was the correct term, not intelligence-gathering – one needed specialist training, particular qualities and, above all, experience. It was no longer the province of the enthusiastic amateur.

For perhaps the thousandth time he scanned the horizon in the hope of seeing a light amidst the heavy rain. He froze in dread. Above the howl of the wind he thought he could hear voices. He realised in a panic that if discovered, he still had the oilskin package strapped to his chest. Straining his ears to listen intently, all he could hear was the pounding of his heart, the crashing of the waves and the howl of the wind. He must have imagined it. No! There it was again. He backed himself further into the hollow in the cliff face to hide, but to his horror saw two darkly-clothed men approach his hiding place. By their movements they were clearly searching for something or someone. Both men carried partially-covered flashlights and were systematically peering into every crevice of the beach. Peter thought it odd that the flashlights were shaded, but did not move a muscle and hardly dared to breathe. Why had he not hidden the package earlier on? He could have returned to collect it from his hiding place once *D2* was sighted. Now, if searched, he would not only have the evidence on him to prove he was a spy, but it would implicate others. He hoped his parents would understand. What would happen to the guides? Would they be shot or hanged for treason? As further thoughts of his and the guides' fate flashed through his mind, he was half blinded by the flashlight of one of the men. Oh my God, he thought. The game's up. Then he heard his name called in a whisper.

'Peter, is that you? Come out, you damned fool.'

Peter's legs gave way under the almost simultaneous emotions of terror and relief. The man with the flashlight was Richard and his accomplice was a Leading Seaman from HMS *D2*. Thank God for the navy.

CHAPTER 22

March 1912

It was almost the end of March and, although the spring was only in its infancy, it was, nonetheless, a beautiful day as Peter set off on his daily walk around the estate. He was enjoying his last leave before leaving for Gibraltar and his new assignment. He had always loved walking and reflected that he had his mother to thank for that. It was a love she had instilled in all her sons and the whole family often engaged in walking holidays either in Mutti's native Switzerland or the nearby English Lake District. Since his family's return to London, Peter had come to appreciate the peace and solitude the countryside had to offer. It was all a far cry from the subterfuge, pressure and above all, constant fear for his life in Germany, France and the Low Countries these past two years. He thanked God he was now free of the persona of the duplicitous von Trotha at last.

He enjoyed being alone, too, with the exception of the company of a Welsh springer spaniel, Seren, on his walks. Although he didn't speak Welsh, he knew that the dog's name was derived from the star-shaped patch on her forehead. She actually belonged to one of his father's gamekeepers. He hailed from mid-Wales and swore by the merits of the Welshie over its larger English cousin and had started to breed them for the estate. Papa wasn't quite so convinced, but, nonetheless, admired the breed for their hard work, initiative and obedience in the field. Whatever their relative merits, Peter had certainly been attracted to the colour of the breed's rich red and white. Moreover, as soon as he had looked into the young Seren's eyes he had become hooked on the breed. Somehow the dog seemed to have said silently through the expression in her eyes, 'You look as if you need a friend and I need one, too, so why don't we get together?' Whatever it was, she was irresistible and they had since trodden many a mile together on the Lancashire footpaths over the past few months. It would pain him to say goodbye to her in just a few weeks.

He checked his pocket watch. He had no language lesson with his grandmother that day and he had warned Mrs Caunce that he would be out for luncheon. If he was to time his walk correctly to make his accidental rendezvous, he still had plenty of time to kill. Mrs Caunce had packed in his rücksack a bottle of her delectable home-made ginger beer, a small game pie and a piece of her fruit cake. He thought he might take his lunch at the old pack horse bridge. It was not far to the bridge and there he could cross the stream, but first he had to climb a steep knoll.

For every stride Peter took across the lush green fields, Seren must have taken a hundred as she fanned out to one side and then the other, looking to pick up the scent of a rabbit or hare. He marvelled at her energy and commitment. Above, a large bird of prey passed overhead. For a brief moment he was excited by the thought that it might be a hen harrier, but then he heard it emit a mewing sound and he recognised with disappointment that it must be a buzzard. He spotted a second soaring above the copse by the stream at the bottom of the valley. The two birds glided in a wide circle, way above the trees, without any apparent effort or movement. It was such a beautiful day and he envied them their vantage point.

He breasted the crest of the knoll from where he could see all the way down the valley. It was warm for the time of year so he paused to remove his jacket, roll up his shirt sleeves and take in the view. Then he noticed, to his dismay, another walker had stolen his idea and was presently resting on the bridge looking downstream. He was incensed. How dare this fellow stop at one of his favourite spots? It was, after all, Miller land. However, the other walker did not tarry long and began to walk on. Peter then recognised him as his Uncle Phil.

The Reverend Kensett was not in fact a blood relative, but an old friend of the family. Many years before, he had served overseas with Captain Miller, but had left the navy to take holy orders. When the living on the estate had become vacant, Miller had offered it to his old friend. Kensett had never married and, at Johanna's insistence as she didn't trust bachelors to feed themselves properly, had become a frequent guest at Marton Hall. As the boys had grown up, they had become very fond of his company. However, today Peter was in no mood to make polite conversation. He was enjoying his own company and private thoughts. Instead, he offered the rector a polite wave and continued to admire the view. Uncle Phil must have recognised him, even at the great distance, as he responded cheerily before continuing on his business.

With the coast now clear, Peter descended into the valley and made his way to the pack horse bridge. There were in fact two bridges spanning the stream. Another wider and later bridge was set further back. This second bridge had been built to accommodate carts and waggons and now even the automobile. It served as the main crossing for all the estate traffic. The pack horse bridge was barely four feet wide and rarely used these days. It had been built perhaps 200 years before and on both banks the grass sloped gently down to the stream. On the opposite bank to Peter it flattened out for several yards and this made it the perfect spot for a picnic. Some iron rings had been hammered into the stonework of the bridge here so he suspected that many a pack horse man in history had taken his ease on just this spot, and used the ring to tether his horse or mule whilst he took a quick nap. Following this custom, he tied Seren to the ring on a long lead and settled down to his luncheon.

He gazed into the shallow running water of the stream on the Marton estate. In certain parts, foam had collected around some obstruction or slower-moving part of the stream. As a child he had refused to drink the water from rivers or streams wherever he saw such foam present, thinking that the foam was the remnants of urine from sheep or cows upstream. Papa had explained the stupidity of such a notion and how any such urine would be diluted into minute particles, but he had not been able to offer a reason for this phenomenon. Uncle Phil, who took an interest in all matters of natural science, had suggested it could be something either to do with the decay of plants in the water, or possibly related to the interaction of the surface of the water with the air. His theory was that the surface of water must have some form of natural film that allowed insects to walk on it and perhaps the movement of the stream disturbed this film and mixed it with the air to produce foam.

Peter had no idea, but still found it interesting. He had even discussed it with von Hoffman on their surveys together in Flanders. Von Hoffman's family were landowners and farmers and he had suggested that the growing trend to add phosphates to the land as an artificial manure might be the cause. Von Hoffman had studied chemistry at Heidelberg University and he had explained how phosphates added nitrogen to the soil. The foaming could be the result of gas released from phosphates being washed into the rivers and streams. He had cautioned Peter to boil water before drinking it and railed against Man for beginning to pollute the landscape through its increasing use of chemicals for agriculture and industry. Von Hoffman was a clever man and Peter had enjoyed his company.

The swirling of the water and its soothing sound began to have a hypnotic effect on him and, as he thought about von Hoffman, he found himself giving way to drowsiness. Memories of his days in France and Belgium with von Hoffman clouded his thoughts. They had spent some very agreeable days in the wide open spaces of Flanders that summer of 1910.

****

Peter woke slowly to find Seren licking his face. He had not meant to fall asleep, but the combination of the early spring sunshine, the pie and the sound of the stream running beneath the pack horse bridge, had all produced a soporific effect. Checking his pocket watch, he noted the hour had passed two and he had probably slept for over two hours. It was fortunate that his face was still well tanned from the previous summer or else he might have suffered sunburn. Time was marching on and he would have to walk swiftly if he was to be on time for his assignation.

He stretched out his long limbs and let them soak up the sunshine for a minute to re-energise himself before unpegging Seren and continuing his walk. He decided he would take the short cut past the cotton mill, but he would first have to climb the other side of the valley. The mill was sited on the River Breden from which it derived its power and, after agriculture, was now the biggest source of employment for the local population, many of whom lived in the village lower down the valley. His grandfather had set up the factory and it was a substantial source of revenue for the estate. A significant portion of these profits had been invested in the village and today it boasted a thriving local school run by the headmistress, Miss Brockles, and her new assistant, Miss Robson.

His path took him through some woods. The going was difficult, not just on account of the steep rise, but the path remained very muddy after a wet winter. Perhaps he should have brought a stick, he thought. Seren, however, showed no difficulty in mounting the slope and was energetically bounding among the undergrowth in her pursuit of some fresh scent. Pausing for a breather, Peter called her in and she responded without hesitation.

'I'm going to miss you, old girl.'

He tickled the young dog's head and ears. Seren responded to the affection by licking his hand. There were many facets of his life in England

and particularly at Marton Hall he would miss. Moreover, there were many uncertainties and potential risks associated with his forthcoming assignment in Persia. He was under no illusion that it would be difficult as a European to master the many disguises he might have to adopt. A shiver went down his spine as he reflected that the price of failure would not be as civilised as a firing squad. He knew enough of the Mussulman's fondness for cruelty and had no doubt that if he faced death, it would be long and painful. On the other hand, he had more confidence in himself. He now knew he could immerse himself into the skin of an alias and this time there was no risk of him being tripped up by meeting somebody he might have been expected to have known from the past. More significantly, he was wholeheartedly committed to this assignment.

Ever since that last visit to Berlin, he had known that war with Germany would be inevitable. How could he have been so naïve in not recognising this truth? Papa had been right all along, although, to be fair, Papa had never returned to the subject of their meeting in Berlin, nor in any way gloated over the fact that he had been proved right. He resented that. It had cost his pride dear to admit his error of judgement and he had tried to make amends by committing to further work as a double agent. Even so, Papa had kept his word to free him of the clutches of the ND by staging his death during the raid on the naval magazines. Notwithstanding the awkwardness he now felt in Papa's presence on account of his guilty secret, his admiration for him had grown enormously. Who else could have turned the situation to such advantage? The Grand Master had used von Trotha as an agent provocateur. It had been Papa's idea to persuade the Irishman to strike a blow against his former Imperial masters. By doing so, Kell's men had drawn out several actual and potential German agents in Britain and now had control of the whole German spy network.

If anything, the descent into the valley was more difficult than the recent climb. This path, too, was steep and slippery and many a time he had to grasp at the trunk or branch of a tree adjacent to the path, in order to maintain his balance. Soon though, as he descended into the valley, the path became less steep and he could feel more confident of his footing. It was not long before the peace of the landscape was interrupted by the increasingly loud thumping noise of the cotton mill machinery.

Ordinarily, he would have continued to follow the path to skirt the mill, taking a loop well to the left and then crossing the river downstream. He would then follow the river upstream through the village and head for

Bluebell Wood. Here the river passed over several weirs on its descent downstream, and on a Sunday, it was one of his favourite picnic spots. Indeed, it was here that he had first met Miss Robson just a few months earlier. In the valley below he heard the chime of the school clock announcing the time as half past three. He cursed himself. He was running late and he decided to cut right, down the narrow, old coffin path to take a short cut to the village. The path was very overgrown with waist-high vegetation that would make a mess of his clothing, but this was the quickest route and he was in danger of missing his assignation completely. He descended quickly into the cacophony of the looms.

CHAPTER 23

The school clock chimed on the half hour. Lessons had finished for the day half an hour earlier and Alice Robson had finished tidying up. Once more she peered through the mullioned glass windows of the classroom and was again disappointed to see no sign of the dog and its owner. Her own dog, Charlie, a black cocker spaniel, also seemed to be impatient with anticipation. He lay under her desk, semi-alert, with one ear partially raised, listening out for any signs of the arrival of his lady friend. Unlike the children, Alice had no difficulty in seeing through the high arched windows. At five feet ten inches she was remarkably tall for a woman. Slender in build, too, she appeared a little ungainly, but with short, blonde hair and deep-blue eyes she was highly attractive. She was, also, unusually qualified for her post as an assistant schoolmistress. Two years earlier she had been successful in taking the Classical Tripos at Girton College, Cambridge, to gain an honours degree. In between leaving Cambridge and taking up her post the previous summer, she had spent six months touring many of the great German universities to develop her passion for German literature and learn more of the German history and culture. News of her father's sudden death to a massive stroke had interrupted her tour and she had returned to northern England to attend the funeral and to support her mother. With her return, the dreams of a career in publishing or acadaemia had vanished.

The Robsons were sheep and dairy farmers in the Westmorland countryside near Appleby. Alice had helped her mother arrange the sale of the farm and the move to live with her sister in neighbouring Cumberland. Then, instead of continuing her plans to take up a career in London, Alice had chosen to take up a teaching position that would keep her within reasonable travelling distance of her mother, should she need to be on hand. Her situation fell far short of her previous expectations, but what choice did she have, she wondered? Alice's mother had another sister, Aunt Emily, also a widow to a farmer, and when the vacancy for a schoolmistress at the Marton village school had arisen, it had seemed a sensible move to apply for the position and live with her aunt.

It had not taken long for Alice to recognise her mistake. The children were pleasant enough, but they had little aspiration to progress their education. Most were from families who farmed as tenants of the Marton Hall estate and their sole ambition was to help out on the farm on leaving school. The headmistress of the school, Miss Brockles, had impressed on her that it was more than enough to teach the children to read, write, do basic arithmetic and, if the children's interests were so inclined and the talent was there, to ingrain in them an appreciation of music and drawing. Alice was a keen watercolour artist herself, but had been frustrated to discover that despite the many beautiful landscapes of the Forest of Bowland, the ambitions of the more artistic children were confined to drawing and painting sheep, cows and, very occasionally, horses.

The three years at Cambridge had developed in her a thirst for knowledge and a yearning for intellectual stimulation. She remembered fondly the vigorous and sometimes heated debates with her fellow students and residents of Girton College. The life seemed a million miles away from her humdrum existence living with Aunty Emily and teaching the children of the tenants of Marton Hall. She supposed this was why she had recently become so enamoured with the cause of the Women's Social and Political Union, one of the so-called "suffragette" societies dedicated to winning the vote for women in general elections. During one of her vacations from Cambridge, she had attended a rally campaigning for women to be given the vote and at which Emmeline Pankhurst had been the principal speaker. Following the meeting, she had met with Emmeline's eldest daughter Christabel and the two had immediately struck a rapport. Before long, Alice had been offered a prominent role in the organisation of the WSPU, but had declined it in favour of her studies.

With the change in her circumstances over the past couple of months, she had recently become a committed suffragette and had not only attended meetings in Manchester, but also lent a hand in delivering several campaign leaflets. She was even thinking of joining the local committee in Preston. She had never seen herself as a militant, but she saw justice in the cause of the WSPU and considered them more likely to achieve political results than their rival organisations such as the National Union of Women's Suffrage Societies or NUWSS.

Notwithstanding her own moderate view, she nevertheless admired the many women who had suffered the humiliation of arrest, loss of liberty to, and physical hardships of imprisonment and, most abhorrent of all, the shame, pain and ill health arising from force-feeding at the hands of the establishment, merely for the pursuit of the just cause of votes for women.

Charlie whimpered softly to indicate he was impatient for his walk. After one last wistful look through the window, Alice realised there was little point in staying. He clearly was not coming today and she might as well go straight home.

Since taking up her post the previous September, she had made it her routine to take Charlie for a walk through the Bluebell Wood downstream of Marton Mill, before going on home to Aunt Emily's farm. In those early days Charlie had been less well disciplined and one day, scenting a rabbit or some other such exciting prey, had run off. Despite her frantic appeals, he had refused to return to heel and she had already started to become quite distressed when, to her horror, he had jumped into the river in pursuit of a pheasant. The bird had naturally taken flight, but Charlie had found himself balanced on the edge of a weir in fast-flowing water. Realising his peril, he had tried to retrace his steps to the river bank, but lost his footing. Immediately, he had been swept over the weir and down the fast-moving river. Alice had screamed in terror after the retreating dog as he was sucked under the surface. Miraculously, in her opinion, her cries had been heard by a fellow walker downstream. With impressively quick thinking and dexterity, the man had appreciated the situation and immediately leaped into the waist-high water. With one hand clinging to a low hanging branch, he had used the other to grab the petrified Charlie by his lead and collar as he was rushed past by the foaming torrent. On gaining the bank and handing over the remorseful dog to his grateful owner, the handsome stranger had then introduced himself as Peter Miller. Alice's profuse thanks had been cut short as the gallant hero had excused himself peremptorily on the grounds that he needed a change of clothes. It had only been later that she had learned from Aunt Emily that Peter was one of the sons of the landlord at Marton Hall.

Since then, except when he had been in London – Alice understood him to be a member of the Diplomatic Service – Mister Miller had frequently chanced to be passing the school just as she was leaving. She had not been slow to spot that if she left just ahead of him, he always seemed to catch up with her on her way to the woods. On those occasions when he passed the school before she had finished clearing up, he inevitably spotted her to his rear and found a reason to adjust his beautiful Welsh springer's lead or his own bootlaces, so that she had no choice but to overtake him. It was obvious that he was engineering these chance meetings and must be attracted to her, but he was far too shy to make his feelings known.

This was a pity, she thought. She, too, looked forward to these chance encounters and, as the weeks had passed and their friendship developed, she had realised that she was deeply attracted to him. Peter was intelligent, well educated, articulate and amusing. His conversation was lively and engaging and she relished the intellectual stimulation of his company – stimulation she was all too sadly lacking. However, whilst he was so obviously confident in his manner and in expressing himself, he seemed to possess a certain vulnerability that appealed to her maternal instinct. He was often cheerful and brimming with enthusiasm, but every now and then he became introspective and even mournful. It was as if he was sad, deep within himself, or hiding some tragic secret. The mystery intrigued her, but she was frustrated by his shyness and had resolved to give him some encouragement to show her some affection. She had, therefore, arranged with Aunt Emily to invite him home for tea this afternoon, but this was now the one day he had not taken his usual walk past the school. Poor Charlie, he would so miss playing with Seren this afternoon.

She locked the school behind her and turned left out of the school gates. There was still no sign of Peter. Somewhat dejectedly, she trudged past the mill workers' cottages letting Charlie take his time in sniffing out the scents in the walls and trees along the way. At the bridge across the river, she would normally have turned right to take the path up to the woods, but today she could not bring herself to do it. Having taken the decision to invite Peter to tea, she felt flat by his absence and could not bring herself to walk through the woods without him. Resignedly, she crossed the bridge and turned right to parallel the path to Bluebell Wood, out of the village and up towards Aunt Emily's. The path was narrow and steep, including several steps at various intervals along it. The sun beat upon her back as she climbed the path and, at various points along the grass verge, she could see primroses in the hedgerow and clumps of daffodils budding up ready to flower.

She should have been bubbling with cheer on such a day. She pondered why the disappointment of not meeting Peter had dejected her so. After all, she had seen him only yesterday. Could it be that she loved him? How does one know when one is in love? She had read often enough of love in both English and German literature, but had no practical experience. She had read that love can hurt and certainly she felt hurt right now. She could feel the weight of her intestines in her stomach, her breast seemed ready to burst and her leg muscles overcome with tiredness. A feeling of wanting to cry overcame her, just as it had done when as a child she had faced some major disappointment. She knew it was stupid. She was grown up, a graduate of Girton College and a professional woman. She wasn't the simpering type men imagined all women to be. Even so, she gave into her feelings and burst into tears.

After only two minutes or so, the tears quickly subsided and she felt better for having vented her frustration. As she applied a handkerchief to her eyes, Charlie suddenly barked three times and strained against his lead to head back down the hill. She sensed danger and quickly turned to face the potential threat.

CHAPTER 24

Peter knew he was too late to meet Alice at the school, but hurried past the mill and into the village nonetheless, in the hope of catching up with her on her way to the woods. Approaching the centre of the village, he noticed he had broken into a sweat underneath his tweed jacket and this added to his agitation. He was not sure how he would explain his dishevelled and muddy appearance, but he would cross that bridge when he came to it. He debated whether it was now worth going on to the school or straight home. In the distance above and to his left he heard a dog bark three times. Suddenly, Seren stopped and, on turning round, she too barked in acknowledgement and strained at her lead. Peter looked across the river to see the source of the fuss. His heart rose and sank immediately in quick succession. High above him he saw the graceful figure of Alice and her dog, Charlie, on the opposite side of the river. Alice had clearly taken a different path, but he could hardly turn round and follow her without his feelings being exposed. All he could do was give her a friendly wave, despite his inner feelings of disappointment.

Alice returned his wave, but then it appeared to him as if her dog had caught her by surprise. He saw Alice fall and let go of Charlie's lead. On being released, Charlie bounded down the steps without hesitation and on reaching the bridge, greeted Seren most enthusiastically. Peter's chagrin immediately turned to concern and, after grabbing Charlie's lead, he crossed the bridge and raced up the path to Alice's assistance with both dogs in tow.

When he arrived at Alice's side, short of breath, he found her sitting on the grass rubbing her ankle as if she had suffered an injury.

'Are you all right, Miss Robson?' he panted.

'Absolutely. 'Tis only my pride that's hurt. I tripped over that fool Charlie's lead. He really is a naughty dog. Thank you for your concern and for returning him to me once again.'

Neither party seemed sure of how to proceed next, but it was Alice who took the lead.

'I'm sure I've only twisted my ankle a little, but I confess the pain is such that I'm too cowardly to check it properly. Might I prevail on you to check there really is no damage?'

Alice then stretched out her left leg towards Peter. He knelt down on the path, gently feeling her ankle for any obvious swelling or more serious injury and, as he did so, he felt a sensual thrill pass through him to be so intimate with her. On examining her white-silk-stocking-clad ankle, he noticed it was attached to an equally shapely calf. To his horror and delight he could not help but notice that she was seated a little immodestly and he could see right up her skirt. Atop her stocking, the pink-ribboned legs of her bloomers were clearly visible. He immediately averted his eyes, but it was too late to prevent a stirring in his loins. He overcame his embarrassment by offering to assist Alice to her feet. She seemed to have no difficulty in standing with his support, but leaned heavily against him. Clearly her ankle was too tender to support her weight fully. As he held her in his arms, he felt a huge sense of excitement and realised how attracted he was to her.

'I would be much obliged, Mister Miller, if you could assist me to my Aunt's. I'm not at all sure that my ankle will bear my considerable weight. Perhaps if you would fetch me a stick and lend me your arm, I could manage well enough.'

He was more than happy to oblige and play the gallant. It struck him that though he knew of Upper Hulme Farm well enough, he had not actually ever been there. Together they struggled up the path, arm in arm, and Peter reflected that events had not turned out too badly after all. Neither spoke much. Alice, too, seemed content with their situation and he let the two dogs run on a slack lead. All too soon it seemed, but in reality perhaps fifteen minutes later, Upper Hulme Farm came into view. The farmland had been let to other tenants, but Aunt Emily still occupied a fine-looking house. The twin gables of the house were painted white beneath the slate roofs, with intricately cut weather-boarding, and the house commanded a fine view across the valley. As they approached from the eastern and rear aspect, he noted that the back of the house looked over a fine orchard and pottage garden in which a variety of hens were scratching about.

Alice guided them around to the front door and let them in. Within seconds, they were greeted by Aunt Emily, a short dumpy woman about five feet in height with short, bobbed, dark hair streaked with grey, bordering a plain moon face beaming with a smile. Peter had never met Aunt Emily or her late husband, but he immediately took a shine to her.

'Bless you, lass. Whatever could 'ave 'appened?' she exclaimed. 'I was expecting you both a good 'alf hour ago and the tea will be well stewed by now.'

Alice shot her aunt a warning glance, but too late to prevent Peter recognising that he seemed to be expected.

'It's all right, Aunt Emmy,' Alice replied. 'I tripped over Charlie's lead and turned my ankle, but was fortunate that Mister Miller was on hand to assist me home. I can assure you that I am quite well and there is nothing over which to fret.'

Alice gave her aunt a most meaningful glance, but the meaning of which Peter could not interpret. 'I wonder if we might repay Mister Miller's kindness by extending him an invitation to stay for tea.'

Peter could have sworn that he detected a trace of a wink exchanged between Alice and her aunt.

'But of course, my dears. I'll just knock you up a fresh brew. Alice, would you show Mister Miller int' parlour?'

The parlour was one of the rooms that overlooked the garden and the valley. The bay window was mullioned and fitted out with a cushioned bench and a small table on which some blue and white china had been adorned with a variety of sandwiches and home-baking. Again Peter noted that he seemed to have been expected, but he didn't care enough to make enquiries on the matter. He also noted that the fire in the inglenook fireplace was already lit.

The room was simply furnished with a few dark oak pieces upholstered in plain fabrics. A more cheerful note had been achieved by the addition of several brightly embroidered cushions, some strategically placed vases of primroses and daffodils and a series of watercolours hanging on the walls. He assisted Alice to a seat on a trestle bench and cast an eye over the paintings. Many were local landscapes he had no difficulty in recognising, including one of Saint Alfege's, Uncle Phil's church, and the pack horse bridge. He noticed the initials of the artist, 'APR'.

'These are mighty fine paintings, Miss Robson. Are they by chance your own?'

'I grant that they are my own work, but you exaggerate their quality. They merely hang there as they are the ones to which Aunt Emmy took a fancy on account of them being local. Are you an artist yourself, Mister Miller?'

'Not at all. I can't even draw. My mother has some skill, but has not passed it on to any but John, my youngest brother.'

'I am convinced you are being modest. But, if as you say, you are not artistic, you certainly have a talent for handling dogs and rescuing damsels in distress. This is the second time I am in your debt through my poor control over Charlie.'

Right on cue, the door was opened by Aunt Emily with a fresh pot of tea and a plate of bread and butter, but before she could even enter the room, she was preceded by a dark streak across the room as Charlie burst in and leapt onto his mistress's lap.

'Eh, lass, you're too soft wi' that dog,' Aunty Emily scolded Alice. ''E needs a firm 'and or th'll ruin 'im. He's not at all like your bitch, sir. She won't cum in to 'ouse. She's sitting quiet like, on doorstep where yer left her.'

'Oh do call her in, Mister Miller,' Alice begged him. 'She is such a lovely dog.'

'It would do no good, Miss Robson. Seren is a working dog and accustomed to a life outdoors. In fact, I really ought to be returning her home to her true master.'

'Oh, no! You'll surely have yer tea and a bite t'eat first?'

Aunt Emily appeared horrified that her guest should excuse himself so soon.

'It's very kind of you, Mrs Hughes, but I've arranged to dine with my grandmother at the Hall and I must have time to change.'

'I won't 'ear of it, sir. Now you just sit th'sen down and drink yer tea and I'll fix for my nephew Ben to run yer both back int' dog cart. I'll get him to nip over to see old Proctor. He's got a telephone and he could ring big house to tell them you'll be just a little late. You could bide another hour and still be back in plenty of time for yer supper surely?'

Peter could see the sense in Aunt Emily's plan and, indeed, was already feeling weary from his day's walk. He also favoured the idea of spending more time in Alice's company and so was more than happy to surrender meekly.

'Well, if you're sure it is not too much trouble. I confess I would be pleased to be spared a walk of four miles home.'

'Right then. I'll go and see Ben to fix the arrangements and leave you both to sup yer tea.'

Aunty Emily's look across to Alice suggested she was seeking some form of approval, but Peter could detect no change in Alice's expression. Aunt Emily left the young couple alone.

Following Aunt Emily's discreet withdrawal, he and Alice chatted freely on a wide range of subjects, including their own perspectives of places they had both visited in France and Germany. However, Peter was keen not to dwell on these subjects too long, for fear of tripping himself up by forgetting the guise in which he had visited some of these places, or that the visits may have taken place whilst he was supposedly at his desk in the Paris Embassy. When he could, he changed the subject to news of recent events in London.

'I see the suffragettes have started making a nuisance of themselves again. I had rather hoped they would at least have waited until the vote on the Conciliation Bill was known.'

He was surprised to see Alice stiffen slightly and, to avoid any awkwardness, he compounded his error by filling any potential embarrassing silence. 'I refer, of course, to the breaking of shop windows in the West End. I do not denounce the women's right to demonstrate.'

Alice replied in an icy tone he had never previously heard. 'Do you not believe that women should have the vote then, Mister Miller?'

He was immediately alert to the danger and cautious in his reply. 'As it happens, I do believe women should have the vote, but it is the means by which the campaign is waged that meets my disapproval. Smashing windows of innocent shopkeepers or destroying famous works of art does not attract sympathy for the cause.'

'You talk of sympathy, but one cannot live on it. Sometimes you have to be prepared to fight in the interests of justice. My sex has been trying for decades to be enfranchised, but it is a man's world. In such a world, it is the men who make the laws and they do so for the benefit of men.'

'I think that hardly fair, Miss Robson. I read that Mister Asquith is quite sympathetic on the issue and my understanding is that the Conciliation Committee is represented by MPs from all the major parties.'

Alice shrugged and looked away. Peter recognised that he had broached a delicate subject and looked for a way out.

'But you need not persuade me of the justice of your cause, Miss Robson. I merely decry the violence. My dear mother, after all, is a woman and one who is extremely well read, educated and intelligent. I do not see why she is less deserving of the vote than I. Indeed, were I to hold the opposite view, then life at the breakfast table would be less than convivial.'

He could not tell whether Alice had been persuaded of his sincerity, but he noted the pink glow from her neck and under her chin started to recede. After a moment of reflection she replied. 'I'm sorry. I was somewhat tart with you, but you have struck a raw nerve. Throughout my time at Cambridge, I and my fellow students continually had to tolerate often ignorant men putting us down merely on the basis that, as women, we were not deemed capable of intelligent thought. I am impatient for change.'

'Perhaps you should meet my cousin, Elizabeth. She shares your views and frustration.'

'Oh, really? She sounds very modern. Where does she live then?'

'Over in Crosby ... on the coast. She is the only daughter of my father's brother. As the only female amongst my Uncle Edmond's and father's combined five sons, she has always had to strive to maintain her femininity. I fear she has had a rather sorry time, but she's a plucky and independent lass ... By Jove! It does give me an idea. Miss Robson, do you have any plans or prior engagements for the Saturday of the Easter weekend?'

He was pleased to see that Alice became animated at the prospect of a further meeting and she responded enthusiastically. 'I have nothing fixed. Certainly nothing that cannot be changed within the notice.'

'Champion. My elder brother, Richard, is in Liverpool that week on navy business and staying with my uncle over the weekend. I was planning already to join him and the family for luncheon. Perhaps you would care to accompany me as my guest? I am sure cousin Elizabeth would welcome an ally to educate we poor ignorant men on the subject of women's suffrage.'

'I think not,' Alice replied and Peter's disappointment clearly showed for she immediately added, 'I mean I would not presume to bore you or your family on the issue of votes for women. I would very much like to meet your cousin Elizabeth and have yet to visit that part of the world. I have heard that the sandy soil is ideal for asparagus.'

Peter's mood brightened instantly. 'Now, that's just capital. I will make the necessary arrangements on my return this evening, and perhaps I might call on you tomorrow afternoon, after school, to discuss the itinerary?'

'That would be most welcome.' Alice placed her cup and saucer back on the table, wiped the crumbs from her lips with her napkin and asked, 'Would you like to see the gardens?'

'But what of your ankle, Miss Robson?'

'Oh, it seems much better now, thanks to the rest, and I think it would do it some good to exercise it. After all, I don't want the muscles to stiffen overnight if I am to attend school tomorrow. I'm sure we must have a stick somewhere – unless I could again seek the assistance of your arm?'

He was only too pleased to help and took Alice's arm to tour the garden. Although Alice leaned heavily against him, he wryly noticed that she sometimes limped on the uninjured leg. They stopped to admire the last view of the valley as the light faded and he felt Alice tremble. He took this trembling as a shiver from the cold evening air and unconsciously put his arm around her to provide her some warmth. She responded by leaning further into him and before he knew it she was in his arms. A pang of emotion surged through him.

'Miss Robson, may I kiss you?' he asked diffidently.

Alice merely laughed and he pulled away from her completely humiliated and hurt.

'Please forgive me, Miss Robson. I cannot think what came over me. I should not have attempted to take advantage of your situation.' He looked away to avoid eye contact.

Alice put her hand on his shoulder to make him look at her and replied gently. 'You are funny. Of course you may kiss me, but please address me as Alice first.'

'Oh, Alice!' He needed no second invitation and held her tight against him and kissed her hard and passionately. Alice responded eagerly. Time stood still. As the length of his kiss extended, his desire for her became more carnal and he was conscious of a stiffening in his breeches as their bodies were pressed close to each other. He shifted his position in embarrassment to stop her noticing, but Alice followed his movement and pushed her thigh closer into his groin.

All too soon, he released her from his kiss, but still held her within his arms. Alice rested her head on his shoulder and was the first to break the silence between them.

'Thank God. I was beginning to think there must be something wrong with me.'

A feeling of total love welled up within him and he made to kiss her again, but was interrupted by Aunt Emily running into the garden.

'Mister Miller, sir,' she shouted breathlessly. 'The vicar's 'ere. There's been a terrible accident.'

'Is it my grandmother? What's happened?' He saw Uncle Phil standing at the door and rushed over to him.

'What is it Uncle Phil? How did you know I was here?'

'I didn't. I've been looking for you all afternoon. I saw you earlier and thought to look for you in the village. Somebody thought he saw you coming this way. Now listen, Peter.' Kensett took Peter by both shoulders. 'It's bad news about your brother, Richard, I'm afraid. His submarine's missing and the navy thinks it sunk. Your mother's beside herself with worry and your father wants you on the next train to London.'

CHAPTER 25

July 1913

Ahmad Mirza was impressed by the length and girth of the Frenchman's dark bushy beard. It was larger even than his own and unusual for a European. The tribesman continued to watch the young French doctor attending his patients. He was impatient to return to his family as his wife was due to give birth very soon, and he had a long camel ride to Bushehr before he could return to his family. However, the urgency of his mission had been impressed on him and, if Allah willed it, Ahmad would at least return to see a healthy young child. Already the father of three fine young sons, he hoped God would provide him with a beautiful daughter this time. Unlike many of the Bakhtiaris tribesmen, Ahmad had only one wife and he longed for a daughter in the image of his beautiful and serene wife, Atoosa. It was becoming clear that it would be some time before the doctor would be free to receive the despatch carefully stored within his robes. So Ahmad contented himself that he could at least rest in the shade of the trees where, even in the late July heat, it was so much cooler than the Persian desert to the east from whence he had just come. All too quickly, he allowed the weariness of his journey to overcome him and fell asleep with pleasant thoughts of the welcome he would receive on his return to his family. He dreamt of the conception of his fifth child.

****

The doctor attended his patients with much dedication. He was not in fact French and nor was he medically qualified, but this did not stop him feeling a sense of satisfaction that he was doing something worthwhile. Outside the towns and cities of Persia the people were totally bereft of medical facilities or expertise. Before Lieutenant Peter Miller had adopted the cover of a French doctor for his travels in Persia, he had been given some basic medical and first-aid training at the naval hospital in Gibraltar and equipped with a simple medicine chest. He had since discovered that even his limited training was more than enough to alleviate suffering. In one of the villages he had visited recently, several children had already died of diarrhoea. By administering no more than drinks of warm, orange-petal tea made from clean water, he had cured the acute dehydration from which many of the children were suffering. Such a simple treatment was considered miraculous by the villagers and they regarded him as a great hakeem. Posing as a doctor had been one of a number of Peter's ruses these past several months to avoid having to explain his movements through the south-western region of Persia. The cover had brought about many unexpected benefits. Once this mission was complete, he now seriously contemplated resigning from the Service to train as a doctor.

Peter had made full use of his grandmother's family contacts in Bushehr, meeting many relatives for the first time. He had set up a network of reporters to provide information on any news of German or other foreign visitors to the region. He had then gone on to use his cover as a French doctor to tour several of the villages in the vicinity of Maidan-e-Naftan, the Plain of Oil, an area of south-western Persia sandwiched between the Zagros mountains to the north and east, and the coastal refinery at Abadan to the south. So far, none of his agents had reported anything worthy of alarm.

At last, he treated his final patient and, as he sat to accept the proffered cup of sweet tea, he noticed the messenger. Despite his curiosity, he had learned that in Persia it did not pay to rush matters and he continued his conversation unhurriedly with one of the village elders. It was only once he had finished his second cup of tea that he rose to his feet and bade his hosts goodbye. He began to prepare his horse and camel to move on. The movement roused Mirza from his slumbers and he stepped forward to address in his native Persian the man known to all as Doctor Pilven.

'Doctor, I have long heard of your skill and humanity. I have ridden many miles to have the honour of this meeting. Alas, it has been God's will that many of those close to me have need of your learning. May I offer you this note of explanation?'

Mirza made a sweeping bow and handed Peter the scroll. Peter accepted it and read it through hastily. He recognised Mirza as one of his cousin Darius's men and realised that the scroll must contain significant news. Sure enough, it was a message from Captain Arnold Wilson, the British Consul at Ahvaz to the south. The message made little sense to the casual reader, but Peter was well briefed on the current intelligence and it told him all he needed to know. Churchill had presented his bill to Parliament and the Germans had sent an agent with his entourage to Persia. He was to return at once to the British Consulate in Bushehr for further instructions and to meet a high-ranking envoy from the Admiralty. Oil was at the heart of Peter's mission and he was very familiar with its history in Persia.

****

Peter drained the glass of cool water and immediately refilled it from the carafe laid out on the table in the guest wing of the British Consulate in Bushehr. He reflected that never before had he appreciated the true quality and value of water. In Europe, water was a drink one ranked below all others. One used it as the body for beer, cider or spirits. One infused it with leaves to brew tea or added fruit juice to it to form a cordial. Other than on a summer's day in the field, when one might appreciate the cool water from a stream to quench one's thirst, it was rarely rated as a drink in itself and never given a thought as to its taste. It was only since his arrival in Persia that he had really thought about water as a drink in its own right. For example, this water from the consulate well had a slight saltiness from the minerals of the earth through which the waters had passed. It was a cool and refreshing taste, but it made one crave another draught.

He felt human again after the long months in the desert since he had last enjoyed the hospitality of Major Patrick Flynn, the British Consul at Bushehr, and his charming wife Elspeth. Rather than return overland by camel and face the fierce desert heat, he had chosen to travel by boat down the River Karan from Ahvaz to the coast, and thereafter by boat down the Persian Gulf from Abadan back to Bushehr. Even so, it had involved many weeks of uncomfortable travelling. It had been over 120 degrees Fahrenheit in his cabin on the primitive sailing craft in which he had taken passage. He had, thus, forsaken the mattress of his cot in favour of a bedroll on deck where he had benefited from the refreshing cool of the evening breeze. However, during the day, even the shade of the deck awning had not been of great comfort from the harsh summer sun.

Peter suspected that his fellow guests at the consulate, Admiral Slade and Assistant District Superintendent Symonds, would also have enjoyed a less than comfortable voyage, despite the relative luxury of the steamship that had brought them to Bushehr from Bandar Abbas a week earlier. He had only met them briefly on his arrival before being ushered to his quarters for a well-earned bath and rest from his journey, but was looking forward to meeting them again that evening over drinks and dinner. He checked the clock and recognised that he still had a full half hour before he would need to dress for dinner.

Although he had not previously met either Slade or Symonds, naturally he had heard of Rear Admiral Sir John Edmond Warre Slade KCIE, KCVO. Sir John was a good friend of his father. He knew nothing of Symonds, other than that he had formerly been an officer of the Indian Police, but was now working for the Indian Secret Service. Flynn, however, he had met on his arrival in Persia the year before. Lately an officer in the 91st Punjabis, a Light Infantry regiment of the Indian Army, Flynn had been transferred to the Indian Political Department some three years earlier. He was a very jovial Irishman whose charm and bonhomie were perhaps slightly exaggerated in a design to mask his acute intellect. Peter had thought him a huge source of knowledge and practical common sense ever since his arrival in Persia. It had been at Flynn's suggestion that he had bribed the Bakhtiari tribe to refrain from causing damage to the APOC oil pipelines.

Peter lay on his bed and picked up one of the bundles of mail he had collected at the consulate at Ahvaz, on his way back to Abadan. One of the many hardships he endured on this assignment was the irregular access to mail from home. Despite the length of the boat journey from Abadan, he had yet to complete reading every letter and he was deliberately ignoring that from Gieves & Company, his tailors in Portsmouth. There were several from Mutti, a few from Papa and one each from his brother Richard and cousin Elizabeth. Richard seemed in better spirits. After surviving the sinking of his submarine, he had spent several torrid months under the command of a bullying captain in another submarine. Now, it seemed, he was to have his own command at last. The news reminded him of his own short time in *D2* and he mourned the death of her captain. Johnson had been a decent chap.

However, the one letter he wished to read again was written in a large, round hand and postmarked from Marton. It was one of many he had received from Alice since leaving England. Like many from his mother, it complained about the infrequency of his replies and the time it took to receive them, despite the regularity of mail services via the Suez Canal. It was easier to explain the delays in responding to letters on this assignment. Quite truthfully he was able to say that he was not often in Tehran as he was exploring the rest of the vast country.

Looking back over his previous mission playing the part of a German spy, Peter realised how much more he was genuinely enjoying this new assignment. Despite the disguises he had employed, not just as Doctor

Pilven, but as an Armenian horse trader and once even as a holy man, he had felt this mission to be more honest somehow. It was simpler to collect information for the Indian Political Department than to play the role of a double agent. Moreover, it had been easy to be caught up in the romance of his situation. Life in the desert was quite basic and the principal aim was often to overcome the elements. This was a bond he shared with other travellers, including the local tribes, and politics seemed irrelevant. Many nights he had lived under the stars enjoying the warmth of a camp fire, the company of his fellow male companions and the entertainment of their fireside stories. It had given him genuine pleasure to repay their comradeship by doing what little he could for the sick in their tribes and villages. Until the past few weeks, he had sometimes speculated that he could live out his days this way. Then, the letters from home, and especially those from Alice, had made him think again.

It had been well over a year since he had said farewell to Alice, and if he was honest with himself, he had often gone several days without thinking of her when in the desert. Nevertheless, her letters always had the effect of jolting him back, both to think of her and to reflect on his future with her. He had never enjoyed a serious relationship with a woman and nor had he considered the possibility of marriage, but he increasingly found himself in a quandary. Each time he had returned to the civilisation of the embassy or one or other of the consulates and received the latest batch of mail from her, he had found himself considering their relationship more seriously.

There was no doubt that Alice was a fetching woman. Interestingly, Richard had said much the same thing after standing her and Elizabeth tea when they had been down in London. But Alice was not just good looking. She was highly intelligent and well educated, too. Her conversation was lively and Peter liked the fact that she had her own opinions and was willing to challenge him on his own. Perhaps her views on women's rights were a bit outspoken and ahead of the time, but he could see her point. Since he had introduced her to Elizabeth at Easter the year before, the two women seemed to have formed a close bond. After the failure of the Government to pass the Conciliation Bill the previous May, Alice wrote that she was now devoting herself to the cause of obtaining the vote for women and, reading between the lines, Peter suspected she had become a militant. That would be Elizabeth's influence. She had always been a wildcat. He suspected Alice might offend certain members of high society, but thanks to his father, he had sufficient means not to have to care about the opinions of his betters. But a man must work and he could not see Alice fitting into the circuit of the Diplomatic Corps. If he were to marry Alice, he would in any case wish to give up the life of a secret agent. Perhaps he would go to medical school, he pondered, but then again he did not have much talent for the sciences. Maybe he could learn to run the estate to support his father if Richard intended to continue long term his career in the navy.

No, his future was not the problem. He did not know how to recognise love and, therefore, was not sure whether or not he was actually in love. Certainly, he had felt hugely attracted to Alice in his last few weeks at Marton Hall and thought he might even be head over heels in love with her. Her letters to him were passionate and he had responded in kind. However, increasingly when he thought deeply on the subject, a nagging doubt had started to envelop him. Was he being false to her in the expressions of endearment he used to her in his letters? If he was honest, and he was when such doubts entered his mind, the long separation in time and distance was not making his heart grow fonder. He enjoyed the freedom that his bachelor status offered him to do as he pleased, but he also enjoyed the thought that he had somebody at home awaiting his return. Then, as he read her letter to him again, the doubts seemed to evaporate and he yearned to be in her company once more.

He roused himself from his thoughts as he realised dinner was fast approaching. Carefully, he packed away his letters and dressed quickly, a habit he had never lost from his days at Charterhouse. He had some difficulty in tying his tie on account of his bushy beard, but then again, he thought with some amusement, who is going to see that I've made a hash of it? He longed to rid himself of the thing, but no Mussulman would be without a beard and he still did not know what disguises he might yet have to adopt over the coming months.

On entering the main living room of Flynn's house, he was pleased to note that he was not the last to arrive, despite his tardiness and enforced haste. Flynn was dressed in his old 91st Punjabi mess dress, the typically drab jacket being brightened only by the scarlet facings of the cuffs and collar. In the army it was customary for majors and above, or 'field officers', to wear spurs with their mess dress. However, the 91st were considered as Light Infantry and, accordingly, Flynn was not wearing spurs, since no Light Infantry officer rode on horseback when their men had to walk. Slade, on the other hand, had opted for the informality of a white civilian dinner jacket, following the lead of the Prince of Wales. Mrs Flynn had already excused herself in order to allow Flynn and his guests to talk freely, so the only guest outstanding was Symonds. Peter accepted a glass of whisky from the Indian Army steward and joined his host and fellow guest standing before the wall-length set of bookcases dominating the room.

Slade opened the conversation by mocking Peter gently. 'My goodness, Miller, you're a fearsome looking chap with that beard. I almost took you for a Talib tribesman. By comparison, I feel clean shaven. Don't you find it a bit hot, man?' Slade, too, wore a beard, but more in the style of the King.

'Hot it may be, sir, but it helps keep the soup off my shirt front. You may yet have cause to be thankful for it before your return to England.'

'Quite. I've just been admiring Major Flynn's library. It really is a splendid collection of reference works on the region, but I see you take an interest in Africa too, Flynn. I am, of course, familiar with Churchill's *The River Wars* and some of Burton's works on his travels down the Nile, but you seem to have everything he ever wrote. Are you an admirer, Flynn?'

'Well, I am and I'm not, sir,' Flynn replied. 'It's down to my dear old Ma bein' a distant relation of his. She will insist on buying me a few of his books every birthday. Quite frankly, sir, I haven't read the half of them. However, I have found the records of his travels in the Indus and Syria quite useful. Long ago, this part of the world was conquered and ruled by the Assyrians. Now that book you have your finger on there, sir, is a bit more up to date and useful on the country.'

Slade picked out one of the books and examined its spine.

'So, what have we here, Flynn? *Syria: The Desert and the Sown* by Gertrude Bell. My goodness! It's an unusual book to be written by a woman.'

'Ah, she's a remarkable woman all right ... and damned useful to the Political, too. She knows what's what and keeps her ear to the ground. And what would be your taste in literature, sir?'

'I tend towards European literature. Naturally, as the son of a clergyman and Fellow of All Souls, I enjoy the works of Trollope. Now there was a man with a beard to rival your own, Miller. I also like to try my hand with certain German and Italian texts in the original language. It keeps the brain going. What about you, Flynn?'

'Ah well, German is a language I've never thought of taking up. It sounds too harsh for my ear, so I cannot offer you anything in that line, but

I think I can lay my hands on something Italian to amuse you this next few weeks. Now where is it?'

As Flynn searched the bookshelves, they were joined by the former policeman, Symonds. Symonds was quite unlike any policeman Peter had ever seen. For a start, he was short for a policeman at only five feet six inches tall. He was completely clean-shaven, without whiskers or long sideburns, and with blond hair and bright-blue eyes. More unusually still, he was extremely attractive, but effete with it. Peter wondered how well he had fitted in with the Indian Police. Flynn paused his search temporarily to greet him.

'Ah, there you are, Symonds. Can I offer you something to drink? A glass of whisky, perhaps?'

'I don't drink spirits, thank you, Flynn, but I would be glad of a sherbert.'

Flynn tried hard to mask his disappointment and, after signalling to the steward to fetch Symonds his drink, he returned to his book search.

'Now, yes. There we have it. I've always had a hankerin' to learn Italian, but have yet to make a start. Help yourself to any of these, Admiral.'

Slade peered at the books proffered and was pleasantly surprised to find a number of great works of Italian literature.

'My, Flynn! I am spoiled for choice. I am not surprised to find Machiavelli's *The Prince*, but Dante's *Divine Comedy*, Manzoni's *The Betrothed* and Boccaccio's *Decameron*, too. You have not selected the easiest of works to read. What about you, Miller, do you read Italian? I seem to recollect your father married a Swiss. Have you learned any of the language from your mother?'

'Indeed I have, Sir John. I am fortunate to speak French and German fluently, too. However, I confess that even so, I would find Major Flynn's great works hard going in the original text. Major Flynn, you might have found it easier to have set yourself the task of taking up the Twelve Labours of Hercules.'

'Oh well, I'll mebbe get around to it one day when I've a little less on my hands. Now, gentlemen, since we're all here, I suggest we go through to dinner and we can talk through our very own Labours of Bushehr.'

CHAPTER 26

During the progress of dinner Peter became more and more intrigued by Symonds. Brought up in naval and army messes for much of their careers, Slade and Flynn were easy company and lively conversationalists, but Symonds was clearly discomfited by the occasion. It was only once the dishes had been cleared from the table and the stewards had withdrawn, that he seemed to find his voice.

'Admiral, I have been instructed by the Indian Political Department, whose responsibility it is to administer British interests in Persia, to co-operate with you and Lieutenant Miller. I understand my brief is to help you discover and avert any operation by a foreign power to disrupt oil production in Persia. So it would assist me if you could explain, given that Persia's oil has been around for centuries, why the navy's sudden interest in it now? As far as I know, the Persians have only seen its seepages of use to caulk their boats and to bind bricks?'

Slade hesitated before replying, but when he did so, he adopted the patient tone of a master replying to his pupil's stupid question. 'To fuel our ships, of course. It's lighter and easier to store than coal, but if we are to invest in a major programme to convert our ships to burn oil rather than coal, then we need a long-term and secure source of supply for oil.'

'But, am I not right that up to now you have procured your oil from the Burmah Oil Company in Rangoon? And I understand Burmah are already investors in the Persian oil fields. I am interested to know why the Admiralty finds it necessary to intervene now.' Symonds seemed quite persistent.

Slade pushed away his port and folded his napkin carefully. 'Very well, Symonds, but I warn you, it is a long story and goes back to 1901. It's down to geo-politics. Not something of a strong suit, I'm afraid.'

'Really? I believe you to be too modest, Admiral. I understood you headed the navy's intelligence department until 1907.' Peter could see that Slade was surprised by how well Symonds was informed. Slade shot a look of warning at Flynn. Flynn merely moved his chair back to stretch out and Symonds leaned forward, as if keen not to miss a single word.

Slade recovered and continued. 'Flynn, you can help me out where necessary as you're the politico. I presume, Symonds, you are already aware that in 1901 an English entrepreneur, William Knox D'Arcy, purchased a sixty-year concession from Shah Muzzafar al-Din to explore and drill for oil across three quarters of the country.'

'I wasn't, as it happens, so please go on, Admiral.'

'Oh. Well, as I suppose often happens in such situations, the venture ran into many difficulties, including the terrain, fierce temperatures, hostility to foreigners, lack of technical skills and feuds between the many tribes. That sort of thing.'

'Truly, there's nothin' the local tribes round here like more than an excuse fer some local feudin', sir,' Flynn interjected.

'Quite. Anyway, by 1904 D'Arcy was finally successful in establishing a viable oil well, but he was heavily indebted and on the verge of bankruptcy. The Foreign Office had, naturally, provided political support, but no finance, you see. Nevertheless, both the Foreign Office and the Admiralty were concerned that D'Arcy might be forced to sell his interest in the concession to a foreign power such as Germany or Russia, or even lose the concession altogether. Together we persuaded the Government to establish a syndicate to save D'Arcy's venture, and Burmah Oil agreed to finance the scheme. Are you with me so far, Symonds?'

'Yes, thank you. Now I understand the reasons for Burmah Oil's interest. Please continue.'

'If you're sure? The syndicate was floated on the Stock Exchange in 1909 as the Anglo-Persian Oil Company, or APOC, after making a major oil strike on the plain of Maidan-e-Naftan. Burmah Oil became the majority shareholder and established a refinery on the island of Abadan in the estuary of the Tigris, Euphrates and Karun rivers, on the border with Mesopotamia.'

Slade's discourse was interrupted by Flynn breaking wind. 'I beg yer pardon gentlemen. The food was mebbe a little rich fer me. Do continue, Admiral.'

'Thank you, Flynn. As I was saying … now where was I? Ah, yes. The new refinery was not a great success. Despite the backing of Burmah Oil and the public financing through shares, the project ran into difficulties in extracting and refining the oil, and by the end of 1912, had run out of working capital. However, we at the Admiralty had anticipated this and developed our own contingency plans. We planned to persuade the

Treasury to become the main and controlling shareholder in APOC to safeguard the supply of oil for the Royal Navy.'

'I doubt the General Staff would have had the vision to persuade the Treasury to invest two million pounds in an oil field,' Flynn added .

'Two million pounds!' Symonds gasped. 'But that's—'

'£2,200,000 to be precise,' Slade continued. 'It would give HMG a 51% controlling share in APOC. Churchill, as First Lord of the Admiralty, presented the bill on 17 June to obtain parliamentary approval for the deal. In return for the investment, HMG will have the right to appoint two directors onto the Board with the power to veto matters adversely affecting Admiralty contracts or issues of major foreign or political policy. Are you with me so far, Symonds?'

'Indeed, Admiral. It is a bold plan.'

'The crux of the matter, though, is we knew that before HMG would sign the deal, it was going to require some assurances that neither Russia nor Germany could sour the deal with the Shah. This is why Miller was sent here and he can explain that more. My role, overtly, is to check on the technicalities of maintaining a stable supply to the navy, even in the event of war. That said, in the light of recent developments, I am on hand, too, to act for the Admiralty in loco parentis to support Miller and Flynn in any way necessary. You can explain, Miller.'

'Thank you, sir,' Peter replied. 'For the past year, the major and I have been keeping our ears to the ground for any hint of foreign interest in the local oil production. So far, I'm glad to say, it has been fairly quiet. I've set up a good network of informers in the region and had hoped my assignment would be over within a few weeks. However, within a week of Mister Churchill's speech, we received word that Germany had sent a military expedition to Baghdad. Clearly the Wihelmstrasse has recognised the threat a secure supply of oil to the Royal Navy would pose to its own Imperial German Navy and quickly acted accordingly. We understand the German expedition is even now in northern Persia.'

Symonds said nothing for a while. He seemed to be digesting the information whilst drinking his water slowly. Peter was surprised at Symonds's apparent equanimity. At length, he seemed to have made a decision and he broke the bated silence.

'Admiral, I am not at all convinced that the sudden appearance of a German expedition to the north is linked to your mission to finalise the investment by HMG in the Persian oil fields.'

Peter noted that neither Slade nor Flynn spoke. They seemed content to allow Symonds the floor.

'You will no doubt be fully aware of Biswas's attempt on Lord Hardinge last Christmas.'

Slade nodded silently.

'Fortunately, the Viceroy was not severely injured. However, on receipt of intelligence to suggest the plot was masterminded from a revolutionary headquarters in California, we sent one of our Canadian colleagues to investigate. He obtained sufficient evidence to confirm that the plot was part of campaign to spread sedition throughout India by a series of assassinations, bombings and armed robberies. The American end of the operation is now led by a Lala Har Dyal. Sir Charles Cleveland, my Head of the Indian Secret Service, is concerned that such a campaign could spread like hidden fire and undermine our hold over the country ... Forgive me, Sir John, but please let me continue and I will soon come to the main point.'

Slade had started to make a comment and Peter was surprised by Symonds' forcefulness and confidence to cut off a former DNI. Symonds's former rank of Assistant District Superintendent was, after all, a fairly junior one. Once again Peter was reminded not to judge a book by its cover.

'Thanks to Hopkinson's investigation – sorry, Admiral, William Hopkinson is a former inspector in the Calcutta Police, now working for the Immigration Branch of the Canadian Department of the Interior – and us, of course. He is the man we sent to San Francisco. Anyway, thanks to Hopkinson's investigation, we learned of a plan to send a shipment of arms from America to India for revolutionary purposes. The ship is carrying half a million revolvers and one hundred thousand rifles. That shipment was paid for and the ship chartered through the German Military Attaché in Washington!'

Symonds paused to allow the import of his latest statement to sink in. Peter could see that Slade was just as shocked by the news, but Flynn seemed to take it in his stride and only he spoke.

'I'm thinkin' that wouldn't be all. Ye may have a few further surprises for us to explain yer presence here, Symonds.'

'Indeed I do, Major. We had a man on board the freighter, the *Bayern*, and he tipped us off that the arms were transferred to a steamer, the *Batik*, off Java. That steamer is due into Bushehr in just under a week.'

This time Symonds did allow Slade to interrupt.

'I presume the Royal Navy has been alerted to intercept this steamer, or is it your intention to allow it to be landed?'

'You are quite correct, Admiral. HMS *Surprise* was on her way home from the China Station, but has orders to board her, seize her cargo and arrest the crew.'

'I assume you have considered allowing the ship to dock and then observin' the composition of the welcomin' party?' This time it was Flynn asking the question.

'A fair point, major, but it would be at the risk of some secret signal, either being made or not being made, to alert the shore-side party of our intervention. We even considered allowing the cargo to be disembarked and then tracking its movement. However, this is too large a shipment to risk it reaching the end-users and I know very well from your despatches how partisan the local Swedish Police is.'

'Swedish Police, you say?'

'Yes, Sir John.' Symonds replied. 'Perhaps Major Flynn would be the more competent to explain.'

'By all means, Symonds, although it's a gendarmerie rather than a police force as we know it. Admiral, it's a sort of mercenary force the Shah has hired to make the highways safe for civilians and trade caravans. As ye may well know, sir, the country is divided into two spheres of influence: the Russians control the north and we the south. Naturally, neither of us was that willin' for a national force to police each other's sphere, so we agreed to the Shah callin' in a neutral country. Shah Ahmed opted for Italy, but we didna' much fancy givin' them any more power, so we settled on Sweden.'

'Eminently sensible, I should say,' Slade replied.

'Ah well, the Swedes have been here a couple of years. They're a fine bunch, headed by a general in Tehran. They've sworn an oath of allegiance to the Shah, but they have na' renounced their Swedish citizenship. Technically, they're not subject to his laws. The nearest regiment is based in Shiraz where they have a school for native NCOs and gendarmes. In all, the force comprises about 3,000 native troops headed by fewer than forty Swedes. The trouble is, sir, they're not up to much and possibly worse. Only last year the British Consul at Shiraz was shot and trapped under his horse a while, and with no sign of a gendarme coming to his assistance.

But for him havin' an escort of Indian Cavalry, I wouldn't have fancied his chances of survival.'

'But that's outrageous!' Slade exclaimed.

'Aye, well that's as mebbe, but the upshot is that HMG and the Russians have agreed to part-fund the force. I've heard it said we may stump up £100,000 this year and to my certain knowledge we've already funded the purchase of some artillery in Shiraz. My fear, though, Admiral, is that they may be a bit biased in their approach, like, and even pro-German. I've heard reports that some of the officers are looking at stirrin' up trouble between us and the Russian Cossacks to turn the Shah against us. It's only rumours, mind, but my sources are generally right in these matters.'

Slade picked up his port and sipped it in reflection, leaving Symonds to resume his briefing.

'Thank you, Major. So you see, gentlemen, it is possible that the sudden appearance of a German expedition in the north may be related to gun-running rather than oil contracts. There may also be an even more sinister explanation.' He paused for dramatic effect, but nobody gave him the satisfaction of an interruption this time.

'Early this year we believe the Germans sponsored the coup in Constantinople. We know for a fact that the mob was led by three armed men close to Baron von Wangenheim, the German Ambassador. And, of course, the new man in power is Major Enver, a former military attaché to Berlin. It would not surprise me if the Germans now plan on stirring things up, not just in Persia, but right through the Near East and India.'

'The devils!' Flynn exclaimed. 'A revolution in India would be bad enough, but we've met with the like before. Such a thing as you suggest would be outrageous. Now just how would they go about a thing like that?'

'Calm down, Major. I only posed it as one of a number of possibilities. I confess I don't know what is going on. Nonetheless, Sir Charles wants me to pre-empt the likelihood and seek out the lie of the land. Although this naturally comes under the jurisdiction of New Delhi, London has already agreed that I might enlist your help, Miller.'

'And just how might I help?' Peter asked.

'I would like to take advantage of your experience in undercover operations and your network of informers in the region. Both will be invaluable. Firstly, I would like you to arrange that we discover the composition of the German party in Shiraz and its movements. I hope you will then share with me any information your observers obtain. Finally, I request you join me in questioning the crew of the steamer bringing in the arms as my Farsi is not yet up to the mark. Depending on what we learn, it will dictate what we do from then on. Might I also suggest you arrange the continued surveillance of the oil pipeline, just in case the situation is simpler than my suspicions suggest?'

'I will be happy to assist where I can. I can see the potential cross-over with my responsibilities to the Admiralty.'

Peter turned to Slade. 'Sir, it had been my plan to accompany you in person to the oil plain, but under the circumstances might I be excused? You will in any case be under the Shah's protection.'

'But of course. In any case, I think I might take advantage of the presence of the *Surprise* to continue my journey up the coast. I will prevail upon the captain to provide an escort of blue-jackets for my journey to the interior. The poor lads will have to delay their return to England for a few more weeks yet. Flynn, I will just need to send a coded telegram to London.'

Slade chuckled and rubbed his hands in glee. 'It's all dashed exciting. It takes me back to my days in the Intelligence Department.'

CHAPTER 27

The Indian Secret Service's intelligence had been entirely accurate and HMS *Surprise* had successfully intercepted the *Batik* before she had even entered the Persian Gulf. *Surprise* was a cruiser in name only. Being lightly armed, she was more suited to despatch work and virtually obsolete. Indeed, she was to be paid off on her return to England. Even so, her five-inch guns and quick-firing six-pounders had been enough of a threat to persuade the crew of the *Batik* to surrender without a shot being fired and to sail the ship under *Surprise*'s escort to Bushehr.

Peter had been surprised by her captain's appearance. Commander Archibald Percival appeared as a tired, grey-haired and bearded, old man, rather than as an active officer of the Royal Navy. Peter had expected a more youthful officer to be in command. Clearly, three years on the China station had told on his health. Still, there had been a keenness in his eyes as he had introduced himself and he had been happy to offer any help he could to search the *Batik*.

Another surprise to Peter had been Symonds's refusal of a firearm for the boarding of the *Batik*. Whereas Peter had gratefully accepted the loan of one of the navy's Webley revolvers, Symonds had merely borrowed one of the seamen's clubs. Whilst Symonds met with his fellow Indian Secret Service agent, disguised as a lascar seaman, Peter waited in the shade of the awning spread over the fore-deck. The August temperature was dropping as the afternoon wore on, but it was still murderously hot. A gentle breeze from the west fanning him and all on board rendered life more tolerable. He watched *Surprise* swing at her anchor in response to the breeze, about fifty yards off the starboard beam, closer inshore. She, like the *Batik*, was anchored off the entrance to Bushehr, surrounded by dozens of dhows plying their trade. The crew of the *Batik* were sitting cross-legged, under the after section of the awning, as a sullen crowd under the watchful eyes of the *Surprise*'s armed blue-jackets. It did not take more than fifteen minutes before Symonds returned with his colleague in tow. Several of the crew shouted insults as the Indian Secret Service agent passed by. Some made to rise before the blue-jackets made it clear that

174

they should remain seated. Others spat in his direction. The former lascar seaman gave them a sideways glance, but otherwise made no reaction.

'Miller, thank you for your patience. May I introduce my colleague, Constable Dubey? Perhaps you might summon a couple of your sailors to open up the access to the main hold and to accompany us.'

A few minutes later, the party of five descended into the hold. They were immediately hit by a wall of heat that made them all instantly recoil before they continued into the stygian darkness. Using their flashlights they examined the cargo within. With the exception of one section, the space was piled high with crates marked as containing machine tools and kitchen utensils.

'It seems we were lucky with our timing, Miller.'

'How so, Symonds? I wonder why they didn't fill the hold completely.'

'That's just my point. Accordingly to Dubey, there was a change of plan. Instead of off-loading the cargo in Bushehr, the Germans intended to transfer these crates to a schooner and several dhows so that the cargo might be landed in smaller quantities – both to present less suspicion and spread the eggs over more than one basket. Dubey says that several cases had already been off-loaded to a schooner shortly before your warship caught up with her. Let's have a look at what we have. Would you two gentlemen mind opening up these cases for us?' Symonds handed each of the sailors a crowbar.

Initially, the crates seemed innocent enough and their contents to match the descriptions printed on the outside. However, it did not take much probing to discover rows and rows of rifles and hand-guns laid out beneath the upper layers of the tools and utensils. All had been carefully oiled to prevent them from rusting in the hot and humid atmosphere of the hold.

'My word, Symonds!' Peter exclaimed. 'There must be tens of thousands of weapons in this hold alone. Your intelligence is right on the button.'

'I fear so. Thank God we caught up with this lot in time. But it looks as if the ammunition has already been landed. Half a million rounds in the wrong hands would still constitute a nasty problem.'

'Can Constable Dubey not offer any information on the location of the missing cargo?'

'I'm afraid not, Miller. All he knows is that it was taken off by a schooner three nights ago and a dhow was due to meet the ship the evening it was intercepted by the *Surprise*. If you don't mind me saying, Miller, it's a daft name for a ship. It invites all sorts of puns.'

'I cannot say how ships come by their names, daft or otherwise. So what are your plans now?'

'Firstly, I think we should inspect the other holds and check what else might be missing. Then you can help me question the crew. Most of them seem Indian, so my Hindi and Urdu will see me through, but I don't speak Persian. Finally, I want to search the master's cabin for any papers that might offer up a clue as to the intended recipient of this cargo. It might help us to establish the current whereabouts of the missing ammunition. Is that all right with you?'

'Absolutely. Let's get to it.'

****

Peter watched the sun begin to disappear beyond the horizon of Persia off the starboard bow. It was at that point where it seemed to be at its brightest, bathing the land and sea before it in a beautiful, golden glow. Peter had seen many such sunsets before and knew that it would soon be dark, the evening sunlight flaring like a match about to be spent. Symonds was in the master's cabin reading several papers they had found together. The papers were in Urdu so Peter had not been of much help. One of the sailors shared his appreciation of the view as they watched from the bows of the *Batik*. Within a couple of minutes the sun had gone and it was suddenly dark.

'There's something odd about the sunsets in the tropics ain't there, sir?'

'Really? How so?'

'Well there ain't no dusk is there? One minute there's the sun and the next it's as black as a coal hole. I've seen the same in the West Indies. Now it's not like that off China or back home is it, sir?'

'I suppose you have a point there. Although I've never been to China, nor the West Indies for that matter. How long since you were last in England?'

'Nigh on three years now, sir. Smoke, sir?' The sailor proffered a packet of cigarettes, but Peter declined the offer. 'Don't get me wrong. I've enjoyed the China Station, but I reckons it's time I was back with me family.'

'You're married then?'

'Yeah. We've two kids now, too. I ain't met Rosie yet, on account that she weren't born when I left, but I ... You 'ear summit, sir?'

'I think I did. It came from down aft. I'll come with you.'

The blue-jacket tossed his cigarette over the side and unslung his rifle before setting off cautiously down the port waist of the ship. Peter followed him and drew his revolver. Suddenly they heard a shout from the stern. 'A-laar—' but the cry of alarm was quickly cut off and followed by the sound of running feet.

'Jesus!' the sailor said out loud, but Peter had worked it out for himself. He fired one round from his pistol into the air to warn the other blue-jackets and, he hoped, the crew of the nearby *Surprise*.

With the alarm sounded, the boarders began to howl and shriek. It was a frightening noise in the darkness. The blue-jacket immediately kneeled and took aim down the waist with his rifle. Within seconds, a mob of cut-throats carrying swords and knives appeared from the stern into the light of the ship's superstructure. The narrowness of the waist forced them into single file and the blue-jacket fired. He missed the first man, but hit the one behind him. The mob wavered, giving the sailor time to reload. He fired again and this time hit the first man, causing his colleagues to retreat back down the waist.

'Come this way,' Peter shouted. He opened one of the superstructure screen doors and almost dragged the sailor backwards through it. Inside the ship, Peter began to apply all the clips to the door and not just the one he had opened to gain access. 'This will slow them down,' he said.

'Mebbe,' the sailor replied. 'But let me, sir.' He barged Peter out of his way and picked up a metal tube clamped to the bulkhead. Placing one end over the end of each clip, he heaved with all his strength on the other end. 'You see, sir?' he panted. 'A bit of leverage will make it harder for them to undo.'

Peter didn't know what to do. He thought he ought to warn the blue-jackets guarding the captured crew, but he also needed to visit the bridge to check that the *Surprise* understood what was happening. *And what about Symonds?*

His indecision was interrupted by the sound of metallic objects banging on the clips the other side of the door. At the same time he could hear one of the doors on the starboard side being unclipped. 'Leave that,' he shouted. 'Go to the starboard side and hold them off as long as you can. I'm going to the bridge.'

Peter ran down the corridor and found the stairway leading up to the bridge. Before he sprinted up the steps, he had the presence of mind to shout a warning. 'Hold your fire.' It was as well he had as, on mounting

177

the bridge, he came across two extremely nervous blue-jackets with rifles aimed at him. 'It's all right,' he reassured them, conscious that with his long, bushy beard, he probably resembled how they imagined a pirate might look. 'Can either of you operate a signal lamp?' One of the sailors nodded and pointed to the badge of two crossed flags on his right arm. He was a signalman. Just then they heard a rifle shot down below.

'That's one of your colleagues keeping the angry mob at bay. You ...' he pointed at the signal man's colleague, '...keep an eye on this stairway and the ladder up to the port bridge wing. We'll watch the starboard side.'

He indicated for the signalman to follow him to the starboard bridge wing as another shot rang out below. 'Call up the *Surprise*. Tell them we're under attack and need help. Once they've acknowledged, help your friend keep the bridge secure. Got that?'

'Aye aye, sir. But where are you going, sir?'

'I'm going back below to help your mates down there. Now hurry with that signal.'

With his left hand clinging to the rail of the twin stairway leading from the bridge below, and his right arm at full stretch, pointing downwards, Peter gingerly descended the steps. He heard another shot and a series of screams. All the hairs of his body tingled at the sound and he fought to stop bile rising from his stomach into his dry mouth. He tried to remember the geography of the ship. He now recalled that the master's cabin was below and forward of the stairway, so why had Symonds not come out on hearing the first shots? The crew's accommodation and the officer's saloon were in the after-part of the superstructure. Three blue-jackets were keeping the ship's crew prisoner in the saloon. There should have been another four blue-jackets on the upper deck and a petty officer. Including the two sailors on the bridge, that made a party of ten armed men, plus himself and Symonds. He had no idea of how many boarders they were facing.

Peter reached the bottom of the stairway and called softly to Symonds, but there was no response. Aft he could hear a commotion, but no more shots. Should he stay put and await reinforcements from the *Surprise* or spy out the situation aft? It seemed safe here after all. He could hear his quick pulse in his head and he forced himself to take long and slow breaths. Aft the screams had stopped, but he could still hear several voices. He leant against the stairway and wondered what Papa would have done. He immediately realised the absurdity of the question. He had no choice. Papa would go aft.

Just as his resolved was stiffened, he heard a shot from the bridge. 'Are you all right up there?' he called. A moment later he heard the reply.

'No problems, sir. Just a couple of the black, heathen bastards tried to come up on the port side, sir. We've sent them on their way, don't you worry. Higgins 'as got through to the *Surprise*, sir, an' a boat-load of reinforcements is on the way, as well, sir.'

As stealthily as his leather-soled boots would allow him, Peter crept aft down a passageway, either side of which were offices and storerooms. Ahead he could see a cross passage off which would lead the corridor to the accommodation. Just before he reached the cross passage he refilled the empty chamber of his revolver. Every round might count shortly, he thought. He could feel a draught coming towards him.

He rounded the corner into the cross passage and was sickened by the sight before him. The sailor with whom he had shared the sunset lay in a bloody heap, his head almost decapitated and with multiple, bloody wounds to the neck and chest. Somebody, in his impatience to retrieve the rifle from the corpse, had hacked off the right arm below the elbow and it lay a few feet from its host. Peter thought of the child that would never know her father and he snapped.

He ran to his right into the passageway leading to the saloon. Ahead he could see the mob with their backs to him. Without hesitation he began shooting. The men at the back fell forward onto their comrades, causing them to surge forward, but something was preventing them going far. The mob turned and looked at him in anger, but Peter could smell fear, too. He heard somebody shout out, 'Right, lads. Time for pig sticking. Forward.' Shots rang out, but Peter could not be sure of the number due to their echo in the close quarters of the passageway. The mob began to hurry towards him and he fired again and again. This only checked the mob momentarily and one after the other they started to wail and run at him. Again he fired, but quickly ran out of ammunition. He turned and fled. He ran back up the passageway and turned left the way he had come. Then he realised his mistake. The screen door before him, leading onto the port waist, was fully clipped. Turning round, he saw that the door opposite was wide open, accounting for the draught. About a dozen of the surviving boarders were rushing through it and being pursued by two sailors armed with bayoneted rifles and a petty officer with a drawn pistol. Unfortunately, three of the mob had turned left after Peter and he was trapped.

One of the trio was a bear of a man, at least six feet eight inches tall and just about as wide. His turban suggested he might be a Sikh. He twirled a small, blood-stained axe in his right hand and then tossed it to his left to repeat the twirling. Peter looked up in fear at the man's face. The ogre smiled to reveal two of his left upper teeth missing. Peter threw his revolver at the man's face and tried to duck to his left and past him, but somebody tripped him and he hit the deck hard. Just as he fell, he heard a strange cry. He rolled further to his left, expecting a dagger in his back and saw a whirl of arms and legs above him. As he tried to crawl away on his back, he realised that it was Symonds attacking the two smaller men who had only seconds before trapped him.

Symonds was engaged in a style of fighting Peter had never before witnessed. He was wielding the seaman's club and at the same time pirouetting on one leg whilst kicking out with the other. Within seconds, both his opponents were lying senseless on the deck, but that still left the ogre. He struck out with his axe and Symonds parried with his club and simultaneously kicked the ogre's left knee with his right foot. The giant buckled slightly and, like lightning, Symonds shifted his weight onto his right leg, twisted and kicked with his left foot against his opponent's chest and right shoulder. However, it had little effect on the Sikh and he responded quickly. He raised the axe, still embedded in the club of Symonds, and in doing so unbalanced Symonds. With his left fist the Sikh punched Symonds hard in the head, sending him reeling against the bulkhead behind him, but the club came free in his hand.

The Sikh leered at Symonds, wolfishly, and repeated his trick of twirling the axe in both hands before pouncing on Symonds. Symonds was too quick. He ducked under the arc of the swinging axe and jabbed the club into the stomach of the Sikh before landing a vicious blow on his left elbow. Peter heard a gut-wrenching crack and felt sure that Symonds must have broken a bone in his enemy's arm. The Sikh roared with pain and anger, lurched to his left and tried to land the axe in his puny opponent's skull. Peter overcame his shock and began to reload his revolver. Again Symonds avoided the lurching Sikh and attempted an uppercut with his club against the Sikh's jaw as he swayed out of the reach of the swinging axe. The giant stepped back half a pace and leaned backwards at the same time. Somehow the club missed him, but in the same movement he kicked upwards and his longer reach was enough to catch Symonds squarely in the groin. Symonds collapsed forward and the back of his head and neck was at the mercy of the axe being aimed at him. Peter didn't finish loading his revolver. He aimed and shot two rounds into the face of the giant. The force of the almost half-inch-calibre bullets was nearly enough to lift the Sikh's giant frame off the deck. His head whipped up and Peter saw its contents splatter against the screen door in the midst of a fountain of blood. The Sikh fell backwards, instantly dead, and his bloody corpse crumpled against the door and down to the deck.

The revolver suddenly felt heavy in Peter's two hands and he let it drop. He felt stupefied. It wasn't the first time he had killed a man, but he had never seen the results of a gunshot before. He was unprepared for the gore and blood that was starting to ooze down the door and bulkhead. It seemed to be everywhere and then he smelt it – a sweet smell, but somehow acrid at the same time. Never before had he experienced the smell of death. He barely had time to turn to his side before he retched uncontrollably over the deck beside him.

Symonds staggered over to him, putting his arm on Peter's right shoulder. 'Are you all right, Miller?'

'Of course I'm not all right, you bloody fool. I've just shot a man.' He felt embarrassed to have vomited in front of the policeman.

'Well, thanks. You saved my life.'

'It was more like the other way round. What was all that kicking and wielding of a club business?'

'Oh, just something some Chinese monks taught me once. It used to come in handy in a street riot occasionally in my days as a policeman. The monks call it goong foo. The dead troll there didn't seem too impressed by it.'

Peter looked at the remains of the Sikh's head and felt his stomach heave once more. 'Let's go back to *Surprise*. We both need to clean up and change. Percival's men can deal with this lot. Did you find anything useful from those papers in the master's cabin?'

'As a matter of fact I did. Wait. I think the reinforcements have arrived.' Peter could hear an officer's voice barking commands to his seamen on the deck outside. Suddenly, Symonds slapped Peter on the back and burst out laughing. 'I can honestly say, Miller, that today has been full of … *surprises*.'

CHAPTER 28

September 1913

For the umpteenth time Flynn mopped his brow. As usual, it was infernally hot, even though it had turned September, and he was concerned that his sweat would drip onto the despatch he was preparing to send to Tehran with copies to London and New Delhi. Even in the comparative shade and cool of his study the temperature was already well above 80 degrees and he knew it would reach the high 90s before long. The temperatures and lack of rain were a far cry from his native County Clare. He thought it must be at least six to eight months since it had last rained and it would probably not rain again for another month or so. *Ah well*, he thought, *as they say in the British Army, if you can't take a joke you shouldna' joined.*

Although an erudite man, he hated writing reports. His natural instinct was to tell it as it happened, but he was long enough in the tooth to recognise that honest simplicity was too dangerous in the Political. He had learned the hard way that before committing thoughts or even facts to paper, one had first to think of the interpretation that would be placed on the words. Somebody somewhere would seek to infer a different meaning to that he intended, either in the interests of personal advancement or to support a hidden agenda. However, on this occasion, Flynn was less worried about that risk. His was a story of success and every civil servant liked to be associated with success. Indeed, even though he had taken little part in the operation to intercept the *Batik*, he would attract some credit just for being the author of the report.

He wondered how Miller and Symonds were faring up north. Acting on information gleaned from papers they had discovered on the *Batik*, they had headed north to investigate further the destination of the missing cargo. Mysteriously, the schooner had disappeared without trace, but the haul of arms and ammunition was now under the control of the navy, pending the instructions he was presently seeking from his superiors.

Miller's latest communication indicated that the leader of the German party was a Wilhelm Wassmuss. He was in Shiraz, but would shortly take up the position as German Consul alongside Flynn in Bushehr. Miller had wondered if Wassmuss's presence in Persia might not be related to the attempt to import the *Batik*'s arms, but Flynn didn't believe it. It was too much of a bloody coincidence. London and Tehran were both looking into Wasmuss's background and that might shed light on his intentions.

He picked up his pen again and returned to his report. He completed it with an account of how, thanks to the assistance of *Surprise*, Admiral Slade had completed his investigations earlier than expected into the viability of the oil field on the plain of Maidan-e-Naftan. Flynn surmised that the technical problems at the Abadan refinery had been resolved. Slade had already despatched a summary of his investigation back to the Admiralty and would remain at Bushehr to await reports from Miller and Symonds.

Flynn read again his report and, satisfied that he was not laying himself or his colleagues open to any criticism, dried the ink and sealed the despatch. He checked the clock of his study and was pleased to note that it was still only quarter to ten. He had been at his desk a full three hours, but still had fifteen minutes to spare before he and Slade went down to tour the dockyard.

Outside, he could hear the commotion of several horses' hooves, waggon wheels and men shouting. He moved across to the window facing the gates of the consulate and raised the blind to observe a company of gendarmerie taking position around the compound and unlimbering a field artillery piece. To his satisfaction, one of the consulate staff had already shut and barred the compound gates, but that would not withstand an artillery shell very long. Now was not the time to wonder what was afoot. He only had time for action.

He grabbed his revolver from his desk and, quickly fastening his holster and belt, he strode out in to the hall and called for his telegraph clerk. He had only seconds to wait before he was informed that, unsurprisingly, the lines were down. Just then he heard a loud explosion from the courtyard. Taking two steps at a time, he raced up the staircase onto the landing above and, keeping himself close to the wall, he peered through the window overlooking the courtyard. As he had feared, the gates lay in tattered splinters of wood. Already his ten troopers were lined up in two ranks facing the gates with loaded rifles, aimed at whoever might be the first to dare enter the compound. Looking back into the hall below, he noted his wife being shepherded by Slade into the kitchen to the rear of the house.

He judged that there must be thirty gendarmes surrounding the consulate. With the forces under his command he could keep the gendarmerie at bay, but the field gun was a problem. Moreover, what would be the point in resistance? With the telegraph lines cut he could not summon assistance from Shiraz. If they broke out of the compound, where would they go and what was the point of remaining under siege in the compound? No, they would have to surrender, but he first needed to buy time and find out the purpose of this assault on British sovereign territory.

Calmly and slowly he descended the staircase and addressed those of the staff who had by now assembled in the hall.

'Ladies and gentlemen, I have no idea what this buffonery is about, but I advise you all to stay calm. Whilst I go out and have a few words with the fellas out there, perhaps some of you would be so kind as to start burnin' the signal books and ciphers. I have a feelin' we're about to have some uninvited visitors.'

As he stepped out of the front door, he felt a surge of pride in the Indian troopers so neatly paraded to his left. He had no doubt that they were more than a match for the rag-tailed bunch of heathens outside the compound walls. On cue, a scruffy native officer of the gendarmerie hesitantly stepped through the remains of the gates, waving a white flag. The front rank of the troopers immediately came to the present in unison without the need for an order and the unfortunate-looking gendarmerie officer eyed them cautiously. Still watching them carefully, he shuffled over to Flynn, stopped ten yards short of him, saluted lazily and addressed Flynn in Persian.

'Sir, I am here to demand the surrender of you and your staff.'

'The hell you are!' Flynn thundered in reply and in fluent Farsi. 'I have only to give the word and you will have five rounds through your skull within a second. What's the meaning of this outrage?'

He had the satisfaction of seeing the man's knees buckle for a moment and enjoyed the gendarme's discomfort.

'Sir, may I remind you that I have come under a flag of truce. You cannot fire on me.'

The man was trembling and Flynn could not help but feel sorry for him, but now was not the time to show such a weakness. He switched to English.

'I don't give a damn about your dirty piece of white cloth. May I remind you that you and your men have just made an unprovoked attack on British sovereign territory, and you now stand on British soil without my invitation? I give you ten seconds to withdraw before I order my men to open fire.'

The poor Persian clearly understood English and believed the threat. He seemed in two minds whether to flee with his tail between his legs or stick to his orders. His sense of duty must have prevailed over his lack of his courage.

'No, sir! Please! I beg you to listen. My commanding officer, Major Carlsson, will be here very shortly. If you do not surrender the consulate to him within exactly one hour from now, he will order the complete destruction of the compound, with considerable loss of life. I beg you, sir. Major Carlsson is a very ruthless man.'

Flynn noted that the gendarme continued to speak in Farsi, but saw no reason to make life any easier for him, so continued in English.

'And what would become of us, if we were to surrender? I have sufficient men and ammunition to hold you dogs at bay for days. Moreover, there's a Royal Navy cruiser out there with a bunch of sailors just beggin' for some action.'

The Persian officer failed to hide his surprise at the news of the cruiser's presence, but began to relax at the hint of terms.

'Sir, you cannot resist. You have no communications with the outside world and Major Carlsson is bringing more troops and artillery with him.'

Flynn didn't believe there was any more artillery available, but allowed the gendarme officer to continue.

'If you surrender without bloodshed, Major Carlsson guarantees nobody will come to any harm. You will merely be disarmed and taken to a place of safety whilst we search the premises.'

'Search for what man? There's no gold here for yer thievin' hands.'

'Please, sir, be reasonable. I am not permitted to say what we seek. Major Carlsson can perhaps tell you more. Whilst we await his arrival, please remain calm and pack only the most essential of luggage. Major Carlsson wishes you to travel light.'

With his courage restored and conscious of his dignity before his men, the gendarmerie officer saluted, smartly this time, turned about and marched out of the compound.

For the next twenty minutes, Flynn was a whirlwind of activity, organising the defence of the compound and burning of his ciphers and confidential papers. As a contingency, he also asked his wife to pack his and her baggage. When all these activities were under way he called a council of war with Slade.

'Admiral, as I see it, we either stand firm and await help, or we get you out somehow. What do you think, sir?'

'And why, Major, am I so important? You don't really think my presence is relevant to this outrage do you?'

'But why else would they choose now to play ducks and drakes with our diplomatic immunity? They will know there must be consequences.'

'I think motive and consequences are the keys to this action. This Swedish policeman may be acting independently, or else he may be doing so with the connivance of his general. If the latter, then they must be sure of there being no likelihood of consequences. Perhaps the Shah has been deposed and, thus, my presence in the territory will be a tiny part of the wider picture. Moreover, I cannot see what gain there would be in my capture. I have already sent my report on the viability of the oil field with a recommendation to push through the deal. It is now up to the diplomats to ensure the Shah has no objections.'

'We know that your report has already been safely despatched, sir, but do they? Or might they want you for your knowledge in your days heading the navy's intelligence department? I can't think of any other sane reason for such insane behaviour. I reckon we'd be better gettin' you out of here, just in case, like.'

'And how might you do that, Flynn?'

'I'm not rightly sure yet, sir. Perhaps, if we made a stab at resistance, in the confusion I could have a couple of me boys pretend to be lootin' the place. We could wrap you in a tent or a carpet or somethin', and get you down to the harbour and on a boat out of here.'

'Major Flynn, I am impressed by your sense of duty, but firstly I do not speak Persian and would have to lay up in the town until some suitable vessel could be found. It would be bound to put many at risk. Moreover, I remain convinced that I am not the objective here. Remember what Symonds said before he left: there are other games afoot and this attack may be another piece of the jigsaw. My advice to you is to get word to Miller's cousin and see how the situation develops.'

'If that's your appreciation of the situation, Admiral, then fair enough, but I don't like the idea of givin' in to these ragamuffins without a fight. I think I might just set a few surprises for any of the varmints that prove a little light-fingered.'

Twenty-five minutes later, Flynn was informed of a deputation awaiting him in the courtyard under a flag of truce. He noted that this time it included the blond figure of a European in the uniform of the gendarmerie. This must be Carlsson, he surmised. *Mebbe I'll jes let him wait a few minutes whilst I change into me dress uniform. It's always better to let these damned foreigners feel at a disadvantage.*

This time, as Flynn stepped out to parley, the troopers were dispersed under cover of the consulate main building, but their rifles were clearly visible to the gendarmerie officers. Neither officer saluted him and he noted that the Swede seemed to regard him with contempt. *Always better to go on the attack*, he thought. He addressed the officers of the gendarmerie, again in English.

'I presume you're that Major Carlsson and yer here to admit some fearful mistake has occurred and to apologise to me for the behaviour of yer men.'

Carlsson winced at the remark and struggled to control his emotions. He replied in perfect, but accented English.

'No, Major Flynn. I am here to accept the surrender of the consulate and to escort you, your staff and your household to a place of safety. I must take my turn in presuming that you are all packed and ready to move.'

'And just what might happen to us were we to be foolish enough to accept yer terms then, Major Carlsson?'

'None of your party would come to any harm, provided you surrendered your weapons and co-operated. The Indian soldiers would be deported, but the rest of you would remain together. I give you my word you would be well looked after.'

Flynn snorted in amusement and contempt. 'That would be the word of a man who has flounced the international rules of diplomacy. Why are ye doin' this?'

Carlsson started to lose his temper and raised his voice.

'Major Flynn, you are in no position to argue. Either you surrender within ten minutes and be ready to depart, or I will kill you all. Now get ready.'

He turned on his heel and marched quickly back through the consulate gates.

Flynn addressed the Persian officer still standing there. 'What's going on, Lieutenant?'

'Sir, you are to be placed under house arrest, in a safe place, awaiting the orders of a German officer called Woss Moss. My orders are clear that no harm is to befall you and that once you have departed the consulate, my men are to search the embassy for weapons. That is all I can tell you, sir, but I do beseech you to co-operate if you value the lives of your men and women. Major Carlsson is not a man to be trifled with.'

The Persian officer begged him with his eyes to agree. Flynn recognised he was beaten and bad-temperedly returned to the consulate to arrange its evacuation. Despite his situation, he still chuckled to himself. 'Some thievin' bastard's goin' to get a helluva surprise if he attempts to remove the gold from my safe,' he said aloud to himself.

CHAPTER 29

October 1913

After 400 miles of hard riding, Symonds was looking forward to the home comforts of the consulate in Bushehr. He planned on having a proper bath and wearing western clothes once again. Miller and his cousin had persuaded him to adopt the local tribal costume and, after six weeks, he had to agree that it was a more practical garb. It was surprisingly cool and immensely practical in affording protection from the desert sun. He was not so sure he would ever get used to riding a camel, though. One had to ride the damned things side-saddle and the rhythm of their side-to-side, lolloping trot was less regular than the horses to which he had been schooled to ride in England and India. They smelt foul, had a tendency to spit, and every now and then, were extremely stubborn and uncooperative. Thank God it was not far now to the consulate. He turned his thoughts into words.

'By Jove, Miller! If I never have to ride a bloody camel again, it wouldn't be too soon. Give me a horse any day.'

Peter appeared not to have heard the remark, but after a minute of reflection, broke the silence. 'I fancy you have forgotten the nature of the terrain we have covered this past month or so. How often have you had to water your mount? I have never known it possible to drink horse milk, but I note that you didn't seem to object to camel milk when we ran out of water before hitting the last oasis. How ungrateful you are to the dromedary, old chap.'

Both men laughed heartily. 'You have me there, Miller. Truly they are remarkable animals, and none better for the desert.' Symonds stroked his camel's neck with affection. 'But even so, I still long for a gallop on one of Flynn's mares back in Bushehr. So what are you most looking forward to doing, once we reach the consulate then?'

'I am rather anxious to rid myself of this blessed beard. I don't know how the Mussulmen put up with them. They are singularly hot in this climate and I always feel dirty with it. I am hoping I will have no further need of it now.'

'I am sure you can count on it. I would imagine that your duty is quite fulfilled. Admiral Slade should have conducted his business by now. Indeed, he is probably already back in England. I fear that but for your help to me with the gun-running business, then you might well have been home, too. After all, it was India political business rather than an affair for the Admiralty. Even so, there is still time for you to be home for Christmas. I am grateful to you and, have no fear, I will be giving a full account of your invaluable assistance in my report to Delhi.'

'Don't be a damned fool, Symonds. It was only my duty.'

Symonds glanced sideways at his travelling companion. He was a little taken aback by the vehemence with which the last sentence had been delivered. Like Miller, he was caked in sand and what little of his face that was visible, was heavily tanned. It was impossible to distinguish either of them as Europeans. His opinion of Miller had changed over the past two months. Initially, he had considered him an amateur. So many of the army 'agents' – the word 'spy' was never used – he had come across in India, were enthusiastic adventurers, looking to replay the Great Game for a lark. Now he was forced to admit from experience that if Miller was typical of the relatively new British Secret Service, then foreign intelligence-gathering had taken a distinct leap in professionalism. Many agents were talented linguists, but Miller was completely at home in the Persian culture, and also, in the guises as a French doctor one day, an Armenian horse trader another, and even as Mussulman healer and holy man.

Symonds glanced back to the camel train following them. Most of the camels were loaded with rifles and ammunition. To be precise, there were 500 Lee-Enfield rifles and 500,000 rounds of ammunition. With the help of the *Batik*'s papers and informants of Miller's cousin, they had tracked the cargo train north. They had then agreed not to interfere with the progress of the arms caravan in the hope it would lead them directly to the German entourage. After all, Symonds had argued, the Germans had paid for the arms and their shipment; the least one could do was see that they received some of them.

Symonds shuddered at the memory of what they had found at the camp of the German mission. The trail had taken them east to the shore of Lake Bakhtegan, a little north of Estahban. There, Miller's cousin Darius and his hired Bakhtiaris had a few days before found the German encampment

190

under the protection of the Tangistani tribe. Darius had explained that there was no love lost between the Tangistanis and the Bakhtiaris and so the men had raided the German camp with relish. It seemed the Tangistanis resented the Bakhtiaris for the remuneration they received from the British in exchange for leaving the oil pipelines unmolested. According to the scant report sent to Miller from Darius, there had been a fierce skirmish in which lives on both sides had been lost. Whilst most of the German party had eventually escaped, Darius and his men were delighted to inform Miller that they had captured the leader of the German mission and two of his staff. Wilhelm Wassmuss was travelling under the guise of a diplomat and the next consul at Bushehr, but both Miller and Symonds suspected he was a prominent intelligence officer. They had looked forward to meeting him.

Initially, as they had approached the camp, it had seemed much as the two Englishmen had expected. The once orderly ring of tents was a shambles. Some of the tents had caught fire and were no more than smouldering ash, and everywhere there were signs of the detritus of the skirmish. It was as they tethered their horses that they were met with a sight to fill them with disgust. Staked out in the sand and under the remorseless midday sun, were the naked remains of what had once been three men. Miller had fought hard to retain his breakfast. The sight was revolting. The birds had already feasted on the eyes and were now arguing over the rights to the genitals. The men's tongues and lips on their blackening faces had swelled to a grotesque size and flies were already laying eggs in the open wounds resulting from the removal of flesh by the birds. Whilst Miller had battled to control his revulsion, he had been quicker off the mark. In his near fluent Persian he had shouted at the nearby Bakhtiari to untether the corpses. He had been beside himself with rage and had reinforced his orders by waving his revolver menacingly. The rumpus immediately brought Darius running from one of the tents to investigate the cause of the shouting.

'Dorood salam pesar da'i.' Darius had addressed his cousin in his native Persian, but on seeing Symonds had switched to English. 'I am delighted to meet up with you again. But why all the shouting?'

'Darius, my cousin. This is not the way to treat your enemies.' Miller had gestured towards the baking corpses. 'Does not your God insist that the dead are buried quickly?'

'Cousin, you are my kin and, therefore, I do not wish to offend you, but do not presume to lecture me on barbarism. My grandfather, God rest his soul, told me stories of how you British treated those who betrayed you in India. Is it not true that the rebel sepoys were executed by being tied to the mouth of a cannon and blown to pieces? Do not interfere with matters of which you know little.'

Symonds had then joined the two men and the conversation. 'I do not condone the old ways of our ancestors. Surely your religion promotes the respect of your enemies in death? Clearly these men were tortured before they died.'

'You are Mister Symonds, I presume, and of whom I have heard much from my cousin. I am sorry our first meeting is on less than friendly terms. However, I repeat, do not interfere with matters of which you know not the facts. These men are our own, but have been punished for their treachery. I regret to inform you, cousin, that these men took gold in return for letting the European Woss Moss and his men to escape. Permit me to show you.'

Darius had then showed the two Englishmen the tent in which Wassmuss and his colleagues had been kept prisoner and had recounted the detail of their escape. Two nights before, some of their colleagues, who had made their escape during the Bakhtiari raid, had returned and bribed the three guards to look the other way whilst they rescued their comrades. The back of the tent had been ripped open to allow the men to escape through the rear of the camp, out of sight of their captors.

The previous euphoria and satisfaction that Symonds and Miller had felt earlier that morning had immediately evaporated. It had been little consolation that the Germans had been forced to leave behind the ammunition and rifles. They had noted that in their hurry to flee the camp, the Germans had also left behind their baggage. Dispiritedly they had rummaged its contents for any clue as to the party's intended destination. It had not taken many minutes of searching before their blood had run cold.

'My word, Symonds! It seems your supposition was right. Those dastardly Germans are set on fomenting revolt. And guns aren't their only weapons.' Miller had been holding some postcards of Kaiser Wilhelm dressed in the robes of Central Asia and wearing a turban.

'According to these postcards the Kaiser has converted to Islam! It's a damned filthy lie!'

'It's worse than that, my dear fellow. Look at these posters, Miller. They're in several different languages, but all call for a Jihad or Holy War against the infidel British.'

The two men had examined with more urgency the material found amongst Wassmuss's baggage. The postcards had been colour-tinted to show the Kaiser wearing the sacred green turban of a Haji, a pilgrim who had visited the holy city of Mecca. The literature claimed that the Kaiser had converted to Islam and was ordering all his subjects to embrace the faith, too. Some of the pamphlets were written in Hindi and urged the Indian sepoys to mutiny against their officers and to join the holy struggle against their imperial masters. In the wrong hands such literature would prove incendiary and was clearly designed to spark trouble for the British Imperial troops as Germany prepared for a European war. There had been several other papers and a number of books, also, but too many for Miller and Symonds to assess for their significance in the short term.

'Symonds, what was it your head of service, Sir Charles said? "Like hidden fire", was it not? More like, gunpowder, I'd say. My God! If Wassmuss gets his way, we don't just face an uprising in India, but throughout the Near East. The audacity of the plot is beyond belief.'

'I regret, Miller, it is worse than I had previously feared. This man Wassmuss must be stopped at all costs, even to the extent of assassination. We have to go after him, but first we need to get this stuff shipped back to the India Office for proper analysis as quickly as possible. What do you suggest? Send it via the embassy in Tehran for onward shipment in the diplomatic bag?'

Miller had considered the options for a few minutes before replying.

'I think it best we send it to Bushehr and put it in the hands of Admiral Slade. If we're quick, we should just catch him on his way back from Abadan. We might be lucky. The *Surprise* could still be under his orders and he could travel back to London in her with this baggage. If not, he can use his influence to requisition another warship for the purpose. Otherwise, Flynn will be able to take care of its onward shipment. We'll need to brief Flynn on our findings, too, so that he can brief our masters on this Wassmuss's intentions. We ought to get this ammunition secured as quickly as possible, too, before it can go astray again.

'Come on, Symonds, there's not a moment to lose. We've a hard ride ahead of us.'

CHAPTER 30

'Oh, my God! What in heaven's name has happened?'

Symonds was immediately brought back to the present by Peter's startled cry. The two men had just crested the hill on the outskirts of Bushehr and looking down on the British Consulate in the distance, were shocked to see the destruction before them. The Union flag still flapped lazily in the still air, but the previous grandeur of a once-proud outpost of the empire had given way to violence and neglect. The large wooden gates to the compound now hung in tatters on their hinges. The front wall of the residence had been demolished by some form of explosion and the roof above had come down with it. The right-hand side of the residence was still standing, but had clearly suffered fire damage. They urged their camels on and left the rest of the party behind.

As they drew near to the consulate, it became apparent that the barracks seemed intact, but Peter noted that the Indian cavalryman guard outside had been replaced by a section of blue-jackets. Cautiously, he and Symonds rode up to what remained of the main gates, now blocked by two heavily loaded carts. They were promptly challenged by two armed sailors.

For the moment, Peter decided to maintain his alias as Pilven and explained that he was here to see the British Consul. The two sailors exchanged knowing looks before one of them called to a colleague further in the courtyard.

'Oy, Knocker. Fetch the duty PO. Tell 'im we got two dirty Hayrabs here, one which claims he's a Froggy guest 'ere for Major Flynn.' The sailor then addressed Peter in a loud voice, perhaps for fear that he might not understand English. 'Now mate, if you wouldn't mind dismounting 'n' bidin' 'ere a minute or two, we'll soon 'ave everythin' sorted.'

Peter used the delay to survey his surroundings. It was clear that the compound had come under some form of attack and he recognised the influence of artillery on the splintered gates. He worried for the safety of Flynn and his wife. Then he thought of Admiral Slade. Might Slade's mission to secure the oil contracts for Britain have come to nought whilst he had been off gallivanting in the north? What would Papa say about his desertion from his proper place of duty?

Fortunately, he did not have long to stew over his fears. A short, stocky petty officer soon arrived to escort him to the relatively undamaged part of the residency. A window had been crudely converted into a doorway leading directly into Flynn's library. Seated at the Flynns' dining table, which had evidently been brought into the library to act as a desk, were a civilian and Percival, the captain of HMS *Surprise*. Neither rose to greet their visitor after the petty officer had announced him and withdrawn. Peter recognised the civilian as a diplomat on the staff of the consulate at Ahvaz. Evidently Smith-Hyde did not recognise him in turn, but then he thought, nor would my own mother, dressed as I am in these Persian robes and the filth of the past several weeks in the saddle. Even so, he was piqued by the incivility of the two men. He did not know Smith-Hyde, but he immediately took a dislike to him. He was a strange-looking man. He appeared to have no lower jaw bone and, as a result, the thin lips of his mouth, above which sprouted an equally thin moustache, seemed to merge with the upper part of his neck. His eyes were also too close together. His looks, combined with his attitude, seemed to suggest menace. Percival, if anything, looked more tired than on their previous meeting and had clearly not recognised him in his filthy native garb.

After sufficient delay to demonstrate who was in charge, the diplomat addressed him. 'So you are Pilven?'

Peter decided that such a welcome was not worthy of reply and remained silent.

'Come, man. Speak up. What's your business here? *Parlez-vous anglais?*'

'But of course, Smith-Hyde. Given that it is my mother tongue.'

Smith-Hyde was visibly shocked to have been addressed by his own name. He peered quizzically at Peter, but there was still no sign of recognition. 'Who the devil are you, man?'

'Why, my dear fellow. I am aghast you do not recognise me. Pray forgive me a second and I will show you.' Peter reached across to Smith-Hyde's pocket handkerchief and quickly removed it before the man had time to resist. Within seconds he had splashed water from a carafe onto the handkerchief, removed his head dress and wiped his face clean.

What there was of Smith-Hyde's jaw dropped. 'My God! It's you!'

'Indeed it is. Now perhaps you would not mind if my colleague joined me. We have both had a very long journey and it is unfair to leave him standing in the heat of the sun.' He turned to the petty officer. 'PO, please invite my friend to join us. Then, perhaps, you would see to the unloading of the camels and ensure that the guns and ammunition are stowed safely.'

'Guns and ammunition, you say?' It was the first time Percival had spoken.

'Yes, commander. Half a million rounds, bought and paid for by the Germans and intended to be used to foment revolt in the East. I will tell you about it in due course, but first, Smith-Hyde, as soon as my colleague has joined us, pray tell us what in heaven's name has been going on here?'

Within a few minutes Peter was joined by Symonds. 'Gentlemen, allow me to introduce Assistant Superintendent Symonds of the Indian Secret Service. Symonds, this is Smith-Hyde of the British Consulate at Ahvaz. Commander Percival you have already met.'

This time Percival stood and shook them both by the hand. 'Forgive me, Miller. I was struggling to place you in those robes. I'm delighted to see you both safe and well again. It seems I am once again under the instructions of the Admiralty to place my ship and men at your disposal.'

Peter detected a note of reluctance in Percival's tone, but could not fathom the reason. Still, the news pleased him greatly. Until a few minutes ago he had assumed the ship had returned to Britain.

'But tell me what brings you here, Captain. I thought you had left weeks ago. And what has happened to Flynn?'

'After the arrest of the *Batik*, I received orders to remain in the Gulf and to take my instructions from Admiral Slade. My last orders were that once he had settled his affairs here, I was to convey him back to England with all despatch. I don't mind admitting we were looking forward to the return home after a long and difficult commission. But the men enjoyed the diversion of the arrest of the *Batik*. However, when I called on the Admiral at the appointed time, I discovered the shambles here and that he had disappeared. On reporting this news back to London, I was ordered to delay our return and remain offshore, pending further orders or being relieved on station. That was four weeks ago.'

Peter could see the commander's frustration. He clearly wanted no more than the opportunity to take his ship home. No doubt he was having some difficulties with morale onboard. Whatever, that was not his concern for the time being.

Smith-Hyde then took up the story. 'On learning the news from London, the Ambassador in Tehran sent word that I should investigate Flynn's disappearance. I found the place much as you see it now … and completely deserted. Until just a few days ago, I still had no idea what had happened to the members of the consulate here. Then the wives of two of the junior staff were brought here under escort by the local gendarmerie. They explained how the party had been arrested, but they had been released in order to deliver a message.'

'Arrested my foot, man,' Percival interjected. 'It's more like bloody kidnapping.'

'Kidnapped? My word. For what purpose? Message, you say?' Peter asked in bemusement.

'One of them carried this letter from Flynn,' Smith-Hyde ignored Peter and addressed Symonds. 'I think you will find it explains everything. It was addressed to you. I'm afraid I hadn't heard of you, so I thought it best to open it myself. Even so, I'm damned if I can understand it. Tehran then instructed me to wait here with Percival until you turned up. Anyway, your presence now explains the reference to the arms and ammunition. Here, read it for yourself.'

Smith-Hyde pulled out a letter from a pile on the desk and handed it to Symonds. Symonds read it slowly and then passed it to Peter. 'Let's see what you make of it, Miller. Some of it refers to you. It's a bit odd and probably contains a code. You might be able to make more of it.'

Peter took the letter and read through it slowly:

'My dear Symonds,

By now you will have heard of my arrest on some trumped up charges or other. In truth, I am being held as a "guest" of friends of your German quarry. I understand that our mutual friend felt an urgent need to decline the continued hospitality of your Persian friends, but in his impolite failure to say farewell, made no arrangements for the forwarding of his baggage. He accepts with some reluctance that there is little likelihood of retrieving the rifles, ammunition and certain literature, but amongst his possessions are a number of personal items he is most anxious to retrieve, including some of great sentimental value and historical significance. He has, thus, asked me to inform you that he would happily relieve you of the responsibility for his possessions and, in return, to allow me, my wife and staff to return to our quiet life in Bushehr.

197

I can assure you that we are being well treated. Our friend is a gentleman and not at all like his ancestor, Attila. However, I fear a long absence from my work might result in boredom. Man cannot live by bridge alone. Our friend, Mr Slade, the shipping surveyor from London you met on your last visit, has, therefore, kindly consented to teach me the Italian language. After careful consideration, he has recommended to me three books and I wonder if you would contact Doctor Pilven, whose collection of Italian literature is more varied than my own, and arrange for them to be sent to me forthwith. They are, Rascaldate Sul Fuoco, La Parta Bianca *and* Di Questa Lettera. *I am sure that in reading and understanding fully the meaning of these books, my time as a guest of our friend will pass that much more quickly.*

Yours aye,

Flynn'

Peter tingled with excitement and then stood up so suddenly, he sent his chair flying. 'Quick! I need a fire. Send for some matchwood and fuel for the grate.'

'Have you taken leave of your senses? A fire in this heat?' Smith-Hyde responded.

'For God's sake, don't quibble. Just do as I say.' Peter rushed out of the room and repeated his instructions to a couple of blue-jackets. Whilst they dutifully laid a small fire in the hearth, he offered his explanation to his three colleagues.

'Don't you see? Flynn was an intelligence officer and he knew Wassmuss would read the letter before it was sent. This letter sends us a message.'

Smith-Hyde sighed wearily. 'As a mere Political officer I am, of course not blessed with the intelligence of those in the Secret Service, but even I had worked out the letter contained a message. It's a ransom note.'

Symonds, however, took Peter's meaning. 'You think Flynn chose his words very carefully, don't you, Miller? It is a code.'

'Exactly. He tells us that Wassmuss has not yet discovered Admiral Slade's true identity. But more than that, consider the words of his final sentence, *"understanding fully the meaning of these books"*. He's telling us to consider what the Italian titles mean in English. There are no such books and Flynn knows I speak Italian.'

He read again the choice of words and burst out laughing. 'You clever rogue, Flynn,' he said out loud. 'We have you, Wassmuss.

'Gentlemen, it doesn't need a cryptographer to decipher the meaning of the letter – just a knowledge of Italian. The message contained in the titles of the books reads: "*Heat over the fire. The white part. Of this letter.*"'

This time it was Percival who caught Peter's meaning and he took hold of the letter to examine it minutely. 'So that's why you need a fire. You think the letter contains a message in secret ink that will be revealed by heating the paper. It's a dashed ingenious idea.'

'Precisely, commander. Good – the fire is catching. Another minute or two and we can get started.'

'But, Miller, where would Flynn find a supply of secret ink? He is bound to have been searched before being allowed to write the letter.'

'A good question, commander, but I regret the answer is rather indelicate. Experiments by our service have found that one of the best inks available is produced naturally and available to most agents. You might wish to put that piece of paper down.'

'I don't follow.'

'Human semen, sir. It works very well and there is rarely a shortage.'

Peter retrieved the paper from the disgusted Percival and carefully held it before the small fire. Slowly, several brown characters began to appear between the lines of the original text. He read the words carefully and contemplated their import.

'Commander Percival, I regret I may need to detain you further. This message reveals the whereabouts of Admiral Slade and the consulate staff. Once I have confirmed the information, I could well have need of your men and firepower to provide a rescue party.'

'I would of course be pleased to help, but I fear I cannot see what support I can offer you.'

'I'll be the judge of that, sir. You underestimate the impact of a small force of disciplined armed men with a field gun. It could be decisive. But first I need to communicate back to my superiors in London. I have no secure communication facilities here so perhaps you would assist me by relaying a signal via the Admiralty. We can then await both their Lordship's pleasure and that of my own masters. Perhaps you would be kind enough to wait whilst I compose a despatch.'

CHAPTER 31

October 1913

The Admiralty lies barely half a mile to the north of the Foreign Office and, for a man of Rear Admiral Miller's fitness, fewer than ten minutes' walk. Today, however, that was not far enough. He was in an angry mood and needed time to cool off before returning to his office. It was a typically dull and chilly autumn day, but there was little prospect of rain, so he decided to take a tour of St James' Park to collect his thoughts before his next meeting.

Taking stock, he thought that overall he had much with which to be pleased. Over the past four years he had seen the fledgling Secret Service Bureau thrive and he was satisfied with the form it now took. Now the two sections had developed into two autonomous services. Major Vernon Kell headed the Security Service responsible for home security and counter-espionage; Commander Mansfield Smith-Cumming ran the Secret Intelligence Service with responsibility for worldwide foreign intelligence.

As a member of the Committee of Imperial Defence (CID), Miller had also persuaded his superiors at a meeting the previous year, that in the event of war, then all Germany's underwater telegraph cables should be cut. Crucially, it would mean that communications with their navy would have to be via high frequency (HF) wireless. Thanks to his influence, the Royal Navy now had a wireless station on the east coast at Stockton to listen in to German Navy transmissions from their high-powered transmitter at Norddeich. Arrangements were already in hand for Marconi and the Post Office, in the event of war, to establish rapidly a chain of other wireless intercept stations. However, there was a fly in the ointment.

He struggled to decide whether it was the timidity or the naïve snobbery of the Foreign Office that had so angered him at the conclusion of the meeting he had left just a few minutes ago. There he had presented his quite sensible and modest proposals to the Permanent Under Secretary of State (PUS), Sir Arthur Nicolson GCB, GCMB, GCVO, KCIE and his top officials. The meeting was fixed indelibly in his mind.

'So, in conclusion, gentlemen, if we can cut Germany's overseas cables, she can only communicate with her colonies by telegram over those owned by us or by letter. The latter will be slow and, naturally, the ubiquitous nature of the Royal Navy leaves them vulnerable to interception. Obviously, we also have it within our means to intercept traffic sent over our own cable systems. Left intact, once war is declared, the German-American owned Liberia-Brazil cable would be the Germans' only means of communicating with the Americas. I, accordingly, seek your assistance in persuading the Americans to agree to sever the cable once hostilities commence. Any questions, gentlemen?'

The two Foreign Office officials attending the meeting had looked balefully at their superior before one of the aides to the PUS replied.

'Look here, Admiral. What you are asking is quite impossible. You must realise that the United States would be a neutral state in any conflict in Europe. Quite apart from the fact that any action of the kind you propose might potentially undermine American neutrality, HMG could not ask it of them. It would put us in their debt.'

Miller had not been surprised by the civil servant's response. He had developed close links with the Foreign Office over the past few years, even to the extent of having the ear of the Secretary of State, Sir Edward Grey. His contacts had already warned him to expect such a refusal. He had merely wanted it recorded that the request had been declined. He was certain he would get his way in the end. However, he had not been prepared for the next statement from the official.

'Now, turning to your other proposal, Admiral, for the establishment of a department for the decoding of intercepted diplomatic telegrams. That would be quite unacceptable for reasons I am sure I need not elucidate.'

'I'm sorry, but I think you will. I do not understand.'

'You disappoint me, Admiral. I understood you to be brighter.'

Sir Arthur had winced visibly and interjected. 'Hold hard, Evans. After my years in chairing several committees concerning the SSB, I can personally vouch for Admiral Miller's intellect. I would ask you refrain from insults and to stick to the matter at hand.'

The civil servant, Evans, had blushed at the rebuke, but recovered himself.

'I apologise, Sir Arthur, and to you too, Admiral. Please forgive me. Naturally, HMG greatly values intelligence and is more than happy to act on it when the occasion demands. But a diplomat has no business eavesdropping on private conversations and I must regard the reading of private telegrams and letters in the same light. We are horrified to hear that your plans to read the contents of letters to and from abroad include those of private citizens, as well as those of diplomats. It really is an infringement of the personal liberty we in Government profess to hold so dear. 'We are, of course, grateful to those who go about the grubby business, but to set up—'

Miller had begun to rise from his chair, causing Sir Arthur to wave animatedly to his assistant. 'I am sorry,' the tactless Evans continued. 'We are grateful to our intelligence services, but to set up a department under the auspices of the Foreign Office would set completely the wrong tone. As you know, Sir Arthur has always taken a great interest in the work of the SSB, but the department feels it important to maintain the work of the Secret Service at arm's length from that of the world of diplomacy...'

Miller had begun to lose interest in the thoughts of Evans and to fiddle with his watch. The man didn't seem to know when to shut up.

'... After all, deniability is a strong defence for any minister or ambassador. May I remind you of a section of the minutes of a meeting you attended in 1909, when it was agreed to establish the SSB from the Foreign Office Secret Vote?'

'You don't need to remind me. I recall it clearly,' Miller had growled, but Evans had shuffled some papers and assumed a pompous air as he read from the minutes: ' *"By means of the Bureau, our naval and military attachés and Government officials would not only be freed from the necessity of dealing with spies, but it would also be impossible to obtain direct evidence that we had any dealings with them at all."* I cannot see how signals intelligence differs in this respect and must insist you hold hard to these tenets.'

Miller had considered walking out of the meeting there and then, to take his case to the Foreign Secretary, but for the sake of Sir Arthur had decided to maintain his temper.

'Mister Evans, on my estate I employ highly experienced gamekeepers to keep down the vermin. Nevertheless, it sometimes happens that the build-up of vermin is such that other measures are required. Then we call in the rat-catchers. I see an analogy here.'

'I do not take your meaning, Admiral.'

'Despite the experience and cleverness of my gamekeepers, circumstances do not always accord with the plan. Then it is time to take action, and it is best done swiftly and decisively. One does not take away the tools of the rat-catcher's trade. Catching rats may be a grubby business, too, but it is a necessary one. Accurate intelligence is not just a critical tool to enable the navy to take action, but valuable to diplomats to prevent that action being taken.'

Miller had not won the argument and had come away exasperated by the meeting. He accepted that it was the role of politicians and diplomats to set British foreign policy, but in the Royal Navy they had a powerful weapon which, if exercised properly, had inordinate influence on the execution of that policy. Why would the diplomats deliberately tie not just the navy's, but their own hands behind their backs? No, it would not do. If necessary he would have to take matters into his own hands, but it was delicate. It was not something he could discuss with his superiors at the Admiralty, but he was used to acting independently.

He would waste no further time on a tour of the park. He had work to do that would brook no further delay. He had a paper to write on his plans for the interception of foreign communications in preparation for war. The Foreign Office be damned!

CHAPTER 32

Observing the Armenian horse trader and his party approaching the mud-built fortress near Ahram, Commander De Montfort wished he could use his telescope to gain a better view of the events about to unfold. He had to contain his impatience. Any reflection of sunlight off the lens would risk indicating to the fort's occupants that he and his party were not in fact a bunch of Persian ragamuffins. De Montfort was the Executive Officer of HMS *Swiftsure*, the battleship acting as the flagship for Rear Admiral Peirse, the Commander-in-Chief of the East Indies station. *Swiftsure* had relieved *Surprise* on patrol off Bushehr and *Surprise*'s captain had been only too pleased to receive his orders to return to England with Wassmuss's baggage embarked. De Montfort was presently commanding a mixed detachment of *Swiftsure*'s Naval Brigade, a platoon of Gurkha Rifles and, less comfortably in his own thoughts, a rabble of Bakhtiari horsemen. This strange assortment of men was all dressed similarly in the robes of native tribesmen. De Montfort was pleasantly surprised by how well suited the garb was to protecting him and his men from the hot Persian sun.

The fortress was situated near the village of Ahram, about thirty miles east of Bushehr and standing on the last stretch of plain leading up to the base of the Zagros mountains, the parallel ridges of which run almost the length of Persia. De Montfort found it a little cooler than in Bushehr, but still thought it deuced hot, despite the approach of winter. He carefully surveyed the small fortress before him and his men. The central part was perhaps forty feet high with parapets and loopholes. It was surrounded by an outer mud-wall of about twelve feet in height, built into which were two great wooden doors. He knew neither the doors nor the fortress walls would be able to withstand a pounding from his two 4.7-inch field guns. The guns had been dismantled and hidden in the carts behind him. The beauty of these guns was that they did not need to be towed behind horses for transport. Indeed, these were the same type of guns that had been transported overland in the hands of sailors to raise the siege at Ladysmith during the Boer War. The Naval Brigade was justly proud of this achievement and, since 1907, had been reminding the British Army of the success by recreating the event in the Command Field Gun Competition at the annual Royal Naval and Military Tournament.

No, with his artillery, De Montfort had no doubt about success in overrunning the fortress. The challenge was the rescue of the British Consulate staff inside, including Admiral Slade, being kept hostage by a Tangistani Shayke and his German paymasters. However, there was a plan and he had to hope that the Armenian horse trader would succeed.

****

As the Armenian and his party of six other traders approached the fortress, the great doors were swung open and three Tangistanis stepped out. The short and rotund one greeted the party affably in his local dialect.

'May God be with you. Welcome to my home. I am Shayke Kamran Haydar. Please follow me.'

The traders followed Haydar through the gates and they and their cart were directed into the left-hand of two small inner courtyards. Their Armenian leader carefully scanned his surroundings and Haydar was embarrassed that the half dozen riflemen guarding the other courtyard appeared quite lugubrious. He had only eighteen men to guard the parapets of the fortress and something in the Armenian's manner suggested that this was too few. It would not do to appear weak. He pointed to the cart.

'I was led to believe that your consignment was much greater than this. Is there not more?'

'Haydar Khan, there is most certainly more. In all I can offer you 500 Lee-Enfield rifles, but you would surely not expect me to deliver them to you until I had seen the colour of your gold. The remainder of the guns are under the guard of my men over yonder.'

'But what of the ammunition? I was told that there could be up to a million rounds.'

'Alas, the ammunition is in the hands of the British. These rifles had already been unloaded onto the schooner when the British Navy attacked the ship. The ammunition was still onboard. It is of little consequence. My men know where the ammunition and the other guns are being kept by the British. For only the smallest of reward, a mere trifle really, I would be happy to pass this information on to Woss Moss. I do not have enough men to overpower the guards. Where is Woss Moss? I was told to deliver these guns to him.'

Haydar wiped away the sweat around his mouth nervously. Casting his eyes over the trader's party he noted that four of them were very short, with different eyes and facial features. Perhaps they were from the north. He had no doubt he had enough men to kill them easily. He wanted these guns badly, but they were no use to him without ammunition. Moreover, the trader had clearly suspected a trick and left most of the guns with the larger party on the plain. On reflection, he would have to let the Armenian live a little longer.

'Woss Moss is not here at present, but may return tomorrow. First, let us inspect the rifles you have brought and then, perhaps you would accept my hospitality. You and your men would be welcome guests under my roof.'

****

Gently, the sailors placed their ladders against the rear, outer wall of the fortress. De Montfort listened carefully for any sounds of alarm, but so far there was no cause for worry. He had decided that the next stage of the operation would be more suited to the Gurkhas under his command. They were much more accustomed to stealthy manoeuvre in the dark. Earlier in the evening, Miller, disguised as the Armenian horse trader, had signalled by flashlight for the operation to begin. The Gurkhas' first task was to release Miller, the two Bakhtiari tribesmen and their four fellow Gurkhas from their quarters in the north-east quarter of the fortress tower. The sailors would be responsible for setting the explosive charges to bring down the great gates. Other members of the Naval Brigade were, even now, lining up the sights of the two re-assembled field guns on the entrance to the fortress.

It was a new moon and, thus, very dark. De Montfort consequently had to use his carefully shaded flashlight to check the time on his pocket watch. It was 01.25, so he only had another five minutes to wait.

Miller seemed to have been very pleased when HMS *Swiftsure* had relieved *Surprise* with orders to assist him to release Flynn and the other hostages. De Montfort had learned from Miller how Major Flynn had used secret ink to describe his location in an apparently innocent letter requesting some Italian books. De Montfort was impressed by the ingenuity of these intelligence types. Then again, he thought, if my life depended on it, I might find my way to becoming ingenious. He had also heard of the plot by Wassmuss to destabilise the region and was determined that this time Wassmuss would not escape their clutches. Indeed, amongst the brigade's baggage was a set of leg irons.

Checking his watch once more, De Montfort realised it was time to let loose his Gurkhas. Quietly, they ascended the ladders and, as he watched them reach the parapet, he saw the glimmer of light from inside the fortress reflected in their kukris as they were drawn. The sight sent a shiver down his spine.

****

'Sahib, are you there?' Corporal Pun opened the door carefully.

Inside the room, Peter and his party were wide awake in expectation. A few minutes earlier they had heard the footsteps of men running, but nothing bar silence until the soft knocking on the door. After being entertained to dinner the evening before, they had been shown to their quarters for the night, this single room in the tower of the fortress. No attempt had been made by Haydar or his men to search their guests as that would have been beyond the bounds of local hospitality. However, they had been asked to surrender their weapons on their honour for the night and warned that a guard would be posted outside the door.

Peter followed the Ghurka corporal back into the corridor, at one end of which lay the corpse of the Tangistani guard. As he passed it, he felt a pang of queasiness. The sentry's eyes remained open, upturned in surprise. His throat had been cut and the ugly wound still oozed blood down the man's sodden front. Quickly and quietly, he gave the Gurkhas their orders to accompany him to the prisoners' quarters. These lay in a long, single-storey building overlooking the courtyard on the right of the main gate.

He let the Gurkhas lead him down to the courtyard by which he had arrived the day before. He knew the corporal to be competent and this was not his line of country. Instead of descending via the staircase, the Gurkhas led him back the way they had come; – out of a window and down a rope ladder attached to the side of the tower. Without waiting for him, they fanned out at the base of the ladder and searched the dark shadows for any sign of life. Their colleagues had already taken care of the two sentries on the parapet of the outer wall, but had earlier spotted two above the main gates. Thankfully, no alarm had yet been raised. As Peter finally touched ground, the corporal approached him.

'Sahib, there are two men on watch above the gates, but we have no means of approaching them unobserved. I fear they may see us cross the courtyard.'

'Thank you, corporal. I think we may have pushed our luck too far already. Can you get a man back over the wall to pass a message to the naval commander? Very well. Tell the commander to blow up the gates and we will use the distraction to get into the other courtyard.'

Ten minutes later, as he and his Gurkha escort crouched hidden in the darkness, a great flash rent open the curtain of darkness, immediately followed by a deafening noise. The air became thick with dust as great clods of earth and shards of wood rained down on the surrounding area. The Gurkhas did not stop to gaze upon the scene of destruction. Sprinting across the courtyard and around the corner, they lunged at the two Tangistani sentries still reeling from the shock of the explosion. As Peter raced past them, he saw in his peripheral vision the flash of the kukris through the air.

To his front he could see a door opening and from it a man emerged holding an old Jezail rifle. Quickly assessing the situation, the man raised the rifle and aimed it at Peter. It was only then that Peter remembered he was unarmed. Continuing to run headlong at the rifleman, his lifetime memories started to flash though his mind. Everything seemed to be happening in slow motion. A bullet zipped past his ear, followed by a loud crack sound. He thought he must be dead, but then realised he was still running and the bullet had passed from behind him. Then his adversary started to crumple and fall forwards. Thank God! One of the Gurkhas must have shot the Tangistani first. He started to hear more sounds of gunfire behind and from the other courtyard, but he ignored it. Another bullet whistled past him, he knew not from whom. Leaping over the corpse in front, he threw himself into the open doorway and found himself in a small kitchen.

He gasped for breath as he rapidly surveyed his surroundings. To his shock and horror, another tribesman stood to his side on the other side of a low table. On the table lay his Jezail rifle. Yet again he regretted his folly in charging ahead without a weapon, but in the same instance the man threw himself to his knees and wailed in his native dialect, 'Don't shoot. For the love of God, please don't kill me.'

Perhaps only five seconds later, Corporal Pun and his men bounded into the room. On seeing the cowering Tangastani guard, one of the Gurkhas advanced towards him and, before Peter could speak, drew his kukri and slit the man's throat. Peter could not believe his eyes and shouted angrily to Corporal Pun.

'That was murder. He was unarmed and had surrendered.'

Pun was silent for a moment and looked back at him sadly.

'Sahib. These men are cut-throats themselves. There is his rifle. Two minutes ago he might not have hesitated to have killed you or any of my men. I have no pity to spare for him. I am sorry if I have offended you, sahib. Now let us do what we came here for. Let us find the prisoners.'

As if on cue, Major Flynn chose this moment to make an entry, dressed in his bed clothes and carrying a lit lantern. He briefly cast his eyes around the room, first at the Gurkhas and then at the dead man, before fixing on Peter.

'Be Jaysus, Miller. I'd recognise that beard anywhere.'

CHAPTER 33

Careful questioning of the prisoners established that Wassmuss and his lieutenants had been quartered in the nearby village. However, on making enquiries and a search of the village, Flynn, with the support of the Gurkhas and blue-jackets, discerned that as expected, Wassmuss had moved out quickly once the attack on the fort had begun. Flynn called Peter, Slade and Symonds to a council of war.

'It's a pity this Wassmus character has flown the coop. He and his kind have the potential to cause me a heap more trouble afore they're finished, but that's as may be. I think, for now, the best thing we can do is to ship you back to London with the admiral, Peter. The guns and ammo are in the safe hands of the navy and this is, after all, India political business rather than Admiralty business. You've more than fulfilled your duty on the latter's account.'

'But, are you saying you no longer need my help, Patrick? I don't like to leave a job half done.'

'Don't be a damned fool. Of course I'd welcome yer help, but you have your orders and surely you're overdue the return to England.'

'Balderdash, Flynn. My orders didn't foresee this sort of situation. I know where my duty lies.' Peter banged the table hard and leapt out his chair.

'Look, Peter, don't take on so. Sit down. No offence was intended. You've more than done your duty, as I'm sure the admiral will concur. All I'm sayin' is that your purpose in bein' out here is now served and I expect London will be wantin' ye back for another job, or even a spot of leave. In any case, somebody ought to be escorting the staff and ladies back to Bushehr. What d'ye reckon, Admiral?'

'I quite agree, Flynn. Miller, my boy, you've done a splendid job. More than anyone could have expected and I can't wait to regale your father with tales of your derring do, as well as the authorities. But Flynn's right. You're back under Admiralty orders now.'

'Strictly speaking, sir, I don't come under Admiralty orders and, with respect, that includes your own now. I'm a member of the Secret Service and expected to take my own initiative. If Symonds here, as a member of our sister service in India, requests my help then I would be justified in providing inter-service cooperation. After all, Symonds, you don't speak Farsi as well as I do.'

'But *I* do, Peter,' Flynn replied heatedly. 'This is my territory and, moreover, you don't know what it's goin' to be like. Accordin' to my information, Wassmuss and his men have split up. He's headed off to Madagascar, but his henchman has taken a bunch o' ragamuffins over to Herat. That's not an easy journey.'

Symonds cut in. 'Why Herat, Flynn? What have you not told us?'

'It's bad news, Symonds. I was goin' to tell yer, right enough. One Hauptman Kruse has a letter on him from the Kaiser. If he can get to Kabul, he plans to persuade the Emir of Afghanistan to invade India once the Holy War has started. You know he's got to be stopped at all costs, even assassination.'

'This journey, Flynn,' Peter interjected. 'I assume we're talking about crossing the Loot salt desert, right?'

Flynn nodded.

'For heavens' sake, man. Forgive me for saying it, but having been cooped up here all this time, are you really in a fit state to make that journey? It must be all of a thousand miles and, according to my cousin, not for nothing is it called the Emptiness Desert. Surely you'd be better off going back to Bushehr, making your report and instigating enquiries into Wassmuss's whereabouts? I've already told you. I'm happy to accompany Symonds.'

Symonds laid a hand on Flynn's shoulder tenderly. 'Nobody is doubting your courage, Flynn, but I think Miller is right. Go home, spend some time with your wife and rest up. We'll take care of Kruse. You tend to Wassmuss.'

Flynn's shoulders sagged and he seemed to shrink in his chair. 'I'm not happy about it, but you two seem set on goin' yer own ways. I grant I don't feel quite my usual vigorous self just now. But trust me this'll be no picnic. You've first to cross the Zagros mountain range and at this time of year it'll be freezin'. Then, by contrast, you've to cross possibly the hottest place on Earth. As well as the heat and the sun, you'll have to contend with poisonous snakes, scorpions and insects. No doubt ye'll fare no worse than Kruse in these conditions, but you may need to keep your identity secret. The English are none too popular with some of the tribes for your pals' efforts in preventin' the smugglin' o' guns from the coast into the north-west corner of India. Several of the tribes rely on the income the trade generates. I don't envy you yer task.'

Symonds placed a hand lightly on Flynn's upper arm. 'Thank you for the warning, dear fellow. But to put a stop to this work of the Devil, I would happily travel beyond the gates of Hell itself. Come on, Miller. Let's work out a route to hunt down this Kruse.'

****

The two Englishman drew nearer to the fire for warmth. Their two Persian guides were camped with the horses a little further away and around their own small fire. Although the temperatures during the day were very pleasant, indeed much as those of a fine English summer, it was a chilly thirty-five degrees at night, barely above freezing. After seven days of exhausting riding, they had reached the depression of Sirjan, a mere 5,000 feet up. Despite pushing themselves mercilessly, it was clear that Kruse was driving his men equally hard.

For much of their journey, Peter and Symonds had always seemed to be two to three days behind. They had correctly guessed the route Kruse would take and regularly received reports of their quarry's progress as they passed through the same villages. It was logical that he would make use of the passes through the Zagros mountains and head for Kerman, and they still had high hopes of catching him before he entered the Loot desert. The two men lay head to head on their backs, examining the clear, starlit sky.

'There goes another one, Miller. Did you see it?' A shooting star had just disappeared into the indigo sky.

'Yes, I saw it. Look. There's another. And another. I used to do this at home, you know. Just lying in the garden, looking up into sky, only it was considerably warmer. What about you, Symonds?'

'I don't think I did. I was brought up in Richmond and the stars never seemed as bright. You come from Lancashire, I hear. I thought it was meant to be even smokier up there than London. What, with all those factories and everything.'

'Come, Symonds. If you're thinking of Blake's "dark satanic mills", you'll find he had in mind the churches of your own Lambeth and not our factories. In any case, the mills on my father's estate are driven by water power. We're lucky to live in some beautiful countryside.'

'It's odd that we should both be here now. If you don't think me impertinent, why did you join the Secret Service?'

'Probably the same reason you joined your outfit. I sort of fell into it. I wanted to join the navy and follow in my father's footsteps, but I get vertigo and they wouldn't let me join. So instead of going to Dartmouth, I went to Charterhouse. From there I joined the Diplomatic Corps and then my father persuaded me to do some work for the Service … and the rest is history. How about you?'

'Both my parents died when I was young and my uncle became my guardian. He was in the Civil in India and I followed him out there. I didn't fancy life in the Civil or as a clerk, so I entered the Indian Police. One thing just led to another … Are you close to your parents, Miller?'

'That's a strange question. Why do you ask?'

'I don't mean to pry. I'm just interested. I never really knew my parents.'

'It's no matter. Since you ask, I'm very close to my mother. I love her dearly. There was a time when I thought myself close to my father, too, but lately we've become virtually estranged.'

'How so? Did he cut up rough when you couldn't join the navy?'

'Not at all. He was very decent about it. I was the more upset as I so wanted to emulate him. No, it came later. Three years ago I behaved in a manner of which I'm deeply ashamed and Papa has since thought of me as a coward. Whenever we are together at home, he always seems to find an excuse to avoid my company. I let him down terribly and I'm still trying to make amends.'

'You a coward? That's hardly credible. I saw you in action at the fort only a few days ago, remember. And you saved my life on board the *Batik*. Look at you now. When you had the chance to go home, you opted to stick it out and hunt down this Kruse character. I would have imagined your father would be very proud of you. Think what you've achieved these past few months.'

'You don't know my father. He's the only man I know of to have earned both the Victoria Cross and the Conspicuous Service Cross, the navy's two highest awards for gallantry. He's clever, decent, strong, and devoted to the navy and his country. All my life I have only ever wished to be half as good a man as he. I might as well seek to measure up to Zeus.'

The two men lay in silence for a few minutes. Symonds felt a curious affection for his companion. How could a man with so much to offer feel so inadequate? He had seen for himself Miller's courage, selflessness and zeal to carry out his duty to the utmost of his ability. Having lost his own father early in his childhood, he had never experienced having to seek a father's approval.

Peter broke the silence between them. 'If I'm honest with myself, I wonder if my pursuit of Kruse is merely an excuse to delay going back home. I confess I love the sense of freedom this country offers. The nomadic lifestyle and sleeping under the stars, it's so real. It's enough to survive the day and give thanks in the evening with others. Others who have shared the same hardships and challenges. There's nothing else to it. I feel so alive here.'

'If you think that, then you really are running away.' Symonds lifted himself onto one elbow and turned to Peter. 'I'm surprised at you. For God's sake, Miller, there are other considerations. If we're not careful, we're going to have a bloody war on our hands. A war in which thousands of people will die. You've got a family for pity's sake. Surely you care about them?'

'Of course I care about them. That's just the problem. I so much want to run away. To be a little boy again. Protected and cosseted. Free of real responsibility. But I know it cannot be. I have to face up to my duty. It's like a powerful magnet drawing me back.' Peter covered his face with both hands.

Symonds decided to turn the conversation and lay on his back again. 'I, too, like the outdoor life, but have seen little of the world outside India. But you should see the North West Frontier. The landscape is dominated by the Himalayan Mountains – mountains so high that they are permanently covered in snow. The melt cascades downstream in great torrents of crystal clear water and the air is equally pure. Sometimes you can see as far as three hundred miles. I judge it's as close to heaven as I'll ever get in this life. Perhaps one day I might be buried there. You should go there.'

'It sounds wonderful and perhaps one day I will have the chance to visit. But would you not prefer to be buried in England?' Peter turned onto his front to face his companion.

'Not at all. I've not been there for so long, I barely remember it and I've no ties there.'

'Don't you have family there?'

'Just an old aunt who lives in Sussex.'

'My word! I couldn't imagine having no family. My relations are spread all over the globe and you've met my cousin, Darius. When I die I want to be buried in the churchyard of my Uncle Philip. His church has a fine view of the valley... But this is a morbid subject. It's all a long way ahead – I hope. For now we have to catch up with Kruse. I fancy we are gaining on him at last.'

'I would agree. He can't be more than a day ahead of us now. We'll have a better idea at the next village. That's up to you, Miller. I can't make out a word of this local dialect.'

'Have you thought any more about what we're going to do when we do catch him? It's your show, old man.'

'It will depend on how we come upon him and his reaction. I expect we are going to have to resort to some force to relieve him of that letter, but there are only two of us, up against six of them.'

'What about Flynn's suggestion that we just surprise and shoot Kruse? With him dead, his Tangistani guides are hardly likely to carry on to Afghanistan, are they?'

Symonds turned onto his front, too, and looked into Peter's eyes. 'And you're prepared to shoot a man in cold blood, are you, Miller? Because it would have to be you. I'm no assassin.'

Peter met Symonds' eyes. 'Point taken.'

Symonds turned away from the fire and prepared to go off to sleep, but Peter seemed in the mood for conversation. After a short pause, he went on. 'Tell me, Symonds. Is there any woman who holds a special place in your affection?'

Symonds might have been surprised by the question and change of tack, but he answered truthfully. 'No. Not yet anyway.'

'If it's not too personal a question, why's that? I mean, are you interested in the opposite sex?'

'It is a personal question, but I'll answer it. I've sometimes thought I would like to meet somebody, but firstly I have been too preoccupied with my work to stick around long enough for courtship. Moreover, I've been a bit limited for choice. The type of girl one meets in India is hardly my type. What about you? You raised the topic. Is there some sweet thing pining for your return?'

'Hmm. In a way, I suppose there might be. I met someone before I came out here. Back in Lancashire. She's a schoolteacher. Good-looking, very intelligent, but also highly independent. I did think she might be Miss Right, but now I'm not so sure.'

'She sounds delightful. What's the problem?'

'I'm not sure myself. She seems a bit too independent. She's got herself mixed up with my cousin Elizabeth's suffragette friends and holds some rather unorthodox views that she's not afraid to express. I don't mind that so much. It's nice to meet someone with brains and the conversation is stimulating. But she seems to want me a bit too much ... Oh, it's difficult to explain, but I value my freedom and independence, and there's another thing. She's a bit willing, if you follow my meaning.'

'For goodness sake, Miller. What's wrong with that?'

'Oh, I don't know. It might sound silly, but it should be the chap that does the wooing. It's part of the thrill of the chase, as it were.'

Symonds turned back to face Peter. 'Not having met the young lady in question, I can hardly comment. But if you don't mind me saying, it's all bosh. You don't know when you're well off. To someone like me, you have it all and I've no patience with your self-pity. Those who have the opportunities owe it to chaps like me to make best use of them. Come now, we need to sleep. We have another hard ride ahead of us in a few hours, mercifully on a proper horse rather than one of your dromedary creatures.'

'We've discussed this before, Symonds. We'll have to switch to camels before we enter the Loot desert.'

'In which case, let us hope we catch up with our quarry well before then. Thank the Lord we have elephants in India. Goodnight. Dream pleasant thoughts of that girl of yours back home.'

****

A couple of hours later, Symonds got up to relieve himself. The fire was down to its embers and giving off little heat. As he returned to his bed roll, he noticed that Peter was sleeping only fitfully and shivering slightly as he did so. He added more fuel to the fire and watched it catch. As he was about to lie down again, he had another thought. He took up one of his own blankets and cast it over the sleeping Peter. 'Sleep well, my friend. I wish I could exorcise your demons,' he whispered.

CHAPTER 34

'Are you sure that's them?'

The guide nodded.

'Right, we'll split up as agreed. Good luck, Symonds.'

After three more days of the pursuit, Peter and Symonds had overtaken Kruse's troop and were waiting for them in a narrow part of the mountain pass between Kerman and the entrance to the Loot Desert at Sirch. They had finally run down their quarry in the town of Kerman the day before. One of Flynn's contacts, a Russian horse trader, had not only supplied a change of horses and the offer of proper beds for the night, but information on the whereabouts of Kruse and his escorts. Symonds had taken the precaution of sending one of their own guides to observe the members of this escort so that he could later identify them. After some discussion, Symonds and Peter had decided that it would be better to intercept Kruse in the open, rather than in the town. They had politely declined the Russian's hospitality and a good night's sleep, and pressed on to the nearby mountains.

The November sun was casting long shadows as it set, silhouetting the approaching horsemen. Using his field glasses, Peter counted six men, one of whom was dressed in European clothes. Against the sun they were indistinguishable to him, but the guide had been quite certain that this was the right party. It was a risk they had to take. He raised his rifle and resting it on the rocky ledge, he took careful aim. He had taken position about thirty feet above the road and was well screened by the many rocks surrounding him. Symonds was similarly positioned about two hundred yards to his right. He let the mounted group pass until it was half way between him and the waiting Symonds. Without warning, he shot the rear horse through the flank. Its rider was catapulted to the ground. The other horses reared up in confusion and fear, but their riders retained their seats. As he reloaded, another shot rang out, a second horse fell, and then a third as Peter fired again. Those still in the saddle quickly dismounted, withdrew their rifles and headed for cover on the opposite side of the pass. The two remaining horses and their remounts bolted back the way they had come.

Peter called out in German, 'Captain Kruse, lay down your arms and I promise you no harm will befall you and your colleagues. I am a British officer and give you my word.'

It was obvious by the way some of the prone men looked towards the man in European clothes, second furthest away from Peter, that this must be Kruse. A murmured conversation was taking place between Kruse and his escorts, but he could not make out what was being said. It resulted in two of the Tangistanis who had the better cover, firing in the general direction from which they had been hailed.

The bullets were wide of their intended target and Peter chose to ignore them for several minutes. The men, as intended, found this disconcerting and did not know in which direction to face. However, the light was failing and he knew he did not have much time for parley. Again he addressed Kruse.

'Captain Kruse, you are completely surrounded by my men. You have lost your baggage and horses and have no means of escape. Unless you surrender immediately, I will order my men to open fire.'

Another short discussion ensued between Kruse and his men. One pointed in Peter's general direction. Immediately afterwards, the group recommenced firing. Under the covering fire, Kruse and one other started to climb the rocks on the other side of the pass. Conscious that darkness fell quickly in these parts, Peter shouted to Symonds.

'He's trying to get away. What's your decision?'

Symonds's response was a shot in the direction of Kruse, but he missed. Peter followed his cue and managed to hit the man following Kruse. He could not tell whether he had wounded or killed him. All that mattered was that Kruse was getting away. Meanwhile, Symonds had started to shoot at the other three Tangistanis. When another of their number was hit, they decided to call it a day, threw down their weapons and started calling for mercy.

'Symonds, cover me. I'm going after Kruse.'

He half slid, half fell down the rock face and charged after Kruse, ignoring the supplications of the surrendering men. The sun was bathing the pass with its crimson rays. A half-moon had revealed itself, but he knew it would be dark within minutes. Kruse was climbing quickly and had already reached a height of about fifty feet. He was tempted to shoot him, but not in the back. Instead he discarded his rifle to free his hands for climbing after Kruse. In his peripheral vision to his right he noted

Symonds and their guides' cautious approach down the pass. Symonds would take care of the prisoners. He ducked as several rocks clattered by, no doubt dislodged by Kruse.

His chest began to heave with the effort of climbing. Sweat dribbled down the side of his head. As the ascent became steeper, he had to search for hand-holds, frequently grazing or even cutting his fingers. Often he had to stop to take cover from the shower of rocks spilling liberally down the slope. He could just see the dim shape above in the shadows cast by the moonlight. Kruse was getting away, but there was no choice. He had to go on.

The next time he flattened himself against the face of the mountain to avoid the falling stones he looked down to see what Symonds was doing. It was a mistake. By now, nearly two hundred feet up, the figures below distant and hardly visible, he felt giddy. His world began to spin and he felt a magnet drawing him away from the safety of the rock face. It was tempting to give in to the force, to let go and let gravity do the rest. Why not, he thought. It's better than climbing this damned mountain. Another voice barked at him within his head, scolding him: *'And what about your duty?'* it said. Then he recalled his father's words, *'You're a coward and I'm ashamed of you.'*

'No,' he shouted, or perhaps he merely thought he shouted. 'I am not a coward and I'm no longer afraid of you.' He shut his eyes and hugged the mountain. He breathed deeply and felt an inner strength pulse through his veins. 'Symonds was right,' he muttered to himself. 'It's down to us to stop this infamy. I must catch Kruse.'

Unconsciously, he started to climb again. His fingernails tore into the crevices of the rock and his fingers bled profusely. The knees of his britches were in tatters, and the flesh beneath bruised and grazed. His chest hurt from his exertions, but he hardly noticed. His only thought was to keep going. Even so, he stopped to draw breath and examined the terrain above, but not below. With his eyes not fully acclimatised to the dark, he could see the landscape clearly by the light of the moon and the bright stars. It looked as if he had just climbed some sort of near vertical chimney that was now levelling out into a wide channel. His keen ears heard the noise of running water and he suspected that this channel had once been cut into the rock by a waterfall. Indeed, narrow fissures fanned out from the channel. However, there was no sign of Kruse and, other than the sound of the water, silence enveloped them both.

Now he was unsure what to do next. He knew that Kruse must have continued his climb up the channel, but beyond that he could have gone in any direction. He decided to press on a bit higher before reviewing his options. Just then the silence was broken. He heard a scrabbling well below him. It could not be Kruse. He could not have passed him in that chimney. Perhaps it was a large bird or a goat.

Stealthily, he crept up the channel, trusting to his ears to warn him of Kruse's presence, but the path was clear. The channel ended at a solid wall of rock, on either side of which led a narrow gully, just wide enough for a man to pass along. He listened carefully for any sound of Kruse, but to no avail. His instinct told him to go right, but there was no reason that Kruse might not have turned left. Doubt entered his mind. Might Kruse yet escape? If he could lay up for a day or so, he might still be able to continue his journey to Afghanistan, potentially with catastrophic effects on the empire. Then he saw it.

Something in the right-hand passage gleamed dully. On investigation, it turned out to be the brass case of a bullet. The hairs on his neck rose in excitement. He recognised the bullet to be of a type manufactured for the German Army. He was on the right track after all.

He proceeded cautiously, careful not to make more noise than he need. It was possible that Kruse was waiting patiently to ambush him. Kruse was armed and might easily cut him down round any bend or corner. Very soon the passage opened out onto a grassy sward, surrounded on three sides by the mountain. The grass was wet and beginning to turn white, betraying the recent footsteps of a man crossing it. Peter squeezed his eyes in concentration, looking for any movement ahead. The noise of running water had increased to a roar from his right, but he could not see its source. The air had become cool and clammy. He started to suffer a headache as the sweat in his hair cooled. The moisture on the face of the mountain ahead twinkled in the moonlight, much as he had seen the granite of Aberdeen reflect the sunlight.

Suddenly, he thought he saw a flash of white higher to his right. He scrutinised the spot until his night vision improved. There looked to be a ledge there, skirting the side of the mountain. Nothing moved. It could have been a bird, but something of a different shade of grey to the rock was sticking out, silhouetted against the starlit sky. He reached out for a pebble and threw it well to his left. It bounced off a rock, making only the slightest sound, but in response there was definite movement on the ledge.

He skirted the grass sward to the right, using the wall of the mountain to keep him out of sight from the ledge above.

****

Symonds was grateful that he was wearing his usual riding clothes, rather than the local style. He had to admit that the traditional Persian dress had much to commend it in the heat of the desert, but for climbing up rock faces, boots and britches were serving him better. He had seen Miller go after Kruse, but had been too preoccupied with rounding up the Tangistanis to follow immediately. Once he had been satisfied that the men were completely unarmed, he had sent them packing back to Kerman on two horses between the five of them. He chuckled at the memory of the fifth man running behind his colleagues on horseback. His friends didn't seem to be keen to wait for him to catch up.

Shaking himself from his reverie, he continued the slow and difficult climb. The light of the moon was of little help. It only cast odd shadows on the rock above. Potential hand and foot-holds had to be searched for by feel alone, a painstaking task and one to which he was not accustomed. Despite shedding his coat, he was sweating hard from the exertion.

At length, the rocky chimney levelled out and turned into a V-shaped gulley, at the end of which he had a choice of routes. The path directly ahead was blocked by a wall of rock, but two passages, wide enough to be passable by a human, led away, one to the right and one to the left. He opted to go left.

Initially, it was relatively easy going as the slope upwards was slight, but after about fifty yards he had to resort to scrambling over boulders, before again having to resort to climbing the wall of the mountain. He seemed to have spent an eternity of climbing the face of the mountain, but to his intense relief, he eventually found himself able to haul his exhausted body onto a rocky shelf hollowed out in the side of the mountain. Briefly, he lay there resting his weary body and allowing the rate of his breathing to return to normal. As he lay on his back, he surveyed the rocky overhang above. He had never had any interest in mountaineering, but he thought this spot would be ideal as an overnight camp for up to a dozen people. It was much like a shallow cave. From this vantage point he could make out two tall pinnacles of rock to his left and a gap to their right, below which must run the pass.

He now felt sure that he had taken the wrong route up the mountain, but he deemed it too dangerous to attempt to climb back the way he had come.

Instead, he searched for an exit from his temporary refuge. The light of the moon did not penetrate to the back of the cave so it was with some difficulty that he eventually discovered a narrow, but navigable fissure leading upwards and deeper into the mountain. 'What choice have I?' he muttered to himself. 'I can stay here until daybreak or chance my arm in the darkness.'

****

Kruse cursed his lack of height and not for the first time in his life. Many years ago the other kids had teased and bullied him for it, but whilst other kids grew taller, he had grown broader and now had the strength of an ox. He could just make out what looked to be a cave in the mountain only a few feet above him, but he could not reach any form of hand-hold to allow him to climb up to it. Ahead, the ledge on which he was carefully balanced, narrowed to nothing and to his right lay a sheer drop of several hundred feet into the water below. His only option was to return the way he had come, but he felt sure one of the Englishmen had followed him. He could not see any movement behind, but a few minutes ago he had heard a definite noise. If he was being followed, then he was trapped, but he wouldn't be caught easily. Silently and carefully, he refilled the magazine of his Mauser pistol and felt the reassuring presence of the knobbly edges of the two cast-iron Kugelhandgranaten attached to his belt, introduced to the German Army earlier that year.

He strained his eyes for any movement along the ledge, but saw none. Nor did he hear any sound other than that of the water below. Again the thought crossed his mind that he might be worrying unnecessarily. After all, he was well hidden and if he could sit tight until daybreak, he might yet evade his pursuers. He had no doubt that his good-for-nothing band of Alis would have taken flight, but he was probably better off without them. All he needed to do was ambush a passing caravan and secure himself transport, food and water to continue his journey to Afghanistan alone. At least he would not have the worry of being murdered in the night. Those Ali cut-throats weren't to be trusted. 'Ach, if I'm going to sit it out, I might as well make myself comfortable,' he quietly muttered to himself and sat down with his back to the stone and his legs hanging in the void below.

Only a few minutes later he was startled to hear himself addressed again in fluent German. 'Captain Kruse, you are trapped. Give yourself up.'

The voice came out of the dark below, but Kruse could not see who was shouting. With surprising agility for such a stocky man, he switched to a prone position and drew his pistol in the same movement.

'Lay down your weapon, Captain. My men have you covered.'

Still Kruse could see no movement below, but in the direction from which the call had come he saw a flash of metal reflected in the moonlight. Taking careful aim at the spot, he fired two rounds. His shooting was immediately answered by a single shot from the same direction. The bullet struck the rock above him and a stone chipping hit him hard on the back of the head, causing a trickle of blood down his neck. At the same time he heard a scuffling from above and another man called, this time in English.

'Hands up, Kruse. Go on, Hande Hoch, man.'

Kruse saw little point in further resistance and threw his pistol into the darkness below. Slowly, he stood up and raised his arms as instructed. Within seconds, his attention was drawn to a scrabbling from the cave above and a man slid down onto the ledge alongside him.

CHAPTER 35

'My word, Symonds, was I glad to see you. I'm not sure what I'd have done if the blighter had refused to give himself up. How did you end up above him?'

Peter and Symonds were making their way back down the mountain with Kruse as their prisoner. Both kept their pistols ready in case Kruse, walking a few yards ahead, should attempt to run off. The grass of the sward Peter had encountered in his pursuit of Kruse was now completely white and crunched softly beneath their feet.

'I'll tell you later, but I hope you would have shot him. Any means would be justified to prevent that letter reaching the Emir. Did you retrieve it, by the way?'

'Yes. It's in my pocket, but I haven't had a chance to read it yet.'

'No matter. There'll be time for that in the morning. Keep an eye on him, Miller. I don't trust the fellow.'

Peter had had a shock as Kruse had clambered down from the ledge under Symonds's watchful eye. For a fleeting moment, lit by the moon, he had thought that Semper had returned to haunt him. His legs had turned to jelly and he had not been able to control his speech, to the extent that Symonds had regarded him slightly oddly. From a distance the resemblance had been uncanny and it was only at closer quarters that his fears had subsided.

Soon they entered the gulley through the rock. Its narrowness necessitated that they pass through it in single file. Kruse still led, closely followed by Symonds, with Peter bringing up the rear. The moon had traversed an arc to the other side of the mountain to offer less light to guide the men's path. Not having travelled this way on the ascent, Symonds's progress was slow and Peter realised that Kruse was beginning to draw ahead too much. He cursed his lack of judgement. One of them should have gone ahead of Kruse, but they had thought it better that he remained in view of them both.

'Watch out, Symonds. Kruse's starting to get too far ahead. Let me squeeze past you.'

'Don't worry. He can't get far. In any case, he's unarmed and we have the letter. I'm going as fast as I can.'

Peter let the matter lie and, to his relief, the light soon improved and he recognised that they were approaching the spot where he had found one of Kruse's bullets. Then both men heard a metallic item bouncing towards them. They instinctively halted and looking over Symonds's shoulder Peter spotted a strange-looking iron ball, about three to four inches in diameter with a grooved surface bouncing towards them. He wondered what it was. Suddenly Symonds shouted, 'Get back,' before dashing forward and falling to the ground. No sooner had he done so than Peter heard a loud explosion and saw Symonds partially lifted from the ground, before falling back completely still.

From that moment on everything seemed to happen at once. As he rushed forward to the aid of Symonds, a distant memory stirred. During his time with the German Army three years earlier he had heard about the use of ball grenades during the Russo-Japanese war, but as far as he had understood it, the General Staff had decided there was no future for such a weapon. Simultaneously, a second iron ball bounced in his direction. This time he had no hesitation in leaping over the body of Symonds and, in one quick movement learned from the cricket field, picking up the grenade and hurling it in the direction from which it had come. Seconds later, the peace of the mountainside was rent by the sound of the explosion.

Ignoring his friend, he sprinted down the last few yards of the passage and caught sight of Kruse barely ten yards distant, scrambling down the dry water channel they had all climbed hundreds of years before. Quietly and deliberately, he took aim at the retreating Kruse. As he applied pressure to the trigger, he called Kruse by name. Kruse half turned and Peter fired three rounds in quick succession. Two of the rounds struck home, lifting Kruse off his feet. He didn't have to bother to approach Kruse's body. He had seen the spurt of blood exit the back of Kruse's head. He knew the man was dead. He was similarly sure of the fate of Symonds, but he rushed back to check.

At first sight, it was difficult to imagine anything could be wrong. Symonds appeared to have crouched face down on the ground, but as Peter turned him over, it was as he had dreaded. The whole of Symonds's torso was a scorched mass of blood and pulp where he had absorbed the full force of the fragmentation bomb. His eyes were still open and he had a startled look, but the light within had gone. Peter gently closed the eyes and placed his jacket over the shredded remains of Symonds's chest. He sat down next to the corpse and, taking the head tenderly on his lap, wept quietly for a long time.

****

The next day Peter returned with one of his Persian guides to bury Symonds. Together they dug a grave in the grassy sward. It was not as fitting a spot as the foothills of the Himalayas on the North West Frontier, but he hoped his former colleague-in-arms would find peace there. As he laid him to rest, he could not help but notice how handsome Symonds looked, even in death. Peter had combed his fair hair, washed his face as best he could and dressed him in a clean shirt. The only sign of dishevelment was his blond beard. Symonds looked as if he had merely fallen asleep. Perhaps this was a sign of a clear conscience and the satisfaction that their joint mission was now accomplished. Kruse was dead and the letter from the Kaiser was safely stowed in Peter's baggage. Might Symonds be at peace? It pained Peter that after so many weeks in the desert and hundreds of miles in the saddle together, he didn't even know Symonds's Christian name. Indeed, he knew very little about him. How could one spend so much time together, share so many experiences, save each other's lives and yet know so little of the other's past life?

Standing over the mound of the grave, he thought he ought to say a few words, but lacking a copy of the burial service or even a Bible, it was difficult to think of something appropriate. He wondered if there might be something in the Qur'an he might use. He had memorised several of the texts as part of his preparations for this assignment, but nothing came to mind. Then he remembered that no prayers are offered for the dead at the funeral of the Mussulmen. In the end, all he could think of were the first three verses of a hymn he had learned as a child. With tears rolling down his cheeks and the accompaniment of the sounds of the mountain stream, he sang his heart out in farewell to his dear friend:

'*Now the day is over,*
Night is drawing nigh;
Shadows of the evening
Steal across the sky.

Now the darkness gathers,
Stars begin to peep,

Birds and beasts and flowers
Soon will be asleep.

Jesus, give the weary
Calm and sweet repose;
With thy tend'rest blessing
May mine eyelids close.'

CHAPTER 36
February 1914

For the second time in his life, Peter stood to attention ready to receive a medal. This time he was dressed in the dark-blue uniform of a Lieutenant of the RNVR. He had returned from Persia just the month before, sadly too late to celebrate the beginning of 1914 with his family, but he was now enjoying some leave. He had been at Marton Hall when he had received the surprise news from Papa that he was summoned to a meeting with the First Lord of the Admiralty.

'Bless me, young Miller, you have been the cause of much vexation amongst the greatest minds in London.'

'I'm sorry, sir?'

'Determining the best recognition for your most valuable service to your country these past four years has required much deliberation. There's even been a special committee formed to discuss it. After all, you already hold the Kaiser's Order of the Red Eagle 4th Class. How is His Majesty to compete?'

Also in attendance were Commander Cumming, as head of the Secret Service, Sir Arthur Nicholson representing the Foreign Office and Rear Admiral Miller representing the Admiralty.

Churchill continued. 'Technically, you are still a member of the Diplomatic Service, but then the diplomats do prefer to be disassociated with intelligence matters, even though the Secret Service does come within the remit of the Foreign Office. Or was it, Sir Arthur, that you were not keen in any case to award someone so young the CMG? '

'Minister, we have already discussed this at length. We only fund its activities. Oversight of the department is by the War Office and Admiralty.' Sir Arthur did not seem amused by Churchill's ribbing.

'Commander Cumming here had the answer. He pointed out that your latest mission – to guarantee the security of our negotiations over the purchase of the Persian oil fields – was undertaken on behalf of the Admiralty. He was backed by no less a personage than your father, who remarked that you also hold the King's Commission in the Volunteer Reserve. I am only sorry that, for obvious reasons, it has been left to me to present this medal and not the King. And, of course, it will never appear in *The Gazette*.'

At this point Cumming stepped forward with a blue cushion piped in gold and on which lay a silver cross. Attached to the medal was a dark and light-blue ribbon.

'Lieutenant Miller, on behalf of His Majesty, I take great pleasure in awarding you the Conspicuous Service Cross. You know, you are only the tenth person to receive this decoration, one of whom was indeed your father. I am sure you will, therefore, wear it with great pride. I presume your father has often regaled you with the tales of how he won his own decoration in China?'

'I confess, sir, that I have never heard my father speak of how he won any of his medals. I did, of course, read the public citation in *The Gazette* as to how he came by his VC in South Africa.'

Peter blushed slightly uncomfortably and Churchill shot his father a look of reproach.

'Your father is clearly as modest as he is brave.'

Churchill pinned the decoration to Peter's chest and Cumming replaced the cushion with a salver of five crystal flutes filled with champagne . After handing a glass to each person present, he raised his own glass in a toast.

'Gentleman, to the health of a very brave young man.'

'So, Cumming,' Churchill asked after the toast had been honoured. 'What are your plans for this young man, or am I not permitted to know?'

'As it happens, sir, I am able to answer that question. I very much regret that young Miller has designs on a career outside the Secret Service.'

'What?' Churchill exclaimed, laying a hand gently on Peter's upper arm. 'Can this be true?'

'Indeed it is, sir. For some time I have entertained the notion of studying medicine and if I can pass a crammer in the sciences, there may be a place for me at a medical school in the autumn, sir,' Peter replied shyly.

'Well bless my soul. Medicine is indeed a noble profession, but it seems a pity that this country should lose your talents quite so soon. But come. Now is not the time to discuss such things. Let me top up your glass and you can tell me all about how you came to earn the Kaiser's medal.'

*****

Back at Cumberland Terrace, Peter carefully packed away his medal. As with the decoration he had received in Berlin, it was not something for public display. This was a pity, he thought, as he would have liked to have worn it for dear Mutti's sake. After all, he had actually earned this award. He turned around at the knock on his bedroom door and saw his father enter.

'Hello, Peter. May I come in?'

'But of course, Papa. I'll just clear this chair and you can take a seat.'

'No, dear boy. You sit down. For what I am about to say, I would rather stand.'

Intrigued, Peter sat in the armchair. He wondered if Papa was going to try to dissuade him from leaving the Secret Service. Then again, they had already discussed it and it had been Papa that had fixed the meeting with Professor Andrews at the medical school. Oddly enough, Papa usually saw him in his study, too.'

'It's a shame your mother could not have seen you this morning. She would have been damned proud. You looked very smart. The second ring suits you well, but it looks as though you've filled out a little since Gieve's fitted you out for the uniform, though.'

'Indeed, Papa. You should have seen me in Persia. With all that riding I was mere skin and bone, but alas, the passage back offered little scope for exercise and I confess I have been a little over-fond of English cooking since my return.'

'I'm sure once spring returns, you'll get plenty of opportunity for exercise.'

The admiral paused for a few moments. He seemed to Peter to be girding himself to broach a topic of some discomfort or delicacy. However, after the short pause his speech became urgent.

'Peter, I won't mince words. I've seen Admiral Slade and he briefed me on your conduct in Persia. I owe you a huge apology. When we met in Berlin … When we met in Berlin I called you a coward and told you I was ashamed of you. For the past three years I have regretted those despicable words.'

The last sentence had been delivered in a croak and, before his father turned away, Peter thought he saw tears welling up. He had not been expecting this from Papa.

'But, Papa, there is no need.' Peter was embarrassed by this rare outburst of emotion from his father and looked for a way to stem it. 'I can see now I was a coward. I was opting out of my responsibilities and I wasn't measuring up to the standards by which you and Mutti raised me.'

Miller turned back to face his son and there were indeed tears in his eyes. 'No, Peter. You are wrong. I have thought much about courage these past few years and concluded there are different forms of it. I've been privileged to have been recognised for courage on the battlefield, on a few occasions—'

'I know, Papa. Everyone admires your courage.'

'Hear me out, Peter. I've wanted to say this for so long and will not be put off longer.' Peter was pleased to see that his father seemed to have his emotions back under control.

'I'm not modest enough to say that I didn't risk my life in those actions, but it was done in the heat of the battle, and I merely saw it as my duty in order to win an objective or save my men's lives. In each case the events were short-lived. You, on the other hand, were living for months with the constant threat of being unmasked and shot for it. It must have gnawed away at you and I didn't understand. I'm so sorry.'

The tears had returned and now poured freely onto Admiral Miller's chest to dull the many polished medals pinned there. Peter covered his eyes to avoid seeing them.

'I now believe courage must be like a bank account. It's fine to have a quick spending spree, providing you have time to replenish the coffers afterwards. On the other hand, if you are constantly drawing on your capital, then there comes a day when your funds have been completely expended. I and Cumming should not have left you in the field so long, without a period to rest and deposit more funds into that bank of courage. It's a lesson we have learned for our other operations. Believe me, Peter … I'm very proud of you … I could not have lived if I had lost you.'

Peter was astonished to hear his father choking on his words and shocked by the fast-flowing tears. He could not bear to see his hero in such an emotional state. He felt desperate to end the situation and could feel tears welling up in his own eyes, too.

'Papa, please stop. I can't bear it. You don't need to say anything. You've no need to reproach yourself. Believe me.'

It was no good. Something seemed to have been unleashed in Papa that could not be stopped. He broke down completely. Peter had seen plenty of grown men cry, but never dearest Papa. He was always too composed and, except with Mutti, always held his emotions in check. As his father came over to him, sobbing, Peter could no longer control his own feelings. How he longed to tell this great man that he worshipped, admired and above all, loved him.

'Peter, my boy. Please forgive me. I'm so proud of you. Indeed I'm more proud of you for your courage as von Trotha than as Pilven.'

By now the admiral seemed to have his emotions more under control, but it was too much for Peter. He threw his arms around his father and the two men gently sobbed on each other's shoulders.

CHAPTER 37

Admiral Miller was having a good day. It was not the fact that it was his birthday causing him such satisfaction. Miller didn't normally bother with birthdays, but for some reason Johanna was making a fuss about this one and seemed to think he wanted a party. As a result, he would have to spend his evening talking to a range of distant relations and senior officers. Miller enjoyed small dinner parties, where he had the chance to talk to all his guests, but had always hated cocktail parties and superficial conversation. This had not been an ideal trait for a naval attaché, but he had quickly learned that such parties were an essential source of gossip and minor intelligence. With the conscientiousness he applied to any matter related to his duty or profession, he had, accordingly, learned to play the part of the consummate host or guest. He cast his mind back to his first cocktail party, as a cadet at the governor's residence in Tortola. Struck with shyness he had tried to hide out on the veranda, but had been winkled out by the wife of the deputy governor. She had kindly taken him under her wing and made a point of introducing him to several charming young ladies. He had gradually found his tongue and learned to behave more confidently in large gatherings. However, if Johanna enjoys herself tonight, he thought, then he would again play his part.

The cause of his joy today lay in front of him on his desk. Seated opposite him was the bringer of such glad tidings, Fleet Paymaster Charles Rotter, the Naval Intelligence Division's German expert. By chance, a few days before, Peter had asked if there had been anything of significance in Wassmuss's baggage to merit the kidnap of the consul and his party at Bushehr. Miller had not been aware that the baggage had been returned to England, but he had immediately smelled a rat. Enquiries had revealed that the India Office had merely stored Wassmuss's effects in the basement of a country house, without any investigation of the contents. One of Miller's staff officers had been despatched to search out the baggage and had eventually returned with two diplomatic codebooks.

'So, Charles, do you think these codebooks up to date? After all, Wassmuss would not have reckoned on the incompetence of the India Office and must have presumed them to have been in our hands for weeks.'

'I would not be so sure, sir. I know the Teutonic mind and suspect he would not wish to report the loss to his superiors. The problem I have is that I have no way of checking.'

'But could you not try decrypting a recent communication? After all, the pile of intercepts is growing daily following our instructions to ships to send us copies of all intercepts of foreign wireless transmissions. I seem to recall HMS *Glasgow* has been particularly assiduous on this.'

Miller fixed Rotter with one of his famous stares, but Rotter just broke eye contact and looked at the green safe as he replied. 'The problem I have, sir, is not a lack of material. It's how to process the mountain that is piled up already. Moreover, the German Navy uses different codebooks for it signals. As you know, I am achieving some progress in making up crib sheets based on routine weather reports intercepted from the station at Stockton. What I really need is more manpower and access to diplomatic telegrams.'

'I take your point,' Miller sighed. 'However, I might be able to help with the latter. I've had a useful meeting with the directors of the Eastern Telegraph Company and they have agreed to send me copies of any German telegrams passed over their cables. I confess to a shortage of ideas on where to find a team of specialists to help you, though. It doesn't just require a certain type of mind and good knowledge of German, but secrecy is paramount. I've even had to swear the heads of Marconi and the Post Office to secrecy with the threat of death by firing squad should they become responsible for a leak on the plan to set up more intercept stations.'

'I understand the problem, sir, but we need a proper organisation.' Rotter resumed eye contact with his superior. 'I do have a suggestion, however. Sir Alfred Ewing might be the man we need, sir.'

'I can't place the name, I'm afraid.'

'He's currently the Director of Naval Education, sir. He was brought into the post by Jacky Fisher. Prior to this appointment, he was engaged for many years on engineering research for a number of cable companies. I understand he has a deep interest in cryptography and in his present position he is well placed to recruit some bright academic types for the work we have in mind.'

'Fair enough. I'll make my own enquiries and consider the idea. In the meantime, I want you to start work on some of the diplomatic telegrams once they start coming in and find out whether these code books are still extant ... And one last thing, Charles. My wife is throwing a great soirée this evening in honour of my birthday. You and your good lady would be very welcome to attend.'

'Why thank you, sir. We'd be delighted ... and happy birthday.'

CHAPTER 38
August 1914

Seamus O'Malley had decided to profit from the warm sunshine on this first day of August by walking to Victoria to catch the boat train. The underground trains were too stuffy at this time of year and the omnibuses too crowded with weekend tourists. He was annoyed by his sudden recall to Berlin. It could not have come at a more inconvenient time. After months of drilling members of the Irish Volunteers in military tactics, he was at last able to teach them how to shoot in preparation for armed conflict. Just a few days before, Erskine Childers and Roger Casement had been successful in importing 900 Mauser rifles and 29,000 rounds of ammunition from Hamburg into Howth harbour. Until now, O'Malley had thought little of Casement, as being too moderate, but he was now starting to revise his opinion.

O'Malley reached Piccadilly and glanced at the newspaper billboards. The headlines still related to the crisis in the Balkans and the mobilisation of the Fleet. He soon hoped they would be broadcasting news of the coming armed struggle in Ireland. It was ironic, he thought, that the flashpoint for the conflict was likely to come from Ulstermen, supposedly loyal to the Crown, but now on the point of taking up arms against the British Army and police. He and his colleagues in the Irish Revolutionary Brigade were almost ready to take advantage of the ensuing turmoil to further the cause of Irish independence, even if the latest Home Rule Bill was again not passed. Glancing at his pocket watch, he noted it was still not three o'clock and, thus, he had plenty of time to kill before his train was due to leave. He decided he had time to take a leisurely tour of Green Park. Yet again, he wondered with indignation, what could be so important to justify this urgent summons to Berlin.

****

Peter watched the retreating figure of his head of service, Commander Cumming, with a small degree of amusement. He chuckled at the memory of the stories with which 'C' had just regaled him of his latest motoring

236

holiday. 'C' was an ardent motorist and enjoyed nothing better than racing his Rolls Royce around the country roads of France. By all accounts the cyclists, pedestrians and other road users did not find the experiences quite as funny. Despite the amusing stories and Cumming's affability, the purpose of the meeting in the sunshine of Green Park had been a serious one. Peter had rightly guessed that the Service wanted him back.

'Miller, my lad, we need you back.'

'I'm not surprised, sir. Indeed, I had assumed you were going to ask me that when you sought this urgent meeting on a Saturday. I presume something has come up in these past few months?'

'I'll be straight with you, lad. I'm desperately short of agents and especially of good intelligence from Germany. Other than the report of your meeting with Tapken, I have absolutely no evidence of Germany's intentions towards Britain. Everything points to the inevitability of war, but we need to know for certain.'

'Can Kell's ring of double agents not elicit something, sir?'

'Naturally, we've thought about that. They're still being asked to provide intelligence on our navy, but there's no particular urgency for anything specific. I'm with Kell that if we ask too many questions, we might raise suspicions that the agents have been turned. The matter has become desperate as now Austria has invaded Serbia, it's only a matter of time before Russia comes to the aid of Serbia and Germany, in turn, takes Austria's side. Events are unfolding too quickly for anybody's liking. The Admiralty has already advised the government to close the Channel to the German Navy for fear they might launch a pre-emptive attack on the French coast and the Germans could well take umbrage over it. The Cabinet is in a complete shambles over it all.'

'So what do you want of me, sir?'

'I want to place you in the Blohm and Voss shipyard at Hamburg. With your fluent German and field experience you're ideally qualified for the task of gaining intelligence on Germany's shipbuilding programme. More specifically, we need to hear wind of any plans to move against the Home Fleet. The absolute top priority for all the intelligence departments is early news of any move by the Germans to strike against England.'

'But I know nothing of shipbuilding, sir. What would be my cover story? And surely my cover in Germany is already blown."

'You're quite right, of course. The plan would be for you to take a job in the yard as a cleaner. We've done it before successfully. As a cleaner you would have access to the drawing office and you could use this to photograph any plans lying around, or whatever you came across.'

Cumming handed him a tiny camera, no bigger than a pocket watch. 'C' had a reputation within the Bureau for his fascination with gadgets and had even been known to invest in promising inventions himself. Peter was impressed by this latest addition to Cumming's collection. He handed it back gingerly.

'After all, who takes notice of the cleaners and you would have the perfect excuse to be nosing about after hours. Your father has even agreed to arrange for you to spend some time at your cousin's yard, to learn more about the sort of information that might be significant. Are you game, old chap?'

Peter was dismayed to hear his father being connected with this mission. 'Has my father said I will go then, sir?' he asked acidly.

'Not at all, my dear fellow. Naturally, I consulted with him. However, he was adamant that it was your decision alone, and he would not persuade you either way.'

Peter's hackles settled down once more. 'I'm sorry, sir, but there's still my blown cover to consider and I don't believe you are being as straight with me as you promised. Why the urgency? I note you say you have tried this operation before. What happened to the other agent?'

'Oh dear, you are a suspicious cove. It must have been the training we gave you. It's a fair question. Firstly, it is highly unlikely you will come up against Tapken or one of his staff, and in any case we can disguise you. As for your suspicions about another agent, I'm forced to admit they are well founded. We did have an agent in the yard; a young fellow by the name of Marsh. To our dismay, he appears to have hanged himself from a crane two weeks ago!'

****

Peter settled in a vacant deck chair to one side of the band stand and listened to the music. He gazed at the other visitors to the park. Several were lazing on the parched grass and some were enjoying the remains of a picnic. To his left, he smiled at two nearby children playing with a large hoop. Their clever little dog was darting in and out of the hoop as they rolled it down the path. The little boy and girl shrieked with delight. It was odd, he thought, that as he and the rest of the audience sat in the tranquil setting of Green Park on a glorious Saturday afternoon in August, a war had started in a remote part of Europe and at any moment the Russians

238

might be mobilising to intervene. As if tuned into his thoughts of Austria, the band struck up Mozart's overture to *The Marriage of Figaro*. He wondered if he had been right to accept 'C''s plea to return to the Service. Somehow though, in much the same way as war in Europe had been inevitable, it had probably been certain he would return to his old trade. The past few months spent cramming the sciences in preparation for a place at medical school had been increasingly tedious and he craved not just adventure and excitement, but a life outdoors. Naturally, he was disturbed to learn of his predecessor Marsh's fate. He readily understood the pressure Marsh must have felt in leading his double life undercover, but he could not help wondering if the apparent suicide might have been arranged by others. His spine tingled at the suspicion. He would have to be especially careful to learn from his mistake in France. That was all four weeks ahead, though. For now, he had other things to consider.

He checked his watch again. It was almost three o'clock and he had arranged to meet Alice and Mutti for tea at the Ritz at half past. Papa was too busy to join them. Indeed, since the Balkan crisis, he had barely seen him. There was no hurry, but perhaps it was time he ambled back through the park to his rendezvous in case Alice was early. Alice had come up to London for the weekend, both to see her old friends from Cambridge and to see him. The night before, they had dined together at the Café Royal and afterwards he had escorted her to her friend's apartment on Hyde Park corner. He unconsciously licked his lips at the memory of their parting. During their passionate embrace and kissing he had again felt that familiar stirring in the loins he experienced whenever he kissed her these days. However, as he had attempted to move to hide his embarrassment, Alice had pressed herself closer towards him and whispered softly in his ear.

'Darling, I wish you didn't have to go. My friends are out for the evening. You could spend the night here.'

He had been shocked by her forwardness and was caught off guard. Lamely, he had replied, 'I'm sorry, Alice. I have to go. Mutti will be expecting me.'

Alice had withdrawn sharply from their embrace. 'Oh, Peter. What must you think of me? Of course, you must run back to your mother.' Peter had noted the flushed cheeks and look of disdain on her face.

'My dearest thing,' he had answered in an emollient tone. 'Believe me. I want to stay with you. I have longed for that very thing for months, but I really do have to be back. Papa has been working all hours at the

Admiralty these past few days and all my brothers are away, so Mutti is completely alone and having a miserable time of it. I promised not to be late and she will be waiting up for me. But I'll fix it for tomorrow, if you can? I promise.'

Alice had visibly brightened at the prospect and rested her head on his shoulder. 'That would be wonderful. Leave it to me.'

The young couple had embraced and kissed again and this time Peter had made no attempt to shift his stance. 'Tell you what,' he had offered. 'Let's all have tea together tomorrow and then we can chuck supper after the theatre and come back here early. Would that be all right with you, my dear?'

'Hush, my darling. Everything will be perfect.'

****

As a rule, Admiral Miller preferred to walk rather than taking a Hansom cab, but today he was short of time. He was due to meet the First Lord of the Admiralty at 17.00, prior to Churchill's Cabinet meeting at 18.00. There was little else he could do before then, so he thought he might just have time to join Johanna and Peter for tea at the Ritz Hotel. He hoped it would make a nice surprise and he was keen to meet Peter's lady friend. Johanna had already met her and seemed to have taken to the girl. Miller knew her to be called Alice, good-looking and well educated, but with the situation at the Admiralty at present, he had had no time for a more detailed description. He was now curious to learn more and looked forward to being introduced.

The irony was that he was now early for the appointment. The cabman had dropped him off in Piccadilly at 15.00 and that meant he had thirty minutes to kill. No matter, he thought, it's a fine day and he could stretch his legs in the park. He walked the short distance to the entrance and just as he was about to pass through the gate, spotted Peter walking in the opposite direction. Capital, he thought. This gives us an opportunity to discuss the meeting with 'C' before we join the ladies. I'll just wait here to surprise him.

As Peter approached the exit from the park to Piccadilly, he was too preoccupied with his plans for the evening to see his father or to avoid bumping into the burly man using the same gate to enter the park, also engrossed in his own thoughts. Each swung round to apologise to the other and, as their eyes met, neither could avoid betraying the mutual recognition. O'Malley's face paled as if he had seen a ghost. The blood

240

drained out of Peter's face, too, as he recognised the Irishman. His heart seemed to stop and he was completely transfixed in terror, rooted to the spot. O'Malley, however, was the quicker thinker. In one movement, he withdrew a switchblade from his right pocket and lunged at Peter.

'Von Trotha, you traitorous fucker,' he called quietly. 'This is for those patriots you murdered, you cowardly bastard.' As he started to swing the knife upwards towards Peter's chest, he was distracted by a manic yell to his right and behind.

'Peter, look out!' Miller threw himself at the tall figure between him and his son. O'Malley had half turned to his right to determine the source of the cry when Miller collided with him, knocking him sideways and backwards. As the two men fell to the ground, Miller grasped O'Malley's right wrist with a vice-like grip. The Irishman was surprised by the power of his assailant, but recovered quickly. He head-butted Miller hard, causing him to loosen, but not abandon his hold. With an agility belying the size of his frame, O'Malley twisted to his right and, with his left hand, pushed the stunned Miller off him. His knife hand now free, the switchblade once more flashed in the August sunlight, before O'Malley plunged it into Miller's abdomen. Without pausing to withdraw the knife, he jumped to his feet and scampered down the steps of the adjacent underground station.

Peter had been too stunned by the chance encounter to move, but the sight of his father lying on the pavement, with both hands clutched in the centre of an expanding pool of blood, immediately transformed him into a man of action.

'Somebody get a doctor, quickly,' cried a member of the gathering crowd. 'Call a policeman,' another called.

'Forget the doctor,' Peter shouted. 'There isn't time. Flag down an automobile. We need to get him to a hospital quickly.' Simultaneously and in one swift movement, he removed his coat, waistcoat and shirt. After tearing his shirt into several unequal-sized pieces, he knelt by his father's body and placed his coat under the head. He then twisted the pieces of cloth into strips which he placed in rings around the handle of the knife, to form makeshift pads. Gently, he applied pressure to the wound, in an attempt to stem the flow of blood, and quietly addressed his still-conscious father.

'Papa, you can't leave me now. You must stay conscious. I can save you, but you must fight.'

Miller moved his head to look at Peter through half-closed eyes and murmured, 'Pity you weren't a doctor, after all, my boy.'

Returning his father's look, Peter noted that behind the slight misting of those dark, deep eyes, the light was beginning to fade. 'No, Papa,' he shouted. 'You're not leaving us. Now be strong and help me. You must live. I'm depending on you.'

Now was the time to see if he was truly a great hakeem, after all.

CHAPTER 39

The Hanoverian infantry colonel resented this audience with the young major seated before him on the evening of the fourth of August in the headquarters of the Tenth Army Corps, attached to the German Second Army. He recognised that General der Infanterie von Emmich would be preoccupied with the first day of the assault on Belgium, but even so, he felt that as a full colonel and commanding officer of an infantry regiment, he should have merited an audience with the Chief of Staff instead. Moreover, the young pup was from one of the Bavarian regiments and not even a Prussian. Like all officers of the staff corps, the young major wore the carmine doppellampassen – double-width trouser stripes – but this one was distinctive in that he also wore the white-with-orange-striped ribbon of the Order of the Red Eagle. The major had clearly served with distinction and was in favour with the High Command. The colonel decided that a civil tongue might not go amiss.

Major Maximillian von Hoffman may have recognised the stiffness in the colonel's attitude as he adopted a conciliatory tone. The colonel decided that perhaps this was not one of those staff officers accustomed to assume the authority of his general.

'Thank you, Colonel, for a most comprehensive report of progress on the front line. General von Emmich very much regrets that he was not able to receive your report in person, but is busy with a conference to discuss the coming passage of the army through Liège. He has asked me to assure you that he very much appreciates how difficult it must have been for you to have spared the time to make this report in person, but he was anxious to receive the most authoritative news possible.'

Von Hoffman smiled affably as he spoke and the colonel began to relax a little. Before he could go on, the two officers were interrupted by a mess waiter bringing a tray of coffee. Once the waiter had poured their coffee and retired, von Hoffman continued.

'I would imagine that your men are in high spirits, Colonel.'

'Indeed, Major. We only faced minor resistance from the Belgians as we crossed the border at Gemmerich this morning. Not much more than a few gendarmes firing from their sentry boxes *"pour l'honneur du pavillon"*. Sadly, they caused a few casualties, but nothing serious. So far, we have seen little of the Belgian Army, but we have had to contend with sniper fire from francs-tireurs. My men already have control of the right bank of the Meuse at Visé. At daybreak the Uhlans will take the bridge and we will cross and take the main town. Does the general think the Belgian army will make a fight of it?'

'He is not yet sure, Colonel. We will know more tomorrow when we approach the fort at Liège. The General Staff, naturally, hopes the King will order his army to offer only light resistance for the sake of honour and then to allow our armies to pass through to the French border.'

'But what are our instructions should we face stiffer resistance?'

'General von Emmich intends that any serious resistance, including the destruction of bridges, should be punished most severely.'

'That is understood. And what news of the British, Major? Have they made up their minds as to whether or not to come to the aid of the French?'

Von Hoffman refilled the colonel's cup. 'Right now, Colonel, I have no definite news, but I fear they will. There is talk at Army HQ of an ultimatum having been issued.'

'They would surely not be so foolish. And for what reason? Their Entente Cordiale is not an alliance. It's nothing more than a gentleman's agreement to keep out of each other's hair abroad.'

'I quite agree, Colonel. But the objection seems to centre on our perceived violation of Belgian neutrality. The General Staff seems to think that the British may choose to stand by the 1839 Treaty of London to guarantee Belgium's neutrality.'

'Mere piffle. What a fuss over a mere scrap of paper.'

'Indeed, Colonel, but Prussia was a signatory to that scrap of paper, too, and forty-odd years ago the new Germany signed another scrap of paper to confirm we would abide by the treaty. The British may see our action today as perfidious.'

'Hah! Even so, I cannot believe the British Government has the stomach for war these days. Their liberals can't even cope with a bunch of women setting off bombs in Westminster.'

'I quite agree, Colonel, but there may be other factors than an old treaty. Remember that Britain has twice before gone to war in its anxiety to see the Channel ports remain in the hands of neutrals. Moreover, the latest intelligence from a friend of mine on the Naval Staff is that if our navy enters the Channel to commence hostile operations against the French, then the British Fleet will come to the aid of the French.'

'I have heard that rumour, too, Major, but that does not amount to war.'

Von Hoffman finished his coffee and dabbed his moustache with a napkin. 'I hope you are right, Colonel, but I am less optimistic. Apparently two English ministers have resigned and Lloyd George is likely to follow them. My naval friend predicts the Liberal Government will fall very shortly and be replaced by the more hostile and interventionist Conservatives. The navy is convinced there will be war with Britain.'

'Well, what of it in any event? You know very well, Major, that the British can only muster an expeditionary force of six divisions and our intelligence department predicts that it cannot be in France for fourteen days. By then we will be well on the way to Paris.'

'That, Colonel, is also how General von Emmich perceives the situation, but first we must not let the little Belgians delay our advance. I must now let you return to your regiment.'

Von Hoffman handed the colonel a sealed envelope. 'Your orders, Colonel, are to take whatever measures are necessary to discourage any form of serious resistance. Francs-tireurs are to be executed "*pour décourager les autres*". Stick to the timetable and the general will be standing us all breakfast in the Café de la Paix in Paris on Sedan Day, the second of September.'

Acknowledgements

Like any author, I have been fortunate to receive support and encouragement from many people, and too many to list. My first draft of this story was written three years ago, but without the advice, editing and encouragement of a literary consultant who I will call Mimir, I would never have persevered with it. Writing can be a lonely business and I am, thus, grateful, too, to crime novelist and scriptwriter, Roger A Price, for his continued mentoring. My wife, Hilary, has also been a rock of support. Naturally, I owe a huge debt of thanks to the team at Endeavour Media for having the confidence in me once again to publish a second book and for their support in helping make my first novel, *The Custom of the Trade*, a success. Most importantly, however, I wish to thank all the many readers of the first book who sent me feedback on it. I have tried to incorporate much of the advice in this new work and hope it is the better for it.

Author's Note

In writing this novel I have tried to reflect accurately some of the significant decisions and events of the early development of today's Security Service (MI5) and Secret Intelligence Service (SIS), as well GCHQ's forerunner, Room 40. The overlap between 'C''s fledgling Secret Service and the Naval Intelligence Division did occur, and there were plans to capture Heligoland and the Frisian Islands as forward bases to pen in the German naval forces. There was, indeed, too, a ring of spies operating in England prior to the war and much of Peter's alias as von Trotha is based on true events. Nevertheless, this is a work of fiction and much of the action has been born of my imagination. There was no raid on the naval magazines in Chattenden, but in his history of WW1, Churchill does write of actions he ordered to safeguard against such an attack. Similarly, I have discovered no evidence that Britain took any measures to prevent the Germans interfering in the talks on the purchase of the Iranian oil fields, but the purchase by HM Government is true.

However, the attempted jihad in what we now call the Middle East was true. John Buchan was a former officer of SIS and he based his novel *Greenmantle* on the actual events. I am grateful to the book, *Like Hidden Fire* by Peter Hopkirk, for the inspiration for my tale. However, I have used my author's licence to set the story two years earlier than it actually occurred.

We will have to wait for another book to learn the fate of William Miller, but now we have met his sons, Richard and Peter, next we will become more acquainted with his youngest sons, Paul and John.

About the author

Shaun Lewis was born in Rutland and educated in Shropshire and Scotland before joining the Royal Navy. In a career lasting twenty years, he served in surface ships and submarines, as well as in appointments in intelligence and as a Chinese interpreter. He now lives in Lancashire with his wife, Hilary. His debut novel was the naval thriller *The Custom of the Trade*.

17418005R00146

Printed in Great Britain
by Amazon